THE VISCOUNT'S SEDUCTION

BOOK TWO
SONS OF THE SPY LORD

BY ALINA K. FIELD

Copyright © 2017 Mary J. Kozlowski
ISBN No. 978-1-944063-22-1
Havenlock Press
PO Box 1891
La Mirada, CA 90637-1891

Second Edition March 1, 2020

This is a work of fiction. Names, characters, places, and incidents either are the product of the author's imagination or are used fictitiously, and any resemblance to actual persons, living or dead, business establishments, events, or locales is entirely coincidental.

Cover Design by Dar Albert

She's lost her family, her home, and even her fey abilities.

But somehow, the fairies have handed this Irish earl's daughter a chance at a Season in London.

From her place on the fringes of high society, she seeks the truth about her brother--and revenge on an English spy lord.

The hoyden he'd met years earlier was still as wild as her Irish roots.

And just as unlucky, and still an Irish traitor's sister. But her beauty, her charm, and her courage can't be ignored, no matter his spy lord father's objections.

When danger strikes, he'll risk scandal, the *ton's* disapproval, his father's ire...and his own heart.

Dedication

To all you believers in romance and
magic

And to Maddox James, who arrived
just in time for this book's dedication!

CHAPTER ONE

County Donegal, Ireland, 1809

The *whisk-whisk* of the curry comb always soothed a girl's jitters. With Papa on edge, and Mama in one of her sinking spells, the great beasts were the only creatures Sirena Hollister could rely on.

Last night, Mama said there'd be bad news coming.

"Ye've about taken all the hair off her." Old Patrick came up alongside and rested a hand on the horse's swollen belly. "It'll be soon for this foaling. Mayhap today. Nipped you yet, has she, fiddling about with that comb?"

"Nay, and you know they never nip me," Sirena said.

She had the touch, Jamie had always told her.

Old Patrick chuckled. "Fey girl."

Like Gram, Mama had the sight to know what was what with the people she loved, and Sirena could whisper a horse off the worst sort of snit. Any horse.

Pity she hadn't that skill with her papa.

One of the dogs bayed, and old Patrick's gaze swung to the open stable doors.

A rider was coming. Around them, hooves began tapping and the mare's nostrils flared.

The bad news was arriving.

Sirena eased in a quelling breath and let it flow out over the mare, fixing her gaze on the rolling eyes. "Shush then," she whispered. "There now. There's a good mama."

She followed the gimping Patrick past stalls humming with the sense of a predator, the great beasts drawing the life from inside her, emptying her.

Death was a predator, wasn't it?

Not the sleep that had taken her gram one soft summer day before Jamie left them for good. No, not *that* death. For all she was no more than a girl, barely bleeding yet, she knew this death coming wasn't that peaceful sleep.

Her heart hollowed more and the shell of it crumbled down to her belly. By the time she reached the gate, the rider was circling the house and trotting back down the Earl of Glenmorrow's lane, his message delivered.

Sirena hiked her skirts and raced past old Patrick, down the path, through the kitchen garden. She slammed into the kitchens, through them, past the laundry and the still rooms, past the butler's pantry with its rows and rows of whiskey, up the narrow servants' stairs and down the hall to the parlor, where she crashed through again, panting, every breath burning her chest and stabbing her side.

Papa's hand shook with the weight of a slim parchment packet, a yellowing lump folded over and over upon itself and sealed with a huge purple-red bruise of wax. Something inside rattled.

In the new world, there was a snake, Jamie had once told her, deadly and venomous, and it shook its tail to warn of its presence. He wanted to sail there and see it. He didn't want to stay home, here, where she needed him.

He needed to go, he'd said. Even her father had allowed it, and so it must be. She'd dropped the chain with Gram's magical Brighid knot round Jamie's neck—the old magic of Queen Brighid, not that of the upstart saint—and made him promise to bring it back to her.

Outside the clouds shifted and the room brightened, thickening the air with dust motes that winked like the fairies. Mama stood gripping her chair, the hoop of white cloth in one hand dripping red thread, her cheeks as white as the bit of linen she fingered.

Papa's face hardened.

She'd seen that same rigid cast when he'd put down a horse, her huddling behind a great oak, thanking the tree fairies it had been Papa astride when the horse tripped.

She clutched the door latch, her breath frozen, watching the wafer snap, the paper unfurl, a length of gold chain dangle.

"They've found a body. They say it's his." Papa said the words the fairies had whispered to Mama last night.

All of her numbed. Time stopped.

She'd prayed—how she'd prayed, and all for naught. *For naught.*

Queen Bridghid, you traitor, carry me away down the hole of your witch's knot. Fairies, open the floor and let me fall through it.

Only, it was Papa caught in a knot, one that tied up his throat and turned his face the same purple as that wax seal. And it was Mama who fell through the floor, her head hitting the edge of a table with a sickening *thump*.

Her dearest brother, Jamie, was, after all, truly dead, and the twisted gold charm that dropped to the floor noiselessly was the proof of it.

Two Years Later

Sirena patted the dappled patch on Pooka's nose and slipped the filly a carrot. "They'll change your name, you know," she said, blinking back moisture.

Pooka's jaws worked and she turned away. Already the two-year-old was ignoring her.

Pooka had taken to the dark, arrogant lord who'd come calling the day before. Tomorrow, he would ferry the horse away, along with most of the best of their blood stock.

What could Papa be thinking?

Angry tears spilled over and she swiped them away with the back of her hand.

She yanked at the waist of her drooping trousers, picked up a shovel and began mucking the stall, tears streaming. Papa needed money, of course, to buy more spirits.

A stable door closed and boot heels clacked on the bricks. She turned her head away. Old Patrick didna need to see her so weak.

"What are you doing in there, boy?" The haughty words filtered through the slats, as if the speaker had got his nose caught in the gate. Or maybe he was pinching it to find the right accent and tone, the ones her last governess had tried to beat into her.

Her chest burned, and she swallowed her anger. She'd been confined in her room for two days. Papa had bade her stay out of the stables, out of his lordship's way. The housekeeper said 'twas not against Sirena, 'twas only her papa's worry about her breasts coming in.

She couldn't let Pooka leave without saying goodbye.

It would be all right. She was just a scruffy stable boy fiddlin' about with his lordship's new horses, seein' to their needs. For all she knew, this lord didn't know *she* existed.

"Muckin', sir," she said, deepening her voice.

Pooka, the disloyal beast, sashayed over and sniffed through the slats.

"And what is she chewing? You'll not foist a colicky horse on me tomorrow. I've already paid your master too much for the beast."

"Too much?" Sirena's blood rose, and she risked turning to face him. In the dim light, only slivers of white linen and skin showed. All else was blackness, and wasn't that a sure sign?

"This beast's granddam won first at Thurles. She's good Irish Connemara and the best hotblood lines, as fast as any of your English hacks, I'd b-bet you." She coughed and went back to her shoveling.

Shoveling shite. Aye, it was a perfect picture. She'd make her way in the world shoveling shite, she would, with her father drinkin' away their horses and her dowry.

And now this man, whose eyes burned her back, let him discover her sex, let him try to take a pinch at her breasts. He'd have this shovel up his arse, he would.

"If I were to stay longer," he said. "I'd take that wager."

And lose it. She straightened. Perhaps this lord was a great gambling fool like the rest of them. Perhaps he'd wager Pooka. Perhaps they could have at it tomorrow at the crack, like the fools who fought duels.

Her shoulders sagged again. What did she have to wager? Naught but her valueless person.

She shook her head. "No."

"No, my lord," he said.

She gritted her teeth. "No, your esteemed English lordship. I've naught to wager."

"No? Even a stable boy has a ha' penny tucked away. What is your name, lad?"

Her name? Papa would bring out the strop again if he thought she'd caught some randy lord's eye. Her mind raced through the names of their dwindling staff of grooms. Dark, they all were. Though her cap hid her yellow hair, the rest were all older, all shorter. There was naught for it. "Patrick," she said.

Old Patrick would cover for her, that much she knew.

James Everly, Viscount Bakeley, heir to the Earl of Shaldon, wished a good night and tromped off, creaking the stable door open and closing it without passing through.

He found a dark corner and waited. Soon enough, he heard it—quiet sobs, weeping, and a choking voice talking to a horse.

A girl's voice.

The pall of hopelessness dogging him since he'd come through the gates of Glenmorrow descended fully upon him, shame flooding in with it. He was here on his mother's behest, buying the Earl of Glenmorrow's prime bloods, no expense to be spared, and even beyond, the only high limit being Glenmorrow's pride.

A crooning song started and seeped into his bones, soothing him in just the same way it was settling the whole stable.

Bloody Ireland. Fairies and gremlins, and a horse named Pooka.

The Earl of Glenmorrow had been tied up with Father's schemes somehow, and it was clear from the state of the roads and the linens, the man needed money. This purchase was paying both men's debts.

And anything left over, Glenmorrow would drink away.

Well, why wouldn't he? The man had lost his son and his wife, and surely that crooning girl in the stall was the daughter who the stable boys whispered had a spooky way with the horses.

She would need some of this money set aside for a dowry. She would need a keeper when her father drank himself to death.

He watched as she slid out of the stall, extinguished her light, and left.

Ye gods, it was true what he'd heard— Glenmorrow's daughter *was* as wild as this unlucky country.

Mother had been hinting about a wife for him. Thank all the stars he'd come for the horses and not the girl. Let her be some other man's to tame.

CHAPTER TWO

London, 1821

"You may meet a young man at this ball, Sirena." Lady Jane Monthorpe sent a sly look to Barton, her maid, who simply lifted her eyebrows.

Lady Sirena Hollister cast her own glance at the able-bodied and sadly underpaid lady's maid and winked. "So, you've dragged us from Dublin to London to be rid of me, my lady?" she asked.

Barton clamped her lips tight on what Sirena knew would be a smile and went back to straightening the pleats on Lady Jane's bodice.

Lady Jane pressed the back of her hand to her still smooth forehead. "Ah, fair Sirena, let us get thee to thy ball, the better to bring forth some dashing young seafarer to your siren's call."

Sirena laughed out loud. "'Tis a poetess you are, my lady. You look lovely tonight, and I daresay there will be a host of handsome lords taken with you also."

"And will you stop wriggling," Barton said.

"Well, I suppose I must if you order it, Barton." Lady Jane smiled and the final primping was completed. "We have done well in these dresses. And it is all due to your skill, Barton. No one will suspect they were once last year's fashions."

"Indeed not." Sirena gathered Lady Jane's wrap. In her own case, there would be no suspecting. The ladies in attendance tonight would know her cerulean blue silk was made over from one of Lady Jane's three-year-old dresses.

She smoothed the skirt. No matter. With its tucks and trims it was still the finest dress she'd ever had.

"I do believe, Barton, you must open up your own shop, right here, in London. Why else should we have made the journey? Lady Sirena will entice all of her wealthy friends to patronize your establishment."

Why indeed come to this wretched, expensive, smelly city? All teasing about dress shops aside, her benefactress had insisted they must come to London for the new king's coronation, though they were having to pinch extra farthings out of every half-pence.

Barton's smile was kind, as always. In the short time Sirena had been with both women, she'd heard them speak often of this fairy dream of a dress shop.

"Then I must truly ignore dashing young sailors and direct my song to someone in commerce," Sirena said. "I wonder, will there be anyone like that attending tonight?"

"Most certainly." Lady Jane nodded. "Lord Cathmore, and he is in trade."

Sirena propped her hands on the smooth silk covering her hips. "And he is most certainly taken.

Lady Cathmore would object to a strange girl cooing at her husband."

Barton chuckled.

"Barton is laughing at us, Sirena. For shame. Now, Barton, you are not to wait up. Sirena will help me out of my stays. And Sirena, my dear, we are late. We will miss the first dance."

James Everly, Viscount Bakeley, all but leaned his tall frame against the wall of Hackwell House's ballroom, wishing he could fade into the damask wallpaper.

"Here you are, your lordship." His younger brother, Charles Everly, smiled slyly and handed him a glass.

Bakeley swirled the dark liquid. "What swill are the ladies serving tonight?"

"Taste and see, brother. Taste and see."

He put his lips to the glass briefly, then tipped it back for a deeper draught.

Charley chuckled. "Hackwell's a good chap. Serves a proper punch. I first met him in Brussels, you know, at Lady Devonshire's infamous ball."

Bakeley stifled a sigh. Charley had been at Waterloo, not fighting exactly, but engaged in some scheme of their father's. Charley had been there, their eldest brother Bink Gibson had been there, as well as their host and any number of his friends in attendance tonight.

He, Bakeley, had been in London, seeing to the routine business of the Earl of Shaldon.

It was another reminder of his lot in life.

He schooled his face into a bored mask. "You failed to appear tonight at dinner, Charley." He'd been counting on his brother diverting their father.

"You're not the only one with another interest. By the way, where is Lady Arbrough tonight?"

He firmed his mouth to fight the grimace that threatened. "This is not the place to discuss—"

"Oh, excuse me, I forgot, this ball is too bluestocking for her tastes," Charley went on. "Not quite as fashionable. I know you have a far better allowance than I, but how ever do you keep her in silks, brother?"

He didn't. Her late husband had settled her quite well, and he was not going to discuss it.

"So gloomy, you are, Bakeley. I take it you had the talk again tonight from Father?"

"Tonight, this afternoon, this morning, last night, and so on, and so forth."

"Father just will not do the noble thing and pass on so you can live the life of a wealthy bachelor earl, gadding about town, fighting with the Commissioner of Sewers about the stench."

Charley grimaced. "Though I must agree, if London could conquer the miasma, we could conquer the rest of the world." He paused for a grin. "And there's not even a need to beget an heir, since you have me."

He fought the urge to sigh. Charley was almost bosky again. "One of us will have to procreate and produce a legitimate male. It might as well be you."

"Pity that Bink is a bastard—his boy would do. No, Bakeley. I'll be like the royal dukes, leaving the business until the very end. And perhaps you, like Bink, will find love and save me the trouble."

Not likely. "Cupid's arrow was surely a woman's invention."

"Hmm?" Charley had been diverted by something across the room. Bakeley followed his gaze.

Charley snickered. "Perhaps, but Bink is well and truly shackled, and a boy produced. He does look happy."

Bink was dancing, of all things, with his wife.

Bakeley handed Charley his glass. "Cheer me up more by bringing me another one of these, will you?"

"Do I look like your footman?" Charley took the glass. "Very well, and...I say. There's a fine piece stepping up with her mother."

Bakeley refused to look. Charley spotted fine pieces everywhere. And he doubted any woman attending Lady Hackwell's bluestocking ball would appreciate being called such.

His brother perched the glass in a potted plant and meandered across the ballroom, leaving him to steadfastly examine the wainscoting on Hackwell's restored walls, and wonder who he could send for more refreshments.

He would not dance tonight. He would not mingle. Not because Lady Arbrough had teased him about attending—she had no say in such matters. No. It was because of the complicated *dance* with Shaldon. The crafty old man had grumbled about attending this ball given by people who were not good *ton,* and Bakeley knew it had been one of his many ruses. What game was afoot, he didn't know.

He'd been competent and able until Father's return to England. Now, he never felt quite nimble enough to keep up with the old man's wanglings. Perhaps there would be rich, titled, women of child-bearing capacity—his father's three bridal requirements for his heir—in attendance tonight.

Lady Arbrough might meet those requirements, except that her elderly husband hadn't been able to get any children on her, all the blame falling upon her of course, and except for the fact that Bakeley would rather harvest the cesspit than marry the temperamental widow.

And what the devil was Father about tonight? He'd tottered in on a cane and collapsed in a chair. Not complaining of any ailment though. Father didn't complain. It added to his mystery.

He must wait the old man out. Shaldon had pretended to die two years earlier in order to catch a traitor, almost getting Bink and his wife killed in the process. One day Shaldon truly would meet St. Peter, and Bakeley would be free to go on as he pleased.

"Get out there and dance, boy."

Bakeley groaned. In his musings he hadn't heard the *tap-tap* of the cane. A fine spy he would make.

"And who would you have me stand up with, Father? Have you spotted a rich, titled, nubile maiden here?"

His lordship stood very erect, his face void of expression. "No. There is no one here for you to marry. And I am glad to see that your *cherie amour* did not attend."

He bristled inside. If he but allowed it, his father would try to pick his mistresses also.

"Arbrough was a cagey fellow. Fattened his calf entirely too much while serving in the Ministry."

Lady Arbrough had been barely out of leading strings then, Arbrough was gone, and the war was long over.

"He's dead. There's no loose end to tie up there, Father."

"No doubt you're right. No doubt. And...*what* is your brother up to?"

"He's dancing with his wife."

"Not that brother." Shaldon brought his quizzing glass up to his eye and *tut-tutted*. "Unsuitable. Woefully, unsuitable, even for a younger son."

He knew when he was being baited. "Do not rouse an apoplexy, sir. Charles has even less intentions of marrying than I do."

"He's dancing."

"He's had more than one glass of Hackwell's punch. Shall I bring you one?"

"No." Shaldon raised a hand and Perpetua Everly, his youngest child and only daughter, appeared.

"Perry," Bakeley said. "Must you wear those spectacles to a ball?"

Taller than most of the men, with mouse-brown hair and a penchant for wearing eyeglasses she didn't truly need, Perry's only hope of marriage was her enormous dowry.

And whoever hoped to gain it would have to be worthy. Bakeley would see to it.

She shrugged. "Father, should you not be sitting down?" She pushed her spectacles higher and examined the old man.

Thump-thump. The cane hit the floor. "Who is that woman?"

Perry followed his line of sight and pressed her lips on a grin. "I don't know. She's not a member of Lady Hackwell's charity."

Perry had found a keen friendship with Lady Hackwell and her circle, all wealthy bluestockings sneering at the foibles of the men in their lives. Father hated it. Or seemed to.

Perhaps he should pursue one of *them*, just to rile the old man.

He discarded the idea immediately. He couldn't abide the continual managing these ladies could dish out. Since Father's return from the Continent, *his* managing had been enough to bear. Plus, though some of the ladies were attractive, most of the single ones were past their prime, and prime was what he was looking for in any woman who shared his bed, even a wife. Where Father wanted rich, titled and fecund, he was looking for plump, obedient, and welcoming in bed.

If he *were* to marry.

The music ended and the orchestra members flipped sheets, preparing for the next dance.

Thump-thump. "Go and rescue that fool. He's attempting to stand up with her again."

Bakeley sighed.

"Go. I know you're in no danger of beguilement."

"I'm in no danger of getting another glass of punch either." He patted Perry's hand. "Find him a chair."

He searched the room for his brother's tawny hair. Charley was indeed preparing to stand up again with the same partner. Nodding to acquaintances, he wove through the crowd, reached his brother, and moved him aside.

And his heart launched into a gallop. The beauty that Charley was with—and she was a rare beauty—stared soulfully up at him. The blondest of hair shimmered and gray eyes glowed luminous in the light of many candles.

"How do you do?" Only manners honed by many years of encounters with the fairer sex kept him from stumbling over his words. He bowed. "Charles, Father commands your appearance. I am Bakeley, miss. I hope you do not mind dancing with an older brother."

Charley sighed, and then shrugged, a grin spreading. "My apologies, my lady. This is not a proper introduction, but it will have to do. This is my brother, Lord Bakeley."

The lady's cheeks went unaccountably pink and she ducked her head in a curtsey.

Drat. She perhaps knew him, but he didn't recognize her. So she was a lady, and beautiful. Was she also rich?

They took their place in the line. Damn, but he should have examined her when Charley had picked her out.

When she moved in a turn around the next gentleman, he looked her over as discreetly as possible. She was a thin little thing in her blue silks, not as plump as he normally liked. What he knew about dresses was almost nothing, but this one seemed to fit with the current fashions, though it had less of the flounces, ribbons, and fluttering pieces.

Which, in his estimation was good.

And it was not white, which meant she was not making her first bows.

A widow, perhaps. She smiled up at him on the next turn. A young widow, and not terribly willing. That smile had been tight and polite.

They went down the middle together and waited through a set. "I don't believe we've met before. Is your family in town for the Season? Is your husband active in Parliament?"

She blinked and her eyes widened.

Not married, then. "I beg your pardon. Your title is from your father?"

They were interrupted again by the need to turn, and he concentrated momentarily on the dance.

When they came together again, her lips had curved up and her eyes gleamed with humor. "You are Shaldon's heir, are you not?"

"Yes."

More infernal turning. Would this dance never end so he could find out who she was?

They marched down the center together again. Where her hand touched his arm, he felt a delicate heat.

"And isn't this always the problem, Lord Bakeley, when a lord and lady dispense with a proper introduction?"

He heard it then: the slightest lilt, the tiniest burr. They parted to go round the next couple in line and came together again.

"You are Irish."

The dance ended and she curtsied, dipping her chin and rising again with a grin. "It was more than kind for you and your brother to dance with me. Indeed, I'm Sirena, Lady Sirena by birth. But now I'm the paid companion to Lady Jane Monthorpe, so I'll just take my leave and return to her."

She chuckled low in her throat, in a way that sent more heat through him.

"Thrilled she'll be at my social success tonight. Thank you for that, and the dance." She bobbed again.

"Wait just one moment." He offered his arm. "You must have some refreshments. And you must tell me all about your home in Ireland."

Her gaze slid over his shoulder. "Is that not your father, Lord Shaldon, there? His eyes are all but glowing. I shall free you, my lord, and return to my lady."

He took her hand and placed it on his arm. "Then we shall both go and speak to your Lady Jane."

Sirena drew deep inside searching for the whisper she used when controlling a particularly hotblooded horse. If she could but call it up—and since leaving home, she hadn't been able— perhaps it would work on the high bred stallion beside her. Lord Bakeley danced a bit less like a dream than his brother Charles, but only a bit less. And while the younger brother had wild fun in his eyes, this heir to Shaldon held a bubbling cauldron that she could sense but not see inside his handsome exterior.

Yow, but she'd not had a good, close-up look all those years ago when he'd come to buy Pooka. Father had been right to keep her away from this devil. And hadn't Bakeley turned the wary Pooka into an obedient sop before they'd left Glenmorrow? The man's looks alone would have horses and women swooning.

And fancy her, he did. She could feel it in the hot press of his hand over hers, even through the fine gloves. She could see it in the pulse at his neck, just over his ornately tied neck cloth.

And wouldn't she like to pull the ends of that neck cloth tighter and make his villainous father squirm?

CHAPTER THREE

Sirena smiled as Lady Jane rose from her chair and greeted them—a lady through and through, and still quite lovely. No one could question Lady Jane's character or bearing, and Sirena could tell even Bakeley could see that. He was ever so aristocratically polite as he maneuvered her patron into a proper introduction that, for all his prying and gabbing, did not include any more details about herself than what she'd given him. In fact, Lady Jane included less, omitting that business of Sirena being a paid companion.

And well, it was not really a true fact, since the lady was sure to be short of funds on Lady Day.

"It is a lovely soiree tonight, is it not, Lord Bakeley?" Lady Jane asked.

"Indeed."

Gad, but the man was fine-looking. Tall, he was, and dark, of both hair and eye, with a jaw that could crack a bushel of nuts.

Lady Jane babbled on about the room and the orchestra, the ladies' gowns and the refreshments. She glowed like the sparkling springs on a moonlit night back home. The poor thing had gone without such splendor for too long.

Sirena slid Lady Jane a glance. "Are you not acquainted with Lord Bakeley's father, my lady? Perhaps Lord Bakeley will escort you to greet him."

When they'd entered the room, they'd spotted the stately, quite fit-looking man tapping along on a cane he surely didn't need. Lady Jane had whispered his name right away.

It might be forward of Sirena to suggest the introduction, but Lady Jane knew Sirena wanted to meet the great Lord Shaldon. Needed to meet him.

Bakeley's handsome face went blank, as though a curtain had dropped on the end of a theatrical scene.

"Oh, good heavens." Sirena began vigorously fanning her benefactress. "You are quite flushed, my lady." She winked unobtrusively. "Let us get you to a chair and I'll fetch you some lemonade."

"Yes. Oh, dear." Lady Jane added a hint of a quiver. "The punch will be more restorative, I believe." She latched onto Bakeley's arm and all but dragged him off toward a vacant chair.

Next to Shaldon. Excellent that the heir was such a finely bred gentleman and followed Lady Jane's lead.

Sirena found a footman, ordered a glass of punch, and hurried over to be introduced.

Bakeley settled the lady into the chair next to his father, lifted his shoulder in the shrug the old man hated, and watched Lady Sirena cross the room, a young footman in hand, the man as bedazzled as he'd been.

She was like a boulder barreling down a mountain.

But no, that wasn't apt. Her back was straight, her step light. Perhaps, more like the alpine avalanche he'd read about recently, or a white frothy tidal wave sweeping all in her path.

A lady. Beautiful, not likely obedient, and certainly not rich. Not for him, but excellent for goading his father.

He informed his father that the lady seated next to him was Lady Jane Monthorpe. Then he did the unthinkable and introduced the vastly unsuitable Lady Sirena, poor, pushy, and worst of all in his father's eyes, Irish, and whose family name he still did not know.

The tight line of Shaldon's jaw and the grim sag of his lowered eyelids both shouted displeasure. "Good evening," he said, inclining his head to first the older lady, then the younger.

Bakeley expelled a breath. No cut direct. That would have been out of bounds even for Father.

Though, he thought, he'd not truly seen his father in many social settings outside of their country estate, Cransdall. Father had been away on the King's business for most of Bakeley's life, and on and off too *ill* for the last two years to take up his seat in Parliament.

"We did meet, Lord Shaldon, many years ago," the older lady said coolly. "I was not much more than a child. But of course you won't remember."

His father's eyes slitted further, Lady Sirena's eyes widened, and Perry pushed her glasses up and smiled too sweetly at Bakeley.

The skin on his neck rippled. Father had been too ill to take up his seat in the Lords, but that hadn't kept him home every day, nor had it kept his old companions away.

There was something afoot here, some scheme. Monthorpe. *Monthorpe.*

Then he remembered. "Lady Jane Monthorpe. Daughter of the Earl of Cheswick."

"Daughter of the last earl. Cousin of the current one." She smiled tightly and looked at the glass of punch. "I believe I don't want this after all." She handed the glass to Lady Sirena.

"I shall find that footman to take it back."

"Wait." Bakeley reached for it, and his fingers covered hers, sending his nerves dancing.

Now that was interesting. Her eyes flared with a bit of unexpected heat, quickly concealed.

"May I?" he asked. "I'm parched."

She released her grip and even colored slightly. Not easy to fake, that. And she had incited a deep glare in Father's eyes. Even better.

Perry came round their father's chair. "You are in good hands now, Father. I must go and chat with Paulette. Lady Sirena, Lady Jane, it has been a great pleasure to meet both of you. We are hosting a musicale next week. All the best people will be there. I would very much like you to attend."

Lady Jane smiled. Lady Sirena glanced at her benefactress, but he saw a hint of tension around her eyes and felt a strong desire to poke at it.

"What an excellent idea, Perry. Ladies, we would love your company. Are you musical, Lady Sirena?"

"She sings like a lovebird." Lady Jane's gushing was more that of a proud mama than a mistress.

"Oh, go on with you, your ladyship. She would have you believing I'm better than I am, she would."

The thick brogue sent one of his father's furry eyebrows shooting up. Lady Sirena laughed that deep womanly laugh, the one he wanted to hear again.

"It is time that we take our leave." Shaldon got to his feet. "We'll send the carriage back for you, Perpetua. I will require your assistance, Bakeley."

Bakeley made his farewells to the ladies with a mix of relief and regret. Perry would learn their direction. Perhaps she would pay a call and would need an escort to accompany her. He would see the fair Sirena again.

"I saw the gleam in your eye," Shaldon said as Bakeley settled across from him in the town coach. "She is off limits. Better the war profiteer's widow than that one."

"Because she's Irish?"

And why would that matter? Bink's mother had been an Irish girl Shaldon had met while posted there. He'd never talked about Ireland, not with Bakeley. He'd shared no more about his time in Ireland than he had anything else.

And of course that had all been before Bakeley's time. A few slips by members of Shaldon's network had given him a picture of how bad things had been. Atrocities and horrors had been carried out on both sides.

The old man thumped his cane on the roof and the carriage pulled out. "Because she's unsuitable." He clipped the words as if they were his final statement on everything.

And if Shaldon thought they were done talking, he would have to have one of his fake swoons. "Come, Father, tell me why she's unsuitable. I don't even know her family name or where she comes from, but apparently you do. Do I have to snoop around to find out? Perhaps I shall ask Denholm when I see him riding in the park tomorrow. He was in Ireland for a bit, as I recall."

The coach lights outside lit Shaldon's sharp profile, but it was too dark to make out his expression.

"Why will you not just agree to marry Denholm's daughter? You will unite two of the oldest titles in England, and I hear the girl is not ugly."

"I have not yet met her."

"You will. She is coming to your sister's musicale."

"Ah, well, perhaps she and Lady Sirena will become friends."

His head swiveled in Bakeley's direction. "*She* is not coming."

"You would make Perry withdraw the invitation? You would humiliate the cousin of the Earl of Cheswick?"

"I have it on good account they have taken rooms. How they arrived tonight, I do not know." They passed under a street light, dimly illuminating a scowl. "Though I suppose, Lady Hackwell no doubt persuaded her husband to send his carriage."

His father could make many things happen, including sending a carriage to pick up two ladies. He was up to no good.

"Denholm will remember a daughter of one of the Irish lords named Sirena. He waxes eloquent on all things Ireland. Perhaps I shall seek him out at the club tonight."

"You would, wouldn't you? Forget your rich widow altogether and go nosing about town. And just to spite me. Well then, boy, have at it, but remember you won't be hurting me so much as the lady. And if you care anything at all about her reputation, you won't bring that family's history to any one's notice."

The carriage stopped. Shaldon jumped out, far too spryly, leaving Bakeley to ponder.

"To St. John's Wood, sir?" the coachman asked.

St. John's Wood was where the dowager Lady Arbrough had settled into a gilded new townhouse. She would greet him with supper, and perhaps a clinging negligee, and after both appetites were quenched she would peck him to death about the Hackwell ball. There would be sly innuendos about gauche country girls and unfashionable bluestockings, and there would be the latest *on-dit* about someone's daughter marrying in haste.

"White's tonight."

"Very well, milord." The door shut. He settled back, closed his eyes, and conjured a vision of his mistress naked. Nothing.

Hell. He'd only just turned two and thirty. Was he losing his virility already?

Outside, a blonde-haired whore stood close by a building, and his mind went directly to a vision of Lady Sirena in her blue dress.

He smiled. The problem was not with him. It was merely time to part company with Lady Arbrough.

And pursue Lady Sirena. Though he didn't pursue virgins. That was a sure way to get leg-shackled, and he wasn't one of those villains who seduced a girl and abandoned her to her fate. He didn't even flirt or raise expectations.

Which meant that Lady Sirena really was unsuitable, though perhaps not in the way his father meant.

Unless he married her.

Oh, hell, what was he thinking?

Brandy was what he needed. Lots of it.

*****

"We have had a social victory, Barton." Lady Jane handed the faithful maid her wrap. "Lady Sirena danced with five gentlemen, including the heir to the Earl of Shaldon. And we are invited to a musicale at Shaldon House next week."

"That is wonderful, my lady."

"Yes. He is quite handsome. So many prefer the younger brother with his fairer coloring and carefree nature, but I do believe the older one is more to my taste. What say you, Sirena?"

"I won't compare. They're equally handsome. But Barton, her ladyship spent time in conversation with the handsome men's father, who I believe very much resembles the son more to Lady Jane's taste. Sat right next to him, she did, and made him remember that he met her years ago. And he's still not half bad to look at."

Lady Jane's face grew serious, belying the blush coloring her cheeks.

"He was great friends with my beau and my brother."

Lady Jane had once had a chance to marry a cavalry officer who'd died without ever setting foot into battle, and her brother with him.

Blast it. She'd stirred a bad memory. She ran her hands over her mistress's dress, smoothing it, and folding it into the clothes press. "He's widowed. Perhaps—"

"Such foolishness." With Barton's assistance, Lady Jane slipped on her nightrail, and the maid left. "Old spinsters don't marry. It wreaks havoc with settlements and inheritances, and even widowed lords want to breed more spares. You, on the other hand, will find a husband this season if it's the last thing I accomplish on this earth." She knotted the belt on her robe. "But, Sirena, my dear, you mustn't set your cap at one of Shaldon's sons. Especially not the heir. I'm afraid the younger one is wild, and the older is, well, he's the heir. He'll be expected to marry...oh, I'm muddling this. You know I esteem you above all of the silly girls we'll meet this season—"

If we receive invitations.

"But you're lacking a dowry, and Shaldon will insure his son marries great wealth, as he did himself. She was a lovely woman, his wife. I was acquainted with her as well, though I was much younger, of course. Her grandfather had an interest in one of the big banks and settled her well." She reached for Sirena's hand. "There now, you don't have wealth, but you do have great beauty and the pleasantest of demeanors, and you *are* an earl's daughter, and that will count for something."

Barton returned with a steaming chocolate pot. She poured a cup for each of them and then gathered up Lady Jane's discarded undergarments. "Is there aught else, my lady?"

Lady Jane sent Barton off with a goodnight.

Sirena lifted the cup and sniffed. Celebrating with chocolate was a great indulgence, given Lady Jane's straitened budget, and Sirena was grateful for it. "Why would I want to give up a cozy talk and fine chocolate for marriage? And anyway, do you think a daughter of Ireland can find a husband here among these English, my lady?"

"You are a daughter of the United Kingdoms of Great Britain and Ireland." Lady Jane sounded fierce. "Never forget that."

How could she? Her brother had disappeared fighting against that union and the bloody aristocrats who enforced their intolerance on the people of Ireland.

She fixed a smile on her face. "To be sure. And I am a Protestant to boot, and not one of those Latin-spouting Catholics."

They sipped chocolate until Lady Jane broke the companionable silence. "It probably wasn't his fault, you know."

"Whose fault, my lady?"

"Shaldon's. He probably didn't bring about your brother's demise."

Her pulse quickened and raced, the way it had when they'd talked about attending the Hackwell ball. She'd confided her great desire to meet the Earl of Shaldon, else the older lady's pride would have caused her to turn down Lady Hackwell's most courteous offer of a carriage.

And, Sirena was certain Lady Jane was wrong on this point. Shaldon had run the network of spies who had reported her brother as one of the United Ireland men.

Well, what if he was? There were rebels of all stripes, and she knew, her brother would never have countenanced the kind of violence that had led to wholesale atrocities. In her young eyes, he'd been noble, kind, and so much more level-headed than their horse-mad father.

Because of Shaldon, her brother had been lost, along with the title. The new Glenmorrow had failed to provide for her. Worse, he'd forced her from her home.

She shook off the thought. It had been a blessing from God and Brighid that Lady Jane had been a guest at the neighboring estate where she'd sought refuge.

"Yes, of course not," Sirena said. "In times of war, there is plenty of blame to spread about."

It was a comfortable fiction, this not blaming Shaldon. For now.

*****

Bakeley drove the gray gelding through the morning fog, finally reining up to avoid a group of riders. He did not exchange greetings. He did not wish to converse this morning.

He'd had a night of sheer boredom, followed by an hour or two of dreams of a blonde siren. Sirena. How aptly she'd been named.

Charley had met up with him in the wee hours, plaguing him with speculation about whether Sirena could be a prospect for an affair of the heart, wondering where a lady's companion who was herself a lady fit into the spectrum of eligible women.

It had taxed Bakeley's carefully nurtured aplomb until he'd wanted to whack Charley, like they were boys again. He'd reminded Charley that swiving such a woman would move her into the ranks of the demimonde in one fell, well, *stroke*. He reminded him that a gentleman did not go about seducing the daughters of other gentlemen, and most especially not the daughters of peers.

Charley had looked at him, stunned, and laughed. And laughed some more. Club rules or no, even under a heavy lid of boredom, he'd come a hair's breadth from pummeling his younger brother.

"I'll yield the field then, brother," Charley had said.

Fortunately, two sods who were friends of Charley joined them, eager to discuss horseflesh.

Unfortunately, failure to discuss the woman in question meant that all of her secrets were still buried.

Never mind. Perry was paying Lady Jane a formal call today to deliver the musicale invitation. He would accompany her.

As the sun lifted the layers of fog, Bakeley headed for the park gate.

On the street outside he spotted a trim woman in the distance, her basket held close. She turned her head at the crossing, and a spray of golden curls peeked out from her bonnet.

CHAPTER FOUR

His pulse buzzed. It might be her. On the other hand, he might be following yet another blonde head through the streets of London. Since leaving Hackwell's home last night, he'd noticed every wench, every streetwalker, every shop girl.

He kept pace with this one. A gentleman did not call out to women on the street, and this one walked with the poise of a lady, though her dress was a plain frock in one of those shades of brown that reminded him of horse dung. She moved quickly, the toes of her dark boots poking out with each stride. Her bonnet brim concealed much, at least from this angle. Blast it, afoot he could come abreast of her.

Abreast. Yes.

He spotted a boy sweeping, hailed him, and gave him a coin to hold his mount. He plucked a turnip from a stall and flipped the shop man another coin.

She was fast for a woman, but he caught up. "Miss," he said, "I believe you dropped this."

She increased her pace. "Miss. Miss." He was alongside her now. He touched her elbow, and she froze.

Astonishment lit her face, kindling a burn in him.

"It *is* you." He swallowed the schoolboy smile that threatened and said regally, "Here is your turnip."

She opened her mouth. Closed it. Took a deep breath. "Good morning, Lord Bakeley. You may have that turnip. 'Tis not mine. And now I must be on my way."

She took off walking again.

He kept pace. "You are out and about alone early, Lady Sirena." Too early, and too alone. It wasn't safe, not for a girl as lovely as her.

Her lips firmed. "I'm on an errand for my lady." She stopped abruptly and glared, the basket held tightly in front of her. Or perhaps she was preparing to bash him with it.

He reached for the potential weapon, depositing the turnip. "Allow me to carry your burdens and escort you home."

She colored deeply. "At this hour of the morning? You must not. Where is your carriage? Your horse?" She scanned the street behind them and her eyes narrowed, her lips turning down in a frown. "There. That fine gray trying to bite the unfortunate boy. You must return to him for he is thinking about bolting. And we must not be seen like this."

"Yes, well. My sister and I will be calling on you later today. With the musicale invitation."

"Your sister is all genuine kindness. You, however, are confirming my conviction that we shouldn't attend."

"You must."

"We have no carriage."

"We will send ours."

She sighed. "Lady Jane may go. I shall have a megrim."

He so wanted to chuck her under the chin. "You do not have megrims."

"How would you know?"

"I know women, Lady Sirena. You are not the megrim sort."

Good heavens. He was bantering like Charley.

It felt rather good.

"Now give me that basket."

Astonishingly, she complied. He patted the cloth as they started walking. Something plump and warm nestled there.

"'Tis bread," she said. "Do not be squeezing it so."

"*You* fetch it?"

"Lord and Lady Cheswick are the generous sort with everyone. Consequently, Lady Jane has enough to support three retainers, of which I am one."

She was letting him know that Lady Jane was poor, and Lady Sirena was poorer, the clever girl. "You keep saying that she is your employer. And you've not told me your family name. Are you not related to her in some way? That is the usual thing in these cases."

"I am not. The Cheswicks are friends of the family that owns the estate next to my family home."

"And where is that?"

"In Ireland." She smiled sweetly.

He decided on a different tack. "So you became acquainted during a house party?"

"Nay."

She turned the corner onto a residential street, lined with smallish dwellings, their elegance fading, and stopped in front of a door needing a fresh coat of paint. "These are our rooms." She took the basket and heaved in a deep breath, fixing him with a gray glare.

He should let her go. Father would surely relent and share her story. Or he could ask around about her...but Father had been correct, it would only draw attention, unwanted if he were to pursue her.

And he wanted to pursue her. "I'm not a gossip," he said. "My sister has her heart set on yours and Lady Jane's friendship, and—"

"As you wish." She shifted the basket. "If harm comes to my lady, I'll know who to blame. And so here it is. Lady Jane all but fished me out of the woods where I was preparing to hide and took me back to the neighbor's house. She shamed them quite unmercifully and insisted they give me refuge until she could find a way to help me."

"You were hiding?" His mind had snagged on that point. The wars were long over. Even Ireland was more or less settled, wasn't it? "From whom? Irish rebels? British soldiers?"

She laughed ruefully. "Well, he was once a British soldier, I know, but he was, like me, another bad mix of the Irish and English. My cousin, the new earl, arrived to inspect his property. Angry, he was, that the house was in disrepair, but he was keen on the horses." She looked hard at him, her eyes taking a blue cast, the irises lined with an edging of gray. "Every bit as fine as your mount here were our horses once upon a time." She pressed her lips together and took in an angry breath. "He said he did love a fine mount."

His heart thudded to a stop and then picked up and raced. Fine cattle and a house in disrepair. Perhaps there was more than one such estate in Ireland. Could it be?

And the rest... If that cousin had harmed her in that way...

She nodded. "In truth, I was not living any richer there than I am now, except that I was home and I could ride through those woods and shoot game when we were hungry. I could have stayed, but...the cost was too dear. You should know that my family name was ruined long ago." Her chin jutted forward. "Honor I may not have, but I have my pride." She gave him another forced laugh. "And my daily bread. Good day, my lord."

Her foot hit the first step.

"Wait."

She looked back at him, the curve of her cheek burnished pink in the morning chill, a chill that seeped into him and raced through his veins.

Brave. Saucy. Proud. This woman stirred him. And terrified him.

"What?" she asked.

"We've brought some very fine cattle to town. Perhaps you and I and my sister Perry could go riding one day."

She turned fully around on the step, her eyes level with his, her face serious. "Plain-spoken, I will be, sir. Lady Jane has a wild idea of me marrying this Season, yet she told me that you in particular are out of my respectable reach. You will be marrying a girl of good family and great wealth, which I am not. And thus I must decline your kind invitation. I wish you all felicitations on your marriage when—"

Bellowing erupted around the corner, and the pounding of hooves. His mount came dragging the boy.

"Blast you," the boy screamed, adding a stream of epithets no lady should hear.

"There, boy. Easy, boy." Bakeley rushed over and grabbed for the reins as the horse shook the boy loose.

And suddenly stilled. Peace swept through the startled beast. Bakeley could almost hear the quiet rush.

A small hand had settled on the horse's dappled gray head, the lady's gaze locked on the beast's dark eyes, a soft, soothing croon sounding deep in her throat. Before he could speak, her hand dropped and she was up the steps and in the door, the basket clutched under her arm.

The gelding looked after her with longing in his eyes.

Bakeley blinked and caught his breath.

Damn this world. Damn the *ton* and propriety and earldoms and... Shaldon. What the devil was father up to? And did he himself give a damn about it?

This beast's granddam won first at Thurles. She's good Irish Connemara and the best hotblood lines, as fast as any of your English hacks, I'd b-bet you.

The gelding snorted, drawing his attention. He was one of a number of dappled grays in their stock, and he had a bit of his dam's cantankerous spirit. They'd not been able to breed out the worst parts of Pooka and her hobgoblin curse.

He'd brought her and the other Glenmorrow horses home to Cransdall all those years ago, and then, upon Mother's horrifying death, promptly forgot the girl in the stall.

Surely this was the Earl of Glenmorrow's wild daughter, the one who whispered to horses. The one whose brother, heir to an earldom, had betrayed England.

He'd paid a high bounty for Glenmorrow's fine horses, but Mother wouldn't tell him why. What had his father done to Glenmorrow? Lady Sirena's plight was all tied up in it, as well as her unsuitability.

Someone would know, someone who would not run to his father with tales of his snooping.

His father's man, Kincaid, who now lodged with his brother Bink knew all the stories, but he was also the surest one to tattle. He could ask Bink, but Bink's investigating might stir up the kind of troubles his father had warned about.

There was Lady Hackwell. She seemed to have a finger on the pulse of every distressed damsel in London, and she had seen fit to bring both ladies to her ball. But paying a call on her was sure to pique Hackwell's curiosity.

And Father would get wind and cause one sort of trouble or another.

He turned his horse toward Berkeley Square. Bink, it would be. His brother was close to both of the Hackwells. He'd been the Hackwells' steward two years earlier. He could get to her ladyship unobtrusively, and Bink had his own past grievances with Father. He was the lowest risk.

CHAPTER FIVE

Sirena hurried into the tiny room they used as a kitchen, greeted Molly, their maid of all work, and dropped her basket. Her heart galloped like Bakeley's horse must have done that morning before his master stopped her on the street.

She'd not lost her gift after all. She'd not lost it, and Bakeley's horse proved it. That dappled nose had drawn calm from her and stirred up a memory of Pooka. Perhaps that gelding was her issue, though in truth, that sort of coloring was common enough.

Her breath hitched. And how was Pooka? Bakeley had made his poor lathered fellow stand waiting in the morning's cold air. Was he careless of his cattle?

Or was he just that taken with her?

"What happened, my lady?" Molly asked. "Ye're pale about the gills."

She forced a laugh. "'Tis the stench of this city, Molly. Will I ever get used to it?"

"Nay, nor will I." Molly reached for the basket. "A turnip. How ever did you know I was wanting one for the stew? A fey one you are, my lady."

Sirena laughed and shooed her away. "A lucky guess."

It hadn't been lucky at all, drawing a rich lord's attention, in the street, of all places. She went about the preparations for Lady Jane's breakfast, letting her overcharged heart cool.

How far had he followed her? How much had he seen?

Jamie, her brother, was lost to the world, but not to her. She'd never truly believed it before, and she didn't believe it now.

She lifted the heavy tray and went down the short corridor to the drawing room.

Lady Jane sat at the small table in her dressing gown, a frilly white cap hiding her still-dark hair, a scandal sheet spread before her.

"Good morning." Sirena infused the greeting with cheer. "What news then? Did they report on our appearance at Lady Hackwell's ball?"

"Not so far," Lady Jane said. "You went out again early."

"Yes. And you'll be ever so happy I did when you taste what I've brought you." She set out the plates, cups and steaming pot.

"I don't like to think of you walking the streets of this town without one of us. I don't like you going out alone."

Lady Jane had a sharp look about her. Perhaps the run-in with Shaldon had unsettled her also.

"Well, and I'm not alone. There's the baker's boy I chat with each morning, and the street sweeper who walks ahead of me chattering for a farthing. And the grocer's wife whose rheumy knee tells the weather each day. I inquire about the forecast with her."

And making other inquiries, she was.

"You know what I mean," the lady grumbled, flipping a page of newsprint. "I feel a responsibility for you."

Sirena steadied her hand and poured Lady Jane a cup of tea. Six and twenty she was, as much a spinster as Lady Jane. And though she hated dissembling with the lady who was her only friend, the O'Brian boys were in town. It was Brighid's own luck that she'd run into them. Like her, they'd hied themselves out of the new earl's grasp, working here and there, wherever a strong back was needed.

"It's grateful I am too, ma'am. But you mustn't worry."

"The streets are teeming with people up from the country. Of course I worry."

"This is out of the norm, then?" Sirena asked. "Are they here for the coronation? It's months away."

'Twas also the old king's death that had brought the O'Brians to town—as if that would stay the executioner's blade for an Irishman fallen out of favor. They'd come not for pomp and glitter but for work and food. Meeting the boys had seemed a miracle to her.

"Yes, but the preparations have begun, and there's work here," Lady Jane said.

Sirena had hired the boys. A strong back she didn't need, but open ears on the docks and seedy places where a girl alone would find only trouble, yes, for that she'd offered every bit of her savings, and they'd agreed. Gossip, news, any loose word about the shipwreck so many years past—what better place than the docks of London, where sailors from all over the world passed in and out?

She must know if anyone survived the wreck of the Honey Bee. If Jamie lived, she must know the truth. A chat with the first mate on the packet from Ireland had stirred him back to life in her heart. If he lived, she would find him.

She felt certain the English government would know. Shaldon would know.

Lady Jane stabbed a finger at the paper. "Here it is." She cast Sirena a grim look and went back to the newssheet. "*Wealthy Lord S was seen frowning as his heir danced with a golden-haired lady reputed to be of a noble family fallen from favor.*"

Blast the man, Bakeley. For certain, she'd found a way into Shaldon's home through Lady Perpetua's kindness, but she'd hoped she'd be merely another speck-on-the-wall genteel companion, unseen, unheard, invisible. Not prey to a randy lord who'd never be anything but above her, and in all the worst ways.

Bakeley found his brother Bink alone in the breakfast room of the townhouse he shared with his wife, Paulette, their infant son, her uncle Kincaid, and a handful of servants.

None of them footmen, unfortunately. Bakeley walked straight to the sideboard and poured himself coffee.

Bink looked up from where he was scanning the morning news sheets and raised a bushy red eyebrow, in much the same irritating way as their father. "Went home to shave, I see."

"Just had a jaunt in the park with one of the Connemara geldings."

Bink grunted. He didn't share the Everly passion for horses.

"He's a spirited fellow. Where's Paulette this morning? Still abed?"

"She's in the nursery. Our son is always hungry. Do you want breakfast?"

"I wouldn't mind."

"Ring the bell."

He laughed. Only at Bink's home would the heir to an earldom be required to summon his own breakfast. "Anyone else would have the food on the sideboard."

"And footmen fetching and carrying, but this here is a commoner's home." A maid appeared and he looked up from his paper. "Fanny, bring a plate for his lordship. Some of everything will be fine—no, make that plenty of everything."

Bakeley plopped into a chair, feeling envious. Bink could breakfast at his leisure without being harped upon. But of course—his marrying according to the old man's wishes hadn't been easy either. "What a difference marriage lines make."

He had Bink's full attention now. "Feeling sorry for yourself, your lordship? The old man pairing you up with some white-clad lass?"

His stomach rumbled. "Denholm's daughter."

"And? Let me guess, she's a pretty young chit who can discuss the weather in twenty different ways without offending anyone, and can execute a perfect country dance as well as sing *The Yellow Hair'd Laddie*. Will she be performing at Perry's musical evening?"

Lord, but he hoped not. "I have not yet met her."

"Ah, well, I'll hover nearby and watch the fireworks as love strikes."

The maid entered carrying a steaming plate. Silence reigned until the door closed on her.

"I don't plan to marry on Father's whim."

Bink sent him a quizzical look. "Like I did, you mean?"

He sighed. "I've already apologized for my part in that."

"Yes, well, as it turned out, Paulette and I do suit, quite well." He grinned. "I would never say it to his face but he was right about this match."

"Well, he is not right about the Denholm chit."

"After the musicale, you might wish to eat those words as avidly as you're plowing through that bacon."

He took a bite of toast. Bink might be right. Perhaps he should keep his options open, at least until after he'd met Shaldon's intended candidate.

"I did hear that you were quite taken with a young lady last night."

That got his ears twitching. It was the same sly tone their father used when he was up to something. "She *was* quite stunning," he drawled.

"An Irish lass." Bink watched with an amused intensity that left him feeling confused. Bink had an Irish mother, a girl Shaldon had met on some government mission, when he was still the younger son, before he'd inherited. Shaldon hadn't been able to marry her, of course. He'd been called back to England by his brother's death, and anyway, Bink's mother had been too low socially.

Unlike Lady Sirena, an earl's daughter. She'd be within Bakeley's reach, if he were so inclined.

Bink laughed.

And Bakeley knew—his brother knew more. Perhaps this time Bink was the one in on Father's manipulations. Well, turn-about was fair play, wasn't it?

And forewarned was forearmed.

"What do you know about her?" Bakeley asked.

"Besides her bonny looks?" Bink leaned back and cocked a foot across his knee.

"You are baiting me, just like Shaldon would do."

Bink grimaced and threw the papers aside. "Her brother, Roland James Hollister, was lost at sea escaping the Crown. He was much older than her. Word was he fought under Corcoran and was connected to Emmet before the nationalist movement was finally stopped."

"He was a traitor."

"Aye. The father disavowed him and hung onto the title."

His hair rose on his neck. "Glenmorrow." He sliced through a sausage and chewed calmly while inside his nerves danced, remembering. The sudden mission to visit and buy up Glenmorrow's best stock. The bedraggled estate.

The stable lad he'd argued with, who was no lad.

He carefully swallowed. "That business would have been years ago. Ancient history."

Bink grunted. "The worst of the rebellion was years ago. He was lost sometime after that."

She was unsuitable, Father had said. "Even then, she would have been a child."

Bink harrumphed. "In war, who suffers more than the women and children?"

The thought of Sirena suffering disturbed him. Her shadowed, defiant face as she'd proudly stated her horse's lineage and challenged him to a race, reared up at him.

He pushed away from the table and began to pace. "Might Shaldon have been in Ireland then?"

"Who knows? Quite possibly."

"What are you not telling me, Bink?"

"I haven't been drawn into any conspiracy, if that's what you're asking. I learned all of this from Hackwell, who learned it from his lady, who learned it from Lady Jane Monthorpe." Bink stood also. "And I made the inquiry because, from the look of you last night, I assumed you'd want to know."

"Funny. Father dared me to investigate. Said it would bring her background to light and ruin her reputation."

"Well then, see that you don't blab this among those fools at your club."

"Or that fool brother of ours."

Bink laughed. "He's the perfect sort of spy, shagging his way through every foreign delegate's wife's bedchamber. He won't ruin her reputation if you tell him not to." He quirked an eyebrow. "But what about you, Bakeley?"

Heat rose in him. Bink always suspected the worst of his brothers, as if being born on the right side of an aristocratic bed lowered a man's character. "What do you suppose Father had to do with her brother's downfall? He told me most emphatically that she's unsuitable, and that I'm to stay away from her."

"I imagine Shaldon has a file tucked away somewhere with the name Hollister on it. Whether he has one for her, I don't know. She's a young woman with only a spinster to protect her. She deserves the benefit of discretion, and to be safe from bored aristocrats tired of their mistresses."

That was pointed enough to spike his anger, but he bit back a retort and picked a spot of lint off his coat, counting to ten. Shaldon's return to England had driven Bakeley from sole management of the Shaldon empire into this noble boredom, much more frustrating than either Bink or Charley could imagine.

He forced a laugh. "Did you know Father is scheming to get you a barony?"

"Bull. He wants me in the Commons where he thinks he can control my vote. And you're changing the subject."

"I don't ruin young ladies of any class or rank."

Bink's shoulders lowered on a deep exhale. "My faith is restored. Now you must come and see what can result from a quick trip to Gretna Green. Your nephew is sprouting a new tooth."

He rolled his eyes, but it was only a pretense, one his older brother would expect. His nephew was crawling now and starting to be interesting. "Lead on."

Besides, if he went home, he would only encounter Father at breakfast. By late morning, the old man would be gone, making the rounds of his cronies, and lining up his chess pieces for Parliament, where Bink and Charley had entered the lower house.

While his heir twiddled his thumbs and pursued Shaldon's choice of a bride.

No. After Shaldon went out, he would peruse the files Father had locked in the study. And then he would accompany Perry when she made her call on the ladies.

CHAPTER SIX

Bakeley set a quick pace away from the Shaldon townhouse.

"You are frowning most prodigiously," Perry said as they trod the several streets to Lady Sirena's lodgings. A rare sun had come out in force, and Perry had insisted they both needed a brisk jaunt in the fresh air. "Are you not glad I tore you away from Father? He was most displeased I insisted you accompany me instead of a footman. That should make you happy."

A muscle in his jaw ticked. Father, as it turned out, had decided this morning to stay at home, preventing a search of his private study. For the first time in months, Father had wanted to discuss some aspect of the estate operations, not to obtain Bakeley's opinion but to inform him of the instructions he'd already issued to their land steward.

It was all a ruse, of course, just like most of Shaldon's other doings. Staying a step ahead of him was difficult.

He should have gone ahead with a move into the house he'd quietly taken when Father had returned, but the man's ill health—or alleged ill health—had kept him tied to the family's grand London townhouse.

Perry nudged his arm. "Bakeley. Do you not appreciate your liberation this day?"

"Yes, Perry." He patted her hand. "You were very clever. And naughty, telling Father we were visiting the book shop."

"Oh, we will, after we visit Lady Jane and Lady Sirena." A smug smile played on her lips. His little sister was finally coming out of the shell she'd entered when Mother had died. He'd never thought to say it, but he was glad to see the mischievous girl reappearing. A beauty she might never be, with her square jaw and Everly nose, but hers was a kind face, and her children would appreciate it even if her husband—whoever Father picked for her—didn't.

"I've done something else Father will not approve."

"What? You've sneaked off to a gaming hell? You've published a scientific article anonymously? You've—"

"No, Bakeley. I've invited Lady Arbrough to our musicale."

No. He stiffened. He had ordered a bouquet delivered that day, along with a note of apology.

"I...I thought you would be happy, since you and she are—"

"You are not supposed to know anything about that." He squelched the urge to chastise more. "But it's fine. You've invited all the fashionable world. It would have been odd to leave her out."

"Good. Thank you. Father and Charley argued about it, but Charley said the same thing, that it would be noticed if I left her out."

His brother was up to mischief.

"Did Charley also suggest you invite Lady Jane?"

A smile lit her face. "That was my own idea. I thought Lady Jane's presence would be good for Father."

"Matchmaking are you?"

Her laugh was merry. "He was terribly rude to both ladies, don't you think? He won't be so again to Lady Jane, but we must look after Lady Sirena."

"I'll let you look after her."

"Oh. Yes, I forgot. Lady Arbrough." She inhaled sharply. "And Lord Denholm's daughter." She waved a hand dismissively. "Pah. When you marry, she'll have to get used to you having a mistress."

"*Lady Perpetua.*"

"This is not my first season, Bakeley. I understand how marriage in our class usually works."

She had steadfastly turned down at least one offer each year from bounders who were after her dowry. His sister was holding out for a love match, and good luck to her with that.

"You must beget the heir. And of course you won't flaunt a mistress in front of your wife. But Denholm's daughter hasn't even met you and I'll warrant she's too innocent to know of your arrangement. I'll have to think on this, but in the meantime we've diverted from what we were discussing, which was protecting Lady Sirena from Father, who'll no doubt be horribly rude to her. I'll be too busy to look after her. Perhaps I'll leave her to Charley."

Not Charley. "You've persuaded me. I'll make the sacrifice and protect Lady Sirena from Father." It would allow him to dodge both Lady Arbrough and Denholm's daughter.

'Twas the Hackwells conveying Sirena and Lady Jane to Shaldon House the night of the musicale. Sirena followed the other ladies out of the town coach aided by the handsome Lord Hackwell himself. His military background had apparently not soured him on all things Irish. He'd been quite kind to her.

She'd made a half-hearted attempt to decline this invitation and allow Lady Jane to go alone, pleading a headache she really felt, and then she'd chastised herself for her cowardice. Soldiers carried on, notwithstanding an ache in the head, and so must she.

Aye, but she'd got bad news. Walter O'Brian had come up with a sad report. Jamie was very likely dead, according to a seaman who'd known another man who'd sailed on the *Honey Bee*, a man who, with any luck, she'd meet on the morrow.

Did he see him die? Walter had asked, but the man hadn't known.

She'd not felt this low since Papa's death. Not even her cousin's insulting treatment of her had depressed her so. Actually, that hadn't depressed her at all, it had made her hungry to know more about Jamie...and to exact a suitable revenge.

And perhaps her pulsing head would be the perfect excuse to slip away and begin searching. Her father had left many of his mundane tasks to her, and she knew the general way men managed their papers. A spymaster would be more careful, but she'd take her chances on finding something.

Glittering eyes turned on them as they stepped across the hallowed portal of Shaldon House. The Hackwells were not considered good *ton*, she with her charitable pursuits, he with his Whiggish tendencies.

Aye, but she was lying to herself, wasn't she? She was the reason for the stares. Even after the Hackwells moved on to greet guests, the quizzing glasses stayed trained on herself, bloody owl eyes searching for the night's prey.

"Ladies, how lovely you look this evening." Lady Perpetua squeezed Sirena's hand. "The primrose becomes you wonderfully. I, myself, look like a spoiled sausage in that shade."

"That's exactly what Lady Hackwell said about herself when she offered the frock to me. 'Tis the truth that this is one of her old gowns made over, Lady Perpetua." That came out less jaunty than she'd hoped, and she couldn't help it. She had a mission, her head hurt, and she was more than a little irritable.

But Lady Perpetua's smile only grew. "How practical and honest you are. Call me Perry. We shall be fast friends, I think. I'm going to have a go at plucking a tune on my harp. Will you also participate tonight?"

"I must beg off. I've a wee hammer pounding nails into my head, but Lady Jane was a complete dragon and insisted I come anyway."

Lady Jane turned from the couple she was greeting and tapped her fan on Sirena's arm while Lady Perry giggled. "You dreadful girl. You must at least stay for your hostess's performance before running off to the retiring room."

Sirena forced a chuckle. "Do you see how she bullies me?"

Lady Perry laughed and excused herself.

Sirena looked around. She'd memorized the route and counted the doors from the entry to this room.

"Is this the ballroom, Lady Jane?"

"I believe so."

It was much grander than Hackwell's, though not nearly as inviting. Paned glass doors opened out onto what must be a garden, but the room itself was all gilded and burnished in the style of the last century. The heiress Lord Bakeley would marry could have a go at refurbishing it.

Her gaze found him, and she chuckled. He wore a tight mask, ever so polite, but she saw well enough his desire for escape. Surely the young lady next to him in her white ruffles, and her mama next to her—for that must be the relationship—could notice it also.

"I'm glad to see you enjoying yourself." Lady Jane linked arms with her. "Come, I see an acquaintance of mine. We'll greet her and find seats."

"Where is the great lord himself?" she whispered.

"Over there." Lady Jane tilted her head toward a kind of dais, and Sirena saw Lord Shaldon nearby, leaning on his cane. He was engaged in deep conversation with an ancient man in an old-fashioned wig and he'd not noticed her, else he would be gamboling down the aisle between chairs, clacking that cane on the polished floor, getting ready to thwack her with it.

"Will you mind ever so much if I find a seat at the back?" She pulled her arm free and touched her hand to her forehead. "This pounding is quite more than I can bear." And if the musicians were as awful as she anticipated, well...

"Go to the ladies' retiring room," Lady Jane said. "When the music starts, come back. If all the seats are taken, some gentleman will yield one for you."

She asked a maid for directions, and hurried along the corridor, counting doors. The room designated for the ladies was, as yet, empty and she settled onto a chair. When two ladies entered, she fiddled with her shoe, as though she'd picked up a pebble, or her stocking had bunched. She didn't know them, and they ignored her. Not exactly the cut direct, yet she felt the full force of their superiority.

Lord love the English. The boys at home had whispered that, at Belfast, they'd locked women and children in a barn and burned them to death. She could withstand a mere haughty attitude. While they turned up their noses, she would nose around, and wouldn't invisibility make it easier?

And what would his esteemed English Lordship, Shaldon, do if he caught her sneaking? She closed her eyes and imagined her punishment. The English had a great many means of persuasion, but most of them came with a fist— to the head, the stomach, the limbs. If she were caught searching his things, she would not be catching a husband with that battered body.

"Are you quite all right?"

She opened her eyes to a most fashionable woman. Her gown cupped her upper arms and two half-mooned breasts, bared down almost to the very nipples, and all about the rest was a rich, sensuous fluttering of silky stuff in the most seductive shade of red. It was a rousing dress, designed to establish her friendliness, especially with the male guests.

The astonishing blue eyes set against pale skin and ebony hair, those were not friendly, no matter how warm her words.

With such haughtiness, and in such a dress, she was surely fashionable and wealthy. Sirena should stand for a creature like this, who was so clearly above her.

She kept her seat. "'Tis only a slight headache. Thank you for your concern."

"Have you taken a powder? I have always found Dover's Powders to be quite effective."

She did not take headache powders. "Yes, yes. I will be fine in a moment, thank you."

"Shall I send for your mother?"

She sighed. A moment alone preparing her spy craft was too much to ask, but she knew how to drive this one away. "You'll be sending to heaven then, if 'tis my mother you're fetching, for sure and she's been gone these many years."

The lady's look sharpened.

That was interest there, Sirena decided, stifling a groan. There'd always be interest in her. She'd hoped for an interested cut. Instead, she saw a decided thawing, and more questions coming.

"You are Scottish?"

She shook her head. "Worse, madame. I am a daughter of Ireland."

"Of course." That came with the start of a sneer.

Sirena felt more hopeful. Perhaps she could move this lady on with some blarney. "I suppose 'tis not polite to say, but I must. Your gown is the most wonderful thing I've seen since arriving in London."

That brought a smile. The lady was as vain as Sirena had suspected. Ah, but vanity was the least of the seven deadly sins.

"No one has told you that primrose is out of fashion?" the lady asked.

"Why, yes." *You just have.* "But it's this or my cerulean blue, which, you'll be telling me, is also unfashionable." She added a smile to soften her impertinence. One must be clever with the most high and hope they didn't notice one's own retaliatory rudeness.

The lady in red laughed and actually curtsied.

"I am Lady Arbrough. Come, you must tell me your name."

"Sirena Hollister. *Lady* Sirena Hollister, there's the amazing thing."

"Indeed."

Sirena could see the wheels turning in the lady's head, clicking down the list of peers, looking for the Hollisters. Good luck to her.

A fiddle bow squealed in the distance.

"They're about to start," the lady said. "Come, take my arm and we shall return together."

So her plain Irish primrosiness could set off the lady's fiery beauty. Fair enough. She would be invisible, and upon arrival could shed the persistent woman.

"Very well." She linked arms and proceeded down the hall. "My lady will be worrying about me."

Lady Arbrough stopped and dropped her arm. "Your lady?"

"Lady Jane Monthorpe. She's taken me in, as it were. One might say she's my employer." Her head was feeling better. She held back the grin that wanted to break forth. "Though I suppose, if one were employed, one couldn't expect to be a guest of the *haute ton*? So I must call her 'my lady' instead of my employer." She curtsied. "And you may precede me, my lady."

Lady Arbrough froze. Her gaze raked the yellow flounces of Sirena's dress, as though peeping under each pleat to see what was squirming there.

"You are a sly one." She twined her arm with Sirena's again. "We'll make a grand entrance together, you and I." She chuckled. "Sly and impertinent. We shall be fast friends, I think."

That fairy hammer twinged in her head again. Another fast friend. She had even less in common with this lady than she did with Lady Perry.

When they stepped into the ballroom, several musicians were tuning up instruments. Some forward gentleman would claim Lady Arbrough immediately, and Sirena would deposit her own self in the far corner of the room between a potted plant and a door. She was counting on it.

Bakeley skirted the edge of the room, greeting guests and secretly searching for a golden-haired lady in a yellow dress.

The moment she'd entered, he'd spotted her speaking with Perry. But he'd just caromed from Lady Arbrough to Lady Denholm and her daughter, Lady Glenna, and when he'd finally detached from that excruciating snare, Lady Sirena had vanished.

Lady Glenna was a pretty girl, with a figure that matched her generous dowry, and what she said had been very pro forma, just what one did say when one was a first season girl meeting one's possible future husband—which meant just enough to show that she was well-bred, virginal, and obedient.

In short, she was perfect.

Blast it all. Father could marry her himself.

Speaking with Lady Glenna had only rekindled the need to see Lady Sirena, to speak with her, to know her better, to find out her secrets.

And to touch her, perhaps even to taste her and see if her lips were as saucy as what came out of them.

He stiffened his spine. He would not touch her, because he would not ruin her. He was not that sort of man.

Perry stood by her harp. Two other young ladies had trotted out a violin and a violoncello and were preparing to accompany her after her solo. She was speaking now, trying to bring the roomful of disorderly aristocrats into submission.

"Your attention, please," he boomed from his spot in the back. The room instantly quietened. From across the room Perry's smile warmed him. Whoever she married must be the best of men. He would not let their father impose some aging roué on her.

A rustle behind him drew his attention.

Lady Arbrough and Lady Sirena entered arm and arm, and he stifled a groan. He wouldn't dare sit with either of them—Lady Arbrough, because it would be too public a display of their relationship, and Lady Sirena, because it would be too public a display of his interest in a relationship that did not exist yet.

And it never will. You may not touch her.

Lord Pelham rushed to greet both ladies and carry Lady Arbrough away, tucked a little too closely at his side.

Bakeley did not feel one whit of jealousy.

Lady Sirena had detached herself, shaking her head vigorously, refusing to accompany them. *Good girl.* Jocelyn was drawing her in, or at least trying. He'd warn Lady Sirena to stay away from the widow.

Jocelyn's dress was provocative enough to have every man staring bug-eyed. She'd been irritated by his failure to appear at her home for the last week. Or had it been longer? He'd sent flowers daily, along with excuses.

Pelham was welcome to her.

He spotted Lady Sirena hunched near the wall and irritation spiked in him. She was a guest. She could drop the meek companion performance tonight.

If he joined her, he'd prove to her and to everyone, that in this house, she was an equal.

He shook himself. Joining her wouldn't help the lady, it would only incite gossip.

The tones of the harp washed over him, striking on every nerve. Normally he enjoyed his sister's musical attempts. Now, he could only wish he might find the right, polite moment to leave his station in the back of the room.

Father's head swiveled, his lips pressing into a frown when their gazes met.

And perhaps he would join the fair Lady Sirena just to poke the old man's goat. And drag her off to a side room where he might kiss her silly.

He eased in a breath, and tried to let the flat notes and jumbled chords divert him. Shaldon turned his gaze back to the dais, and finally the first piece ended. Jocelyn cast a smirk his way, then leaned to whisper in Pelham's ear. He in turn said something to make her laugh.

The next piece began, an ensemble with Perry's friends, drawing all eyes to the front.

His gaze sought out Lady Sirena like a bee searching after a flower and—she was gone

CHAPTER SEVEN

B akeley backed stealthily to the door, thinking. Soon after her arrival, Lady Sirena had left the room, and had only returned as the performance was starting, with Lady Arbrough in tow. Both had most likely been in the salon set aside for the ladies.

Lady Sirena might truly be ill. She might not have been lying about megrims.

As the host, he was entitled to check. It was more properly left to the hostess, but she was thick in the middle of an étude.

He knocked at the retiring room door, and the maid in attendance said no one was there except herself. He opened his mouth to ask about the lady in the yellow dress, but then remembered— the maid, like every other servant in this house, was likely to share his questioning with the housekeeper, who would speak to the butler, and sooner or later, Shaldon would hear of it.

The strands of music filtered through the corridors. Where would she have gone?

That was the wrong question. *Why* would she go off exploring the home of the Earl of Shaldon?

Why, indeed. Shaldon was all tied up in her family's troubles. Perhaps she, too, would be looking for the same thing he'd searched days in a row for—a file on the Hollisters.

His father's study wasn't on the first floor, and it would be locked. Even if she could find the room on her own, she wouldn't be able to enter.

Unless she could pick a very complicated lock, which, being Irish, she probably could.

The other places to search were his father's bedchamber and the library. Even if she found her way up the stairs to the correct bedchamber, the valet might be there, fussing about with his father's things.

The library it was.

He followed the corridor to the other side of the house and listened a moment at the closed door, then turned the latch. A low fire burned in the fireplace, and the room was disturbingly quiet.

Yet he sensed a presence, heard a rustle suddenly *shushed*. The only scent in the air was the stale smoke of cigars. Lady Sirena used no scent that he could recall, or perhaps her perfume was too subtle amongst the cloying perfumes of the other ladies.

As his eyes adjusted, he spotted a candelabra and went about lighting the tapers. "I do hope Perry is not disappointed that I have a megrim...also," he said.

When he looked up from the lit candles, she had moved in front of the fire.

"I shall return then." She stepped out toward the door.

He blocked her path and heard her small gasp. And smelled her, a faint hint of some flowery soap.

She stepped to one side, and he matched her, as in their dance at the Hackwells' ball.

"Pray, sir, what are you about? Sure, and I mayn't be here all alone with you."

The lilting words warmed him. "Whatever are you doing in the library?"

"Have I offended? I am sorry. I do have the headache, and I could find no peace in the ladies' retiring room."

"Ah. Is that where you befriended Lady Arbrough?"

Her low chuckle moved over him. "Aye. I walked up to the fashionable lady and asked her to help poor me back to the music room." She clucked her tongue. "Do you think? For some reason, it was the lady befriending me. Said we will be fast friends, which Lady Perry said also tonight, and her I may believe."

"Lady Arbrough is starting trouble."

"Are you and she friends then? Two peas from the same pod?" She tried to skirt him again, and he matched her—again. "Let me pass and the trouble will be less."

He took a step closer, close enough to feel the swirl of her skirt, and his heart lifted. "Lady Arbrough...until very recently was a *very* close...friend."

And that friendship was over. He would talk to Jocelyn on the morrow.

He felt a shock travel through her, and when she spoke her voice trembled with it. "Your amorous congress—isn't that what it's called?—is nothing to me. I'm leaving now. Take your sorry self out of my way and let me pass."

"No." He snatched up her hand. "You look lovely tonight. Stay. Keep me company."

She tried to pull away but he reached for her other hand.

"Do not do this, sir."

The anger was giving way to fear, though whether it was real or feigned he couldn't tell. He drew her closer to the light. Her eyes glowed with that same luminosity he'd noticed at Hackwell's ball, her lips were plump and inviting, and gold highlights bounced off her dress and her hair. She was a beauty in daylight. By candlelight, she was a goddess, a golden siren. No wonder she'd had to run away from the cousin.

And that thought brought him up. He didn't ravish women, unless they wanted it. This girl didn't want it.

Unless he convinced her she did.

He eased in a breath. No. At least, no, not tonight.

"You and I, my lady, we're looking for the same thing."

She swallowed hard, her lovely throat jumping. "You are mistaken."

"Am I? What do you think I'm talking about?"

She pursed her lips. Opened them. "A liaison."

"An improper one?"

Her brow furrowed. "You're mocking me now. Let me go."

"First we should search together."

"I don't know what you mean, and we'll be missed. Both of us gone? Together?" Her eyes became shiny. She'd drummed up some tears. "I'll be...on the street. I'll be fortunate if I'm sent back to serve as my cousin's, my cousin's—"

"Files, Lady Sirena. Files that say *Hollister* on them."

A tear ran unchallenged down her creamy cheek and her mouth dropped. "Oh."

He swept the tear away with his finger. So soft her skin was, as he dragged the moisture down to her lips and traced a path over them. Her chest rose, her breasts straining the modest bodice of the yellow gown.

He yanked her closer and settled his lips on hers, and a sharp gasp escaped her before she clamped her mouth shut.

"Just one kiss," he whispered. He nibbled around her locked lips and stroked the line of her jaw until she shivered in his arms and her lips parted, allowing him entry.

He kissed her then, sweeping his tongue against hers, for long minutes, then tasting her skin, following the path of his fingers along her jaw and down to her neck, inciting a sharp gasp and a moan, and more wriggling. He wanted her, and she wanted him, and—

"Stop." Her hands locked on his shoulders, pushing.

Heart pounding, he froze. He was a gentleman. Even if she had been no lady—which she most definitely was—he would have stopped. No matter how hard his cock screamed for release, as it did now. "Right." He stepped back and straightened his neck cloth.

Sirena's heart pounded so wildly she could barely find breath to speak. "The files," she said finally.

"Yes. He wouldn't keep them here in so accessible a location."

Oh, he was lathered, she could tell, almost as much as herself. This was what was meant by seduction—not the graspy, slobbery, forced thing her cousin had attempted. If not for the housekeeper and butler and a strong dose of laudanum...oh, this was very different, and this man a far more powerful lord than her cousin.

She'd be lucky to survive this night with her maidenhead intact. But she wanted that file. She needed to know what happened to Jamie. "His study then? My father had a room like that."

"Yes. We'll look there." He gazed down that bored nose, straightened his neck cloth, though not so much as a hair of the man was out of place, while inside herself, every nerve was dancing a jig. She pressed a hand to her throat and hoped her heart hadn't pounded her bodice askew. She daren't look away first.

Music still played, and a wobbly contralto could be heard. Finally, he turned away, blew out the candles, and took her hand, leading her up the servants' stairs.

Using the backstairs—it tweaked her pride, but she quickly dismissed the emotion. Lady or no, she was an Irish girl in London with no money or family, and no right to put on airs. And now was no time to take offense. If Shaldon's heir required her to mop or dust, she'd do it and gladly, and mayhap have more chance to see what the old man was hiding.

She'd not willingly spread her legs for him though, and as he squired her down the dimly lit hall she decided he'd not likely try to force her either. He'd stopped immediately upon her request, like the gentleman he claimed to be.

No, like a true gentleman of any country, his would be a sneaky attack on her virtue. She must be strong and forbearing of carnal pleasure. Not even dear Lady Jane would rescue her if she cheerfully surrendered her virtue to Bakeley.

Men's voices on the grand staircase brought Bakeley to a sudden halt, and she collided into him. Her cheek bumped his shoulder and she uttered an *oof.*

He turned quickly, hooked an arm around her, and placed a finger over her lips. The voices had paused and picked up again, and she recognized Lord Shaldon's deep tones.

Bakeley quietly opened the nearest door and twirled both of them in, shutting it without so much as a *click*, turning the key. Under his fine coats, his chest rose and fell against her breasts.

Oh, heavens. The man was all muscle and lean strength, and he smelled—wonderful. Some manly perfume mixed with hints of tobacco and leather. And just a touch of the stables. Her father had smelled almost wholly like horses and whiskey, which were wonderful in their own way. But this?

His hand crept up her back, and the other— there were two wrapped around her—the other moved down, and... *Oh.* His hot breath caressed her ear in a long *shhhhh* that sent warmth curling through her.

Voices came through the smoky fog in her brain. In the corridor, Shaldon was speaking.

She strained to hear his words, tried to discern who he was with, but that *whoosh* of hot breath, like the brook near her home rushing over the boulders, swallowed the voices.

The men retreated and a door slammed, cutting them off. She unwound her arms, realizing she had been holding him as tightly as he held her.

You are a fool, Sirena.

Dim light penetrated the room through the drawn back curtains. Her eyes had adjusted and she saw the outline of a grand bed. She could make out no scattered garments, no books, no clutter of any sort. Perhaps this was an unoccupied guest chamber, and they at least wouldn't be discovered by an occupant turning in early.

You cannot stay here with him. Get out now.

She pushed against his chest, so solid and strong, her hands itching to slide under the layers of coats.

"Well, that's that," she whispered. "I'll be off."

"Not yet." The low masculine murmur stirred her, as did the hand traversing her bottom. The thin muslin, the delicate petticoat, the fine gloves, they were the flimsiest of barriers for his lordship's heat.

CHAPTER EIGHT

Bakeley settled his hand on the swell of Sirena's hip and held it there. The heat coursing between them was like the exchange of a blood oath. Need, want, and anger did battle with his finer senses.

His father had entered his study down the hall, and that had been Lord Denholm's voice he'd heard too. Making plans for his future they were, to settle him with the little miss down below who deserved someone better than him, someone younger, someone who wanted her.

What he wanted he had in his arms right now, in a dark bedchamber. She'd tried to push him back, but that had been no display of maidenly airs—it was a fine-honed sense of survival. A maiden she was, he'd guess, and had never been properly kissed before, yet every instinct in her had made her respond. And damn it if he didn't want to take that further, to show her just how sensual she was.

He could. He could do this. He could have her.

His heart quickened and began to pound fiercely against the hand she had planted on his chest.

He could have her, but not this way. He moved his hands to her shoulders and let his thumbs sweep the soft skin there. "My sister's rooms are on this floor. She told you to go up and lie down there if you needed. You got lost."

He could feel the movement of her throat as she swallowed.

"She will back you up," he said.

"Yes. I'll go now."

"No. I'll go to my father's study. Wait until you hear the door close again. Then go. Take the main stairs."

"Thank you."

He dropped a chaste kiss on her lips. "I'll call on you tomorrow."

He rapped once on the study door and sauntered in. Surprise lit Denholm's face, but Shaldon merely sunk deeper into his chair, as though he'd been expecting him. Both men were seated comfortably at the low coal fire, drinks in hand, settling his future.

"Just the man," Denholm said. "Join us."

"For a moment." He poured himself a drink and pulled a chair over from the writing table. Why Father had brought Denholm to his chummy, cluttered study was a mystery. No one but two trusted servants were ever allowed to clean, and they only delivered coal and dusted around the piles of paper and books.

But perhaps Father had looked for him in the library. Father was a cagey one. He would have noticed that both his son and Lady Sirena had disappeared.

To hell with it. "I hear you have a horse running at Ascot this year," he said. His father's interest in horses had necessarily waned, what with having to save England from Napoleon. But with Denholm, horses were a safe subject.

"Indeed. And I have a fine filly downstairs in your music room. What think you of her? She'll give you some fine foals. Good stock she is, like her mother."

Shaldon watched, as ever, unreadable in a crisis.

"She's a lovely young *girl*."

Denholm slapped his knee, immune to sarcasm. "Indeed she is. Kept a tight rein on her, I did. None of these young ladies' academies for my chits. Have another one at home just like her. The settlements will be easy. Shaldon and I have already come to terms and we'll have you married in no time."

He sipped his drink and stared back at his father. This desire for an alliance with Denholm was baffling. Father had claimed to be too ill to attend Parliament, but he was no doubt busy meddling behind the scenes of government. Of course, Denholm's would be an easily controlled vote, but he would follow Shaldon's lead anyway. The man had no political aspirations, unless a horse was involved. And Shaldon had plenty of fine horses to bargain with.

There was the Denholm money, of course, but the Shaldon earldom had plenty of that also. No, his father had some other motivation.

"Well, boy, what say you? Will you marry my daughter?"

And have a lifetime of Denholm at one end of the table and Shaldon at the other?

"I have spent all of five minutes with her, Denholm. She's lovely and very young, and my strong sense is that she deserves better than me."

The man's thick eyebrows drew together as he sorted through the words. "Ah. Because of Lady Arbrough." He rubbed his hands together. "A man wouldn't want to give that up. Glenna has been taught the way of the world. She'll not mind."

His stomach roiled and his head began to ache, the revulsion he felt seeping inward. Lady Arbrough had seemed a great prize a few months earlier. That she'd picked him as her first liaison in widowhood had raised his spirits. But marrying a young innocent and keeping his mistress on, like some eastern potentate? Bink would not do so, nor would Hackwell. Nor, he suspected, had his father so many years ago, else he would have brought Bink's mother to England.

He didn't give a damn if that were the way of the world. It would not be the way of *his* world.

"Denholm, she's a lovely young girl, but still a girl. She needs some seasoning, a year making her way through the *ton*. Let us all understand one another—I am not going to marry her."

"Wife won't like it. She wants her girls married off in their first season like she was, to the best catch. We can agree to a long engagement."

"No, Lord Denholm."

His eyes wheedled. "Ah. You've been snared. Lady Arbrough has set her cap."

His head felt like it was gripped in a vise. "No. However, I did hear about a stallion coming up on the market down in Kent. Descended from the Darley Arabian, they say. You were in need of a stud, were you not?"

Denholm was soundly diverted. They talked through another drink about horses and racing, giving Sirena plenty of time to escape. Shaldon observed in his quietly menacing way, and then they all returned together.

At the door of the music room, Denholm left them to find another drink. The music had stopped and the guests were mingling.

"You have dodged for the last time," Shaldon said. "You *will* marry."

"Or?"

His father actually sighed. Another fake sigh, because there wasn't much he could threaten him with. The estate was entailed, and his mother's settlements had provided generous portions for all her children, even the heir.

"I should like to bounce the next Viscount Bakeley on my knee before I die."

Perry smiled at him over her shoulder and pivoted to reveal Lady Sirena, whose smile disappeared when she saw him.

"Denholm, Father? What were you thinking?"

"You would have the damned horses in common. And his money is not soiled by war profits."

And he is not Irish. "Yes, well, I'm done with the war profits." He strode away before his father could add a snide remark.

He must make a trip to the jewelers tomorrow.

Sirena sat very still on the coach ride home. Her head no longer hurt, but her insides felt filled with bubbles. Excitement trembled within her, and why, she couldn't tell, except that all she could think of was the feel of Lord Bakeley's warm hand resting upon her bottom and his whispered promise that he would call on her tomorrow.

And why would he promise that? She didn't want to know. She didn't want this troublesome lord interfering. She needed to find out about Jamie.

And she couldn't share any of it with anyone, not Lady Jane, nor Lord and Lady Hackwell. All of them conversed, and she pretended to listen, but heard not a word.

"Sirena, are you still unwell?" Lady Hackwell asked.

"I'm better. Only a little fatigued. London is so very exciting after Dublin."

"You must sleep late tomorrow," Lady Jane said. "None of this running off to the market."

"A good night's rest will set me straight, and you shall have your warm bread, my lady."

The Hackwells exchanged a glance but said nothing. Thank heavens. Good people they were, and not inclined to pry. A pox on Lord Bakeley's kisses, his promise to visit. She'd rise early tomorrow, as usual. Walter and his brother were bringing a man to meet her. It had taken all of her persuasion and most of her meager funds to arrange it, for this was a man well and truly on the run, much more so than the O'Brians.

Early the next morning, Sirena saw Walter's tall, lean figure in the shadows of a shop doorway, and he was not alone. The other man moved, and the twist of tension in her stomach relaxed. It was Josh, Walter's brother.

Walter tipped his hat to her. "We'll both be going along with ye, milady. He'll not come here. And we must go to him, and not a good place neither."

That hadn't been the plan.

"I mustn't be gone long. How far is it?"

"The East End, milady, near the docks. A place called the Sign of the Bull. Faster, if we can hire a carriage."

She thought of the coins tucked away in her pocket alongside her gram's good luck charm, the quaternary knot. She'd brought it along just in case...well, it was the only identifying thing she had of her brother.

Gram had used up all the good luck in Queen Brighid's knot, which was probably why this morning was going awry, and money spent on a hackney left less coin to buy information. "We'd best go afoot. We've walked farther at home."

She set off and they came up on either side, escorting her into a part of London she'd heard of but not seen. Lady Hackwell had spoken of it in the one meeting of her Lady's Relief Society she and Lady Jane had attended.

There'd been no more meetings. Not that she and Lady Jane didn't sympathize, no. They sympathized aplenty, but they had no money to help.

And back in Donegal, she herself had seen plenty such hardship.

A poor woman with two urchins in tow shouted out for a coin.

"Off with ye," Walter growled.

Her heart lurched, but she kept her eyes straight ahead. She needed every farthing to find news of her brother.

At the end of the block she turned and saw the woman shaking a hand at her.

"A faker, that one is," Josh said. "She'll be in the gin mill drinking away her coins."

"And the children?"

"They'll be with her, chewing a crust of bread and swilling gin also. Not much further now."

But it was. The sun was full up before they'd stopped at a tavern with a swinging sign of a bull.

"Wait here with Josh, miss. I'll get the man."

Bakeley rapped on Lady Arbrough's door just as Lord Pelham was making his exit, at an extraordinarily early time of day.

Pelham opened his mouth and seemed to not know what to say. A bachelor also, he had inherited his title when he was still in leading strings. Pelham had far more experience in keeping well-bred mistresses, yet this awkward moment was making him nervous.

"Be at ease, Pelham. I won't call you out."

"You always were a good egg, Bakeley." The butler hovered at a discreet distance. Pelham leaned closer. "Yielding the field are you?"

Bakeley nodded. "Yes."

Pelham's eyes brightened. "Denholm's daughter? I thought congratulations were in order when I saw you enter with the old man. Everything's settled then?"

"No. Denholm's daughter is still on the market. Beware, old man."

Pelham laughed. "Dodged the parson's trap, did you? Thank you for the warning." He clapped Bakeley on the back and left.

He found Lady Arbrough quite at her leisure amid a field of flowers that occupied every spare inch of table. Pelham wasn't the only one making overtures.

She extended her slender hand and he kissed it.

"That was very courtly of you, Bakeley, but not quite what I was reaching for."

So, she was going to make this easier. He pulled the box out of his pocket.

She opened it. "Ah. Rubies." She studied them for so long she began to remind him of his father.

"Is a speech required?" They had always been direct with one another.

She smiled, and it seemed almost wistful. "Heavens, no. And you may tell Pelham it will not be quite so easy as he might think. I have not at all settled on your replacement."

He would miss this aspect of her. But, Lady Sirena was a plain-spoken woman also.

She rose and rang for a servant. "We'll have a last tea together." Aside from that glorious bosom, she looked altogether too thin, her skin tightly drawn, her years starting to show.

No different than before, but how had he not noticed it? "Will it be poisoned, Jocelyn?"

"No, my dear. It is well past time for you to marry. I was a young bride once, and I would not play the distraction for a young woman's husband."

Servants brought tea and closed the door on the way out.

"You *are* going to marry?" She finished pouring and met his eyes.

"Shaldon wishes it so."

A grimace. "And whatever Shaldon wishes he gets."

"Lord of the realm." He popped a biscuit into his mouth.

She settled back like a cat, kicked off her shoes and curled her feet under her. "I know what you're up to."

"Really?" He sipped some tea. Denholm's wife must have set the rumor mill turning.

She nodded. Her eyes slitted and her lips curved up. "And I approve. We had quite a chat last night."

"Indeed." Well, Denholm did say his daughter was broad-minded.

"Pity you won't be able to tell me about Shaldon's reaction to the news. But perhaps she will relate it to me eventually. I believe she and I will be fast friends."

The hair on his neck rose. He leaned back and stretched out his legs. She meant Lady Sirena. And if she thought his wife would be friends with a courtesan, even an aristocratic one...

But Jocelyn's reputation was not such a wild one. She'd been faithful to her husband, as far as anyone knew. In fact, she'd waited two years after the man's death to take Bakeley as a lover. Though there were men who whispered of their conquest of her, they were all well-known liars, the sort who claimed imaginary trysts, not worth the aggravation of a duel to defend his mistress's honor, if he were so inclined. Which he wasn't.

He opened his mouth to protest, and then closed it. There was no sense attempting to argue her out of the idea "Why?"

"I like her. And, your little fiefdom does not need another infusion of cash." She shrugged. "And really, Bakeley, she needs you."

A scratch at the door brought the butler announcing another caller.

He got to his feet. "What do you know about her?"

She bit her lip and looked away. "Only what I've said. Though, I suspect, she guards her cards. To truly win her may require all your arts of seduction." Rising, she kissed his cheek. "You may count me as an ally, my friend."

The walk to Lady Sirena's lodgings gave Bakeley a chance to think. Why did Jocelyn care about Lady Sirena? Years before, Jocelyn had famously swept the elderly Arbrough off his feet, but she had not been an impoverished orphan adrift. She'd come from Welsh gentry, she'd said, and he'd heard she'd brought a respectable dowry.

And how had she known of his interest in Lady Sirena? Well, that was obvious. He and Sirena had been absent at the same time. If Jocelyn had noticed, so had at least some of those at the musicale last night. Pelham hadn't, because his brain had been filled with the vision of Jocelyn's breasts.

Shaldon would have noticed, yet he'd said nothing about it at breakfast.

She is off limits, Shaldon had said. *You have dodged for the last time. You will marry.*

Uneasiness crept through him. He should have brought that intemperate horse for a brisk ride instead of taking a brisk walk, something to settle his mind.

Shaldon's opposition to Lady Sirena. Jocelyn's support of the girl. Rumors and obsession. All because of a few stolen kisses, which reminded him how well his hand had fit upon her bottom, and how smooth her skin was at her shoulders.

Perhaps he should point himself toward Shaldon House, or better yet, the bachelor lodgings he hadn't visited in months. A bottle of brandy and some time to brood in peace might soothe him.

He turned a corner and found himself on the same street where he'd met Lady Sirena, mere doors from her rooms.

Yes, well, he hadn't promised to do more than call on her, and that he would do.

The door of Lady Sirena's lodgings opened before he could knock. The thin woman who answered was not the same maid who'd admitted them the day he'd visited with Perry. She was older, perhaps Lady Jane's age, and plainly clad like an upper floor servant.

"Oh, sir, thank you for coming. Lady Jane is aflutter." She ushered him into a sitting room. "Lord Hackwell has arrived, my lady."

Lady Jane's mouth dropped. "Oh, Barton, this is not Hackwell. This is Bakeley."

"I do beg your pardon." The servant called Barton, a lady's maid, he'd guess, settled a shawl on Lady Jane's shoulders.

"I did not know what to do," Lady Jane said. "Cheswick is still in the country. I sent for Hackwell."

His heart quickened. "Where is Lady Sirena?"

"That's just it. I don't know. She went out this morning as usual and she hasn't come back."

CHAPTER NINE

Barton directed Bakeley to the shops Lady Sirena frequented. Yes, the shopkeepers had seen her that morning. No, they hadn't seen where she'd gone. No amount of coins could pry that information from them. He wasn't sure if they were suspicious of him or if they genuinely didn't know.

He stepped outside the last shop and a boy ran after him. "Sir, I did see something."

Bakeley's heart quickened.

"The Irish lady, she talked to two men, both of them Irish also. I was cleaning the windows round the corner. They didn't notice me, I think."

"What did they say?"

"They was to meet someone in the East End, by the docks. A tavern, something about a bull. The men wanted her to hire a hackney, but she said no, they would walk."

Bakeley handed the boy a coin. "Describe the men."

"They had rough clothes and caps. Sailors, maybe. Not gentlemen like you."

"Thank you." He handed him another coin.

"It's usually just the one she meets."

He froze. She'd been meeting with an Irish sailor. Could it be her lost brother? Or a conspirator, like one of the Cato Street ilk?

"Do you know him?"

"Walter, she called him. And he called her my lady."

"Why would you remember this?"

The boy blushed deeply, and he realized the lad was older than he seemed. "Only that the lady was so pretty and always so nice."

"What is your name?"

"Henry."

He pulled out a card. "If you think of anything else, find me here. Speak only to me. No one else, understand?"

"Yes, milord."

The East End. The docks. With two Irish sailors? Was the woman mad? His heart raced and he hailed a hackney and climbed in.

He had no knife on him, no pistol, no weapon of any kind, not even a walking stick. He gave the driver an address and told him to make haste. Bink's home was right around the corner.

Sirena's hopes crashed when she saw Walter step out of the third tavern they'd visited, alone. The man they were supposed to meet was, once again, missing.

"We must get you out of here, milady." Walter's hand kept going to the side of his coat. He was armed, she'd guessed. So was she. Her heavy wool shawl draped her from the top of her head to her hips, hiding her bonnet and fair hair and covering the sheathed knife tucked into a very unfashionable sash.

The docks were busy with arriving ships offloading cargo. Josh's mere presence had kept lookers at bay, though they'd kept up their leering, the sailors stumbling from drinking all night, other seamen making their way from the arriving ships, porters, cart drivers, merchants, pickpockets, and street whores, even at this hour.

She set off with her two protectors. A group of rough men blocked their way. "How much for your whore?" The big man who spoke had glittery dark eyes that made her shiver.

A taller man shoved him aside. "I'm to be first." He lurched at her, and Josh blocked him.

She drew herself up. "Here now." She used the King's English her governess had tried to pound into her a decade ago, before the woman's wages had to be put to buying whiskey. "I am *not* a prostitute. You will move out of my man's way this instant and let us pass."

That at least made them pause. She slid the knife from her sheath, hiding it under the edge of her shawl.

The taller man stepped back from Josh and scratched his head.

"There are lasses down on the next corner who will gladly take your coin," Walter said in his most pleasant brogue.

The bigger man, the one who had spoken first stepped up. "Go on with you boys, if that's what you want. I had my heart set on a real lady."

He lurched again, knocking into Walter. Sirena stumbled out of the way and her head covering slipped bringing her bonnet down with it.

"A yellow-haired lass," a man shouted in a heavy foreign accent.

Someone pawed at her, and Walter's fist lashed out.

"Behind you," she shouted, trying to move out of the way. She heard a whistle. The river police would come in time, she hoped.

Fists flew, and there were strange oaths and the sound of cracked jaws and *oofs*. Walter and Josh were taking a beating for her. She must stop this. A crowd had started to form, ringing them, shouting out odds and wagers.

In front of her, the tall man pushed Josh to the ground and bent over him, pounding. His cap had flown off, and a greasy black queue slid over his back.

Bam. Crack. Oof.

She must *do* something.

She threw off her shawl, jerked him back by his queue, and dug the point of her dagger into his neck.

"Leave off," she shouted. "Or I will slice this devil. Leave off."

He squirmed and the point pricked him. The crowd quietened. The men hitting Walter looked up.

Josh crawled onto his knees. Whistles and pounding footsteps approached and the watchers started to slip away, including some of the men who had started the melee.

"Get him up." She made eyes at Walter, jerking her head.

He gripped his assailant and one other by their necks, and let Josh help himself up.

Her heart twisted. The O'Brian boys might have a price on their heads from the new Lord of Glenmorrow. They had risked everything to help her. If they swung from the gallows it would be her fault.

Two respectably clad men ran up, the river policemen, she guessed, by their dress, and in the distance behind them she saw the blur of two other dark-clad men.

The policemen stopped short in front of her. "Put down the knife, lass, there's a good girl."

She summoned the English again. "I am not your lass or your good girl, sir. I am a lady, and these men beat up my servants and threatened to violate me."

"She's lying," the man in her grip said. "She wanted more money."

Josh was up by now, fist raised, but a look from Sirena stopped him.

The policemen exchanged glances. "Yes, yes, well, we'll take all of you in and sort it out."

"Lady Sirena." A deep voice boomed through the crowd, as if the man who owned it was taking charge of everyone from the East End to Mayfair and every street in between.

Her heart jangled and she sucked in deep breaths to quell the dark spots that appeared. She would not faint. She would not.

A dark handsome head bobbed high over all the others, a ginger one following, shoving the curious out of the way.

Relief flooded into her, followed by dismay. She had no right to warm feelings. Lord Bakeley was not her friend. His brother, she wasn't sure about, but he was Shaldon's spawn too, and that made him also suspect.

"Lord B-Bakeley." Drat, her voice shook. Moisture flooded her eyes and she blinked hard.

He nudged a policeman aside and covered her knife hand with his. "My dear." He spoke with such tenderness, she blinked hard. He eased the knife from her hand, while Mr. Gibson fell upon the villain.

Lord Bakeley drew out a handkerchief, wiped off the blade, and let the cloth fall to the ground like the tainted object it was. "There. I've cleaned off that scurvy rat's blood. Sheath this, will you, my lady?"

She couldn't move. She couldn't see. He found the sheath at her waist, his hands touching only the leather, not her. Not like last night.

"I don't have another handkerchief," he murmured. "Hold those tears, love."

That swelled her eyes more. She wiped at them with her sleeve and then she squeezed her eyes tight for a moment.

When she opened them, she saw Walter and Josh, rounded up with the villains. "What are you doing?" She summoned her English yet one more time again, imitating a duchess she'd heard speaking to Lady Hackwell. "These two are my men. They were protecting me. Unhand them right now."

Mr. Gibson eyed his brother. "And it looks like they took the worst of it."

"At least five against two. Such valor will not go unrewarded. Gentlemen, I'm Lord Bakeley. Her ladyship and her men will come with me. I'll see that they get medical attention."

One of the two policemen looked speculatively at her.

"I am the daughter of the Earl of Glenmorrow. I am not a...a woman of the streets."

"Odd that an Earl's daughter would be here."

She opened her mouth and clamped it shut. *Peeresses did not explain themselves to lesser beings.*

"Milord, they must give statements. All of them, including the lady."

"I'll see to the statements," Lord Bakeley said. "Brother, explain please."

Mr. Gibson drew the more suspicious officer aside.

Lord Bakeley fixed his gaze on Walter. "Who are you?"

Walter had propped Josh against the wall and was busily mopping blood from his brother's poor battered face.

"These are the...the Smith brothers," she said. Oh, she was a poor liar, yet she must protect them. "This is...Michael, and this is...John who was beaten so fiercely. You boys saved me." The dratted tears came and she swiped at them, angry with herself for being such a crying ninny.

"Well, you saved me, milady," Josh said.

"I am so sorry, boys." She glanced at Lord Bakeley. He should not be here. Why was he here?

The memory rushed back. He'd said he would call on her and he'd done it. But how had he tracked her down?

Fear rippled down her spine. His father was having her followed. If that were so, then the O'Brians were in danger. She must take them somewhere. The money she'd planned to use for a bribe—that would pay for a room for a time. They'd know where to go, and she'd throw her own self upon Lady Jane's mercy.

"Bakeley," Mr. Gibson said, "I'm taking these men with me. Come along, then, John, Michael. I'll find us a hackney."

"No," Lady Sirena said fiercely, "they'll go with me."

Neither Michael nor John budged at Gibson's order. One of the officers took a threatening step toward her.

Bakeley drew her a few steps away from the men. "You'll all come with me. They need medical attention, and you and I need to talk."

She shook her head, her face going pink even while she blinked away tears.

Blast it. His only concern was getting her to safety. To hell with her men.

Her men. Who were they? Bakeley looked from her to the two *boys,* who were both well into their thirties. The names were no doubt fraudulent—the shop boy had mentioned a Walter—and why they were here, he knew not. He could kick their arses for letting her come down here.

Though, knowing her, she would have come by herself without protection, so he must thank them for not abandoning her.

Two Irishmen using aliases. They were wanted by someone, probably his father.

"I won't turn them over to Shaldon, I promise you. Now, is that yours?" He pointed at a large heap of black wool. She wore no pelisse or mantle and was shivering.

"Yes."

He held on to her arm and retrieved the shawl, draping her with it. "What you're feeling is shock."

He was feeling it himself. That first horrific vision of her with a knife to a ruffian's throat, the man at her feet beaten, had sent a panic through him.

He should have been quicker. She should have not come here. Foolish, foolish girl.

He scooped her up in his arms.

"I can walk," she cried. But her face was wet, and her tears were shredding his composure.

His sister, Perry, never cried. But she might if someone had beaten up her footmen and tried to assault her. The mere thought made his blood boil.

"Shush." He hurried back to the hackney that had brought him and, flipping a large coin, sent a boy for another.

Her servants, the Smith brothers, staggered up behind with Bink at their heels. Both men looked wild-eyed, tired, afraid, like the fox after a long chase. He set Lady Sirena on her feet while they waited and kept her locked at his side.

"None of this was their fault," she said.

"I told you I'm not turning them in."

The man called John sagged in his brother's arms.

"Listen," Bakeley said. "Both of you need a surgeon. I'll see you patched up. Then you may leave."

"Get in." Bink hauled John up as gently as possible. "And don't think to stab me with that blade you have hidden. Bakeley, take the lady in the other transport."

She tried to push away. "You will take them to—"

"We will all go to the same place, lass," Bink said. "Bakeley, where is that to be? My home?"

"No." Bink's home included Kincaid, who was deeply loyal to both of the Gibsons, but he had served as one of Shaldon's operatives for more years than anyone could count. He would see this situation the same way Shaldon would. "There is another place. Get in."

He gave each driver the same direction and helped Lady Sirena into the hackney.

This second carriage was a small affair, only big enough for two. She slid into the corner and huddled there.

He planted himself in the center of the seat and hauled her onto his lap.

"What are you doing?"

Lord, how she trembled.

He tucked the knitted shawl around her, a shawl for a fisherman's wife, not the wrap of an earl's daughter. The coarse texture of it angered him. She should have something finer against her tender skin.

"Stop fighting me, woman. I'm not going to hurt you. I'm sharing my warmth."

Her fidgeting settled and she allowed him to finish arranging the shawl around her.

"It's colder now. There's a storm coming in, I fear, and there's a storm inside you. You've had a great shock and that's why you're shaking. Now," he pulled her close and settled her head on his shoulder, "you must think about your story."

He heard a tight breath.

"My story?"

He let his hand drift over her back and began to stroke there. "Yes. Let me see. Why would a lady be walking the London docks with two working men?" He let the words hang there a minute and when she didn't speak, went on. "Oh, yes. You ran into the Smith boys at a shop where they were making a delivery of, of—"

"Grain."

"Grain. Yes. You knew them from your home to be good, honorable men. Perhaps you knew their mother or some such."

She had gone very still.

"Are they Catholic?"

"No."

"Presbyterian?"

"No. They are Church of Ireland, like me."

"Excellent. They'll be more practical about oath taking. The others can be unnecessarily scrupulous about what they say with their hand on a bible. Now, the Smith brothers could see that your circumstances had been reduced, and they heard of a ship docking with a great store of cloth that would make you a few fine dresses."

She had stilled and her breath warmed his neck. That and the swell of her bottom were heating him. When he pulled her a little tighter, her lack of resistance sent a surge of arousal through him.

"The cloth would have to be for Lady Jane. She has a birthday upcoming and I have naught to give her."

"Then so it shall be."

He held her, and felt her stiffness relax a bit more, and heard her breathing slow, while his own accelerated and his insides burned.

They were lies and he didn't care. He didn't care why she'd gone to the dock alone except for the two Irishmen with prices on their heads. He wanted her, and whether it was simple lust or to spite his father, he didn't care. For once in his carefully managed life, he was acting a fool, and so it must be.

He let her rest against him, both of them keeping their peace until he thought she must be sleeping, poor girl, after that long walk and such excitement.

The carriage came to a stop and the driver descended, and she quickly slid onto the seat and straightened her garments.

She hadn't been sleeping at all. She'd been, most likely, plotting.

He helped her out to where Bink and the Smith brothers stood waiting. Well, one stood. The one called John still sagged against his brother.

"What is this place?" Bink asked, staring up at the brick-faced townhouse.

"This, brother, is my very own refuge from the world, my bachelor lodgings."

Sirena pulled her shawl close around her, contemplating escape while Lord Bakeley himself stoked the fire. That, she supposed, was better than the task his brother, Mr. Gibson, had taken on, that of stripping and washing Josh.

It was unaccountably colder inside than out, like the house had stored every bit of the winter's chill in its brick walls and heavy draperies. It had been all but closed up, clearly not much lived in, and not even yet fully decorated. He must keep it for bringing his mistress, Lady Arbrough, though such a fashionable lady surely found this place laughable.

Or perhaps Lady Arbrough was looking forward to decorating it, though it didn't seem grand enough for a viscount with a wife.

This bedchamber sported a full sized bed, plenty big for the man stretched out groaning there. The housekeeper, a competent, congenial sort, had brought out sheets, and Sirena had helped her make up the bed before Josh had been laid there. While Mr. Gibson sponged Josh, a male servant—the housekeeper's husband, she guessed—worked on Walter's face.

Michael's, she reminded herself. Slipping from John to Josh was not so noticeable, but if she called Michael *Walter,* Bakeley would have at least a first name to give to his father, and Shaldon would easily rifle through the Home Office's Irish files and make the connection to Walter O'Brian.

Josh groaned out an oath.

"Sorry, lad," Mr. Gibson said.

Bakeley stood and dusted off his hands. "How bad is he?"

"Warm the blanket," Mr. Gibson told the housekeeper. "I'm guessing a bruised rib or two, or maybe broken. I'll send for a surgeon."

"I'll be fine, sir." Josh tried to sit up and gasped, falling back. "We'd best be off."

"The surgeon is my man, not Shaldon's," Mr. Gibson said. "And you'll rest there and let yourself be treated."

CHAPTER TEN

The same lady's maid he'd met that morning ushered Bakeley into Lady Jane's sparsely decorated drawing room. Lady Jane rose to greet him.

He handed off his hat to the maid. "She's safe."

"Thank heavens. Lord Hackwell couldn't be reached." Her face flashed a momentary relief and then clouded again. "Where is she?"

The maid still hovered near the door, her face stricken also with suspicion, and he fought the anger that rose in response.

"Barton, bring us some tea. Lord Bakeley, come and be seated. I will hear this story."

While the maid slipped out, he took a seat. He'd spent the journey here wondering how much to tell the lady about the young woman she'd taken in.

"We found her near the docks."

"We?"

"My brother, Mr. Gibson, and I. He lives very near, and I sought his assistance."

Lady Jane's finger tapped the arm of her chair, but her gaze remained steady, pinning him.

He sighed. "She was with two Irishmen, two men she knew from home."

The lady pressed her lips together and studied her hands, now clasped in her lap, before raising her eyes again. "She's not a traitor, Bakeley. She merely has a notion her brother's alive. Where has he put her?"

"Who?"

"Your father."

"No." He stood. "He knows nothing about it. She's..." He cleared his throat. "That is, I've come to—"

"No." The lady shot out of her chair also. "Not Sirena. Far away from Shaldon and every Everly is where she should be. I'll take her—"

The door creaked open, the servant Barton carrying a tray. "Molly had the kettle boiling already," she said, laying out cups and sending her mistress a questioning look.

"Thank you, Barton. That will be all for now."

The lady's hand shook as she poured from the chipped teapot into faded cups.

"My lady," he said, taking the cup and setting it aside. "I have a note from her, but first we must talk. Please hear me out."

She shook her head and sighed. "Very well."

Hours later, Sirena jerked herself up from a chair set before another fire, the one in Lord Bakeley's small study.

She'd fallen asleep. *Asleep.* How could she when they were still in so much danger?

She fingered her gram's necklace in her pocket, tracing the loops of the knot, and pulled it out to look at.

She should leave it here, in this English lord's home. All the good luck of it had turned to bad. She sighed and set it aside on the round study table and went back to the fire.

After the surgeon had departed, both Walter and Josh had signed the vague, brief statements Lord Bakeley had prepared for them. She'd left the boys in the housekeeper's care to write out her own statement, and a note to Lady Jane, telling her she was safe and in the care of Lord Bakeley and a chaperone.

She couldn't leave while Walter and Josh were in danger. It was the least she could do for them, though her heart broke from knowing Lady Jane might not take her back.

Lord Bakeley's brother would not count as a chaperone, but she had to claim one. And it was only a small lie, one she prayed would save her from being dismissed.

Trying to pretty this up was like putting a bonnet on Mrs. O'Brian's goat. She'd done a foolish thing, and she didn't care, except that if she was booted out by Lady Jane, she wasn't sure where to go.

She squeezed her watering eyes shut. She wouldn't give up. She wouldn't lose heart. There *were* honest things a young woman could do. Lady Hackwell's orphan home might need a helper—in the kitchen, in the garden, in the stable yard even. Or she could teach—arithmetic, needlework, how to care for livestock. There were many things she could do.

But surely Lady Jane would understand. Sirena would tell her the truth. Or something of the truth.

The door opened and Lord Bakeley entered, his housekeeper and her husband behind him carrying a covered tray as big as a carriage wheel.

Lord Bakeley's cheeks glowed pink and the ends of his hair glistened.

"You went out," she said. He hadn't told her he was going. She'd thought he was merely sending a servant with messages.

Fear jolted through her. He'd been to see his father. Or even if he hadn't, if his father were having him followed—and who wouldn't put such a thing past his evil lordship—he surely had led the man's minions back to his house and placed Walter and Josh in danger.

Perhaps she would be locked up too, in some Secret Service dungeon, and flayed until she'd admitted to seeking out Irish rebels.

"Yes, I went out." His servants departed, and he poured two glasses of claret, handing her one.

She set it aside. "I should leave now, except that I fear for the, er, Smith brothers' safety when your father shows up here."

"Have a sip of the wine, Sirena. It will help settle your nerves." He lifted a cover off a dish. "I'm afraid it's plain fare for us tonight. Mrs. Windle has done her best with a mutton stew."

Indeed she had. The food smelled divine. "Have the Smith brothers been fed?"

"Yes, we had a few crusts of bread and drams of water for them."

She rolled her eyes at him.

"Of course they've been fed, before us even, and the same meal. What must you think of me?"

She'd not had a bit to eat yet this day, and the tasty aroma took some of the edge off her suspicion. That, no doubt, was his crafty intent.

"I think you're an English lord, and the son of Lord Shaldon. Where did you go?"

He glanced at her and went back to dipping out stew into two dishes.

"Your father—" Her stomach growled loudly and she gritted her teeth.

"Is not coming after you or your Irish rebels. Come." He took her hand and seated her in a chair by the table. "Eat. I command it."

"You do not command me, sir."

"Oh, no?"

"No." Another growl escaped. "I'll eat because I wish to keep up my strength, and because I'm fair famished."

She let a spoonful of broth slide down her throat, enjoying the warmth and the savory flavor. The hearty broth would do both brothers good. She hoped they were resting now, sleeping, after their ordeal. What she would do with them next, she wasn't sure, but her money, such as it was, was theirs. Perhaps they could take a packet to Ireland, just to be on the go. Or even to the Continent, except the poor souls had no French.

When she looked up, he was watching her intently. "I delivered your note personally to Lady Jane."

She paused in her chewing and quickly swallowed. "What did she say?"

"She did ask who the proper chaperone you mentioned was."

"Oh."

"Yes. I told her that the Irish must have a different idea of what constitutes a proper chaperone, but that we most certainly are not alone. Mrs. Windle has been here all along."

"And her husband."

"He has been in and out running errands."

"Oh. But Mr. Gibson is here, and he is very respectable."

He laughed out loud at that. "That must be another Irish notion. The respectable by-blow chaperoning."

She ought to be irritated but she knew he was right.

"Besides, Bink—Mr. Gibson—left as soon as he felt assured the Smith brothers wouldn't stab Mrs. Windle on their way out the door."

Her heart beat faster. They couldn't yet be gone. She hadn't given them her money. She pushed up from her chair. "They've left?"

"No, no, I looked in on them. They're snoring away, and Windle is back sitting with them. Bink will return shortly also. He's arranging a shipment of new nursery furniture to his country estate. The wagon will leave in the middle of the night, and they'll be on it."

Her heart eased and then picked up its pounding again.

"But if Shaldon finds them—"

"Don't worry. Bink will accompany the wagon and be back in a few days' time. For now, he's bringing a maid and some clothing for you."

The loud thumping about her temples must be coming from her heart. He expected her to leave with them. "You're thinking to send me off to the country also?"

That would mean leaving Lady Jane. It wasn't right. She'd rather stay and risk the dear lady's rejection, or even weather Shaldon's beatings, anything rather than abandon the lady who'd been her only friend.

"No. You're staying."

"Then I'll go home as soon as the wagon leaves." If Lady Jane was willing to take her back.

She set down her spoon and took a sip of the wine, a hollow sensation making her heart feel small.

"When you spoke to her, was she angry?"

"She should be, should she not?"

Indeed. Hot guilt made her cheeks warm.

He shook his head. "She wasn't though. She expressed great relief. She'd been terribly worried."

"Oh." Tears rushed her again. *Damnation.* It had seemed such a wise thing to seek out the man who might have information about her brother. Yet, she could have been carved up and thrown into the Thames, and Lady Jane would never have known, all of her kindness to Sirena going for naught.

"What is this?"

She opened her eyes and Lord Bakeley was there, on his knees, by her side.

"I can't abide tears," he said sternly, handing her a napkin.

His scent, far too familiar than was proper, rose dangerously around her, threatening to addle her brains more. His hands, broad and strong like a working man's, gripped the back of her chair and the edge of the table, boxing her in.

She swallowed hard. "Nor can I. I'm not generally a weeper." She dabbed at her cheek. "There."

He didn't budge.

"Lord Bakeley, go back to your dinner."

"I've finished. You didn't notice me cleaning my dish because you were eating with such relish I thought you'd lick out your bowl."

She gasped. "I would never—"

"I'm teasing you." He cradled her chin in two fingers and his eyes gleamed with humor.

Oh, he was muddling her mind. She must concentrate. She must return to Lady Jane and assure her of her safety and sanity.

"Perhaps the wagon could drop me off at my lodgings."

"Would that be wise? If my father has watchers there, all they need do is follow that wagon."

He was right.

"Would you call a hackney for me?"

"Would I put you in a hackney in the middle of the night—for that is when they're leaving—and send you out by yourself?"

"Would you escort me then?"

"And blithely bring you home after you've spent a day and a night in my company?"

Those strong fingers had found hers and were rubbing circles over the back of her hand, sending warm bursts of sensation up her arms, down her back, and into her loins.

An uneasy certainty crept over her.

Perhaps the claret had been drugged. She must be firm. She lifted his hand off hers.

"Lady Jane will understand, I think, when I explain to her."

"Will she? Perhaps the Cheswicks won't, when they find out, and she's dependent upon them, isn't she?"

"Oh, surely they won't learn of this."

"You were to attend a rout tonight, were you not? She told me she sent excuses and stayed at home, but you know how the *ton* will talk. Perhaps someone will learn that the river police almost arrested a pretty earl's daughter named Sirena."

A sickening feeling flushed all the warmth out of her and brought with it a chill. Her hand went to her roiling stomach. "You mean to seduce me.

You mean to pressure me into being your mistress, to replace Lady Arbrough."

He frowned. "Is that what you think of me, Lady Sirena? That I would save you from street thugs, only to abuse you myself?"

Her heart quaked and her body stirred with conflicting desires. She wanted to leave, she wanted to feel his touch again, she wanted him to kiss her, and she wanted to be back safe with Lady Jane and Barton.

And she wanted very much to smack him.

"Whatever am I to think after the kissing the other night?"

"Last night."

Oh. Her heart thundered. It had been that recent.

His tension altered, his eyes going darker. "Perhaps you might think that I'm an honorable man."

"You're Shaldon's son."

"Yes, yes, you have said that before, but I'm not Shaldon, running about Ireland and the Continent spying. I'm the heir. I was trained to run a vast agricultural empire and manage a fortune in investments. I'm quite boring really."

His hand rested on her knee and the very air around him vibrated, sending a thrill through her that was anything but boring.

"We also breed horses. Very fine ones. Some of the best in all England."

He paused and the air crackled.

"As you know," he said.

His gaze held hers, as dark as the night when she'd caught him peering through the slats of Pooka's stall.

"Horses," she said stupidly.

He nodded. "Very fine horses. Even some with Connemara blood. And I try to be very good at managing our other investments, since horses are a costly indulgence."

And didn't she know that?

His thumb stroked the side of her knee. She clamped her hand over his.

"Where...where is our best Connemara mare? Is she...is she..."

He frowned. "She's in Kent."

"Pooka?"

His face went blank, as if he was hiding something. "Yes."

His family home was in the north, Lady Jane had said.

"You *sold* her?" she gasped.

He shook his head. "I have a small estate in Kent. We moved her because—well, we simply moved her."

Because Pooka was trouble, and didn't she know it?

A wave of sadness washed over her. She could have worked with the mare. She could have helped her. Pooka had not had a chance to get better. "Did you...did you get any foals from her?"

"Yes. A few."

She thought of the sprightly horse trying to shake off the boy in the street. "Your gelding?"

"Yes. He's one of them. None of them are as ill-natured as their dam."

Anger flared in her. "And so why buy her? Why were you so keen on her?"

His eyes sparkled and he leaned in close enough for her to see a small scar on his jaw. "It was my mother's wish that I buy the mare whose granddam had won a first at Thurles."

Oh, that sly word-for-word remembrance spiked her temper higher. All of the grief of that day roared in her.

She gritted her teeth and forced down the feelings. "Was she happy, your mother, with her ill-natured purchase?"

A shadow passed over him as he backed away. "She died before she got to see your hobgoblin horse."

She shivered. There'd been nothing but trouble since Pooka had appeared in her mam's belly. Jamie's disappearance, her mother's death from striking her head, her father's death from the whiskey.

"How did your mother die?" she asked.

"A coaching accident."

She'd seen one or two mishaps on the rutted roads at home, though none bad enough to take a life. "I'm sorry." She squeezed his hand.

She daren't ask more, not now. Lady Shaldon was long dead, but the pain of her passing still worked in this man. And though Pooka had taken to him that long ago time at Glenmorrow, his distaste for the mare was clear. He blamed her for his mother's ill luck, dying too young.

A curse on that name Pooka—why had she picked it?

His gaze met hers and she could see he'd steadied himself, while she was still all jumbled up inside. A bloodless Englishman, he was—horses were a business for him, not a passion. Not his life. He was boring, he'd said, a boring man with his hand on her knee and eyes beginning to glow like dark coals.

Her face picked up the warmth. She was still gripping that firm, strong hand. "I *am* sorry for your loss, my lord. And now it's best you get to your point today, sir."

His mood shifted again, and he grinned, knocking her off balance. "You're so lovely when you're heated, whether from a brisk walk or an angry dispute, or a passionate touch."

She leaned away from his lips and encountered the back of the chair. With no further escape, she was trapped.

His kiss was a chaste peck.

He wanted more though, that she could see. His eyes fixed on her lips, his breathing quickening, and fear raced through her.

Or—was it excitement? Oh, aye, hadn't she been here before with her cousin? It had felt nothing like this, which made it twice the danger.

She glanced over her shoulder. She could clout him with a bowl, but the lovely bone china would just shatter on his thick skull. The only knife was on his side of the table. He'd left her armed with naught but a spoon.

"Lady Sirena." His sharp tone brought her round. He reached into his pocket and pulled out a box too small for anything but...

Oh. Her heart quaked and her body tingled as if all of her insides were dancing. A shimmering sapphire stone twinkled up from its place on a band of gold.

"Will you do me the honor of becoming my wife?"

The room filled with a bleating of noise, like the swarming of bagpipes when all the pipers had drunk too much.

CHAPTER ELEVEN

*N*o. No, of course she could not be his wife. She lifted her gaze and saw a glint of— uncertainty, yes. It had clouded out the desire, well, mostly it had, because there was still that bit of tension around his mouth like he was wanting to take a big bite out of her.

And if he was uncertain and desiring, then he'd want his wedding night now and he'd change his mind in the morning, and then she'd be one more girl for the houses in St. James's. Nor would she find her brother if she was having to spend all her time flat on her back.

But...if he was true, if they *were* to marry, she'd have access to that great house over near Berkeley Square. She could even tell the great lord what she really thought of him.

And yes, wouldn't that make you welcome in the family, girl?

"It is customary in these circumstances to say *yes*." The wee bit of irritation made his eyes flash, as they seldom did with these great bored lords. Bakeley had some spark in him. And strength, yes, especially in the hand that had started stroking her leg through her skirts. He might be an honest fellow, too, not making any pretense of his amorous intentions.

Or he might be dishonest. He might just be a craftier seducer than her cousin had been. He might still change his mind in the morning.

"Sirena," he said.

His hands paused and his gaze pinned her.

He was...earnest. Determined. He wanted an answer, this English lord whom she knew nothing about. Practical and boring. And English. How could they possibly suit?

She swallowed hard. The simple answer was, Lady Jane was correct—they wouldn't. He belonged with a rich, noble, English girl, a girl with good blood lines. A girl with a father who could force him to marry her after he'd tupped her.

"It's a mad idea." Her voice shook with the quiver that ran up one leg and converged at the spot where it and the other leg met.

Get hold of yourself, Sirena.

If she but had a horse in the room, she might be able to whisper up some calm.

"No," he said, "It's very logical."

"It's mad and rash. Your father would have an apoplexy, the *ton* would laugh at you, and in six months you'd be seeking an annulment."

A smile drove out the uncertainty in his eyes, but not the heat, which still lingered around those turned up lips. "You are trying to dash my hopes." He set the jewel box on the table, slipped her shoe off and began to massage her foot, one-handed. His other moved to her hip.

"And you are trying to—" She inhaled sharply at the burst of sensation. "To seduce me with your wicked hands."

"Wait until I employ my wicked tongue."

Heat raced through her. Pictures danced in her head, making her dizzy. "Lord Bakeley—"

"Why not call me James?"

Her breath left her in a loud *whoosh*. It was a moment before she could speak. "Is that truly your name?"

The stroking stopped. "Yes, Sirena. What's wrong?"

She directed her gaze to the fireplace. To the door, to the table with its fine linens and china. Anywhere than at that searching gaze. It was too tempting to want to fall in.

"It's my brother's name. The name we knew him by."

"Your brother who was lost with the ship that foundered."

"You knew?"

"Would I propose to a girl without knowing everything I could?"

"You found your father's files?"

"No. The little I know of you, I learned from my brother, Bink. I still haven't found any files. Perhaps when we marry we'll just go and ask him to show us them."

She pushed back her chair and stood, grasping his hands. "Get up before you wear out the knees of your breeches."

That coaxed another smile from him, though she wasn't sure it was any less wicked.

"If my father thinks to cut us off, well, I have a great fortune of my own, Sirena, sufficient for us to live here when we are in the city, and I have that property in Kent when you wish to spend time in the country."

His hands had found her shoulders and he was touching her again, sending ripples of warmth through her.

"I can bring nothing to a marriage. Not even a meager dowry. It is *not* right."

"It's not true, either. You can bring your person, your beauty, your wit. Your ability with horses. And, I would hope, your affection and your loyalty."

Loyalty? Ah, then, they were in grand trouble, for she could never bring herself to love the English, considering all they'd taken from her. "I shall always be a daughter of Ireland."

He turned her squarely facing him. "I'm talking about loyalty to *me*, to the children we'll have, to our family, Sirena. I know you're capable of it. I've seen how you are with Lady Jane."

"Loyalty to your father?"

His eyes glimmered with the same bright desire. "Can you not see the opportunity here? You want to know things, am I correct?"

Arrgh. He'd changed tactics. He was a wily one—no wonder he was rich.

"That's why you were down at the docks today. You want to know what happened to your brother. You want to know if he's alive."

Her mouth dropped open and her heart bashed against her ribs. How could he know this?

He pulled her close, wrapping her in his arms, in a cocoon that quaked with safety, and warmth and desire. She could smell soap and starch, leather and horses, and the musk of a man at the end of his day.

Her arms went around his waist—there was nowhere else for them. He had yanked her up, pressed her breasts to where they wanted to go against his coats, her cheek to the smooth wool of his shoulder. Ah, she could fall into this and perhaps never have to worry again.

"When I saw you today with that knife to that villain's throat...Sirena, you must promise me to not set out on your own like that. If your two men had been less stalwart, if you had been alone, I could not bear to think what might have happened." His grip tightened a fraction more. "It may seem like madness to you, but I've thought this through. I'll get a special license tomorrow and we'll be married immediately. I'll draw up a settlement for you and our children, should anything happen to me."

Fear tightened her embrace. To marry and lose Bakeley, another James, oh no, she could not bear the thought.

And what madness was it that she could care at all?

Perhaps she already did feel affection for him. And perhaps he was worthy of loyalty. And the chance to have children, and to have the means to care for them properly...

A trembling overtook her, and she grasped for a bit of sanity. "You've thought this through, you say. Tell me, what exactly did you argue with yourself? Because other than my fair person, I still cannot see an advantage to you."

"Your fair person weighs heavily in the measure."

He was not going to be honest. She eased herself away. "Fair maidens abound here in London, offering a much better bargain. Proper girls who won't run the streets without your leave. You can get an heir from any one of them."

"What did I argue? That you're beautiful, Sirena, and no doubt brave. And not without good sense. Today you took along your two men and armed yourself." His mouth firmed. "Would you have cut that man's throat, Sirena?"

The memory of that moment *whooshed* back upon her. "I...I think so. I don't know. I couldn't let him kill Josh. I was glad I didn't have to."

He touched her shoulders again. "My father is pressuring me to marry, but I'll be damned if my wife will be chosen for me. It's you I want. And for your part, you'll be provided for, and you'll have a husband who chose you."

Those were no small advantages, providing he chose her for the right reasons. She took a step back and stared up at him.

"And so, you're marrying me to get an heir and to spite Shaldon?"

His gaze skidded away, and her heart fell.

Yet...the honesty was strangely reassuring.

"'Tis a foolish reason for marrying a girl you only just met. A girl you don't truly know," she said, voice shaking.

"And 'tis a fact that I met you ten years ago."

She couldn't stop the snort that escaped her. "Properly introduced through the slat of a stall, with a hobgoblin horse for a chaperone. Whatever do you call Pooka now?"

"She's still Glenmorrow's Pooka," he said. "If you marry me, we'll train her to a sidesaddle and she'll be yours."

"Oh." Tears clouded her vision and she ducked her head. "So I'll marry for a horse, and you'll marry for spite."

And in truth, there'd be some spite against Shaldon in it for her also.

"And the kissing," he said.

And the kissing would lead to bed sport, and she was more than a little nervous about that.

She eased in a breath, quelling that fear. Mares were covered by the pedigreed stallion whether they liked it or not, and it was much the same for the aristocracy. One could endure for the chance of a foal.

"Will not Lord Shaldon wrap me up and toss me down a well?"

"Don't tell me you're afraid of him?"

Was she? She shook her head. "For myself, no, but I do worry about the boys. And...if he discovers me trying to muck up his blood lines, he'll stop any nuptials." And then she would be well and truly ruined.

He slid a finger under her chin and tipped it up. "My brother will see to your men's safety. I'll see to the marriage."

His touch sent warmth slithering through her. She took in a shaky breath. "You'll help me find out if my brother is alive?"

"Yes."

Her breath eased. He'd spoken without thought, so perhaps he meant it. Perhaps he wasn't just trying to trick her.

Marriage to him would bring a sure roof over her head, regular meals, and children. Perhaps a chance at the truth about Jamie.

Aye, but there'd be a price when she stepped out of her front door—the taunts of the *ton* about Bakeley's poor Irish bride.

The *ton* wouldn't matter if...

"I can be loyal, if you'll but show me respect."

"You're thinking of Lady Arbrough. I've truly broken with her, and as long as I have the company of an affectionate and loyal wife, there will be no need for other women."

Well, that was honest enough too. She was to be loyal, or else. They would marry for his spite, for her sustenance, and for a son. Not for love, and wasn't it just as well?

She looked at his hands. "No fingers crossed, my lord? While I'd be grateful to not share a husband, 'twas something else I was thinking of—my Irishness. My poverty. Can you not hear the voices? *Did you hear what Shaldon's heir did? Fell prey to a bog-trotter without two coins to rub together.* You must think ahead to when your father passes on and you take his seat in Parliament. You must think about your business interests. Who'll side with you to make laws, to work out contracts?"

His jaw firmed, but when he spoke his tone was the gentle one he'd used on the horse that day in the street. "I'll have my brother Bink in the Commons, and his mother was an Irish girl. And as for business, my reputation has been established. Men in trade look at trustworthiness and the potential for profit."

"But socially—"

"Socially? I heard you speaking like a queen to those ruffians. If you don't know how to run a great house, we'll find someone to teach you. Perry knows something about it."

She'd forgotten Lady Perry, who had said she would be her fast friend.

"Sirena, it's a fact that this gossip will get out, and both our reputations will be ruined. You must say yes."

Must she?

His reputation no doubt weighed heavier than hers, else they would not be at this point. Spiting his father played some part also. Would there be any chance at happiness?

Her heart twisted with aching. For one such as herself, happiness didn't come in this life, certainly not in a marriage. It was daft to expect it. The best she could hope for was shelter, meals, and a babe or two, if the birthing of which didn't kill her.

And then there was the matter of finding Jamie.

"Sirena."

She looked into his dark, intense eyes. He was a determined sort, and surprisingly warm behind closed doors. Not prone to tantrums, else he would've had one with her on the way back from the docks. He'd not raised a hand to her, as many men might have done.

If he didn't truly have an interest in her fair person, he was doing a grand job of acting. An answering need spiraled through her. Lust it was, but at least they would have that.

And it was true. This time she wouldn't be able to escape the ruin, and by all that was holy, she didn't want to find herself alone on the London streets.

She nodded. "Yes."

He tugged her close and set his lips to hers. She didn't bother to fight, surrender being what she wanted, what she'd yearned for the first moment he'd taken her hand in the dance the other night. Her lips parted for him, her tongue met his, her head bent back, and at the place where their hips joined, she felt the hardness of him. She'd lurked in the shadows of the stables often enough while the men and boys talked to know what that would be, and the thrill of it shot through her, sending hot moisture pooling between her legs.

He cupped her head firmly, and with the other explored every inch of her person, settling on her breasts and lighting more wildness within her. She moved her hands up his hard chest, around to his neck, threading her fingers through his thick hair.

He would want her tonight. That was clear.

He plunged a hand into her bodice and flipped the fabric down, freeing her breast, and then stopped to watch his finger make swirls around the bud of her nipple.

Pleasure shot through her. "Oh," she breathed. "Oh, my," and, when he bent his head and let his tongue take over, "Oh, Bakeley."

She squeezed his shoulder, his arm, the back of his head. More pleasure rippled inside her, wrapping around her heart.

A knock at the door made him go still.

A male throat cleared, the sound muffled by the heavy wooden door. "It's Bink."

Bakeley tucked her breast in and arranged her dress, his face such a grim mask she had to laugh.

"Caught in the act. Does he know your intentions?"

He grinned. "Yes. He wouldn't have left you alone with me otherwise."

Her heart lifted that someone who knew nothing of her should care. "Truly? Who else knows?"

"Lady Jane. I asked for her blessing." He searched her eyes. "Do you mind that I spoke to her?"

Lady Jane stood as the closest thing to family for her. Her eyes started to water. "Did she give it?"

"Yes, but not right away."

"I'm coming in." Mr. Gibson rattled the door latch.

Bakeley bade him enter and then turned back to her. "I had to go through a litany of objections with Lady Jane—my father, your nationality, your lack of wealth, your social standing. It was a good rehearsal for my dealings with you."

Once again, a throat cleared loudly next to them. When she looked, Mr. Gibson had an amused gleam in his eyes. A bonnie girl in a simple gown stood behind him, holding a large bundle. She bobbed a curtsey, and cast her eyes down, but not before Sirena saw a flash of interest.

He'd brought her a saucy maid.

"Lady Sirena, this is Jenny," Mr. Gibson said. "She'll be yours as long as you need her."

"Oh, I couldn't. Mrs. Gibson—"

"It's no trouble. We have plenty of help. Jenny is blessed with the ability to hold her tongue, and she likes a little adventure now and again."

The girl peeked from under her eyelashes and bit back a smile. She couldn't be more than eighteen. "My mistress has sent along some clofing, miss."

The cockney accent was thicker than gruel and made Sirena smile. "How very thoughtful. It's grateful, I am."

Lord Bakeley squeezed the slim hand he was holding. The look on Sirena's face reflected her gratitude, knit together with kindness toward the maid, and a keen humility. That last they would have to work on if she was to run his household. "I didn't think to bring any of your things from Lady Jane's. Thank you, Bink."

"It was Paulette's doing." His gaze flitted from Bakeley to Sirena. "Have you settled your business then?"

The pink that tinged her cheeks made him want to grab her and kiss her anew. Yet the night would be a busy one. Best not to get started down that path.

"Brother, you are the first to know. Lady Sirena has agreed to become my wife."

Bink's approving look was gratifying. From the time he'd first met this brother, his nine-year-old self had looked up to the bigger boy. A by-blow, Bink was, but a man of courage and character also. Not long after Bink's mother's death, he'd been shuffled from a cruel stepfather to a cruel headmaster. He'd run away and joined the army, had served in the Peninsular War as a sergeant under Major Steven Beauverde, now the Earl of Hackwell. Upon Bink's return to England, Bakeley had found him working as Hackwell's steward.

Bink's approval of his choice of a bride meant the world to him. He'd have at least one ally when he faced their father's disapproval.

"Welcome to the family, Lady Sirena," Bink said. "Paulette will be most happy to have another sister."

She flushed more deeply. "A sister. I had not thought about that."

"A sister and a great burly Irish brother here." Bakeley kissed her hand. "Why not go with Jenny and see what she's brought. The housekeeper will have a room ready for you by now. You may rest for a while, and you'll want to say goodbye to the Smiths when they leave."

"All right then." She turned back to the table and picked up a chain he hadn't noticed, pocketing it, and led Jenny out.

When the door shut, Bink's expression darkened. "Kincaid smells a game afoot. I don't keep secrets from Paulette, but I did make her promise to conceal it from Kincaid. She'll do it for the lady's sake."

"Paulette is still angry with me, I take it." Bakeley had been involved in their father's scheme to bring Paulette and Bink together.

Bink laughed heartily. "No more so than with Kincaid, who she's forgiven. And I don't think she was ever truly angry." Bink slapped his back. "Yet it would've been so much easier had you at least told us the truth."

"Yes, you're right." It had been his lone invitation to immerse himself in his father's gambits, and it had almost got Paulette and Bink killed.

Shaldon's retirement had brought him home to England after years of absence, and the man had not really left his games behind, as he'd proven by using Paulette to lure a traitor into the open.

Well, damn it, Bakeley was done with that. It was time he moved out of Shaldon House and into his own home.

"Father will find out," Bakeley said. "I wonder what the reaction will be. Swooning? An icy cut? An attempt to lock Sirena in the cellar?"

Bink grumbled low in his throat. "I'm going with that wagon tonight. Those boys will make it to my place safely, and I have men who'll do as I say. Your biggest danger will be at Doctors' Commons tomorrow."

He would visit Doctors' Commons for the special marriage license first thing in the morning. "I don't give a damn. I'll marry the woman of my choosing, even if I have to carry her off to Scotland as you did with Paulette."

"That's a very long trip from London." Bink poured two glasses of claret. "Here's to you and your bride and to getting those two Irish boys out from under the wily lord's nose."

"Here, here." He took the glass. "I've been thinking about this, you know. I've been thinking that he won't give me any problems with the special license because he's up to something."

Bink frowned and took a bite of bread. "Casting Lady Sirena as a lure?"

Anger shot through him. "She was down on that dock looking for information on her brother."

"Meeting someone?"

"I haven't got to the details yet. Can you get the real story from one of the Smith brothers?"

Bink snorted. "No doubt Kincaid could."

"Can you do it without using his methods?"

"I'll try. I can't stay long at Little Norwick though. I have Parliamentary meetings to deal with before those fools in the Lords come up with another set of Six Acts. And I'll reckon those boys will want to be off as soon as the one called John can stand up to piss."

"Josh."

"Eh?"

"She slipped. One of them is a Josh. The other is Walter."

Bink chuckled again and shook his head. "Are you sure about this, Bakeley? This girl will lead you a merry chase, and what do we really know about her?"

"About the same as you knew about Paulette."

"Aye, but Shaldon knew everything about *her*."

"My point exactly."

Bink sat down, the better to reach the untouched food and the wine bottle, and poured another drink, rapping his fingers on the table. "He's the devil, is our father."

"The night we met at the ball, the night I led her over to him, the look he gave her was condescending, yes, but it was also a look of...interest. Was he in Ireland then, do you think?"

Bink stirred in his seat, his eyes glowing, wary. "You think she is his?"

"*No.*" The thought sent a chill through him. The dalliance that had produced Bink had occurred in Shaldon's bachelorhood. As far as anyone knew, their father had been a faithful husband. Bakeley's mother would still have been alive when Sirena was born. "Mother sent me to Glenmorrow to buy up his best cattle. As if paying a debt. What I mean is, was Shaldon in Ireland around the time her brother fled? It would have been around the very end of the last uprising."

"I've no idea. This Cato Street business might have somewhat to do with it."

"Plots and uprisings," Bakeley said. "Yes. That would fit with Father's games. What did you think of the Smith brothers?"

"Not conspirators, I'd say, unless Sirena is their leader."

The idea was absurd. "We must shield those men from father."

"Aye. I'll be leaving in the wee hours. Where will she be when you're out getting the license?"

He had thought to leave her here in his townhouse, but Bink was right. The housekeeper and her husband would be no defense if Father showed up and raised a row. Jenny looked tougher than both of them combined. "Would Hackwell help?"

Bink grinned broadly. "What a scary thought, Bakeley. We're beginning to think alike. That's exactly what I was going to suggest. And here," he handed him the jewelry box, "best give your bride her ring."

CHAPTER TWELVE

It was long after midnight when Sirena heard a knock at her door and rose from the chaise where she was reclining. She'd washed and changed into the fresh chemise and dress Jenny had brought, and had started another letter to Lady Jane, which she tore up and threw into the fire. She'd even dozed for a bit at Jenny's urgings.

Bakeley stood in the doorway, looking fresh and only a little fatigued. "The wagon is here. Do you want to say goodbye?"

"Yes."

At the door to the bedchamber where Walter and Josh were still resting, she gripped his arm. "May I have a few moments alone, or will you be insisting on making your presence known?"

"We are betrothed, Sirena. We'll do this together."

She sighed as loudly as possible so he would know her displeasure. What she had to say—that she would write to their mother as soon as she was able, that they should tell her if they'd heard any more of her brother—she wished to say none of that with Bakeley around.

The O'Brians were in danger because of her, and what did she truly know of their comings and goings? She'd had to take them at their word, much as she was taking Bakeley.

Walter rose when she entered the room. Both men wore fresh clothing and had washed. Poor Josh had a bandage around his head, and his jaw had sprouted a whole goose egg.

Because of her. "Please sit down, er, Michael." She pulled a purse from her pocket. "I want you to have this. It'll tide you over. And I'm more than sorry for the trouble I've caused you."

Walter looked at the purse she'd placed in his hand. He looked at a spot over her shoulder. "His lordship has already given me coins. I can't take it, milady."

"You must. This is my money I've saved."

"His lordship said you'd be wedding."

"I'm not wedded yet. Please do take it, my small compensation for all the harm I've caused. If you had not been there..."

"Mam would skin us alive if we'd let you go to the docks by yourself, Lady Sirena. You know she would. No, Josh and I, we've talked. We're going home, and the devil take his lordship. Better to hang than to live on the run."

He'd slipped and called his brother Josh. "Michael—"

"No, milady. Your lordship here knows our true names," Walter said.

Bakeley nodded.

"An' he's not the lord causing trouble. That would be your cousin, milady."

"Accushed ush of poaching," Josh said.

She looked from one to the other. They'd often poached—her father had turned a blind eye to it, generally, as he'd had so little money to make the tenants' lots better. No doubt they were guilty.

"Once you left, Mam was starving."

Anger burned through her, flashes of light behind her eyes shooting tension all the way to her fists. She wanted to punch someone, stomp on something.

Damn him. Damn this new Glenmorrow who wanted nothing more than to rape his Irish estate and all the people upon it. Damn the English for driving her brother away. Damn her father for his drinking and spendthrift ways. And her brother...

No. If Jamie lived, he was all she had.

Grief followed the anger. If Jamie Hollister lived, there was naught they could do for their family home or the people who lived there. This new Glenmorrow was firmly ensconced. Finding her brother was for her. It would do their people no good.

And it would do Jamie no good if she found him and he was snatched up by Shaldon, tried for treason and hanged.

"We've told your lord here you were looking to meet a man on the docks about your brother. I'm sorry my lady, but lies do not come easy and we've had our fill of 'em."

She took his hand and closed it around the purse. "At least give this to your mother if you won't take it for yourself. Tell her I think of her every day."

He nodded. "All right then. For Mam."

She wished Josh farewell and a rapid recovery and waited while Bakeley shook their hands. It was a sight for sore eyes, a lord shaking hands with poor Irish men, nothing that her father would have done, nor the new lord of Glenmorrow.

She was trembling when Bakeley led her downstairs and scarcely noticed him wrapping her in her shawl.

Jenny appeared, carrying a valise.

"I'm going with them?" she asked, unease threading through her. Was he sending her away?

"No. Bink will accompany them. You and I are going to spend the rest of the night as Hackwell's guests. I'll be up early and out to Doctors' Commons. You may help Lady Hackwell plan our wedding breakfast."

"May I not go to my own home?"

"Lady Jane has courage, but if my father decides to interfere with our plans, Hackwell will be a more formidable adversary and a better protector."

"But who will protect you?"

He froze, and then laughed. "Do you know, you have a point. Well, Hackwell has one or two stout footmen with military backgrounds." He lifted her hand and kissed it. "You forgot this earlier."

He slipped the sapphire ring on her finger and it twinkled in the light of the servant's lantern.

It was a beautiful ring, dainty, the stone perfectly sized for her own small self. She'd forgotten it, but he'd remembered. Bakeley was a determined sort.

"And here I thought I might let you slip away from the leg shackle, if you had a mind for it," she said.

"Not a chance." He squeezed her shoulder. "Don't be afraid."

"Afraid? Not a chance for that either." God's truth, she was terrified, but she must bluster through this.

She lifted herself up on her toes and kissed him in front of Jenny and the footman holding the door open. "A promise is a promise, Lord Bakeley. If you do not return for me, you shall see how an Irish lady takes her revenge."

He leaned in close and whispered, "'Tis lucky for you we have all these servants hovering, else you'd see how an English lord takes his lady."

Her heart thumped wildly. "No," she whispered back. "Not lucky at all." She squeezed his hand and hurried away before he could see the heat overtaking her.

"Yes, oh, yes." Lady Jane clasped her hands together. "Barton has been working on this for days, and we'd meant to surprise you with a new gown, but here you are—you've surprised us. A pinch more at the bodice, Barton. Inhale, Sirena. Is this fabric not lovely? This is called *gros de naples.*"

The words floated over Sirena while she dutifully obeyed, surveying herself in the mirror. The golden threads of the bodice and overskirt caught the faint light of the dimming day and set the red underskirt afire.

"Princess Charlotte was married in a dress of gold," Lady Jane said.

Barton removed a pin from her mouth. "Hold still now, my lady. And you'll have much better luck than the unfortunate princess."

The princess had died in childbirth. After all Sirena had been through, that didn't scare her. To have a child of her own would be worth the risk.

"Why, yes," Lady Jane said. "Barton and I will find a good midwife and keep away all of those men with their leeches and knives."

"We're putting the carriage before the horse," Sirena said. "First the bridegroom must appear with the license and the vicar."

Barton plucked at the poufy sleeve caps. "There." She smiled broadly. "Jenny has done well with your hair."

Lady Jane looked her over. "He was head over ears for you in your made-over dresses. He shall swoon when he sees you in this."

She couldn't help smiling. "Perhaps I shall myself swoon in these stays." Her breasts threatened to spill over the top of the tight lacing. It was nearly indecent, and a march on Lady Arbrough's bosom-baring campaign.

The door opened and Jenny slipped in. "He's here."

She straightened and smoothed her skirts.

"Wait, Sirena." Lady Jane flipped up the lid on a slim box and lifted a delicate chain, and she pulled another from her pocket.

Sirena's heart pounded fiercely, the drumming resounding in her ears and pushing against her eyes, clouding her vision.

"I found this box amongst your things, my dear," Lady Jane said, "and the other was on the night stand. I thought you might want to wear one of them."

Queen Brighid's knot swung gently back and forth, its complicated turns pulling Sirena in, twisting up her heart, pressing on her lungs. Images flashed before her eyes, the knot resting in her gram's gnarled hand, the knot against Jamie's broad neck, the knot on the worn carpet at Glenmorrow.

"Sirena." A hand clutched her elbow.

She sucked in a deep breath, closed her eyes, and opened them, glancing at the other dangling item, her mother's locket.

At Papa's death, there'd only been a few items of her mother's jewelry left, and this one she'd purloined from the Glenmorrow estate, risking a charge of theft by her greedy cousin.

She fingered the locket. It was cold, firm, the etchings worn under her own shaking fingers, and thank God for it. Had she Gram's and Mama's Sight, the thing might be warm and buzzing as fierce as her head now.

"Perhaps something borrowed," Barton said, moving in front of Sirena and fluffing a sleeve cap again. "It's one of the traditions where my people come from."

"Of course," Lady Jane said. She moved behind Sirena and fastened a chain around her neck.

'Twas Lady Jane's own small amber cross, the one she always wore.

"Will this do, then? It was my grandmother's, and she had a long and happy marriage with many children."

Sirena's heart settled and warmth rushed her eyes. "And was that not her wish for you, my lady? I shall give it back directly."

Lady Jane smiled. "I should like it back, but I'm afraid my time for marriage and children has passed."

Sirena grasped Lady Jane's hand and studied her, a knowing quaking inside of her for this friend she'd grown to love. And perhaps she did have some of her mother's gift. "No, Jane," she whispered. "It hasn't."

Lady Jane's mouth opened and closed.

"Lovely." Lady Hackwell said, sweeping into the room, tall and elegant-looking. "Lady Sirena, I'm so sorry, I must rush you on your wedding day." She smiled, but there was a tension about her eyes. "He's here, as is the vicar, and wishes to make all haste."

Which meant, his lord father, Shaldon, might be hot on his heels. She put a hand to her stomach. She'd slept so little that morning.

Lady Hackwell's eyes narrowed. "You don't have to do this if you're unwilling. No matter what has transpired—"

"Lord Bakeley has been a perfect gentleman." Well, *almost* perfect.

And what was she to do? She was trapped, by the simple need for shelter and food. If she ran off from Bakeley, Lady Jane couldn't take her back and still be respectable. She didn't love Bakeley, but God's truth, he was handsome, and his kisses were magical.

And...he was the son of Shaldon, the man who might tell her where to find Jamie. She might find the truth. And if her brother truly *was* dead, by all that was holy, when she knew the how and the who of it, she'd take her revenge, even if it meant going against her husband's father.

She straightened her shoulders. "I do want to go through with this."

That was the terrifying truth.

A few squares over, a valet held up a dark coat for Edward Everly, Lord Shaldon, to ease into. The tight sleeves pinched at his shoulder, causing the old wound where a bullet had been dug out to throb. Even that could not bring him down.

His obstinate heir was taking a wife, finally.

"I couldn't persuade you out of this?" The man speaking stood erect and alert. "No. By the grin on your face, I suppose not."

"You shall accompany me and save me from the worst of my folly. As usual, Kincaid."

"An Irish lass. Is it not poetic justice that the next Lady Shaldon will be Irish? Bink's mother is laughing in her grave."

He took his cane from his valet and dismissed the man. "But she would approve, and so would Felicity." His late wife's generous spirit had left hefty bequests for all the Shaldon offspring, including his Irish by-blow. "As do I. Imagine the boy saddled to that milksop lass of Denholm's?"

"Would Lady Sirena have killed that man at the docks yesterday, do you think?"

Yesterday, his future daughter—or perhaps the wedding ceremony had been completed and she was his current daughter—had had a gleam in her eye to test the devil. Bakeley had chosen a strong woman. "I would have wagered on it, Kincaid. But she'd only have done it to save those men fighting in her behalf. My grandchildren will be in good hands."

Kincaid snorted. "They'll be Whigs, every one of them."

He laughed. "No they won't. It's the plight of the parents to have their children oppose them. It seems all my children have Whiggish propensities. My grandsons will be good solid Tories."

"It was good Bakeley appeared when he did, else we would have had to intervene," Kincaid said. "You'll not hold it against her that she ruined the day?"

"I should, but I find I cannot."

"That was more than the usual mayhem. I'd say she was very close to the man."

Shaldon frowned. "Any news of her brother?"

"The rumors are churning. But why the devil come back here and now? You'll take an extra guard with you when you're gadding about."

"Hmmph. Come, we'll be late."

The town coach waited in front, and they climbed in.

"Hello, Father." Perpetua smiled up at him, her lovely, bookish face framed in a most becoming bonnet. Here was another political contrarian. Finding a husband acceptable to her was proving to be quite a challenge, though he doubted she'd yet realized he was making the effort.

Kincaid climbed in and greeted her.

"What did I say about Whigs, Kincaid? You should not be attending today, Perpetua. I'm afraid your brother is becoming a bad influence."

"Because he supports the Poor Laws, Father? Or is it on account of his interest in London sewers and the Fever Hospital?" Her smile grew bolder. "Or, because he's given up his mistress and is marrying happily?"

He grunted. "One Spanish daughter-in-law and one Irish—cannot anyone marry a good English girl?"

"Perhaps Charley will, Father."

Kincaid's gaze barely glanced off of him but he caught the hint of a smirk. Since returning from the Continent, Charley had wormed himself in with the entire foreign diplomatic corps, primarily the wives. What he learned he passed on to Kincaid. What Kincaid learned, he passed on to Shaldon.

She smiled. "Though I doubt it will be any time soon."

Bakeley paced the length of the library again.

"Good God, man, she'll be right along. She hasn't fled the premises, and no one has been by to snatch her up today. My lady wife is bringing her along." Hackwell poured a finger of brandy and marched it over to Bakeley. "Down the hatch. Vicar, would you like a tot?"

"Perhaps just a little." This vicar was not the scrupulous sort, nor one of the wealthy younger sons settled into an easy living. The generous sum Bakeley offered had pulled him expeditiously out of a parish meeting.

"Take a seat and review those documents, will you?" Hackwell pointed at a sheaf of papers on the library table. "I had the solicitor follow your requirements precisely, but you'll wish to double-check."

He sighed as he pulled out the chair. "I thank you." No doubt he could trust Hackwell, but he could hear his mother's voice telling him that honest men never minded having their work checked. Besides, this document would commemorate an irrevocable choice. He wanted it correct from the start.

A lifetime of reading legal documents allowed him to skim through the text and determine that all was in order. As he was straightening the papers, the door opened.

Lady Hackwell entered, her serious expression sending a jolt of worry through him.

Sirena had changed her mind.

But no, Lady Jane followed behind her and smiled at him. He jumped from the seat and went around the table just as Sirena entered.

His heart tried to pound its way out of his chest. She was a vision in a golden dress that glowed. Or she glowed, he wasn't sure. Her breasts perched daringly high, ready to spring out.

Into his mouth.

Stand down, old man.

"You're frowning," Sirena said.

He took the several steps to meet her, like walking on soft pillows, or through a deep water. He couldn't get there quickly enough, but he did finally reach her. He took the hands she gripped together and kissed them.

She was wearing his ring.

"Say something, then, Bakeley."

"I am dazzled."

"Displeased?"

"You look like a shining star."

She laughed and he heard relief. "Are we to marry then?" she asked.

"I am not much of a poet, am I? But you are blindingly lovely. And, yes, I have the license here." He patted his pocket. "And the vicar over there. Come and I'll go over the settlements and we'll sign them and then be married."

The little frown returned to her face, as if she were steeling herself for the business ahead, perhaps for the life ahead. Indeed, as he explained the provisions he was making for her and their children, she listened intently, gripping her hands as if she were about to jump off a cliff. They signed, and Hackwell witnessed, and when he looked up, he realized everyone but Hackwell had departed.

And Sirena's face was as pale as a snowdrift.

Hackwell must have noticed it also. "Come into the drawing room when you're ready." He stood and walked out.

Left alone with her, Bakeley squeezed her icy hands, then began to chafe them with his. "Don't be afraid. I won't cheat you over your pin money. I won't lock you away in the country. I would never strike you, Sirena. And I won't let my father harm you in any way."

"I'm not afraid." Irritation laced her voice, and her deep inhalation made her breasts rise to greet him.

He had only the wedding and the small celebration to get through and then he could partake of her loveliness.

He stroked a finger along the top of her breasts, and her cheeks pinkened. "Bakeley," she whispered. "What are you doing?"

"Bringing your color back. You were looking pale, as if you were going to faint."

"I'm not a fainter."

"Nor are you a coward. Shall we proceed?"

Her eyes searched his. "You're quite certain you want me?"

"Yes. I'd be willing to show you right this moment, if you wish. Hackwell wouldn't mind much."

Her eyes went wide and her mouth dropped open in a breathless laugh. "You rascal, you."

"Are you quite sure you want *me*, Sirena?"

She stared at him for a long moment, her cheeks going pinker, her eyes smokier, a glazed look settling over her. Finally, she nodded. "It's madness, Bakeley, but I do."

"James."

She took a deep breath. "Yes. James."

"Let us proceed then, my lady." With her on his arm, he led her down the corridor and through the open door of the drawing room.

Her grip on his arm tightened, and a high wave of tension hit both of them at the same time. He heard her sharp intake of breath, and his own heartbeat quickened.

Two other men had joined their party. One of them turned around and cast both of them a grim glare.

"I am not too late." Lord Shaldon raised his quizzing glass, his scrutiny directed at Sirena.

Bakeley's blood spiked, but he patted her hand and noted she had lifted her chin, as regal as the dress she wore. Her bravery settled him.

Lady Hackwell, Lady Jane, and Perry moved around Shaldon. If he planned to start trouble, the ladies would reckon with him. Lord Hackwell had taken his station near Mr. Kincaid, along with Bink's wife, Paulette, who shoved her small son into Kincaid's arms, an effective means of disarmament. Two maids hovered just inside the door, Lady Jane's abigail and the girl Jenny.

"Where is the Vicar?" Bakeley looked around.

"Right here, sir." The man pulled opened his prayer book. "Shall we begin?"

"Yes." Bakeley tucked her arm more firmly and marched her over. His father's glare was like a piercing wind, or an icy spike, or a fragment of shot from a misloaded gun.

The vicar's voice droned with the beginning prayers. Hackwell stepped up to give Sirena away. There were more droning words about the sanctity of marriage. Then the vicar started to ask if there were any objections and he could hear Shaldon clearing his throat.

"Move on," Bakeley said. "Quickly, as we discussed."

The vicar's jowls fluttered. "My lord, I—"

Another throat-clearing.

"Don't do it, Father." Perry's chiding whisper filled the room.

"My son is right," Shaldon said. "Move on."

After that command, the clergyman set a dizzying pace, and before he knew it, he was kissing his bride's soft, chilly lips and then being congratulated by their friends. Their circuit of the room ended at his lordship.

"So you have married," Shaldon said.

The frosty manner spiked his ire. Worse, his bride had matched Shaldon's comment with an impenetrable sheet of ice.

Lovely. She should be glowing with happiness and warm anticipation, not icy anger. Shaldon was throwing a dampener on the wedding, which had no doubt been his intention.

"Did you not wish me to marry, father?"

"Of course I did."

Next to him, tiny tremors rippled through his bride. "You didn't wish him to marry me, though, did you, my lord?"

Shaldon looked at her again, with that studious gaze, as if he was looking at another species of earthworm, and he said nothing. He used this technique to intimidate his children. Bakeley was tired of it.

"Father, Lady Sirena is my chosen wife. If you plan to be rude to her, you may return home, and please, don't bother to extend invitations to visit, as I will not subject her to mistreatment from anyone."

"What are you talking about, Bakeley? You and she will be living at Shaldon House."

"I have taken a townhouse."

"Have you? That narrow building is no place for the next Lady Shaldon." Shaldon brushed at his sleeve.

Bakeley exchanged a look with Sirena. "What are you about, sir?"

"I would speak with the both of you after the celebratory meal. Will you indulge me then?" He cleared his throat. "I will be brief."

He looked at Sirena and she nodded her agreement.

"Yes. We will," he said. He led her off to the dining room.

"I'll have some things to say also, Bakeley," she whispered.

"James."

"James. I do hope you weren't counting on a quiet, meek wife."

A frown line was etched between her eyebrows. He hoped she would save some of that spirit for later.

"I believe I knew you weren't quiet and meek when I saw you with a blade yesterday. I do hope you'll limit your challenges to sharp words."

"Of course. Unless your father threatens my person."

"No, my dear, I mean with me. Over the course of our marriage, we're bound to have a disagreement or two."

She rolled her eyes. He had distracted her from worry about his father, he hoped.

Leave Shaldon to him. His lordship was up to something, and it was his job to make sure it didn't ruin the wedding night.

"I'm looking for a man," Lord Shaldon said. He'd taken a wing chair set near to the fireplace in Hackwell's library.

Sirena turned her gaze to the man called Kincaid, who didn't so much as shift against the mantle. Honestly, he would burn his breeches should he keep leaning so close.

While everyone had toasted the bride and groom and nibbled at the generous repast, Paulette's uncle—for that was Kincaid's kinship— had alternated Paulette's wee baby and the Hackwells' two little ones on his knees and played a game he called skat with Hackwell's young nephew and brother, all without his dour face breaking a smile. Paulette said that her uncle and his lordship were thick as brothers, two men who could finish each other's sentences, that was how long they'd fought side by side.

On the chair next to her, Bakeley was as stiff as one of the Beltany Stones. Waiting his father out, he was. Quite patiently. And so should she bide her peace also, if ever so impatiently. She'd hold her tongue and see which way this conversation uncoiled.

Well, but it seemed his lordship was being direct, and what did that mean?

Shaldon cleared his throat. Bakeley remained mum.

Oh, good Lord. 'Twould be left to her to spur the talking. "And who would you be looking for, Lord Shaldon?"

His lordship's hard eyes turned on her. "Father."

The hair on her neck rose. "I beg your pardon?"

"I should very much like for you to call me 'Father', Lady Sirena."

Heat swamped her. What was the old man about?

Bakeley's face slipped into a confounded frown. "Who is the man you're looking for?"

"Would it be possible for you to call me 'Father'? I know your own father is deceased. A fine horseman he was." His fingers thumped the chair arm. "It was a bad day when your brother disappeared, but that is the pity and the foolishness of war."

Her heart quaked within her and sudden anger sparked her tongue.

She bit it back. He thought the Irish were fools, including the Hollisters.

Certainly her father had been foolish, spending all on his horses and drinking himself to death. Perhaps if *he'd* sold the rest of the horses she'd helped build up after Bakeley's purchase, perhaps he'd have lived longer instead of succumbing to the black bile. Or perhaps his daughter wouldn't have been left to live as a pauper with Lady Jane.

Shaldon couldn't be any worse of a father than that. Well, except that she still didn't know what his tie was to her brother. If there was a tie.

Her chest quaked like a cauldron boiling. She blinked hard and cleared her throat. "Certainly I'm without a father now, and if you wish me to call you that, then I will."

"It's very hard for a man to lose a son and a wife. Very hard indeed." He looked away, ruminating on something that hadn't happened to him. He'd lost a wife, but not a son. And surely a man this hard wouldn't be *sentimental.*

She felt the press of Bakeley's hand on hers.

"I count myself quite fortunate to have three sons and a daughter, and now two daughters by marriage."

She held her breath. Fortunate to have her?

"Father, who's the man you're looking for, and what does that have to do with Sirena and me?" Bakeley's frown had been a momentary wrinkle. He'd turned back into a standing stone—the bored aristocrat, the dispassionate Englishman—these men all played so well.

That, in truth, was much of what James Everly, Lord Bakeley was. Queen Brighid, help her.

Ah, but she'd learn how to spike his cannon. And she knew, at least on the topic of breeding, that a passionate man hid beneath all that aplomb. When they returned to his townhouse tonight, she'd get his eyes dancing and his blood racing, and once she got through that, he'd damn well help her search for her brother.

Shaldon's gaze narrowed on them. "Yes, of course, it is your wedding day. You are impatient to get away. I am looking for a man named Donegal."

Her hair prickled. "*Donegal*?" Donegal was the man the O'Brian boys were looking for, the man she was supposed to meet.

"You are not going to use my wife as a lure. I will not have Sirena placed in danger." Bakeley might have been describing the weather.

Shaldon steepled his hands.

"Come, Sirena." Bakeley planted his feet as if to rise.

"Donegal may have information on your brother," Shaldon said.

Her new husband never so much as twitched, yet she sensed his rising anger. Her own heart had quickened to a mad race. He took her hands in his.

"'Tis what I hoped for," she whispered.

"What do you want from us, Father?" Bakeley asked, but his eyes never left her face.

She was trembling, she knew, and it irritated her. The old lord was playing with her, she knew that also, in the way a cat played with a broken beetle as it died.

She was not broken, nor would she die for him.

Shaldon folded his hands in his lap. "Donegal might be willing to speak to the sister of Roland James Hollister."

"Aye, but will he share secrets with Lord Shaldon's daughter-in-law?" Her cheeks were on fire. She could never match this English coolness.

"Speak plainly, Father. What do you know of Sirena's brother?"

"Only what you know. His body has not been found."

Her head buzzed with the vision of that day—the rider, the note, the chain, Mama's head hitting the heavy table.

Mama had died the next day.

"But it was," she whispered. "It was."

Shaldon's gaze softened. "*A* body was pulled from the sea, so badly...well, I'm not convinced it was his." One long, strong finger tapped the arm of his chair. "Nor are you, Sirena."

The rush of emotion confused her—gratitude, vindication, more anger. How could he reach into her heart and pull out that knowledge?

"And why do you seek this Donegal?" Bakeley asked.

Shaldon glanced at Kincaid.

"She is family now," Shaldon said.

A chill went through her. She was family to this man who was part of the machine that spread such sorrow through her land.

"You've heard of the Cato Street Conspiracy, and the actions of the radicals last year in Scotland?" Kincaid asked.

When Kincaid spoke, she noticed the burr. "You're...Scottish?"

"I am. But Lord Shaldon and I spent many years on the Continent seeing what happens when radicals rip apart the social order. They promise change and then install their own despots."

"But all the radical conspirators were executed last year."

"There is always a conspiracy afoot." Bakeley's voice sounded leaden. "I will not allow my wife to be placed in danger."

Rebellion stirred in her. This was how it was when one was married. The husband decided what one would and would not do.

She would, of course, try again to find Donegal, though whether she was willing to lead him to Shaldon and Kincaid was an open question. Perhaps not. If he was but an Irishman seeking freedom, she couldn't wholly condemn him to the English Secret Service. And she wouldn't discuss any of this with Shaldon, not without speaking first to Bakeley.

If she decided to discuss the matter with Bakeley at all. Wife or not, he wouldn't control her in that way.

"Perhaps you could tell us something about this Donegal," she said.

Kincaid jumped into the breach again. "He's said to be Irish. Believed to have left Ireland about the same time as your brother, possibly on the same ship. Where he went then, we don't know, but he resurfaced in Scotland two years ago."

Her brain muddled through the calculations. "That's more than ten years since he vanished." And on the same ship as Jamie? The one that sunk? Was he tied up in Jamie's supposed death?

A chill went through her. Donegal had promised a meeting and not shown up, and perhaps sent that crowd of ruffians after her. "Is he...do you believe he's dangerous?"

"Yes." Shaldon spoke. "And quite elusive."

She wanted to ask what he had in mind. She wanted to say more.

Bakeley gripped her hand like she was sliding off the side of the Honey Bee herself and about to fall into roiling waters, which she would, if she loosened her tongue and spoke her mind.

She hadn't survived the years of her father's drunkenness, or the assault by the new Lord of Glenmorrow, or her months of serving Lady Jane without being able to hold her tongue a little. Aye, and wouldn't marriage and the care and feeding of a titled husband and his treacherous father present new opportunities for keeping silent?

Perhaps Shaldon would say more without her there. She wouldn't work for the Spy Lord, not against good Irish people, and she didn't know just what Donegal was yet.

But she knew what she was. 'Twas the sad truth, no matter how many horses she'd bred and trained, she was but a woman, made specially valueless by her lack of a dowry.

Bakeley turned his gaze on her, and her heart did a jig. Valueless, she was, but he'd taken her anyway. Perhaps...perhaps if she handled this husband correctly, he truly would help her.

"Well, then. I'll go and say my thanks to Lord and Lady Hackwell, and leave you to discuss this matter with your father." She stood, and so did Bakeley and her new father-in-law.

Her husband moved by her side to the door. "I shall be along directly," he murmured.

She nodded. "Counting on it, I am." She leaned in and dropped a kiss on his cheek. "Find out everything."

CHAPTER THIRTEEN

Bakeley strode back and braced his hands on the back of his chair. "Father. Have you gone mad? *Call me Father, Sirena*? Only days ago you were telling me to stay away from her."

Kincaid cleared his throat. Bakeley ignored him.

"Did you listen?" Shaldon said. "Did it keep you away from her? No. You were as besotted as a puppy the moment you took her in the dance."

Fire rushed through him. Besotted, yes, and he should be well on his way to taking her in more than just a dance, instead of talking about using her as bait to draw in a radical.

"But we have learned, have we not. Kincaid, that when circumstances arise, one makes the best of the situation."

Kincaid turned away to hide a smile, and then he knew. *He knew*.

Shaldon had engineered his marriage to Sirena as surely as he'd done with the marriage of Bink and Paulette, though he'd used a different set of wiles.

He rubbed a hand on his cheek. He'd been dodging every one of his father's conspiracies and plots, ever since the fiasco with Bink. Shaldon had thrown Denholm's chit at him, knowing he would reject Lady Glenna, purposely telling him to stay away from Sirena.

He walked to the sideboard where Hackwell had bottles of liquor and poured himself an amber liquid from a cut glass carafe. Brandy, he hoped.

He quaffed it back and almost choked. It was a strong Scotch whisky, with a bracing burn that smoothed out on the way down. He poured another.

"Not too many, my son, if you're going to take effective action with your bride tonight."

He cursed low under his breath and drank.

His mind swam with pictures of her in her gold and red gown, and a chuckle bubbled up from the spot where the liquor had settled. His father's wishes for his marriage and his own had coincided, and that hadn't changed. He had no regrets—so far—about the wife he'd chosen.

But she wasn't going to work for the British Secret Service. That he would *not* allow.

"So what is your plan, Father, Kincaid? Or shall I say, what are the parts of your plan you're willing to share with me?"

"Don't be angry with me, boy. You're not unhappy with your wife."

It was true. He wasn't. "Nothing can be straightforward with you, can it, Father? First Bink, now me. And you almost got Paulette and Bink killed."

"Because they didn't trust me."

"And who could?"

"The right spouse makes all the difference in your happiness. I've tried to lead you lads in the way that would be most effective."

"Most effective?"

"Yes. My eldest is a warrior. I knew when he saw Paulette in danger, he'd protect her. And then there was the money settled on them, and the chance to stand for Parliament and right the wrongs he saw in society."

"I see."

And none of those applied to him. He was a steward of the family wealth, not a warrior. He was rich already. And he would, someday, take his place in the Lords when he inherited.

When his father died.

He studied the amber liquid. He had no wish to rush into the Lords.

"And me, Father?"

Shaldon made a rumbling noise in his throat, sending up a fit of coughing from his gut. Kincaid poured him some of the whisky and handed him the tumbler.

"Please. No swooning, Father. No pretending to die before we have this little talk."

Kincaid chuckled, a rare enough occurrence that Bakeley knew the coughing was a ruse.

"I'm waiting."

"You are so like her."

"Like Sirena?"

Shaldon waved his hand. "Like your mother. Never would let me get away with anything. Even when I was on the Continent, her wagging finger followed me. No foolishness, Shaldon, she would say, and I'd see her in my mind's eye."

He snorted. "I fail to see—"

"I didn't see it either. Didn't see how well you managed in my absence after she was gone. I didn't trust your judgment, and so you didn't trust mine, did you? If I said go, you looked for all the ways to stay. If I said buy, you investigated selling. You became a contrarian, Bakeley."

Heat rose in him, but he kept his manner cold. "Indeed."

"And then I learned that Lady Jane had come to town with the late Earl of Glenmorrow's daughter. I had visited that estate once."

The hair on Bakeley's neck prickled. *He'd* visited Glenmorrow also?

"She was far too young to remember me. She's grown into a lovely woman, like her mother. Her father was an affable fellow then. Not yet broken." He handed Kincaid his glass. "Get me another, Kincaid."

When Kincaid returned, he quaffed the shot. "So Lady Sirena came to town. Hackwell's Annabelle liked her well, as did Paulette." He thumped the chair arm and stared at the fire. "And, of course, Jane. The family's problems didn't jade the girl, though they easily could have."

His mind swirled and his head buzzed, but it was the only noise in the quiet room. Very well. He'd been manipulated by the crafty old Spy Lord. In the end, he'd been maneuvered into marrying the wife his father had arranged for him.

He went and got another drink. There was no rush to consummate a marriage so carefully managed.

"Bakeley." His father's voice sliced through him. "You wouldn't have married her had you not wished to. This marriage was your decision, and your doing. I simply made sure you met the lady."

And told me to stay away from her. And there was the matter of the assault at the docks.

"She could have been killed yesterday. Did you know about it?"

Shaldon nodded.

"Were you behind her assault?"

"Most emphatically no."

He set the glass down untouched. His father was right, too much drink would dull his senses, already sapped by too little sleep. He'd gone after the forbidden fruit, and he was damn well going to partake of it. "I thank you for this little father-son discussion. I believe we'll set off for home."

"I should like very much for you to return to Shaldon House after your honeymoon. Your sister is not entirely content with playing the political hostess and this will be a very lively session, I do believe, with both of your brothers in the Commons."

Bink certainly would vote for lifting the more onerous of the Six Acts, and Charley might be amenable to siding with their brother. He himself would not have a place in Parliament, not yet, but as the manager of a grand estate and network of commercial interests, he could still exert influence. It remained to be seen how Sirena's role would play out.

And then of course, there was the man his father wanted to trap.

"Sirena as your hostess, Father?" He tried to picture her at the foot of the great dining table, and shook his head.

Could that wild girl from Glenmorrow's stable play that role? Would she be willing? Should he give her the choice? Certainly, the small stable behind Shaldon House would be a forceful lure for his horse-mad bride.

"You will, I hope, give us a few days for our honeymoon before Sirena must begin fêting politicians and luring radicals."

Shaldon eyed him shrewdly and said nothing.

His hair rose. He must be on his toes. And he must get his new bride to their bed, before his father set another plan in motion. "We'll decide on our arrangements after the honeymoon."

As for Donegal...

"How do you plan to lure your man out of wherever he is hiding?"

"We've not decided," Kincaid said. "We shall, however, include you in our planning. You must know that. You must tell your lady. I fear she is a determined sort."

Shaldon cleared his throat.

"No," Kincaid said. "He must know. The O'Brian boys—"

"Who?" Even as he said it he remembered—the Smith brothers.

Shaldon eyed Kincaid, who lifted a shoulder and spoke. "The two men with her at the docks. Yes, they worked for me upon occasion. Didn't know your father was involved. They knew her from her home, yes, they did. Yet when we asked them, they agreed to help. Had a poaching charge against them, they did, yet they seemed good sorts."

A memory of her on the docks arose.

"And the group that attacked her? Were they with Donegal?"

"We don't know," Shaldon said. "The docks are filled with riffraff."

"Find a female operative, one of your women with yellow hair, to play Sirena's role."

Shaldon pursed his lips. "We'll consider it. It may not work, however. We believe Donegal may have seen her already, if not recently then in the past."

"He's been a decade away, maybe longer."

"True. Or possibly true." His father rose and walked toward him. "Now, take your bride home, son. Kincaid will put a guard around your townhouse." Shaldon took his hand and shook it heartily. "She's a worthy wife. No harm shall touch her."

Kincaid gripped his hand also and then helped the old lord out.

In the years since his return, Shaldon had been turning the world topsy-turvy. And he'd managed to combine matchmaking with his spying business.

All well and good, the sooner they got through the Donegal matter, the sooner Shaldon would move on to Charley.

Donegal. Sirena had surely recognized that name. Neither she nor the O'Brians had shared the name of the man they were seeking. His new wife had kept that secret. He'd have to be on his toes with her also.

He'd have to convince her to share all her secrets, and the only way he knew how to do that was to seduce her until she was witless.

The moment the door of the coach clicked shut, Sirena was pulled onto Bakeley's lap. His big hand pressed her head to his broad shoulder, and then...nothing.

The *clackity-clack* of the wheels and the *clip-clopping* of horse's hooves, all around the carriage actually—strange that—was all she heard.

"Who's with us?" she asked.

"We are being guarded."

"By whom?"

He loosed a hand from her back and waved it. "Kincaid. His men."

"Are we in danger then? And from whom?" She tried to sit up but he clasped her as though she were a piece of Chinese porcelain. "And what about Donegal?"

"Was it Donegal you went to look for yesterday?"

She tried hard not to freeze. Holding her this tightly, he would notice. Yet a little shiver still went through her.

"Please do not lie, my love."

His love. And if she believed *that* there was a tree with a leprechaun she could sell him. Still he was right that she should not out and out lie. Close to the truth was always better. In this case, she might as well say it all.

"That *was* the name the boys gave me."

"Did you know the O'Brians also worked for Shaldon?"

She went even colder, deep into her core, and all of her fingers and toes numbed. Walter and Josh worked for Shaldon?

And then a hot pounding started inside her head. Bakeley was lying, tripping her up. Conspiring with his Awful Lordship to trap her.

She'd tied her cart to this horse for the rest of her life. What had she done? Oh, dear God, what had she done?

He noticed her fear, of course he did, because that paddle hand stroked her back like he was settling a horse, and the motion inflamed her more. She struggled. He tightened his embrace.

"Let me off."

He'd trapped her arms at her sides, and was setting his lips to her face. She turned her head to move out of his way, bucked. Squirmed. All to no avail.

Rage built within her. There was no one to help, no housekeeper to lace his brandy with laudanum, no butler ready to bash him.

She opened her mouth to let out a scream. He planted his lips there.

"Get off," she tried to say, but it came out garbled, and tasted like spirits, and his lips in spite of it all were gentle.

The scent of him flooded her, brought all of her senses alive. The horses outside clopped along steadily. She was surrounded by men—Shaldon's men. Screaming would not help her.

She should think. But, oh, the rascally man would only allow her to *feel*.

His lips moved to her cheek, and between kisses he murmured, "Be still," and "I'm sorry," and "It's what Shaldon said," and "We'll do this together."

And then, "Do not cry, love."

Damn, damn, damn.

She wiped the back of her hand over her eyes, soaking her glove. "I'm a bloody fool. Shaldon's son? I've married Shaldon's son. What was I thinking?"

He handed her a handkerchief. In the dim light of the coach's lantern, his eyes sparkled like fairy dust.

"You weren't thinking. Neither was I. Marriage is usually a rational endeavor, but not in our case. You were using your woman's intuition. Here's a strong, sensible man, you said, rich, too. And he genuinely wants me."

"Oh, yes? And what of you? Were you using your man's intuition?"

"Oh, yes."

The kiss that followed was less gentle, more determined. His hand at the back of her head kept her fixed and held her in place when the coach turned a corner and threatened to topple her. A sigh worked its way from inside her, and when her mouth opened, his tongue touched hers and began to explore.

It was...*oh*. His hand moved up her bodice, still spanning her side and keeping her stable, while his thumb began to search for her nipple. The layers of fabric—her pelisse, her petticoat, her gown, her stays, her chemise—intruded. She grasped the back of his head and hitched herself closer.

He traced the line of her bodice and trailed his fingers under the fabric. The deep curve of her décolletage made the journey a short one, and soon she was gasping while pleasure streaked through her.

He let go of her lips then and nibbled her cheeks down to a spot on her neck, and the feel of it made her groan.

This was not Shaldon's son. This was James, Lord Bakeley, the man she'd just entered into mad holy matrimony with to save her men from his father, the Spy Lord. Only they were really Shaldon's men, not hers. And now the crafty old Lord wanted her to call himself Father.

It was beyond madness, even for an Irish girl.

He gave up on her breast and before she could cry out in protest he had captured her mouth again, distracting her so much she didn't notice his hand had moved up under her skirt to above her knee, where he was wreaking a havoc of sensation. She swept her tongue against his and gave back completely, burying her fingers in his thick hair.

His hand made a rapid advance to the crux of her legs and began a gentle assault, sending such bliss through her that she groaned with it.

When he stilled his hand, she pulled back, and realized the carriage had stopped.

He opened the shade. The lights of the townhouse poured brightly through the open front door where the housekeeper and her husband stood waiting.

"We're home." Eyes glittering darkly, he straightened her skirt and bodice, eased her onto the seat and rearranged his trousers.

CHAPTER FOURTEEN

Bakeley looked into Sirena's wide eyes. She'd noticed his bulge.

He couldn't help grinning. "See what you do to me?" He planted a quick kiss on her swollen lips. "Come along then, Lady Bakeley. They are waiting."

A groom rushed to put down the steps and he brushed the man aside, turning to help Sirena himself.

She lifted her eyes to the bright lights and the crowd of Kincaid's guards that had gathered. "Is there to be company?"

"Company?"

"The lights. This crowd. I had much rather not entertain."

"Heaven forbid. I would send them all away."

That brought a shy smile from her.

Desire roared through him. It took all his control to hand her down gently, but once her feet touched the ground, he swept her up into his arms.

She gasped, the same noise she'd made when he'd fondled her breasts. Another surge of lust swept him.

"What are you doing?" she cried.

Like a conquering hero, I'm taking home my spoils. "Carrying my bride across the threshold," he said. "To placate the house gods. You've heard of that custom, have you not?"

"Am I not too heavy?"

Heavy? He felt as powerful as a savage. "Not heavy at all."

"You're huffing and puffing."

"That is anticipation, love."

In the light of the landing, he could see her face flush.

They crossed the threshold and he set her down. She greeted the servants politely.

The housekeeper curtsied. "I'll assist you, my lady, until you've selected an abigail."

"Not tonight," he said. "You may lock up and retire. If we need anything we'll raid the kitchen for ourselves, shall we not?"

Sirena rewarded him with a smile.

"We've laid a cold repast in your chamber, but should you want more, there's fresh bread in the box and good butter in the cold cabinet." The housekeeper rubbed her hands together. "I've filled a kettle. It will just need to be heated."

"Thank you, ma'am," Sirena said.

"Good night," he said.

"Come along, missus." Mr. Windle took hold of his wife, fighting a smile.

Bakeley turned the key in the bedchamber door's lock, and then hauled his bride up into an ardent kiss.

She didn't seem quite as willing as before. Not wholly stiff, either. He set her back and studied her face.

She was nervous, he decided. Or perhaps hungry. She'd picked at her food during the wedding party. In any case, when the time came, he wanted her willing. He'd never forced a woman in his life.

"Shall we check out Mrs. Windle's cold repast?" He dropped her hand and went to the table, removing covers. He poured two glasses of wine, and carved off a hunk of bread.

She shook her head at the wine. "How can you eat?"

"I'm hungry. Keeping up with Father was spoiling my appetite. Is that why you also limited yourself to two bites of food at Hackwell's?"

She lifted a shoulder. "'Tis a strange way I'm feeling."

He pulled a chair out, sat down, and patted his lap. "Come and tell me about it."

She sighed. "Would you first help me out of this dress? I've never had anything so lovely, and I would so hate to spoil it."

She'd been reading his mind. He fisted his hands to control his own urge to rip the gown from her. "Come here then and turn around."

She looked back at him over her shoulder, a shy smile forming on the lip he'd kissed to a dark shade of pink.

"You've never been undressed by a gentleman before?"

The smile faded, a deep blush formed, and she turned away, so that all he could see was the knot of blonde curls quivering on the back of her head.

Something inside him twisted. He'd assumed she was an innocent. Perhaps he'd been wrong.

And would it matter?

He went to work on her laces. "It's a very nice dress, made lovelier by your beauty. You know you shall have many more dresses, Sirena. As many as you wish."

"The pin money you agreed to is very generous." Her voice was shaky, breathless.

When all the fastenings were undone, he pushed the dress off her shoulders and began to unlace her stays. A tight knot at the top needed extra attention. The smooth skin of her back, and the quivers that rippled through her at his touch, kept distracting him.

"There is a damned knot," he said.

She tensed. He kissed her shoulder. "Pardon my language."

"I *am* still a virgin," she said, her voice low and husky. "He did not v-violate me."

He pulled the knot free, anger roaring through him. Whoever the man was, he was dead.

Rather than speak and frighten her more, he put his lips to a cool stretch of skin, making her shiver, and went back to the laces.

"It was my cousin, the new Glenmorrow. The moment he arrived, I smelled trouble. He w-wooed me. 'Twas improper, and I knew it. There I was, in the same house, a poor relation, no family or chaperone to see to me. I tried..." She paused to swallow, "the vicar sympathized, but he had the living off the new earl."

"Shhhh." He turned her around. "You don't have to talk about it."

Her lips pressed together firmly and she shook her head. "You say you don't wish for lies, my lord. I should have told you before..." She took in another deep breath. "He went after me during the dessert course of Sunday dinner. Gr-groped me. I told him...told him to wait until later, wait until the servants were abed. I knew I would have time to sneak away after the meal. He didn't care about the servants. The footman went to the housekeeper, and she laced his brandy with laudanum, which I didn't know until later. He bade me sit with him while he drank, but I ran to my room for the bag I'd packed. He followed me and r-ripped my best dress."

"But you stopped him."

She shook her head. "The butler bashed him. He was so woozy, you see, from the laudanum, it didn't take much. They carried him back to the dining room. Propped him in his chair with his head on the table."

"He didn't notice?"

"We worked it out so he would blame me."

"It would be hard to have everyone keep the secret."

"They sent a maid to distract his valet. And many of the servants had a half-day. In any case, I haven't heard that he's sacked anyone. Lady Jane wanted me to bring charges against him, but..."

But, no one would take her word against Glenmorrow's, a girl this lovely.

She stepped out of her dress and stays, picked them up carefully, draped them over the back of a chair, and faced him in only her chemise.

Blotches of anger colored her cheeks and her hands fisted.

"'Twas that the servants would've had to testify, and after the man was exonerated, they'd have been put out without references, or worse, perhaps falsely accused of some crime." She pounded her fist into her palm. "My father gave into the drink, but he was a worthy man. This man is not worthy."

If the new earl were here, he'd toss him straight out the window. He looked around the room and could not spot her night clothing. He went into the dressing room, retrieved his dressing gown, and helped her into it. The dark satin swallowed her like the dark trappings of a funeral byre.

An appropriate thought for the way this evening had progressed.

"Thank you," she said, her voice softer.

He raked his hands through her hair, pulling out combs and scattering pins. "Tell me the new earl's name."

"Glenmorrow."

"No. Who was he before he became Glenmorrow?" The coil of hair cascaded over the dark fabric like a river of gold, making his insides clench.

God, she was lovely.

"Sterling Hollister."

"Where is he now?"

She turned to him, face blotched with pink, and his heart all but stopped and started up again, bashing against his ribs. Damn, damn Sterling Hollister, new Earl of Glenmorrow.

"I don't know. I know he was once a soldier but he sold off his commission. He'll be wanting to make his title official. He'll be wanting to enter the Lords."

If he'd been in the army, Hackwell or Bink might know of him.

But he wouldn't be entering the Lords unless he was one of the Irish elected peers, and he'd doubt if an upstart new heir would be even considered. Unless...

"Did your father serve in the House of Lords?"

"No."

"Come," he escorted her over to the table. "You must eat."

"I couldn't." But she came and let herself be seated. He filled a plate for her.

The red rage had drained from her and she looked ashen.

"I've not studied the law," he said, "but I know enough of it. And for what I don't know, I can employ the very best of those who do. Eat, my dear."

She frowned at him and picked up her knife and fork.

"You're looking for your brother to displace this villain."

She stopped her fork midway to her mouth, put it down, and stared at him, biting her lower lip.

"It's a good plan." He speared a piece of ham and chewed. "Eat Sirena. I've heard the French say that revenge is best as a cold meal like this, or some such."

She stared at him, that little frown creasing her brow. He swallowed and took a drink of wine. "Pardon, my lady. One does not speak with one's mouth full. There's also the good Bard's line: 'Think therefore on revenge and cease to weep.'"

She smiled. "'*Caesar's spirit, ranging for revenge, with Ate by his side come hot from hell, shall in these confines with a monarch's voice, cry havoc and let slip the dogs of war.*'"

"You know your Shakespeare."

She lifted a shoulder. "A bit. 'Twas my mother's doing."

"Excellent. We'll have no more tears tonight."

"I was not weeping, Bakeley."

"You are not eating either."

"I won't be able to sleep if I eat now."

He locked his eyes upon hers, set his palm upon her hand, and walked his fingers up her arm, under the dark brocade, watching as her color rose again.

"'Tis our wedding night," she whispered.

"You had forgotten."

"No only... how did we arrive at Julius Caesar?"

"You were explaining that you are still an innocent."

"I am."

He drew his hand away and patted his knee. "Come here."

She paused to drain her glass—for courage, he thought—and settled daintily on his lap.

He kept his hands braced on the edge of his chair. "What do you want from me tonight?"

She looked at him a long moment. "A wedding night." She nodded. She sounded breathless, and her chest was rising and falling like she was having trouble breathing.

"You look very fetching in my robe."

"Thank you."

He hadn't expected shyness. "I've played your maid, yet I'm still fully dressed, as you see."

A smile danced on her lips. "I will valet you, my lord." She went to work on his neck cloth. "Though I shall not be able to tie anything so elaborate for you in the morn. Your valet is quite the artist."

"I tied that myself."

Her eyebrows rose as she tossed the white cloth away. "It's talented you are."

"As you shall see."

She opened her mouth, closed it, and opened it again. "Shall we stand to remove these coats?"

"No." He leaned forward, close enough to smell the scent of lilacs. "Slip your hands under my lapel and push."

"Oh."

Her slim hands on his chest made his heart thump and his trousers tighten as though about to burst.

"Like a glove, it fits. Who is your tailor?"

He grunted as she wrangled the sleeves, her breasts touching his chest, her silky hair floating against his cheek. "Henry Poole." He watched as she put the inside-out sleeves of the coat right, folded it, and tossed it onto her vacated chair.

God, a man should never marry a woman who'd been in service.

He had to find some way to move this event along. "I have an idea, my lady. I fear you are getting a crick in your neck. If you straddle me, this undressing will be easier." He lifted her bottom and pushed at her skirts. "Separate your legs, my dear."

She had her lips pursed. If he had any doubts of her innocence, the color rising there told him all he needed to know.

"There. Now you may unbutton my waistcoat."

CHAPTER FIFTEEN

Sirena settled on the very edge of his legs. Her fingers trembled on the slim shiny buttons of his waistcoat, and she kept her eyes focused on them, trying to avoid looking at his trousers below.

Heat pulsed through her. He'd left his hands bracketing her hips, the warmth of them sending her insides quaking.

When she glanced up, he was watching her in that dark, slack-eyed way that nevertheless seemed to glitter.

"There," she said, keeping her voice nonchalant. She pushed his waistcoat off. "Lean forward, sir."

He did, pushing her robe back, hooking his hands around her back, and pressing himself to her while she slid off the waistcoat, leaving him clad in only his shirt. He fell back, taking her with him, only her chemise and his shirt keeping their flesh apart.

And 'twas only her chemise and his pantaloons keeping her hot center from his hard erection. The pounding she felt might be her heart or his.

He pushed the robe off her, skimming his hands over her bare arms. "There. What do we have left?"

She felt his fingers trail down to the hem of her chemise and underneath, moving up the silk of her stockings to the ribbon garters holding them.

"You have the loveliest legs."

"Go on with you. You've not even seen them."

He gave her knee a squeeze. "I have taken a peek at your ankles. As for the rest, I'm going by touch. Which is telling me that the rest of you is lovely also."

She turned her head to argue and his lips captured hers, at once startling, yet familiar. This was Bakeley, and he was her husband, and he'd promised her she had nothing to fear. She'd shared her last secret.

She let herself sink into the kiss. Perhaps *he* was keeping secrets. He was Shaldon's son after all.

But wasn't this the surest way to gain his confidence?

And she wanted this. The heat that raced through her seemed to pool in the spot where her private parts met his.

His lips slanted and moved, his tongue stroking, and she found herself matching him, kissing him back. The desire he kindled in her roared to life and she trailed her lips down his jaw, savoring the prickle of his stubble. He'd not stopped to shave for the wedding or the party after, and she was glad. She liked the feel of the scratchy dark scruff against her lips and her cheek.

Was his chest hairy also? She undid the button at the shirt opening and slid her hand under the white fabric, over his shoulders, halfway afraid that he would find her too bold.

Instead, it seemed to inflame him more. He bent his head to her breast, suckling her through the thin chemise, making her wet there, also. The heat, the wet—steam should be rising around them. She wanted to be closer, needed to be closer.

She hitched herself up and the movement made him gasp.

All of her froze. "My lord?"

He rested his head on her breast. His dark locks tickled her nose and she could feel his silent chuckle. And then there was the scent of him, the same manly smell that had permeated the robe he'd put around her.

"My lord?"

He lifted his head, propping his chin on her breast the way her best hound used to do. Only the dog's look had been imploring. This look was wicked.

She let out a breath. "You're fine, I see."

"And you, my lady?"

His grin stirred something in her, though she couldn't name what it was. She wanted more. She wanted something.

She wanted to see him. That was it.

Let him be shocked. She was no fine lady, and anyway, he was stuck with her.

She tugged at his shirttails. "Take this off."

"Yes, my lady." He put his hands up and leaned back while she pulled and yanked until the long tail of his shirt came out and she whipped it over his head.

"The cuffs," he said, his voice muffled by fabric.

She tried finding the fastenings, and in utter frustration, ripped the fabric apart, pulled it the rest of the way off him and threw it aside.

Her breath hitched. He was not some soft lord. Muscles rippled from wide shoulders to a tapered flat waist, and in fact, he was hairy. She touched the dark hair, tracing it down the center of him to the top of his fall.

She dare not go further.

"What now, my lady?" he asked, the gleam in his eye belying the ease of his question.

"You've trousers left, and, and probably smalls and stockings. And boots." She jumped off him and knelt. Her chemise was plastered to her breasts but she didn't care. If she was to be practically naked, let him be the first to shed everything. His boots must come first. She grabbed one, twisting and pulling. "You've a fine bootmaker also."

She fell back with the first boot and caught herself on the floor, her skirt riding up, making her gasp. "My stockings are gone."

He sent her that lazy smile again. "Yes. I removed them while you were busy kissing me."

A furious heat overtook her. She grabbed his other boot and yanked hard. "Am I being too forward, sir?"

"It's not possible for you to be too forward with me."

This boot came off more easily, and she went to work on his stockings, eyeing that bulge again sideways.

Curiosity had always bedeviled her. She'd seen men's parts, when they didn't know she was looking, but never a hard member.

If it were not possible for her to be too forward...

"Stand now, sir, and let's have the trousers off."

His steady gaze locked into hers sending heated shivers through her, as though her skin would melt away, leaving her bare to the bones for eyes that saw deeply, and everything.

"You wish to see me." He stood, still watching her, and went to work unfastening his fall. "And I wish to see you. But we shall grant *your* wishes first." His fall came undone and he pushed the fabric to his hips and stopped. "Will you promise to remove your chemise?"

Her eyes must be popping with sympathy for that great hidden beast he had straining to spring out.

Heavens. Perhaps it was a mistake. Perhaps she should blow out the lights, get into bed and ruck up her skirts. Even if she couldn't see, this great well of feeling in her would still carry on, and she'd not see the beastly thing enter her. She'd not fear the pain so much, and thus it would hurt less. She'd not squeal like a mare being mounted.

Before she could stop him, Bakeley had her in his arms. "Close your eyes, Sirena."

"Why?" She breathed the word into his shoulder.

"So I may strip off my trousers."

"You could blow out the lamp."

"But then I would not see *you.*"

He meant to see her naked, but for her to not see him. She pushed away and propped her hands on her hips. "I'll not close them."

His lips twisted in a grin, and as he stripped, his member sprang out at her.

God's bones, how was she to manage that?

He scooped her up and carried her to the bed, flopping her down none too gently and crawling up to kneel next to her. She could not take her eyes off *him*, even as he stretched out next to her and propped his head upon his hand.

He trailed a finger across her breasts, sending ripples through her. "Has anyone explained to you how this works?"

"Of course I know how it works. I grew up in the country. I've seen horses, cows, dogs, chickens—"

"Humans are a bit different."

"Yes, of course." She had no idea what he was talking about.

"Do you know how we're different?" His hand had made its way down to her belly, where he was swirling circles. Another river of heat rushed through her privates.

She sighed. "We're in a bed lying down."

His fingers inched further down and touched the pleasure spot, the one she was not supposed to touch but sometimes did. "Yes, we'll do this lying down tonight."

He'd moved a bit further, pulling the thin muslin tight. Pleasure permeated the thin barrier and shot through her.

"This is so wicked," she said.

"No. Nothing is wicked that brings pleasure between husband and wife." He insinuated a hand between her legs, his fingertips exploring the entrance to her womb, still through the fabric barrier. He hooked his other arm beneath her head and dropped tickling kisses on her neck. "You are so wet," he said.

"I'm sorry—"

His firm kiss stopped her talking, and it was just as well for the way his palm pressed against her pleasure spot, and his fingers found her entrance, and lips and tongue worked over her, she couldn't think. Sorry she was if the wetness annoyed him, but surely it was his fault. Or—perhaps he didn't mind it.

She wrapped her arms around his neck and pulled him closer.

She didn't feel her skirts come up, didn't realize he had raised them until she felt something enter her. She swept a hand over him, down his arm. He still lay facing her, his member rubbing hard against her side.

"That's my finger," he said against her ear. "Am I hurting you?"

His palm flattened and pleasure sparked through her. "No."

His fingers started a rhythm, and her hips danced along with them, completely out of her control, pushing, pushing against an ache that wasn't human, only animal. She'd seen this with stallions but never the mares.

"Yes, love." He kissed her cheek. "That's it." His tongue found her ear. "Come, Sirena. Come, my love."

She turned to him, gripped his neck, and writhed against him. It was...there was...something...and something and...

Pleasure exploded in her, sweeping through her. She keened with the feel of it and held herself against him while it settled.

"That's my girl," he grunted, and pushed her legs apart.

He was going to enter her. She braced her feet and grabbed a fistful of the sheets.

"Don't be afraid."

"It hurts, they say."

"It will hurt less now that you've had pleasure."

His words were as taut as the sinews of his neck and the frown of his face. He needed release, and now she understood what that meant.

Her heart did a flip and she bit her lip. He'd taken the time to show her. She could be generous. She could be brave.

The tip of him entered her, gently pulled away and went in again more deeply. There was no pain yet, only tightness and more pleasure. She squeezed her eyes shut.

He pushed again and she felt a twinge.

"Sorry, love."

Another push and pain pricked her, making her gasp.

"Just once more." He thrust again and stopped inside her, his tight breath rasping beside her ear.

"'Twas not so bad," she whispered.

He lifted his head and looked at her, braced on his elbows, jaw hard, muscles quivering. Below they were tight, locked, with him buried completely. Two were becoming one.

She was reminded of the hounds when they were breeding. "Are we stuck?" she joked.

He blinked and then a glittery grin lit his face, and she understood. He was being gentlemanly.

Pleasure sparked in her again, making her giddy. "'Twas no more than a pinch, Bakeley. You may proceed."

He reached back for her foot. "Will you put your legs around me?"

She locked her feet upon his back and squeezed her inner muscles, surprised at the pleasure that rippled inside her.

"You clever girl." He pulled away and thrust back in and, oh...

It was happening again, joy coming with each thrust, driving that aching need, building it up inside her until the frantic fire consumed them both. She exploded, and then he must have reached his own release, because she felt him pulsing inside the very heart of her.

He propped himself above her again, kissed her soundly, and rolled onto his back.

She hugged the arm he'd hooked around her. "Well. That was very enjoyable."

His soft chuckle tickled her ear. "Are you sore?"

She tightened her inner muscles again and felt a new twinge of desire, and a tiny bit of soreness. "I'm fine. When will we be doing this again?"

He opened his eyes. He wasn't smiling now, but the way his hand moved at her waist, she did not think he was feeling irritation. "Very soon."

That flicker of pleasure within her jumped a little higher. He still watched her through heavy lidded eyes, but as she gazed at him, she saw them slipping lower.

He was completely spent. Getting her to the altar had been his driving purpose for the last two days. And the devil of it was it hadn't even been necessary to hide from Shaldon, who seemed to be happy they were married.

As her new spouse sank into sleep, she watched him and wondered if he would regret this hasty marriage. Tonight he didn't, of course. He'd been plenty satisfied, and satisfied that she was satisfied. In the long run, though, would coupling with an unworthy Irish lady be enough for him?

When his soft snore smoothed into a steady rhythm, she eased herself out from under his arm. The lamp still burned, as did the fire, yet it was chilly in this seldom used home. She covered him and found his robe, pulling it and all its manly scent around her, and settling herself before the fire.

Shaldon was looking for Donegal, the man the boys had been taking her to meet. But the boys were Shaldon's lackeys. So perhaps the men who attacked them on the dock were Donegal's lackeys. And why would Shaldon think Donegal would have aught to do with her now that she was his daughter-in-law?

And he wanted her to call him Father. It defied all sense. It made her head hurt.

Her stomach grumbled so loudly she thought Bakeley might awaken. She filled a plate and began to eat, going through all the facts again.

"You did say we would do this very soon," Sirena said the next morning.

Bakeley propped himself on his elbow and watched a dark beauty spot on her breast move with her breathing. He'd managed to get her fully naked this morning.

"Bakeley. James. Are you listening?"

He touched a finger to the spot and she inhaled sharply.

He'd won the marital sweepstakes. Her passion was worth any sized dowry.

"Yes. Did I say that?"

"Last night. I asked you when we would do this again and you said very soon, but I'd no idea I'd wake up to you prodding me with that great beast of yours." She smiled while she teased him. "We'll do this every morning then?"

Her breasts seemed to swell under his palm. "That would be quite acceptable."

"Shall we share a bedchamber? My parents didn't. Did yours?"

He sighed at the mention of Shaldon. "Most of the time my father was gone."

She pondered that. "You saw him on holidays?"

"He was gone, Sirena, for years. We went years without seeing him. He came home for good a few years ago."

She pushed his hand away and sat up. "And now he wants to know his sons."

"Yes."

"And to manage them."

"That also."

She bent her knees and tucked her arms around them, letting her breasts rest on her legs, no longer shy, it seemed. "Are we to live at Shaldon House, then?"

He couldn't help groaning. They were on to business already.

"Do you want to?"

She pinched at a clump of the sheet where the tiniest spots of blood were drying to brown. In an older time, they'd be hanging that sheet out of the window, as the proof that his bride had been innocent, and that any subsequent issue would be his.

"I don't know what to think. I'm not afraid to work. I know even here I'll have the responsibility of this house, won't I? I don't want to interfere in Perry's domain, yet I'd be happy to help her and learn from her until such time as you become Shaldon." She lay back and turned on her side, propping herself up and mirroring his posture. "I want some freedom to come and go. I don't want to feel I'm in a prison. At home, the last few years, I helped a great deal with the horse breeding. Keeping the records, yes, but also helping with the exercise and training. Even the grooming at times. I'm not afraid of hard work."

His heart filled with the memory of her dressed in her sagging trousers.

She'd not be grooming horses at any of their properties.

"We've a proper mews at Shaldon House. And I've brought up a sweet gelding that Perry doesn't ride often enough."

She kissed his nose. "Not that wild one you were riding the other morning?"

"No."

"May I see *him*?"

"Yes." She might see him, but he wouldn't allow her to ride him. Which might be a tetchy subject.

"And perhaps," he said quickly, "you should have a tour of the house. There's a lovely chamber near mine. And then *you* may decide."

She flipped onto her back. "We'd have separate rooms there." The idea seemed to displease her.

"Only when you're out of temper with me."

She turned her head and her eyes were thoughtful. "What does he mean to do with me, do you think? How does he plan to find this Donegal?"

Ah, Donegal. She'd dodged the bait to tease him back, and now they were on to the next business. "What do you know about him?"

"I asked the O'Brians to find out anything they could about the survivors of the ship my brother left on, and they said Donegal would have information." She frowned. "If they worked for your father, he fed them that information."

"It's possible."

"But, no, Walter said he spoke to the man. I don't think he would lie about that."

"Did he describe him?"

"Yes. A big man with sandy hair and a rough beard, very hard, from a lifetime at sea, and cagey,

Walter said, about my brother. He said he'd talk to me for a price."

"And how would this man have information?" he mused. "He was on the ship himself, or he rescued the survivors, or—"

"Or he shared a grog with someone who'd heard the story and told the tale." She sighed. "It does seem a stretch, and rather foolhardy."

He pulled her close. "Don't lose hope. You're married to a wealthy man with good connections for uncovering secrets and solving mysteries."

Her gentle kiss surprised him. She pulled away, rubbed her palm along his cheek, and smiled.

God, but she roused him. He rolled her over and began to kiss her thoroughly.

A loud rapping at the door resounded.

"Bakeley." A male voice boomed, not Windle's. "Bakeley, it's urgent. Do tell me you've heard me so I don't have to burst in on you."

Damnation. "Wait," he shouted.

Sirena, in all of her lovely nakedness, jumped out of bed with him.

"That's my brother, Charley." He threw her his banyan, but she tossed it back and ran to a trunk on the floor, rummaging through it and pulling on her own robe.

He waited for her to knot the tie and then opened the door a crack.

Charley's hair stood out in wild patches and his neck cloth was so poorly tied it had come undone.

"Bink has been attacked on the road to Little Norwick."

"What happened?" Sirena hovered near his shoulder.

Charley averted his eyes. As well he should.

"Father says—er, asks, that you come quickly."

"Is he injured?" Sirena asked.

"Only minor injuries, the message said."

"And the men with him?" Bakeley asked, because he knew she wondered.

"I don't know."

"I'll be along directly. Have them saddle my horse."

"I've a carriage waiting."

"Fine." He shut the door.

Sirena was already at her chest, pulling out clothes. "I'm coming with you."

He began to dress. There was no point to arguing. If he had to leave and go north, she would be safer with his father and his sister.

CHAPTER SIXTEEN

Later that day, Sirena crossed the threshold into the most magnificent bedchamber she'd ever seen.

"This will be yours." Perry linked arms with her. "It's a bit outdated, not having been redecorated since the last century, but the housekeeper keeps it fresh. It is our grandest suite, even comparing it to Father's. What do you think?"

The fawn-colored brocades all but glittered in the rosy light of early afternoon. It was all opposite to her room at home in Glenmorrow, where truly she had never got out of the nursery.

The bed that graced this chamber was so high a staircase had been set to it. Once they arrived at the top, the bed would easily accommodate her and Bakeley.

That thought warmed her. "It is indeed grand," she said. *Too grand for me.*

"Come, and we'll see the rest, and then you may decide." Perry led her through a door into a sitting room decked out with cabinets and wardrobes. "This room is rather dark, I think."

Sirena viewed the heavy violet covering the one small window. "Lighter curtains would help."

"You see, already you have ideas for making things better. Now come." They continued through another door.

Dark green curtains and wallpaper, and dark, heavy furniture made clear that this was the man's chamber in this suite. And this bed was even bigger and higher than the lady's. "This one has been redecorated more recently, a few years ago when we added the bathing chamber and the water closet."

Sirena's head jerked up. "You have a water closet?" She had seen one at her neighbor's estate, but that was a lowly affair stuck near the kitchen scullery.

"Come and see." Perry's eyes sparkled under her spectacles as she tugged Sirena to yet another door. "Bakeley put it in when he had repairs done to the house, before Father returned. Isn't it marvelous?"

A monstrous wooden tub held center stage in the small room, with pipes leading to and from an enormous metal container.

"Isn't it marvelous?" Perry asked again.

Perry's raptures demanded a response, but she didn't have one.

"Bakeley installed a cistern so the servants don't have to haul up the water for bathing. You must agree it is marvelous."

No water to heat and haul in buckets, and then to scoop and haul away again. Each time Lady Jane bathed, she, Barton, and Molly had been put through their paces. "Indeed. I'm awestruck."

Perry detached herself and went to open a door. "*Voila*. The water closet."

"Bakeley did this?"

"It was his idea, yes. He spent considerable time redesigning the piping and drainage, and pressing the Commission of Sewers for better maintenance in the street. He has plans to install these at Cransdall also, but Father said we must wait a bit."

His father was a demanding, overbearing, interfering man. She must keep that fact in mind.

Perry turned a valve and water rushed into the tub.

Sirena put her hand under the flow of water. "It's cold."

"There's a heater for the holding tank." She closed the valve and the water stopped. "Is it not amazing? One of these in every building, and we will solve half the problems of the poor. Bakeley agrees with me on this, though the cost...well, he's been after Father to take up the problems of the sewer works with the Lords, and now we have Bink and Charley in the Commons. Besides the disease and vermin, it is so demoralizing for people to be dirty, do you not think?"

She nodded. Perry had lofty and fine goals, but Sirena doubted she'd had much experience of true dirt. She couldn't imagine the bespectacled girl in the Shaldon stables, where the grooms rubbed sweat with their charges, or on the track having dirt kicked up at her. And the rookeries, and alleys, and the docks? She couldn't imagine Perry had any more knowledge than the testimony of others.

Still, Sirena counted her as a friend, one that she would learn a thing or two from.

"Do you think they'll be back soon?"

Shaldon and his two sons had gone off to some government office. Bakeley had taken her aside, assuring her he would report back to her, and telling her to wait at home until he returned.

She had said yes, but only because she'd been stunned and flummoxed by the man who wished for her to call him Father.

Upon arrival that morning, they'd invaded the breakfast room where Shaldon had greeted her quite formally, looking down his noble beak at her hastily twisted up hair and dun colored dress. When he'd spoken, though, it had been with a kind reassurance that the O'Brians were safe.

And then they'd had, above all things, a family meal, James and his brother piling on the bacon and buttered toast, waited on by the spritely butler who looked to be one of Shaldon's old spies. And wouldn't there be a houseful of them here?

"Don't worry, Sirena." Perry turned another valve, and they watched the water drain away. "Father is not going to let any harm come to you. He is so happy to have you as a daughter."

And how could that be? She didn't believe it for a second. "The attack on Mr. Gibson was not so serious, was it? It was his lordship's way of getting us to the house."

When Perry pushed her glasses higher on her nose and smiled, she looked much younger, than her years, which couldn't be many less than Sirena's. "That sounds like Father. But you would not mind so much, would you? It wasn't quite the crack of dawn when he sent Charley to you. In fact, Charley had even been abed, and he's one to be out all night. I know because I'm an early riser. I heard him arrive this morning from a night spent carousing at one of his gaming hells." She cocked her head and touched a finger to her chin. "Or perhaps he was with the contessa last night."

"Who?"

"His latest lover," she whispered. "She's a dragon, but I imagine he doesn't notice because he's only trying to get her to reveal state secrets. Father took us to the opera once and I saw her watching us all night through her opera glasses."

"Trying to get Charley's attention?"

Perry shrugged. "Or Bakeley's. Or Father's. Or perhaps she was sneering at me and my spectacles."

"Do you mind?"

"No of course not."

She had spoken too quickly. "Can you see perfectly through them?"

"Yes."

"And can you see at all without them?"

"Yes, of course. It's just, er, much clearer, and I'm in the habit of wearing them."

"So if a gentleman comes up to dance with you, you can see his face clearly?"

Perry led her back into the bedchamber. "The only gentlemen who ask me to dance are my brothers. I suppose I'm too tall for the others, or they fear I'll tread on their toes."

Sirena laughed. "Or they fear you'll see too much—the spot of wine on their neck cloth, or the rip in their sleeve seam that their valet didn't repair, or the bags under their eyes from swilling brandy all night."

"Or the pustules on their chins." Perry giggled.

Sirena followed her into the fawn-colored bedchamber. "Or the stalk of celery between their teeth."

Perry laughed out loud and leaned against the bed post. "Oh, you must come live here, Sirena.

You must. Who knows how long Father will be around? He's just beginning to appreciate Bakeley and to listen to him. And he's so looking forward to more grandchildren, especially an heir."

"Will he be happy if I produce a girl?"

"Most assuredly, but he'll tell you to keep trying for a boy." She closed her mouth, colored brightly, and then burst into more giggles.

This was not the staid girl Sirena had seen the night of the musicale, and wasn't it wonderful? "I'll need to find a good dressmaker."

"Why, the dress you married in yesterday was perfect."

"Barton made that, Lady Jane's abigail. I can't impose upon her. Now with me gone, she'll be fetching and hauling like never before." She could not imagine how the ladies would cope. It was sad to think of Lady Jane reduced yet again.

"Was your work really so...so..."

"So servile? Yes, but no, because I didn't mind it. It was like being a poor relation living with a kindly older sister."

Perry's brows drew together. "Who is also poor."

"Well, yes. But very proud, so do not say I said it."

"It's a wonder Lord Cheswick doesn't provide for her better." Perry's frown deepened. "This house is very large. Three times the size of most London townhouses."

More plotting. The girl was as bad as her father. "No. I don't think—"

"She's almost a contemporary of Father's." Perry's intense gaze fixed upon a spot above the fireplace. "It could be quite diverting for him."

Perry turned that gaze on Sirena, her eyes bright behind the lenses. "Perhaps a diversion for him would benefit us all. And she could be of use. I know I'm to instruct you in managing this house, but truth to tell, I struggle with the task, and the thought of entertaining as Father wishes petrifies me. I spent more time in the stables at Cransdall, you see. As the daughter of an earl, surely you managed such things yourself and likely know more than I."

So she'd been wrong about Lady Perry.

Sirena shook her head. "I grew up in the stables also. I was young when my mother died, and after that, we never had guests."

"Ever?"

"Never. We..." *We were pariahs, unwelcome by all of the quality.* Sirena sighed. "My father simply withdrew. He and I, we took an occasional meal together, but that was it."

"Not even the heir came to visit? He was a cousin, was he not?"

"He was, but I only met him after my father died." And she didn't want to speak of him now. "But I shall ponder the matter of Lady Jane. In truth, she thinks to persuade Barton to open up her own dressmaking enterprise. I can't imagine how much capital would be required, can you? We've all discussed and debated it upon a rainy night, but we couldn't work out the costs."

"Bakeley would know. He's a genius at business."

"Ladies' business?"

"Any business. Business is business, he says. And he's rich in his own right." She tapped a finger on her chin. "And we could tie this in with Lady Hackwell's charity. The girls can work as seamstresses, the boys as porters."

Perry was well on her way to arranging Lady Jane's move and the establishment of Barton's dress shop.

This was a very managing family.

And yet...did it not speak volumes that Perry would undertake such fearless planning? Her constraints were few, it seemed. Perhaps here, Sirena would also find some freedom, with access to the horses she'd seen earlier in the mews, and help with the duties of the lady of the house, and, if Lady Jane was welcomed, she'd have another ally, and most importantly of all, a foil for her new father's scheming.

And there was still the matter of the Hollister files the man must have stashed away somewhere.

"Perry, I'm finding myself more and more persuaded. I wonder, while the gentlemen are away, would you finish the tour of the house?"

Perry clasped both of her hands, her fierce squeezing telling Sirena just how much she wanted her there.

"Truly, Sirena? You *will* be the mistress here? I'll be more than happy to show you the rest of the house. What would you like to see?"

Your father's study. She leaned in close. "Every chamber. Every nook and cranny. Every storage place. Everything."

Bakeley pulled aside the curtain of the town carriage. They'd turned down a street in Knightsbridge lined with modest homes. "This is not the way to the Home Office, Father."

"We're not going to the Home Office. We're meeting with Farnsworth at another location."

So now, at least, he had a name.

Charley lifted his head from his doze. "Who is Farnsworth?"

"A colleague recently returned to town."

"A former colleague." Bakeley waited for his father to correct him, upbraid him, or otherwise reveal that he was in fact not at all the poor sick man who had retired from the spying business, that he was still quite actively employed, but with a better cover.

Shaldon smiled. "And as it happens, Farnsworth is your godfather, Charles, though I don't wonder you don't remember. And by the way, you look like the devil today."

Charley grinned. "Thank you, Father."

Bakeley fought the irritation rising. "He did not mean it to be a compliment."

"I suppose you were with your lady friend last night," Shaldon said.

Charley said nothing. He also had learned to wait out the paternal pauses.

And...of course, Bakeley was present and not supposed to know Charley's affair was more spying.

"It will take its toll. Only compare how fresh your brother looks, and that after two sleepless days."

Charley smirked. "And his wedding night."

"And I did not shirk my duty last night. Perhaps it's time we find you a bride, Charley."

"By your schedule, I have a few more years before becoming leg-shackled. And I do believe it is I who spotted your bride and turned her over to you."

Shaldon's cane cracked. "You are bickering like a child, Charles." The carriage came to a stop. "I don't think we want you with us in your current state."

Charley started to grin and swiped a hand across his mouth to hide it.

Shaldon climbed out of the carriage first.

"Curse you, Charley," Bakeley said. "This is one of his traps. If I don't return by nightfall, send runners to search for me."

"I confess, I'm relieved. And after all, this concerns your lady, does it not?"

"So he says."

"Bakeley," Shaldon called.

Bakeley gritted his teeth. "There's another matter of Sirena's I'm looking into. Can you meet me later at White's?"

Charley yawned.

"You *did* disrupt my wedding night."

"It ran into the morning, did it? No wonder you're looking so refreshed and pleased. You shall have to tell me all about it. Or...not." He laughed. "Stop glowering. Yes. I'll meet you there."

The carriage drove off and the front door opened. A strapping footman greeted them, eying them up and down, and when they'd passed his examination, leading them up a set of stairs.

A man rose from an armchair near the front window. He was younger than Shaldon, shorter than his visitors, with a wiry physique and dark hair streaked with iron gray.

"Lord Shaldon." He bowed. "Lord Bakeley."

"Be seated." Shaldon waved both of them into chairs, exactly as if he were the lord of this manor.

The room was a study or library, and from the disorderly arrangement of books and periodicals, clearly a gentlemen's room.

Shaldon sat erect. "So what have you learned, Farnsworth?"

"As you expected, he's disappeared again."

Bakeley's head spun. They'd been plotting behind his back for far longer than a few days.

A sense of betrayal gnawed at him. He shook it off and made himself concentrate.

"I received a report from my eldest. Gibson and his people were attacked on the way to Little Norwick."

Silence stretched as though both men were reading each other's thoughts.

Well, Bakeley was not a mind reader. "Mr. Farnsworth—"

"*Lord* Farnsworth, son. Farnsworth is a baron."

"I see. So happy we've now been introduced, my lord. Who is the man you're reporting on?"

"Donegal," Shaldon said dryly.

As if Bakeley should have known that.

"Fineas Donegal, to be exact," Farnsworth said, "of County Donegal."

"Pseudonymous, in other words."

"Indeed." Farnsworth nodded his head in a way that Bakeley took to mean he was pleased.

The patronizing irritated him. "How can we be sure this was not just a random group of highwaymen? Bink was conveying new goods for his home, after all."

Shaldon nodded. "It's possible."

Bakeley had reviewed Bink's scribbled missive earlier that morning. Their four attackers had been injured, but all had managed to escape. "Father, how soon will the men you sent report back?"

"As soon as ever they can," Farnsworth said. "And may I congratulate you, sir, on your marriage to Lady Sirena Hollister? We'll do all we can to keep her safe."

A hard knot formed in his chest. "From Donegal?"

"From any danger, Lord Bakeley."

"And is she in danger from Donegal?"

Farnsworth looked to Shaldon.

Bakeley leaned back casually and crossed his leg. "It is she who wishes to speak to Donegal. She believes he has information about her brother. It's what he told the men reporting to you, the O'Brians. Tell me, why would this dangerous radical Donegal lead her to believe he would have such information?"

"Do you know her brother's reputation?" Shaldon eyed him in that supercilious manner that said he was too rash, too careless.

He brushed some dust off his boot. After his talk with Bink, he'd recollected the story he'd pieced together after his visit to Glenmorrow years ago. "Hollister turned on all that was British and became an Irish nationalist."

"Roland James Hollister, yes," Shaldon said. "That *was* the story. But Fitzgerald's plotting soured him on the rebels. He found he didn't wish to kill his own father. But once ensnared, there was no way out, except to counterspy. In the end, he worked for me."

Red blazes clouded Bakeley's vision. Of course. He had known it in his bones, all those years ago, sent to deliver a hefty purse to the Earl of Glenmorrow. He'd known then that Father had his hand and arm in this business all the way to his shoulder. "So Donegal wants—what? Revenge on Hollister through Sirena?" The thought sent chills through him. "That makes no sense if Hollister has been dead these, what? Fifteen years?"

The silence stretched long enough for his brain to reach across the short space and know what his father was thinking. *Donegal believed Hollister would contact his sister.*

It was up to him to keep her safe, because he did not want to lose her.

"I should like to hear this story from the beginning. Will you indulge me?"

His father sighed deeply, seeming to embrace every one of the lines on his face. "Pour us a brandy, Liam."

The usual cloud of tobacco smoke enveloped Bakeley as he entered White's. He spotted Charley seated with two young bucks whose names didn't come readily to him, especially not now, not while his mind was clouded with the possibilities of danger to Sirena.

Father had dropped him, wondering aloud why Bakeley wasn't returning directly to Shaldon House and his new wife, but promising to check on her.

"Bakeley." Charley raised a hand in greeting. The other two men welcomed him and hastily took their leave.

"Fine fellows," Charley said.

"Your school friends, are they not? I don't remember their names."

"They won't notice. Foxed already, they are."

"Indeed."

"And you'll be anxious to get back to your lady, eh? Too anxious to remember the names of a couple of nonpareils. From the grave scowl, I've hit it, haven't I, Bakeley?"

He had the waiter bring him a brandy and settled into his chair. A robust card game was taking place at the nearest table. Otherwise they could talk in reasonable privacy.

"You're right, of course."

"Hah. I knew it. What part of her business did you want to discuss with me? You don't need money, I know. Is it a government matter? I'm rather powerless but I do have a few friends in the foreign office and the treasury."

"It's a soldier I'm inquiring about, or rather a former soldier. Sterling Hollister."

Charley sipped his drink. "A relation of hers?"

"Her cousin, the new Earl of Glenmorrow."

"Have you spoken with Bink or Hackwell?"

"Not yet. But I don't want too many snooping."

"I have friends in Horse Guards who might know. Yet the name is familiar." He tapped his chin. "I've heard it recently. British is he?"

"Or Anglo Irish. Sirena says he's wanting to enter Parliament."

"He will wait a good long time for an Irish opening in Lords." He sat up. "Hold there. Is he the fellow entering the Commons? I'd heard there was a new Irish Earl wishing to lower himself for a foot in the door, as it were." He rubbed his hands together. "You're in luck. With Bink and I taking seats, we can snoop around without suspicion."

"He's in town then?"

"I don't know." Charley looked around the room. "If I ask one of these fools about him, the word will get out." His eyes lit and he waved at a man who'd just entered. "Penderbrook will know. He knows everything."

"Can he be discreet?"

"Trust me, Bakeley."

"With your reputation?"

Charley laughed. "One that is carefully honed."

Penderbrook joined them, his open face beaming. "Everly, did I not tell you your money was on the wrong horse?"

"Very well, yes. I must accede to your superior knowledge of horseflesh. Never mind that my family raised the horses the Conqueror rode when he crossed the Channel. Do you know my brother, Bakeley?"

Penderbrook bowed. "We met at a boxing match some time ago."

"Did my man win?" Bakeley asked.

Penderbrook flushed. "I believe not, my lord."

"Penderbrook thinks that he never errs, Bakeley, but don't believe it. I can go through the betting book and show you all the wagers he's lost." He waved a waiter over and had him pour a third drink. "You must lift a glass with us. Bakeley has got himself leg shackled only yesterday to the very fetching Lady Sirena Hollister."

A spark lit in Penderbrook's eyes, guileless and eager. He was younger than Charley, one of his brother's many friends making his way in society, wanting to be the man in the know with the first juicy piece of gossip. Bakeley dutifully lifted the glass and drank, swallowing a groan along with the liquor.

"The announcement will go out tomorrow," Charley said, "so we're counting on you, Penderbrook, to wait until then to spread the news far and wide. I know I can count on you."

"Of course. I'm the soul of discretion." The younger man's eyes twinkled. "At least I *can* be."

"Bakeley doesn't wish to be entertaining curious callers for at least a few days, do you, brother? He's fortunate the marriage was carried out with very little trouble, especially from the bride's family. She's an orphan, and Glenmorrow went to some distant Hollister cousin."

Penderbrook frowned and gazed off for a moment. "Sterling Hollister? The new Earl of Glenmorrow? You have married his cousin, sir? But he's also a member of White's. He's in town now. He'll be disappointed to hear his cousin married without his presence, since he's now head of the family."

"Good heavens." Charley looked around. "Is he here now? Will you introduce us?"

"I don't see him, and I believe he said he was going to the country for a few days, visiting a friend in Lancashire. What ho, strange is it not, him going into the Commons when he's a lord?"

Charley frowned. "He gives up his lordly privileges, does he not?"

Bakeley stared at his drink, his vision clearing, an idea taking shape. "A risky business. He can be tried for crimes just like a commoner."

Penderbrook laughed. "Good thing he's a gentleman. Capital fellow, they say, else he wouldn't be a member here, eh?"

"Yes," Charley said. "No rogues here. Perhaps you should call on him, Bakeley, when he returns to town. Do you know where he's lodging, Pender?"

"The Oxford Arms, I believe. He hasn't taken rooms or found a friend or relation to impose on yet."

Charley grimaced. "You must tell him, Bakeley, he's not welcome at Shaldon House until after your honeymoon."

Sterling Hollister would *never* be welcome. "He had no residence here?" Bakeley asked. "Where did he live before coming here?"

Penderbrook shook his head. "At his estate in Ireland, I presume. Though before that, I don't know. An army man. Telling stories about Waterloo, I hear."

"Indeed." Charley's face clouded.

Charley had been at Waterloo, though to hear him talk he'd got only as far as the Duchess of Devonshire's ball.

"You must introduce him to Bakeley and me the next time, Pender."

Penderbrook promised to send round a note when he heard Hollister was back in town.

Which would not be necessary. Bakeley's next stop would be that inn, and with enough coin he could know everything he wanted to know about his new cousin's stay there.

He said his goodbyes and settled into a hackney. Nothing would proceed on the Donegal matter until his father's men returned from up north.

His hair rose and a ripple went through his skin. Hollister had gone north, just as Bink was attacked. Could the two facts be related?

He shook his head. The description of Donegal, rough and hairy, was not the description of a gentleman. No, they were two different men, and two different threats to Sirena. One threat to her person, the other to her person and reputation.

Perhaps he shouldn't bother seeking the man out. Perhaps shutting him out of society and influence was a better tactic.

Hollister would call Sirena a liar. That was a given, so any legal dispute was his word against hers. The Glenmorrow servants might testify, but only if they hadn't been terrorized already, only if Bakeley could protect them from Hollister's wrath.

And then what? A trial that would drag her name through the London gutters? He wouldn't put her through it.

There must be another way. If he were on better terms with his father, he'd mention it to him, but then he'd have to share with him what the man did to her.

Or perhaps his father knew it already. Would Shaldon have declared himself happy with the marriage if that were the case? He didn't know his father well enough to answer that question.

At the inn, he tracked down the proprietor and greased the wheels of his plan. Hollister had indeed kept rooms there for himself and two servants, and was expected to return on the morrow. Yes, the innkeeper would send a message when the Earl of Glenmorrow arrived, and most importantly, the man promised to keep Bakeley's inquiry secret from everyone, including the man he was tracking.

A promise that could easily be bought by a higher bidder.

He must make one more stop on his journey home.

It was near dark when Bakeley returned to the Shaldon residence. He sought out his father and found him in the library with Perry.

"She's safe," Shaldon said. "I've not locked her in the dungeons."

The dry humor caught him up. It was not like his father to joke. "Good to hear. Where is she then?"

Perry smiled. "In your chamber."

He should send Perry away so he could talk to Shaldon in private. Or...he could talk to him after he'd checked on Sirena. Yes, that would be better.

He excused himself and ran up the stairs. His bedchamber door stood open and a maid was dusting. She bobbed a curtsey.

He blinked. All of his things were gone—books, bottles, newspapers, all of the paraphernalia that made the room comfortable. "What the devil?"

"Oh, sir."

The housekeeper entered. "My lord, we've just got everything moved."

"Moved?"

"Yes. Her ladyship ordered, er, instructed, that all of your things be moved to your new chambers. The bathing chamber was very appealing."

The bathing chamber. "You've moved me to the state suite."

"Yes."

"Very well. Carry on."

The bathing chamber was appealing. The great tub there could easily accommodate two.

He knocked on the door of the lady's bedchamber and waited, hearing footsteps crossing the room, anticipation building in him.

Jenny opened the door and curtsied.

"Is Lady Sirena here?"

"Yes, milord."

He pushed past the maid. Sirena's single trunk stood lonely and dwarfed by the massive expanse of space, and another young maid was helping with the unpacking. Sirena was nowhere in sight.

She's in your chamber.

He dismissed the maids, and hurried through the dressing room and into his chamber, clawing at his neck cloth.

His books were stacked neatly, his razor and brushes laid out in order. A side table held an assortment of liquor and glasses.

And the door to the bathing chamber was ajar. He flung off his coats.

CHAPTER SEVENTEEN

Sirena lay back, eyes closed, savoring the heat of the water, and only a wee bit wondering how she had got *here*. Jenny had helped wash her hair, and then Sirena had sent the girl away, content to have these few private moments alone, away from Shaldon's steely gazing and Perry's enthusiastic scheming. And, oh, yes, away from the fretting housekeeper, eager to discuss menus and accounts with her new mistress.

Mistress of Shaldon House—wasn't that a laugh? It had been but two days since she'd gone out to the docks, and here she was, a viscountess living in the home of her country's enemy. Whether 'twas a blessing or a trap she wasn't sure.

She hadn't noticed the ache in her body until she'd soaked for awhile in the blessed heat. Her legs were tired from her long walk, and her arms from the fight on the street. Between her legs, aye, she was sore there also, but not so much as to keep her from thinking of Bakeley and what he'd made her treacherous body feel. She sunk a little lower and blew bubbles in the water.

A door closed and she waited for Jenny to pop in. "It's still quite hot," she said. "I'll stay in a bit longer."

"Then I'll join you."

Her eyes shot open. Her hands flew to her breasts. "Bakeley."

"James." He was shedding clothing willy-nilly—shirt, boots, stockings, trousers.

Water shot up her nose and she choked. His male part was erect, and...and...

She took a deep breath and stifled a giggle. "You're flapping."

He grinned as he climbed over the side of the massive tub, nudging her around and settling her on his lap. "You have that effect on me."

Did she now? "Shall we crash through the floor below?" she asked.

He chuckled. "It will be worth it, will it not? We are christening this tub, Sirena."

"No one has bathed here?"

"It's not the bathing I'm talking about. Unless," he kissed her neck, "you are too sore."

Too sore? Perhaps. His fingers swirled around her breasts, wiping away all thoughts of discomfort.

"No."

A chuckle rumbled through her ear. "I am glad. And don't worry, I had the builder reinforce the flooring to support the weight. We could host ten dancing elephants within this chamber without even shaking loose a pipe."

She nestled back against him, that buzzing awareness blossoming in her and turning her mind to blancmange.

"I see you've decided where we'll live," he said.

"You said you'd leave the choice to me. Are you angry?"

From the way his fingers stroked across her, she didn't think he was.

"No. I'm astonished. You could have had your own house to run without Father and Perry underfoot. And, there's a perfectly good bedchamber next to my old one, but I'm glad you picked this suite of rooms."

She turned around to look at him. His afternoon stubble sparkled with splashed droplets. She let her fingertips glide over the roughness, noticing the dark circles under his eyes and a worry line between his brows that hadn't quite relaxed. He knew something. He'd learned something.

She opened her mouth to ask, and then shut it quickly. One took one's time with a hotblood like Bakeley. One used ones wiles. She turned and got upon her knees, watching his eyes go darker.

"I didn't truly pick these rooms. Perry told me this is where we would be staying, if we chose to live here."

His hands had found her breasts. "Perry is brilliant."

"Full of ideas. You have no idea."

"Oh, I do. And I have ideas of my own."

A while later, Bakeley awoke to a wet, shivering woman in his arms. The water had gone tepid, and Sirena was chilled. He sat her up. "Stay right here."

He found a towel, helped her out, and rubbed her down, then wrapped her in a heavy velvet robe the maid had laid out.

While he dried himself and drained the water, she grabbed towels and mopped the floor.

"We've splashed something fierce, Bakeley."

"James. And do not worry. That was taken into consideration also when the room was built."

"Put on your robe, then, James, so you don't catch cold."

He propped his hands on his naked hips and sent her a baleful look, watching warmth bloom in her cheeks and her gaze soften, making her laugh.

"Well, and I've done my part tonight to keep you happy, and I must try to keep you healthy also, my lord. And I imagine you're hungry."

"You dozed through the dinner bell," he said. "They won't expect us. I'll ring for a tray."

"I'll do that if you'll feed the fire in the bedchamber."

"And then you must sit yourself next to it and dry your hair."

He ushered her into his grand bedchamber, found his robe, and then stoked the fire.

She seated herself next to it and began brushing her hair, the long locks sparkling in the glowing fire. He watched her from the corner of his eye while he lit the lamps and candles. She was beautiful, a lure to any villain, common or aristocratic. What his father had in mind, he didn't know, but no matter where she went, if someone was after her, she was in danger. A trip to Bond Street might as well be a trip to Cransdall, their family estate in the north, for the ease of ambush.

He couldn't accompany her everywhere, and he doubted she'd willingly live with a guard upon her.

"We haven't talked of your meeting," she said. "What did you learn?"

He went to her and took the brush. "Let me."

Her hair was thick and wavy. In his much younger years, he'd dallied with a lady with hair this blonde, but once the hair pieces and folderol came off, her hair had been as thin and straight as a baby's. Not like this.

He lifted a strand of hair and inhaled, then bent to kiss her ear.

"You're dodging," she said.

"No, I'm not. You're distracting me."

A shiver went through her. *She*, distracting him? Good heavens, and well, wasn't it true? It seemed that each time she looked at him that manly part was standing at attention.

She reached for the brush, and he pushed her hand away.

"Very well." The brush moved through her hair. "Fineas Donegal is, they believe, a name being used by an Irish nationalist. It seems, Sirena, that instead of providing you with information on your brother, he may be seeking information from you *about* your brother."

"So Jamie might be alive." Her heart lifted. "But why me? Would I be going to him for information if I knew anything?"

"Donegal disappeared at the same time as your brother. Perhaps they were on the same ship. Perhaps Donegal was pursuing your brother or your brother was pursuing Donegal."

It didn't make sense. "But my brother was an Irish nationalist also." The strokes settled into a soothing rhythm. "Unless there were differences among them in how to proceed. That's possible, isn't it?"

James set down the brush and knelt before her. "Not just possible, but likely. My father says that your brother did portray himself as a member of the rebel cause, but he was actually still loyal to England."

She studied his face, so serious, and his words began to sink in, bringing with them a chill beyond the room's coolness, and making her shiver again. "He was a spy? My brother was a *spy*?"

"So my father says."

His father, who was the Spy Lord. Sirena's gaze dropped. "My brother worked for Shaldon."

James nodded. "So he says."

A wave of anger closed her throat and she had to take in great gulps of air to speak. "And yet," she choked out, "the whole world goes on thinking that the Glenmorrow heir was a traitor."

"True. And yet, it may explain why your father wasn't taken in by the authorities, and why he didn't lose his estate or his head."

She pushed him away and stood, pacing. And it was still true—Jamie was a traitor. He'd turned on Ireland, his people, his country. He'd spied on men like Fitzgerald and Emmet. People had died, cruelly, at the hands of the English. And her mother...

She pounded a fist into her other hand. "You don't know what it was like." She paced to the fireplace and leaned her head against the mantel. "Did he know, my father? Did he know Jamie was playing a double game?"

"I don't know. If he did, would he have told you?"

She shook her head. "No. And it wouldn't have mattered—Mother died inside when that ship went down, and her actual passing killed my father, though it took many years of the bottle to finish him off."

He touched her shoulder. "I'm sorry, Sirena."

She stiffened. *Sorry.* Was Shaldon sorry? Probably not. He would judge by the results, and not worry much about the means. He'd likely sent many men to their deaths. If he was capable of remorse, perhaps her marriage to his son and heir was a means to relieve any twinge of guilt that troubled him.

"What we must keep in mind is the possibility your brother is alive."

Oh, that made her head hurt, to think of her mother dying of grief and her brother still living. And yet, if he were still alive, she would have *someone.*

Someone who was a lying spy, a traitor to the people of Ireland, someone who'd let his family suffer needlessly.

She shook her head. No. She couldn't believe it.

"And if he's alive, he's the Earl of Glenmorrow."

She wheeled around to face him. "But Sterling has already inherited."

"I'm not sure the accession to the title has been finalized. In any case, we can throw up a legal challenge."

Her hands tingled and itched. Oh, to have her cousin in front of her and a knife in her hand. She'd forgive the traitorous Jamie Hollister if she could bring down Sterling Hollister. "Would you do that? For indeed, *I* cannot do it. I have no money, and I imagine it would require a great deal of money and political influence."

"I'd do it for you." He smoothed his hands over her arms. "He's in London."

Hope flashed and then she realized he was speaking about Sterling, not her brother. "I don't wish ever to see him unless I am armed with a dagger or...or a brace of pistols. But...he's come to

London already? Glenmorrow needs management and care." Without her father there, without her, the tenants and servants were dependent upon Sterling and the steward he'd put in place, and God help them if this new steward was anything like her cousin.

"He's here for the Parliament, and for the coronation."

Of course. "I'd forgotten. The new lord taking his place with his peers."

"No. The Irish have elected their members for the House of Lords and he's not among them. He's taking a seat in the House of Commons."

"He can do that?"

"Yes, by giving up his privileges."

Hope stirred in her. "His title?"

"No. His right to a trial by his peers. He can be tried as a common man for any crimes he commits."

Her heart pounded, and she gulped in air. "No one would believe me, Bakeley. No one would take my word over his."

"I would support you no matter what, Sirena, but I would never expect you to pursue a charge." Bakeley's jaw hardened. "A man like that, a man who would attack his own orphaned cousin, he'll have other victims, Sirena. And when he attacks, I intend to have a net waiting to snatch him up."

"Perhaps." She licked her lips, her mouth suddenly dry. "But it did seem very personal from him, like he hated who I was. He hated *me*." She swallowed hard. "And he did make me an offer. He said he would keep me installed at Glenmorrow as his mistress until such time as he took a wife, and then I could live in a croft on the estate with his by-blows."

Her head buzzed with the memory and a new flood of rage.

"It was as if he meant to humiliate specifically me, Sirena Hollister, the daughter of the old earl. And he didn't even know me. So I don't know that there will be others."

"A scoundrel in big things will be a scoundrel in small things." His voice cut like steel. "He will pay."

Their dinner came and all discussion stopped until the door closed on the servants. It had given her a moment to think, and Bakeley a moment to brood.

More had gone on today that Bakeley was not telling her.

"Who did you meet at the Home Office? Is it a name I'll recognize?"

He filled her plate and handed it to her. "Lord Farnsworth. Do you know him?"

"Is he Irish?"

"No. That is, I don't know."

"We shall look him up in Debrett's."

"Yes, well, he's also one of Shaldon's spies. And it wasn't the Home Office we visited. It was a townhouse in Knightsbridge, very likely owned by the Home Office."

His sharing such confidences raised her spirits. "Thank you."

"For what?"

"For trusting me with state secrets."

That brought a smile from him. "And how was your day?"

She told him about Perry's plot to move Lady Jane in and to have him fund a dressmaking establishment. It didn't coax a laugh as she'd expected.

"Would you like to have Lady Jane move in?" he asked. "We could phrase it as an invitation to help you learn as you adjust to your new duties. However, if she lets go of her lodgings and wishes to continue here, it would not be easy to undo, so you could expect something of a permanent arrangement."

"Perhaps. But when her cousin comes to town, 'twill be easier for her to lodge with him if she wishes, now that she's rid of me. And what of the modiste shop?"

"A business is a business. It can't be so very different than other endeavors. If you wish it, I'll consider that also."

Her heart swelled. She'd been treated well by Lady Jane and Barton. To think that she could share some of her new-found prosperity with them made her happy.

A footman appeared at the door.

"We're not quite finished," James said.

"Pardon, my lord. A letter came for you."

She took a drink of wine and watched as James glanced at the letter and closed the door on the servant, a frown marring his handsome face. Instead of returning to the table, he picked up a candle and proceeded into the dressing room.

She found him there, still frowning. "What is it?"

His mouth thinned. "I'm going to dress. I must speak to father." He grasped her hand and placed the letter in it. "After the interview with Farnsworth, I went to investigate your cousin. This message comes from the proprietor of the inn where he was lodging." He kissed her forehead and started pulling out drawers.

"That one." She pointed to the cabinet where his valet had stored his clothes.

She spread the folded paper and read.

The man you inquired about returned tonight with his two servants. You did ask for any peculiar news. Both his men are injerred and we have sent for the apothecary.

"What does it mean?"

James was pulling on his breeches. "I don't know for sure."

A tremor went through her. Oh, aye, he was keeping secrets. She must keep her own guard up.

"He went north, the landlord said, a couple of days ago."

North. And his servants were injured. And Bink went north with the O'Brians.

Yes, James was not sharing everything he knew.

She shed her robe, her skin rippling with the cold, found a clean chemise and tugged it on. "Will you help me with my stays?"

"Sirena, no—"

"Very well. No stays." She ran for the brown dress, the one that shouted *Sirena Hollister, serving wench.*

Lord Bakeley had a taste for keeping secrets, and wasn't that something to keep in mind when she found a few of her own?

CHAPTER EIGHTEEN

As he led her up the stairs, Bakeley let his hand drift along Sirena's waist under yet another ugly woolen shawl. Shaldon had not been in the library and they were on their way to his father's private study.

He liked the feel of her soft curves without the tight boning. "You don't really need stays."

She bounced up the steps. "I saw almost everything today. But not this room. The housekeeper begged off letting us in."

"She doesn't have the key," he said.

Her manner had been chilly, and not from the lack of heat in the frigid dressing room. He'd offended her in some way unrelated to her cousin or his father.

And blast it if he could figure out what was wrong. "I've been told that dresses don't fit properly without stays. Perhaps I shall ask your dressmaker to make you a whole wardrobe that doesn't require them."

She stopped on the stairs, indignation lighting her face. "Aye, your Paddy bride, flopping about in public all over the isle of Britain. I think not. I'm bought and paid for, and you can have me without stays every night, Bakeley, but I'll be respectable when I'm out and about."

The words slammed him. Bought and paid for—was that what she thought of him? Or...was that what she thought of herself.

He drew himself up. "What is really wrong?"

She chewed her lip. "Nothing."

"I see. Or, I don't see. I have a feeling that father can shed some light on your cousin, and if you're coming with me, than you need to be *with* me. We need to work together. Agreed?"

"You want me to what...charm him?"

He ignored the sarcasm. "If that works, yes. And if it doesn't, try something else. You've not had more than one chat with him after our wedding. He seemed inclined to be conciliatory."

"We spoke this afternoon also."

"Did you? Yes, he did tell me he would speak to you. Is he having you keep secrets from your husband?"

Her eyes flashed, and she quickly sent them rolling.

Sirena would keep secrets. She would lie to him. Jocelyn had been right—he'd need to seduce her.

"Oh, now I *am* curious. What did he say?"

"Nothing of import. He hopes I'll be happy here, or some such. The housekeeper came to take me to look at the silver, and that was all that was said. I believe he set her up for the interruption so he wouldn't have to share anything of importance with me."

A flood of affection swept through him and he pulled her closer. "Then your perceptiveness puts you one step ahead of him, love." He squeezed her hip. "Come. Let us find out what he really knows."

Insides quaking, Sirena let Bakeley handle the door-knocking. A gruff voice called out and they entered. Two lamps shed pools of light and a low fire warmed the small room. Half-hidden behind a dark wooden desk, Shaldon sat erect. A brown file lay precisely squared up an inch from the edge of the desk, like it had been laid by the footman preparing the dining table.

Shaldon did not look at all surprised to see them, but, she reflected, in the few times they'd met, his face had worn that same haughty bored look she saw often on Bakeley's handsome mug. Her own father had been like a badly loaded musket most of the time, easy to set off and unpredictable. Not at all like the Shaldon men. It would be her greatest achievement to rouse some emotion in her new father.

"Yes?" Shaldon asked rather impolitely. That one lonely word dropped off into a conversational abyss.

Next to her, her husband had stiffened up like the fireplace poker.

"I received a message tonight I wish to speak with you about." Bakeley moved a chair from before the fireplace for her, but he remained standing.

Very well. She would play the demure lady. She wrapped her shawl a little tighter and sat.

Shaldon took the proffered paper and scanned it. "Who is this about?"

"Sterling Hollister."

Shaldon's eyes flickered, but he shuttered his gaze before turning it on her. "Your cousin."

"Do you know him?" she asked.

"We may have met at some point."

She glanced at Bakeley. His arms were folded under his hastily-tied neck cloth, and his hair still glistened from the bath. And he hadn't shaved. He wore his I'm-a-lord-and-intensely-bored look, and *that* combined with the delicious, disreputable appearance niggled at her hard-won composure.

"The note is from the landlord of the inn where he's taken rooms," Bakeley said. "I went to visit Hollister today, and he was away. He and his servants have been gone. They've returned, as you see, with injuries."

His lordship's chin came up an inch. "And what is that to me?"

Bakeley moved another chair and sat, lolling back and kicking one foot over his knee.

Both men looked at each other. Not as if they were staring daggers, or not even butter knives. They were two icicles facing one another, not even melting.

Anger rolled through her in great waves. At this rate, the conversation would stretch until bacon and toast were laid out for breakfast. Aye, she must intervene. What was Sterling Hollister to Shaldon? If he was another one of Shaldon's spies, some hard facts for his lordship might move things along, and let him hear what he'd got for a new daughter.

Sirena rose. "Father—you did ask me to call you that, sir—Sterling Hollister was a distant cousin of my father, who was, you know, the Earl of Glenmorrow. Sterling appeared at Glenmorrow last summer, coming to claim title to the land, bringing along papers and my father's solicitor from Belfast to explain them all. I'd been expecting it, 'twas true." She paced to the fireplace. "I'd had but a few friends in the neighborhood. My brother was a scandal, and my father became one with his drinking, and in any case he'd given up on everything except his horses."

Shaldon still watched her.

She sensed him thawing, even as icy anger built within her. She forced her fists open and took a deep breath.

"Might I have a season? No. Might I entertain a regular kind of courtship from a respectable man? No. We were outcasts, you see, and also, the meager bit that was to be my dowry was gone. Yes." A hard knot of anger strangled that last word and she swallowed it down. "So, no social standing. No gentlemen callers. I know horses, and I can manage their breeding and training, but I had no dowry. Even a yeoman wants a wife to bring something more than unwomanly skills and her fair self to the marriage. And then along comes Sterling Hollister."

Warm hands settled on her shoulders, and she realized, she'd been trembling.

"Sirena, shall I tell the rest?"

Bakeley had joined her near the fireplace.

She craned her neck around and searched his eyes, glad there was no pity there.

She didn't want pity. She wanted revenge. "I suppose he knows it already."

"Tell it anyway."

She took a deep breath. Bakeley's hands circled her waist, lending her strength. "The vicar's wife told me I could expect my cousin to provide for me, being an orphan. She said that everyone in the neighborhood was whispering he might even propose a marriage, since the rumor was he had no wife. I thought upon it, you know, and decided it wasn't completely impossible. We weren't rich, except in land and of course what horses we had left. If we managed better, if we switched to sheep and put more land to planting..." She shook her head. "Sterling Hollister arrived on Saturday. He accompanied me to services the next morning." She looked down and found her hand resting in Bakeley's. "Lord and Lady Cheswick and Lady Jane were visiting our neighbor. We met one day when both ladies came to see a horse. Well, at church on Sunday, Lady Jane pulled me from his side. She'd seen him touching me. Seen me slapping his hand away."

Heat flooded her at the memory and she bit her lip.

"Do you need my handkerchief?" Bakeley whispered.

"No."

Shaldon had come round his desk, as tall and as dark as his son, ready to catch her the other way.

Well, she would not collapse on either of these Englishmen.

"In short, sir, the new Earl of Glenmorrow did say he would provide for me. Since my father had mismanaged the estate so badly, the cost to me was that I would be privileged to share my cousin's bed, while he looked for an heiress to fill his coffers. And after that, he promised he would only throw me as far as one of the crofts on the estate."

Shaldon's firm jaw moved, and the lines between his eyebrows deepened. Perhaps he had not already heard this story after all.

Her chest tightened and moisture pricked her eyes. She took a deep breath. "Was Sterling another of your spies, my lord?"

Shaldon blinked. "No. Never. And you are a very brave girl."

She turned away and squeezed her eyes shut, surrendering to Bakeley's arms. Not brave at all. Naught but a weak weeper.

"Hollister tried to violate Sirena." His words rumbled through her. "He followed her to her chambers. The housekeeper had slowed him down by dosing his drink, the butler bashed him, and Sirena ran away. Lady Jane rescued her."

She heard a loud audible sigh that did not echo in Bakeley's chest.

"You've sent someone to watch him?" Shaldon asked.

"I borrowed Bink's groom, Johnny."

"A good man. Sirena, my dear, are you all right?"

She had squeezed back the tears, though her face must be blotchy.

Bakeley looked down on her. "I'm glad you've not got my coat wet."

"My dear." Shaldon was next to her, freeing one of her hands from Bakeley, his grip as firm and as solid as his son's. There was none of the papery smoothness of old age in that hand, or in truth, anywhere about the man. He pushed her chair closer to the desk and seated her again.

"Bakeley, pour us all a brandy. You'll have one, my dear?"

"Only a bit." She sat up straight. Brandy weakened the mind. So could a sneaking man's kindness. "Did you know all of this about my cousin already?"

"That he tried to molest you? No. That he's the worst sort of villain? Yes."

He accepted the glass from Bakeley and looked hard at him. "You've done well, son."

Bakeley's mouth dropped open, but he quickly recovered and handed Sirena her drink.

"Let us drink to the next Lady Shaldon." His lordship lifted his glass, took a drink, and promptly had a fit of coughing.

Perhaps the stories of his illness were not entirely unfounded. "Are you unwell, sir?" Sirena asked.

Shaldon shook his head and cleared his throat. "We shall send someone to take a room at that inn."

"Kincaid?" James asked.

"Even in disguise, he's too well known, I fear. Besides, he's not back yet from Little Norwick. I've another man, just returned from the Continent."

He got up, went into the hallway and spoke to someone, someone who hadn't been there when they'd entered.

"Good heavens," she whispered.

"Yes. Will you have another?"

"No." She handed him her glass and glanced back. Shaldon was still in the hall. "Shall we have a look at that file?"

"He means to show it to us, else it wouldn't be there."

But there wouldn't have been time since Shaldon soon returned and took his seat. "Sterling was in the army, did you know that?"

His abruptness took her by surprise.

"Yes, I'd heard that," she said.

"He was in the cavalry for many years and never made it past captain." Shaldon frowned. "A squirrelly, unreliable fellow during the Irish troubles, and one who had a dodgy period of service in the Peninsular campaign, managing to get himself shifted back to England. He was about to be sent to America when Napoleon escaped.

Much to his chagrin, Hollister wound up at Waterloo." He took a drink and his frown deepened. "As did his brother."

She thought back to the short twenty-four hours she'd spent with the man. "He never mentioned a brother."

"Gareth Hollister was the elder, first in line for the Glenmorrow title. Gareth had studied law and had a small income, but otherwise lived the useless life of a landless gentleman. Got caught up in the patriotic fervor and followed his brother to Brussels. He wasn't regular army, but he took his horse out with the cavalry anyway."

"And was killed." Sirena felt sick. "Was he also a villain?"

"He was mainly a fool."

"Gareth died at Waterloo, and Sterling walked away unscathed?" Bakeley asked.

"Quite. Fought side by side, they did."

A hard look passed between father and son, and Sirena's skin quivered. "They both knew my brother was dead. And with Gareth gone, Sterling stood to inherit."

Shaldon's lips thinned. "Sterling sold his commission, took up Gareth's income, and moved himself to London."

"And waited for my father to die. I should count my blessings he didn't come to visit us."

"He wouldn't have dared to enter the county. Your father had no love for Sterling."

Her breath almost stopped. She wanted to shout questions, but she held herself still, like her husband was doing.

Bakeley glanced her way. "So Lord Glenmorrow knew his cousins?" He was asking on her behalf, bless him.

"He knew Sterling. It was Sterling who chased your brother all the way to the coast."

A film seemed to fall from her vision. Sterling had three people between him and Glenmorrow— her father, who he could reasonably expect to outlive, her brother, who was on the wrong side of the law, or so Sterling thought, and his own brother, who'd gone so obligingly to his grave.

"He came back to your father to report on your brother's ship sinking. Your father took a horsewhip to him."

She closed her eyes and a memory rocked through her, her mother in tears, her father with his whip, and a soldier in a red coat receiving the lashes. One of the servants had picked her up and hauled her inside to the housekeeper's room, where she'd done her own crying.

Her head swam with the memory. "That's why he singled me out for his despicable offer." It was revenge against her father, beyond the grave. Anger, hot and powerful, threatened to bubble over.

She took a deep breath. "Did my father know that my brother was spying for you?"

Shaldon grimaced and glanced at his son. "Very well. Yes, he did. And he could not share that word with the world because it would compromise others still working. And later..." He sighed. "I'm sorry, Sirena. War takes its toll on the innocent as well as the guilty. Your mother's death—"

"Did she know?"

"He should not have told her. I don't know if he did."

She shook her head. "She had many friends who dropped her, and the grief of it was unbearable. I think he must not have. I think she would have borne it better if she'd known."

He touched one finger to the file on his desk and slid it across to her. "You've been looking for this, I think."

Bakeley pressed her hand, and she glanced at him. His nod jarred her out of her own reverie.

She wasn't looking to him for permission, nor did she need it. She lifted her hand to reach for the file and noticed the shaking. She clenched and unclenched her fists, and took the brown folder.

Roland James Hollister, Baron Glenmorrow.

She'd forgotten her brother had held the courtesy title.

He'd been very young when recruited. There weren't many original reports in his hand, but she recognized his careless scrawl from her memories of the few letters her mother had saved from his time in school, letters she'd had to leave behind at Glenmorrow. Most of his uncoded, transcribed messages had a guardedness about them, like he was not entirely forthcoming with the names of rebels, though he did report on plots and schemes the rebels had afoot.

Halfway measures from a man who was twice a traitor. Her head ached with it.

His last dispatch said he would provide them with a list of names, and that he was pursuing one particular traitor within the army.

A tight knot formed in her stomach. Did he regret his betrayals, this brother she no longer knew? Was that why he provided no names?

She slid the file to Bakeley and waited as he read through it, her gaze focused on her own clenched fists curled in her lap.

Paper swished and Bakeley cleared his throat. "I take it Sterling Hollister was the traitor providing information to the rebels?"

Shaldon chewed his lower lip. "We watched him closely. Fed him information unproductively. We were never able to prove it. But, yes, I would bet my first-born son he is."

Her breath whooshed out. "Did you send Mr. Gibson north to draw out Hollister?" She shook her head. "I'm so confused."

Shaldon almost smiled. "It is only a figure of speech. I should have known Hollister was here. I didn't." He drummed his fingers on the desktop. "My intelligence was lacking, but it's all the fault of these many plots and schemes against the government, and the preparations for the coronation. We're spread too thinly."

Bakeley's skin rippled with awareness, the two people who should be the closest in the world to him, his father and his wife, were tied together by this intrigue and he wasn't sure he could trust either one of them to share everything. "Sirena, why did you believe your brother might be alive?"

Her momentary press of lips was matched by a widening of her eyes, and his own excitement built, wondering if she would lie to him.

"The first mate on the packet we took from Dublin was, well, he was very friendly with me, and I did tell him about my brother, as I tell everyone so that they...will be warned off, as it were, and he said he'd met a sailor who'd told him there were survivors of the sinking, and that he'd sailed with one of them on an Atlantic crossing. Well, I asked the O'Brians to check at the docks for me, to see if anyone had names of survivors, and they came up with Donegal. I suppose that was your ploy, Lord Shaldon."

He shook his head. "They did make contact with him. Brief, and he was very careful, very cagey. They let him know that you were looking for your brother. And we believe he may have known your brother some twenty years ago. We have no reason to believe he knew your brother was working for us."

"So why would he have any interest in Sirena?"

"Ah, well, about that. What the O'Brians also told him is that you might have clues to your brother's whereabouts."

Her head shot up and color spiked her cheeks. "Which I do not. Which means that Jamie is d-dead."

Bakeley reached for her, but she pushed him away and glared at his father. "You're using me, Lord Shaldon and I know not if this man Donegal is quite so bad as you suspect."

"Perhaps he does have information about your brother, my love," Bakeley said, "or knows something that will set us on the path to investigate more."

Her gaze met his, and he felt the fire melting out of her. This one was not used to gentling. The *my love* had disarmed her.

"You are still willing?" she asked, her voice shaky, as if she expected him to turn on her.

"Of course. I'll do everything to help you find your brother, if he's still alive. Father, tell us about Donegal. What leads you to believe he's plotting?"

Shaldon sighed deeply. "What I tell you must be held in confidence."

"Agreed. Sirena?"

She bit her lip. "Agreed."

He lifted her hands. "See, Father. No fingers crossed for either of us."

CHAPTER NINETEEN

"You have heard of the Cato Street Conspiracy?"

"The plot against the Prime Minister," Sirena said.

"Indeed. Those were not the only plotters against the Prime Minister and the King. It's been reported that a man believed to be Donegal has met with some of the men we're watching."

"Perhaps that's another man."

"That is always the unfortunate possibility. Operatives can be..." Shaldon picked over his words. "Imprecise. When they are led by money, they will always go to the higher bidder. When they are led by passion, well, one impassioned speech can turn them on their head and find them working for the other side."

Sirena stared into the dwindling fire. "Like Jamie. Could he still be alive?"

Bakeley sensed it had been a question for herself, not for him or his father. She couldn't focus on Donegal. She couldn't connect the dots between Donegal, Sterling Hollister, and her brother. Hell, he couldn't yet either, but while she stewed about her worry, it was his job to work out how all three men tied together.

She sighed deeply. "I'm not willing to give up, Lord Shaldon. If catching this Donegal for you will tell me something, I'll do it, but in exchange, there is something I want from you."

Bakeley watched her stand and pace, his unease growing. She was intense, passionate, determined. She'd take information given and act on it, with or without him.

"Or rather I want to help you with something else that will bring me great satisfaction. If 'tis at all possible, I want Sterling Hollister. I want his head on a platter. I want a stake through his heart." She braced her hands on the desk and leaned forward. "And if he *is* truly a traitor, I want to help you prove it."

Alarm bells went off in Bakeley's head. He'd thought to handle the vengeance himself, in his own way, stripping the man of his title. But Shaldon's eyes had lit up in that way they'd done when his brother Bink had finally been lured to his bait. Shaldon would be ruthless, careless.

Sirena might be equally as ruthless and as careless, but she would also be defenseless.

Still, telling either of them *absolutely not* was the sure way to find himself locked out of the plotting, as he had been with Bink.

Sirena sat again on the edge of the chair. "Bakeley said my cousin has given up the privileges of his title, and that perhaps he's not yet officially recognized as Glenmorrow. Could we catch him in a crime and perhaps, um, put him in your dungeon?"

Shaldon's eyes had not ceased to glitter and now his lips quirked. The old man would live another fifty years with Sirena as a daughter.

Of that, he was glad, but keeping her from danger would keep Bakeley on his toes. He must *think*.

"We do not have a dungeon, my dear," Shaldon said.

"Not here anyway." Bakeley snatched the file and opened it, flipping through pages. "The list. He was going to bring a list and the name of the man he was pursuing. Perhaps we can let it be known that we have found that list, and that his name is upon it."

Her eyes flitted back and forth. "Would it matter, so many years later?"

"Father? Would Liverpool's government be interested in a list of old traitors?"

"Indeed." Shaldon steepled his fingers. "We might also find reports from Waterloo survivors, men who have come forward wanting to tell the story of an officer shooting his own brother."

Sirena's mouth dropped open. "Are there such reports?"

He shook his head. "God knows, I have tried to find them. Battle is such that brother shooting brother is not so unfathomable. Soldiers would rather forget."

"It is chaos, Sirena, so Bink says. Brothers in arms can accidentally shoot each other." And that was all Bink would say about battle.

"I see." She nodded. "But he won't know that, and perhaps it will rattle him. If he's the one who attacked Mr. Gibson and the O'Brians, perhaps we should take a journey to the country and lure him that way."

"*No.*" Bink's journey with Paulette had involved an invasion of her inn room and two killings—and he'd seen one of those bodies. No, Sirena would not be put through that.

Her face settled into a stubborn frown, while Shaldon watched, no doubt enjoying the potential for an argument.

She would not go on a journey. Whatever trap they set, it would have to be in town, where he could keep her close, and even then...to keep her at home was better, but that was tricky, unless...

"We'll hold a ball." He sat up in his chair, the genius of it flooding him. She and Perry would spend hours planning menus, writing invitations. "A wedding ball, to celebrate our nuptials. In one week, or perhaps ten days. We'll invite Hollister, of course, as your nearest relative. Don't frown so, Sirena, Father will have men ready to snatch him up and take his head off."

"But a week—"

"It may be too much for you and Perry alone." He snapped his fingers. "Lady Jane Monthorpe. We shall ask her to move in here and help with preparations."

"But—"

"Yes, I know, you'll need a dress. You may spend as much as you want, my dear. Take Perry and Lady Jane and buy yourself a wardrobe, everything you need. Feathers, flounces, some of those bloody pleats."

"And she'll need your mother's jewels, Bakeley."

He stared at his father. His mother's exquisite diamonds had been stored away so long they'd slipped from his memory.

He nodded. "Our marriage has been a whirlwind, and I had forgotten. They're yours now. I shall show you them tomorrow, Sirena."

She waved a hand as if the jewels didn't matter. "How shall we lure him? What if he doesn't come?"

"He's here, taking a seat in the Commons, so he's ambitious. Father, can you muster up some influential guests?"

Shaldon nodded. "Most certainly. We'll make sure he won't want to miss it."

Sirena's breath quickened. "Shall I write him a note? I can tell him I've found something among..." she tapped her chin "among my father's personal papers? Something my brother gave father that concerns him?"

"That may be too obvious," Shaldon said. "Perhaps we'll have a dinner before the ball, with select guests. He'll be one of them. Let me think on this and we'll talk again. We know your cousin is dangerous. We must be crafty."

"And what of Donegal?" she asked.

"He'll be back. We have a man who can drop a story around the East End, where he turned up before."

"You'll need to be careful on any excursions, Sirena," Bakeley said.

"I'll bring my dagger."

"And several body guards."

"They'll discourage him from making contact."

"If he's clever, he'll find a way. We'll need to be on our toes to look out for him."

"How nice if we could invite him to the ball also, and kill two birds with one stone."

"I believe Father does not want Donegal dead. I believe he wants to *talk* to him."

She smiled, and he felt a rush of...blast it, he was about to say *love*. Such a trite emotion. What he was feeling was lust. They'd been here quite long enough.

His father scowled. "You're quite right. We want Donegal alive and talking."

He made no mention of keeping Sterling Hollister alive.

"And the new Earl of Glenmorrow?" Bakeley asked. "Does he have much to say of interest, or..."

Sirena paled. Perhaps she was not so bloodthirsty after all. Which meant that after the inevitable marital disagreements, he would be able to sleep with both eyes closed.

"If there are charges we choose to file, he shall be tried," Shaldon said. "Perhaps."

And perhaps he'd be too dead for a public trial. He caught Sirena's eye and she nodded grimly, no doubt picking the platter for Sterling's head.

"So, a ball," she said. "Seven days hence."

"Or perhaps ten. Make it a fortnight if you must."

She shook her head. "The housekeeper will have an apoplexy."

"Then we'll hire a new one, love."

Love. Sirena's heart squeezed around the word that Bakeley blathered so easily. An endearment that tripped from his lips, so he'd probably used it before on a horse, or a hound, or a harlot.

She would have mere days to arrange a fashionable ball, a thing of which she had no experience. 'Twould all be done for people who held his Paddy bride in abject contempt.

And sure, they'd hire someone for the planning. Several someones if she truly had any say in the matter. They'd need more footmen and maids as well.

A scratching at the door roused Bakeley from his chair, and the butler entered.

"Beg pardon, my lords," he said. "The cellar is seeping again. You did ask me to tell you, Lord Bakeley."

Bakeley swiped a hand through his hair. What had Perry said? He'd designed all the drainage himself.

Well, and perhaps he'd not done a good job of it, a lord dabbling in a working man's trade.

And...hadn't she been lolling around in a great bloody tub all afternoon? That would be her bathwater seeping out in the cellar.

"I have some of the men seeing to it."

"Thank you, Lloyd. I'll be right down." Bakeley closed the door on the man.

"The sewer," Shaldon said. "Threats to the Crown, and you worry about sewers."

Bakeley scowled. "Miasma fevers and marsh gas explosions are also threats to the Crown."

Sirena stood. "'Twas my bath—"

"No," Bakeley said. "The public sewer is backing up again. Come." He reached for her hand. "I'll take you back to your chamber. Shall I send Perry up so you can begin organizing the ball?"

Her heart trembled within her. Dump her he would, after all she'd discovered, and go and deal with his shite.

She forced a light tone. "Lady Perry will be abed, or near to it. You're going down to your dungeons?"

"The cellars, yes."

A part of the Shaldon House tour she'd missed. "Then I'll find my own way." She nodded to Shaldon. "Good night, then...Father, Bakeley."

She rushed out, but Bakeley caught up with her in the corridor outside her bedchamber, touching her waist. Blast him.

"Sirena—"

"Go," she said, trying to sound cheerful.

"Go to bed then. I'll be right along."

"To join me?"

"If you wish."

If she wished? Anger bubbled up in her, like Bakeley's seeping sewage.

She pasted on a smile and faced him.

A lamp had been lit in the corridor. Surely the dim light would hide her falseness.

"'Twas truly not the bath?" she asked.

"No. I've been after the sewer commissioners to clean up the lines. London is growing and..." He shook his head. "Shall I send your maid to tuck you in?"

Tuck her in? Bakeley thought he'd married a meek soul who needed a maid to fetch and carry for her. An Irish lady who'd blithely forget all her countrymen and open her arms to the English at a fancy London ball.

It made her head spin, it did.

She patted his arm. "Go on with you, then."

He dropped a kiss on her forehead and she watched him hurry off.

Inside, all was quiet. Outside, carriages clacked and rattled, rich people off to their parties and balls. And the night stink did indeed seep through the windows.

A year earlier, she'd have run the fields in brisk, chilly air on a night like this. Even two days ago, she'd been free to go out at the crack of dawn.

She pounded a fist on the door frame. They'd trapped her, these English, as surely as Jamie must have been trapped.

She found the same servants' staircase she'd climbed with Bakeley that first night and groped her way down to the back door.

CHAPTER TWENTY

Sirena pinched her nose with the corner of her shawl and picked her way to the stable at the back of the garden. Shaldon House was a grand mansion, standing all on its own, not one of the townhouses wedged up against others. 'Twas as big as her home in Glenmorrow, and if Cransdall was grander, as Perry had said, it must indeed be a veritable palace.

And with Lady Shaldon deceased, it was Lady Bakeley's to run.

She shook off the terrible thought and let herself into the stables.

Horses and hay—a deep breath brought the comforting smells. A low lantern hung in the aisle, casting a dim light, so someone must be about.

She paused. Every stall was filled except the one loose box in the near corner. The box, a great luxury for a London mews Perry had said, still stood empty, Save for some shuffling and snorting, all was quiet. Perhaps the grooms had been needed to help Bakeley shovel the human seepage. For herself, she'd rather deal with horse droppings. And she had every right to be here, didn't she?

A gray nose poked her way—Bakeley's gelding she'd met on the street. And that only a few days ago.

She moved up silently in the stall and laid a palm on him. He buzzed with an excitement and interest that shot up her arm and stirred her. Her fey gifts were truly back. She let out a long breath, letting it float over him, her eyes tearing with the joy of it.

Now, here was a fast friend, a true friend. Ride him, she would. She opened her mouth to speak, but a rumbling whisper down the aisle silenced her.

The gelding trembled.

"Shhh," she breathed, stroking his nose.

"Sure, and they're all in the house. 'Tis only me here."

The lilting male voice made her ears fairly quiver. That was an Irishman, here, in the Shaldon stables. Did their lordships have a Paddy employed?

The other voice rumbled, and the skin on her back rippled. The gelding stirred.

She closed her eyes to hear better.

"No. 'Twon't be that easy."

More rumbling.

"I'll try. 'Tis all I can promise. And—"

Bam.

Down the aisle, a horse was objecting. And wasn't that a sure sign the whisperers were up to no good?

The gelding's nostrils ruffled but he held in his worry.

The voices moved away, toward the door at the end.

Behind her, the door she'd entered opened again. Light from a lantern lit the gelding's rolling eyes and fear shot through her. She swallowed hard and turned.

"See here—"

"Don't be swinging that light at me," she said.

Shock registered in the man's face. She didn't know him.

"Beg pardon, miss."

"You've left a lantern lit and the horses unattended."

"Lord Bakeley called, but there was a man here." He took off his hat, revealing hair that was probably red in the light of day.

"What's your name?" she asked. "Why aren't you wearing your livery?"

"I'm Johnny, miss. Mr. Gibson's man. He sent me over to...er..."

The conversation with Shaldon came back to her. "You were at the inn."

"Yes." He rolled his cap in his hand, looking confused.

He didn't know who she was. Shaldon had said he was a good man.

Behind him, more men trickled in and scattered to the stalls, sending her sideways glances.

"I'm Lady Bakeley," she said. "What are you all on about now?"

"We'll be moving these fellows to a hired stable. Lord Bakeley's orders."

Her heart plummeted. "He wants them removed?"

She'd have no horses to visit and to calm her.

"For a few days, in case the pit down below seeps. Bad for their feet. And any gases are bad for their wind."

She blinked, trying to follow the man. "The pit?"

"The cesspit, my lady. The common sewer is backing up into it, his lordship says."

The cesspit. And sewers. Of course, as his lordship had said to her also.

"Then 'tis not the best time to discuss a mount for me. Do you need my help with the moving? Shall I call Lady Perry to come help also?"

His eyes went wide again. "I couldn't—I mean, we men here have ahold of it, my lady."

We men.

Well, she'd only been Lady Bakeley for one day. It might, perhaps, take more than that to worm her way into the stables. But be there she would, or Bakeley could arrange his own wedding ball.

She patted the horse's nose, wished the man a good night, and found her way back to her bedchamber.

Jenny was sprawled on the chaise longue, fast asleep.

The girl stirred and sprang up, mumbling a groggy apology.

"Poor Jenny. If you've been waiting for me to climb out of the bathtub, I do apologize. We'll make a fast job of it tonight, and you can head up to your bed. I didn't don stays after my bath."

"You could have called me, my lady."

"I was in a big hurry. How are you finding this great house?"

"My lady?"

"Are they treating you well? Your being new, and the staff being so well-settled. I'm grateful to you for joining me here."

"I'm not the only new one. There's two new footmen, and some of the grooms, and a couple of maids they've hired on for the season. They're expecting a great deal of company."

"I see. Good. So you're not the only one trying to fit in. Is all well with the staff?"

The girl's forehead wrinkled and her lips pressed together.

"I'm not asking for secrets, you see. It's just, I'm to be the new mistress here..."

"I don't know as I'd say all is perfect below stairs. There's a great hubbub there now in the kitchens, with all of the grooms and footmen tramping about."

Her voice cracked on the last words and she turned away, shaking out the brown gown while Sirena pulled on her nightrail.

A tremor went through Sirena. 'Twas more of that gift springing up, and not her own with the horses, but her mother and Gram's. Meeting Bakeley had stirred up the fairies. "Where have they put you to sleep, Jenny?"

"There's cots off the kitchens—"

"What? You're not in the attics with the other girls?"

"The beds are all taken, they said."

Unease threaded through her. Her tour hadn't included the servants' quarters. But she'd not have a girl in her care confined to the scullery. Not with the cesspit seeping and men tramping everywhere.

She pulled the counterpane and a pillow off her bed and carried them to the chaise longue.

"You understand, I cannot put you in my bed, Jenny, just in case his lordship wanders in with no light and a bit foxed. He'd not bother you, I'm sure, but 'twill be better to not confuse him and embarrass the either of you." She plumped the pillow and spread out the blanket. "You'll sleep here."

"Oh, miss, I couldn't."

"You can, and you will. We'll lock this door to the corridor, and I'll be in Lord Bakeley's bed." She took the brown dress from the girl, tossed it onto the bed, and crossed to the door, turning the key. "There now. Loosen your laces, take off your shoes, and stretch out."

Jenny let out a breath. "Thank you, my lady."

"Good night and sleep well."

Guilt nipped at her, and anger. Lady Bakeley she was, like it or not, and mistress of this great house. And tomorrow night her maid would sleep in a proper room.

It was the wee hours before Bakeley trudged up to his bedchamber.

At Sirena's door he paused and moved on. It was late, and she'd be asleep, and as much as he'd washed below stairs, he surely carried the stench in his clothing.

In his chamber, a lamp burned. He spotted a shape in the bed, sending his heart into a gallop.

She was here, waiting for him. He stripped off his clothes and climbed in with her, pulling her close.

"Bakeley?" she whispered.

"Who else?"

"Did you fix things?"

"No. Not tonight. We didn't want to nose about too much with the lanterns. There are gases that might ignite."

"Really? And start the house on fire?"

"Or worse. Explode."

"Will we have to move out?"

"No. We'll carry on." They'd clear the stables though, just for a time. For the health of the cattle. "We'll call out the muck men first thing tomorrow."

"Will we still have the ball?"

"Yes. It will all be cleared up by then."

"Oh."

He heard the disappointment in her voice.

"A fine challenge you've set me." She turned her head and scowled at him. "Plan a ball and pray that the house doesn't explode around our guests."

Her eyes went wide and she sat up, the covers spilling to reveal a lacy nightrail. "Could it be done on purpose? Perhaps the man, Donegal—"

"London's growing so fast, there are frequent problems like this."

"But if it's inside, perhaps it's one of your people—"

"No." Though in truth, he'd gone over the list of his staff in his mind, wondering the same thing. But they'd all been checked quite thoroughly, even the new ones.

He traced a finger down the valley of her chest, making her shiver.

She clamped her hand over his. "You're so sure of yourself."

The challenge in her voice sent lust storming through him.

He held himself still. "You wish to sleep. You're probably sore."

"That's not what I meant. I meant, have a care of your staff, is all. For the other, well, I know my duty. I'm to breed the next little Lord Bakeley." She turned to him. "And so, husband, here I am."

Her lips touched his, and he was lost.

Only later, as he was drifting to sleep, the scent of her hair filling him, her words came back, troubling him. She was his chosen wife, not a brood mare. She wasn't bought and paid for. And, by God, he'd be more to her than the man she married to save her reputation. She'd surrendered her body and it wasn't enough. He wanted her Irish heart.

A few days later, Sirena squeezed in next to Perry in the front-facing seats of the Shaldon town carriage. Across from them, Lady Jane sat next to Barton, all but quivering with excitement.

Sirena pushed the curtain aside and peered out. Two riders on each side protected them, along with two men on the coach. "Have we enough outriders?" Sirena muttered. "They'll think a royal princess is tucked away in this carriage."

Perry giggled. "Bakeley would have come along himself had he not been meeting with Father, and Bink, and Charley. It's wonderful the way we've all come together."

"Barton and I am delighted to be visiting Madame Le Fanelle's," Lady Jane said.

Barton had been cooking up her dress designs from her observations in the park, shops, and public byways, as well as whichever Ackerman's fashion plates she could get her hands on. The chance to see the modiste's shop up close had even the level-headed maid grinning.

"It's spying, you are," Sirena said. Perry had whisked her off on the first day to this fashionable dressmaker, where she'd been measured for a wardrobe and fitted with three completed dresses the proprietor had ready for new customers just like her, she'd said. Though Sirena imagined some other poor soul had gone delinquent in her bill-paying.

In spite of Bakeley's plight with the muck men, Lady Jane had moved in—for a short while only, she'd said—and now, two days later, they were off for more fitting and shopping, and the spying, of course. The time spent on the mundane tasks of arranging menus, planning the flowers, and addressing ball invitations had included more discussions of the dressmaking enterprise, and Barton was quietly eager to see how the most fashionable modiste in London conducted business.

James had interrupted his sewer concerns to come with them on her first modiste visit, both to satisfy himself that she would be safe and, he'd whispered, to take his own measure of the cost of setting up such a business. Madame had greeted him more effusively than she would have had she known his true purpose—and had she not already made the acquaintance of his coin. It may have been the first time he'd crossed the threshold of the shop, but they had, Sirena decided, done business together before.

She'd had to beat down a powerful bout of the green monster, as well as a healthy dose of curiosity, reminding herself that he'd broken with Lady Arbrough, and what had taken place before Bakeley's marriage was not truly any of her business. This wasn't a love match, after all. Once he'd got her with child, he'd soon enough leave her bed for another's.

There again, perhaps he'd only paid his sister Perry's bills. Yes, that might well be it.

The carriage stopped and they were handed down into the phalanx of guards.

"The street is a quiet one." Lady Jane bent to whisper to Barton. "And quite respectable. And note the display. Very tasteful."

Perry smiled behind Lady Jane's back. "The windows are also so clean they are glistening, and the fixtures are completely *au courant*. Come. Let us go up these well-swept stairs and enter."

Sirena chuckled and followed her new sister. The shop girl who greeted them said Madame was just finishing with a customer, and indeed, Sirena turned and saw the dressmaker walking from the back with a tall, dark-haired lady in a fawn-colored pelisse.

A buzzing started in her head and she sensed Perry moving closer. Of course Bakeley knew this shop—Lady Arbrough had her dresses made here. Perhaps her more intimate attire also, the kind a lord would buy his mistress.

Now he was paying for Sirena's new attire. A new peignoir, a delicate, frothy thing in white, had been delivered to the great house the day before. He'd removed it from her body not long after she'd donned it.

She felt her face go warm. Lady Arbrough was coming her way, a knowing smile upon her face, yet not an unfriendly one.

"My dear." Lady Arbrough curtsied. "Lady Perpetua. Lady Sirena. How wonderful to see you both. Am I too bold when I say that I read in the paper the announcement of your news? I do wish you and Bakeley every happiness. Lady Perpetua, you must be thrilled to have a new sister."

The chatter gave her time to recover. Perry's initial alarm had faded and now she looked bemused, responding politely. Lady Jane and Lady Arbrough exchanged polite greetings.

Lady Arbrough swept a gaze over Sirena. "I see Madame's hand in your gown. That shade of blue is very becoming."

Sirena smiled. "Perry, will you introduce Madame to Lady Jane?"

"Most certainly. Come along, and Barton too. You must see the collection of trims Madame keeps handy."

Sirena waited until they were out of earshot to speak. "You're saying in your polite way that 'tis good I'm rid of the primrose?" She added a chuckle to defuse her impertinence.

"I shall always be honest with my fashion advice. My dear, I meant what I said."

"That you wish me every happiness?"

"Yes, that too. But no, what I mean is, I meant what I said that night at Shaldon House. I believe we shall be fast friends." She lowered her voice. "That past arrangement is truly the past, never to be reopened, and must have no impact on your current and future happiness. We *can* be friends."

Sirena tried to imagine what her husband would say about that. "I'm not being pert, my lady, but have we anything in common besides Bakeley?"

Lady Arbrough smiled. "I do like your pertness. And you like my fashion sense. That is a good place to start. And so, we can be friends. Perhaps not right away, though. We shall give society a cooling off period."

Lady Arbrough curtsied. "I wish you great success with your ball." There was an edge to her voice.

Wistfulness, Sirena decided. Or, perhaps the woman was waggling her way into an invitation, playing to Sirena's understanding of what it meant to stand outside and look in.

The ball was looking to be a very curious affair. Shaldon had somehow secured the attendance of the Prime Minister, a few cabinet ministers, and a duke or two. Lady Arbrough's name hadn't been discussed, but her friends had omitted her, out of consideration to herself, probably.

It took but a second to decide. "You must come. Your invitation has not gone out, but it will. I'll need every friend I can get at this ball. You may whisper to all of your acquaintances that I'm destined to be a fashion leader."

Lady Arbrough's handsome face softened. "You are too kind, Lady Sirena. You may be sure that I'll tell everyone you have exquisite taste. Adieu."

She watched the graceful departure, and wondered if Lady Arbrough's heart still bore a tiny flame for Bakeley. For surely, she hadn't been talking about Sirena's taste in fashion.

Sometime later she plopped into the carriage seat beside Lady Perry, head pounding, and arms sore from lifting them for fittings. "Well, Barton? Did you see everything that you needed today?"

"Yes, my lady. I even had a peek at the back workroom."

"But not the ledgers," Lady Jane said. "I couldn't find those in her office."

Perry's mouth dropped open. "You looked?" She laughed and shook her head.

"I was trying to fetch a sketch I'd seen on her table," Lady Jane said.

"Heavens," Sirena said. "Best not let Madame know. If she wields a dagger like she does a straight pin, we'll all be poked to a quick death."

"Oh, but I wanted that sketch for Barton to copy—which reminds me. Will you drop us at the stationers? Barton needs fresh drawing paper. We'll walk home from there."

"Why should we not all go?" Perry asked. "I know just the place." She leaned out and spoke to the groom.

When they arrived at the shop, Sirena begged off going in. She lay her head back against the squab and watched Barton and Lady Jane hurry in. Perry paused at the shop window, studying the paintings displayed there.

No, she was transfixed by one painting, a large pastoral scene of green hills, trees, and a patch of blue lake. Sirena's lack of training in the fine arts rendered it just pretty, not worthy of stopping an accomplished girl like Perry in her tracks.

Oh, but wasn't her new sister a bit of an odd one? She closed her eyes. And she would never say that to Perry or anyone. Odd she might be, but she had the makings of a true sister.

Days later, across town, Bakeley took a place across from Shaldon at the dining table at the house in Knightsbridge.

Bink, Charley, Kincaid, and Farnsworth had joined them. Kincaid had planned to bring two of his men, burly Scotsmen he'd brought south to protect Bink two years before and never sent home, but they were shadowing his wife on some other errand related to the upcoming ball.

His plan to keep her home was not working.

The Scottish guards were a small comfort, as was the presence of two additional grooms accompanying Sirena's town coach. Shaldon's men were never just normal grooms and footmen. Hell, even some of the maids had been pressed from the families of his operatives, and paid well. Bakeley knew because he'd followed his lordships hiring instructions and seen to the wages these many years.

He'd had to bring in more servants this year, all well screened. But new, and Sirena's questions a few nights earlier nagged at him.

The newness worried him.

"What of Donegal?" Shaldon interrupted his thoughts.

Farnsworth tapped the table. "He's not been seen since the O'Brians set the meeting with Lady Sirena."

"Has he set sail?" Bakeley asked.

"Not under that name, anyway. We've checked all the lists. We've had our people about in the taverns and gin houses."

"How did the O'Brians find him the first time?" Bink asked.

"He made the first contact with them," Kincaid said, "after he heard they were asking about the Glenmorrow traitor."

"I would bet he was somewhere at the docks when she was attacked, watching for a trap." Bakeley drummed his fingers on the table. "I wonder if he's someone she might actually know."

"A Donegal man? We never settled he was actually from Ireland," Farnsworth said.

"Did you send the O'Brians to London after Sirena?" Bink asked.

Shaldon looked at Farnsworth, communicating permission to speak in that silent way he had.

"No. The O'Brians were already here. Her meeting them was pure chance. Sometimes, pure chance does happen."

Bink exchanged a glance with him. "That's true enough in battle. But where our father is concerned, I'm not a great believer in pure chance."

Charley smirked. Shaldon's lips firmed.

"For the love of God," Kincaid said. "They at first withheld from us their contact with her, did they not, Farnsworth?"

"Yes. She'd been kind to them and their mother. Turned a blind eye to their poaching on the estate, brought them extra food when times were lean. It's all mixed up when Donegal first made contact with them and how they came to arrange the meeting."

"And we won't be talking to them any day soon," Bink said, sounding smug.

His brother had felt a clear sympathy for the Irishmen.

"Unreliable operatives," Shaldon said.

The O'Brians had left Little Norwick soon after Bink's return to London, and whether they feared Shaldon more or Donegal, Bakeley couldn't guess.

"The fight upon the road unnerved them," Bink said.

"So, perhaps your man will come to the ball also disguised as a musician or a waiter." Charley lolled in his chair. A paternal glare brought him up straight in his seat.

"Then we'll have two rogues to contain," Kincaid said.

"We've sent Hollister the invitation," Bakeley said. "We haven't heard from him yet. His injured men slipped away after the apothecary saw to them." The groom Bakeley had sent, Johnny, had lost sight of them.

"Johnny should have stopped them." Kincaid sighed. "But aye, it's easy enough in a busy innyard to be distracted."

"I spoke to the innkeeper and the apothecary myself," Bink said. "Their descriptions, and what they said of their injuries, makes me believe it was them who attacked me."

Charley leaned forward looking suddenly sober. "So if Hollister sent men to attack you and the O'Brians, why? What possible reason could he have?"

A throbbing started up in Bakeley's head. "He thought Sirena might be on that wagon."

"Or might he have thought they betrayed Donegal?" Bink said. "Is Donegal tied up with Hollister?"

"It's possible," Farnsworth said. "There were four men on that road. One might have been Donegal himself. What came of that business with the sewer, Lord Bakeley? Perhaps it's related."

He shook his head. "Routine stoppage, the men say, cleared away." He was certain of it.

"Now there's a bill for us to work on, Bink," Charley said. "New sewer works. Bakeley, we'll leave it to you to draft for us."

He sent Charley a withering look.

"An anonymous note has been delivered," Bakeley said. "It says that the writer stole a list in my possession that I was planning to deliver to the Irish Secretary upon his arrival in London next week. The writer is taking bids from each member on it, or their family members who wish to avoid the scandal. The highest bidder may proceed to destroy it or conduct his own blackmail as he wishes."

"To recover his own losses." Charley laughed. "That will appeal to any scoundrel. I'll try again tonight to run into him."

"I'll join you," Bakeley said. He'd like to size Hollister up before the man showed up on their doorstep.

"Besides Hollister, who are the other names on the list?" Bink asked.

Shaldon blinked. "The list will be fictitious. When it's written, it will contain only one living man's name. The rest will be Irish nationals who were uncovered and...thwarted."

"Excellent." Charley lolled back again. "And who is Hollister to make contact with?"

"We're here to decide that today," Bakeley said. "We'll send a second missive with instructions. Can we assume he'll have the delivery man followed?"

Kincaid and Farnsworth nodded.

"Very well," Bakeley said. "Let's demand an immediate reply. Then we must decide who'll be the blackmailer."

"Not you or Father, obviously," Charley said. "Not Kincaid—too loyal. No one would believe in his betrayal. Not Farnsworth, since he's not a bosom beau. Not Bink. He's too thick-headed and stubborn to engage in blackmail." Charley's eyes glittered. "It must be me, the scatterbrained youngest son with an expensive mistress and gambling debts. Both are merely gossip, Father. You know I'm gathering information from the lady, who has plenty of money of her own, and I have been assiduously avoiding the tables."

The thought of another brother being placed in danger gave Bakeley pause. "It doesn't necessarily have to be one of us," he said. "It could be one of Father's men, posing as a footman or valet, someone who would have access to my rooms."

"Our footmen are known to be rocks," Charley said. "He would sniff that out immediately."

An ache started up in the back of his head. "The new ones—"

"Were screened, were they not?" Charley asked.

Kincaid cleared his throat. "There is another possibility, if she's willing."

CHAPTER TWENTY-ONE

Bakeley's blood roared. "Not my wife. Not Sirena."

"No, no. I wasn't thinking of her at all."

"*Kincaid.*" Shaldon's tone was a sharp rebuke, but his fellow campaigner was not standing down.

"You can trust your sons, Ned, haven't I told you that?"

Charley sat up, and Bink lifted an eyebrow.

Kincaid stood, palms flat on the table. "The foul-up two years ago endangered Paulette, and it was only Gibson's presence of mind that ensured her safety. Enough. We can trust them."

Shaldon sent Kincaid a dark look, and the other man returned the glare.

Well. Perhaps the hazards of war had made them more equal than mere social position would allow for. In any case, none of the sons of Shaldon had seen Kincaid step out of rank before.

Both Shaldon and Kincaid turned their gazes on him, and it made his skin ripple.

Hot anger pulsed in him. "Not. My. Wife."

"Indeed not," Kincaid said.

Farnsworth followed the discussion, his expression a cipher. Bink frowned. Charley grinned.

A very loud sigh floated across the table from Father.

"We are all men at this table," Kincaid said. "Bakeley, we don't have time to coddle sensibilities."

His every nerve alerted. "Sensibilities?"

Kincaid ignored him. "Some years ago, quite a few actually, there was a suspicion about some of the equipment being supplied to the army. Great profits were being made, and not all of the shipments were arriving intact. We set an agent to see what she could find out about this business."

The pulse in Bakeley's ear began to pound louder, sending a pain just above his right eye to join the ache in his neck. He eased in a breath. "Lady Arbrough."

"Indeed." Kincaid nodded.

Had his father set her to spy upon his heir? Had all his careful pursuit of the untouchable Lady Arbrough and her unexpected capitulation been a ruse? She'd had no lovers in the two years since her husband's death.

That question would be asked later. "The whole world knows we've broken off. I wouldn't insult my wife by having anyone believe otherwise. Hollister will do his snooping and discover Lady Arbrough has no access to my bedchamber."

"He's making excellent points," Shaldon said.

Kincaid waved them all away. "The liaison ended around the time your courtship of Sirena began. One might infer that Lady Arbrough might have had access and seen something on your person that you obtained from Lady Sirena."

"But that something is impossible for her to obtain now. I never entertained her at my townhouse or Shaldon House. Hollister will know she has no access now, not after my marriage."

Kincaid frowned. "You don't know then." He straightened in his chair. "Paulette has said your lady is overwhelmed by the preparations for this ball."

"Bakeley."

He turned at Bink's voice. "Paulette spent the evening yesterday helping the ladies with the final invitations. Sirena insisted on inviting Lady Arbrough to the ball."

He eased in a breath and picked a spot of lint off of his coat. "Well, then. Lady Sirena knows I feel nothing but friendship toward the lady."

What a lie that was. He was livid. He would like to throttle Jocelyn for weaseling her way into their wedding ball. "And I would not care to see her life endangered."

Except by him, while he was throttling her.

"As I recall, she was quite adept," Farnsworth said. "Do you believe she has retained her skills?"

"The question is, will she be willing?" Kincaid said. "Shall I undertake to speak with her, or will one of you?"

"Not Shaldon," Farnsworth said. "She hasn't forgiven you quite yet for accusing her of double-dealing."

Shaldon cleared his throat and sent a menacing look toward the two men.

So Shaldon wouldn't have set her upon him, but perhaps she'd set herself in his path so she could wreak revenge on his father.

Much like his wife had done. A tingle crept up his spine.

And anger reared anew in him. Until two years ago he'd been a man, competent, able, and in control of an empire. Now he had tingles and headaches.

Bakeley glared back. "I'll speak to her. That will support the story, will it not?"

"Can we trust her?" Charley asked.

"Excellent question, Charley. You are not as drunk as I thought you were. Can we, Father?"

Shaldon's eyes narrowed on him. "Yes, I believe we can."

"Very well. I'll engage to speak to her." And he would speak to his father later, privately, to spare the old man's *sensibilities*. "Now, let us get down to the specifics of our plan."

Later, as they left the meeting, Bink pulled Bakeley aside.

"It's a bad business, this," Bink said. "I'll go with you to talk to her."

The last person he wanted with him when he talked to Lady Arbrough was one of his brothers. "Not necessary," he said. "And I'm not visiting her at her home."

"What about your wife's feelings?" The steely-eyed glare reminded him of the one Bink had delivered the day they rescued Sirena. Defender of women and children, was his brother.

"What about them? Did you not tell me she insisted on inviting my former mistress to her wedding ball?"

Bink shook his head. "It did seem a bit too fashionable."

Bakeley climbed into the unmarked coach where Shaldon already waited. Perhaps he should rejoice his wife was so open-minded.

Outside the coach, Bink hesitated. Charley and Kincaid had already ridden off on their mounts. "I'll hail a hackney."

"We're going your way," Shaldon said.

"You'll want to talk." He pushed the door closed and the coach drove off.

"Well, Father. We're alone. If I'm to recruit Lady Arbrough, I'll need to hear all about her escapades."

His father sighed expressively.

"If you swoon, do not expect me to catch you."

"Ungrateful pup." Shaldon smiled and then laughed.

Sirena woke before dawn to the sound of a door closing. Her second day here, she and the housekeeper had come to terms, and Jenny now had a proper bed. This night, it had been herself falling asleep on her chaise longue, waiting for Bakeley. She sat up, watching the connecting door and anticipating his warmth, her heart sinking lower with each passing minute.

Finally, she rose, dressed in her old work gown, and went below stairs, surprising a yawning maid who was stirring the kitchen fire.

In the mews, a lone stable boy roused at her passing and pulled at his cap. She waved him back to his doze, and looked down the aisle at the empty stalls.

The brickwork looked dry to her. Why was he keeping the horses away?

A familiar snort drew her.

Lightning turned his great gray nose to her and sudden moisture flooded her, along with the memory of the first time she'd seen Bakeley so many years before.

"Sure, and you *are* Pooka's," she whispered, rubbing the spots. "The same markings. The same spark."

He nosed her skirts and she laughed. "And the same sneaky appetite."

Selfish of her to not stop for a carrot.

"What then, my fine boy?" she asked, patting his side. "Where was your master last night?"

The stable boy came carrying buckets of water, leaving one in Lightning's stall.

She found a curry comb and began stroking, the *whisk-whisk* of it calming her.

For the first time in their brief marriage, her husband had not shared her bed.

She knew why. He'd learned about Lady Arbrough. No one had told her, but no one had to. In this great house, for all Shaldon's secretiveness, everyone had a sense of what all the rest were doing. And Bakeley was angry.

Men liked to be in control. If a wife and a mistress were friendly, well, how could he work them against each other?

Her heart felt like she'd breathed in a load of shot. She'd thought to be kind. She'd thought to be sensible—this *wasn't* a love match, and he being a great, wealthy, handsome man, sooner or later he'd have a woman on the side. Great or lowly, men were gullible creatures where the fair sex was concerned, and it was how it was done.

The ache in her chest rose into her throat, and to chase it away she began to croon a song her mother had sung to her.

Bam.

The gelding shied and snorted.

Bam. The pounding had come from another stall.

"You're not alone then, my boy? And who is that ill-tempered neighbor?"

When she went to investigate, a dark head eyed her, lips pulling back to bare a full set of yellowing teeth.

"Be careful, my lady." The stable boy, a sandy-haired fellow as slight as herself, stepped out of a shadow. "A mean one is this one. His lordship just brought her in."

"Is she now?" She held the horse's curious gaze. "A challenge you will be, will you? Has my wee lullaby discomfited you? Is my singing so bad?"

The boy chuckled.

"Or are we a jealous one?" Sirena said. "Well then, you shall have our attention." She edged closer. "Come on then. Let's have a discussion."

Bakeley was buttoning his waistcoat when he finally heard a stirring in Sirena's chamber. A night spent with Charley—and without Sirena—left him irritated and cross. He'd done far more hopping from club to gaming hell than he had in years, trying to run into Sterling Hollister.

Hollister had moved into rooms, but apparently, he'd not yet settled fully into the club life. That would change—a man looking to make his way in politics would have to show his face socially. He'd not yet accepted his invitation to the Shaldon ball, either—though the landlord at the inn said he'd delivered it himself.

Bakeley had arrived home with nothing but an extra ill-tempered horse that he'd won in a card game, and he was too damned snarly himself to wake up his wife for a tupping.

Nor did he want to be questioned in bed about his plans for the day when he was groggy and half out of his mind with lust. Though now...

He went to the connecting door, tapped gently, and opened it. A maid looked up from her dusting and quickly curtsied.

Disappointment ramped up his irritation. He'd slept through Sirena's rising, and she hadn't come in to wake him.

"Where is Lady Sirena?" he asked.

"I don't know, my lord. I haven't seen her."

Unease rippled through him, remembering her morning jaunts when she lived with Lady Jane.

He hurried downstairs.

Perry sat alone in the breakfast room studying the scandal sheets. "They're not mentioning you and Sirena today," she said by way of greeting.

He helped himself to some tea. "Wonderful. Where is she?"

Perry pushed her spectacles higher and studied him. "Not still in bed?"

The note of surprise and concern, as though her romantic conceptions had been upended, ruffled him more.

And then more worry reared in him.

"She hasn't come down," Perry said. "That I know of. She wasn't in the morning room."

"Are the men at work in the ballroom?" Perry had concocted the harebrained scheme of commissioning an elaborate chalk drawing to cover the dance floor.

"I don't know. Perhaps she went to check on it, though I made her promise not to peek."

He trudged to the ballroom and stopped on the threshold. The gray light outside barely touched the floor, but what he could see was an intricate design of horses, mythological figures, and Celtic signs.

His sister had found an artist to come up with the design very quickly, and paid him—*him*, who the devil was *he*?—out of her own money. He should question her about the man and how she'd learned of him, but this business with Donegal...

He sighed. The fanciful floor art would awe the *ton*, and surprisingly, it would be ready in time. All looked complete, except for a corner where a lone man worked away without looking up.

Bakeley retraced his steps and went downstairs, catching Lloyd, the butler, supervising the cleaning of silver. Lloyd had served the family well, since before Bakeley could remember, and made a point of knowing all the comings and goings of staff and family.

He didn't disappoint. Bakeley's boots clicked on the bricks as he strode to the mews.

He heard her before he could see her. She was talking, her voice low and soothing in a way that did anything but settle his own disquiet.

He sensed a wedge between them, related to Lady Arbrough perhaps, or—he couldn't imagine what else it could be.

Drat, it could be his own guilty conscience. He was off for a private meeting with Lady Arbrough, and perhaps Sirena had discovered it the same way he'd discovered she'd invited his former mistress to her wedding ball.

"Get Lightning saddled."

The groom saluted.

"Handsome, you are." Sirena's voice came from a stall further down, and a sliver of jealousy stirred in him.

He peered into the gelding's quarters and the lonely horse cast him a baleful look. Another jealous male.

"'Tis the new horse she's with, my lord," the groom said.

Alarm must have shown on his face because the young man shook his head. "Softened up like butter, she did. Her ladyship has her in hand."

The girl who whispered to horses.

He approached slowly. In the light of morning, the mare was beautifully built, her black coat sleek over taut muscles.

The horse rolled her eyes and snorted. Sirena's monologue broke off and her hand stilled momentarily.

"Good morning, my lord."

Whisk, whisk, whisk.

The horse noticed the absence of speech and glanced back at her.

"Having a nice conversation, we are." She didn't look at either of them.

She'd worked with horses all her life, he told himself. She could handle this one—was handling this one.

"You've calmed her."

"I'm glad you've brought two of the horses back. This one I don't know." She smoothed her hand down the horse's shoulder. "Does she have a name?"

"Not as I know."

"Banshee would do," she said. "She's a flighty, complaining one. You have a devil in you, do you not, my girl?"

"Yes, indeed she does. I won her at cards last night from a fellow who was pockets to let and happy to be rid of her. As I will be when I can get her over to Tattersalls."

She paused again and still wouldn't look at him. "I should like you to keep her."

"And I should like you to leave her to one of the grooms. In fact, I'm wondering why my wife, who has a grand ball to host in a day, is in the stable brushing a wild mare who won't be ridden."

Her hand paused again, and he saw a tremble. "I've barely touched a horse in so many months. Will you take this away from me then?"

The catch in her voice sent a wave of guilt washing over him.

But she was his to protect. "Sirena, this horse is dangerous. You know this."

"Aye." She made another pass with the comb and turned to him, cheeks pink and eyes glowing. "I don't need a gentle, safe beast. There'd be no challenge to that."

He blinked. A gentle, safe beast. A boring husband.

"And I will ride her one day," Sirena said. "She and I are coming to an agreement about it." She patted the horse's neck. "Though she knows we likely can't be together every day as I'd wish."

Jealousy flared in him and he pushed it back immediately. This was a horse. *A horse*, not a man she was talking about.

Boring though he might be, she was stuck with him. And he would win her, somehow.

Wisps of hair protruded from the cap she'd pulled on. The horse snorted and nosed her arm, and cold fear ran through him. The beast could snap one of her bones so easily. Behind him he heard the creak of leather as the boy readied Lightning.

"I'll have Pooka brought up from Kent and trained to the side saddle for you."

She threw him a glance. "Sure, and I can manage the side saddle, but astride suits me better."

"Perhaps when we're home at Cransdall. But in town—"

"Do not the grooms take them out early to run in the park?"

Whisk, whisk, whisk.

His wife, riding astride, in London, dressed as a groom, for surely that was what she was planning. And he'd never allow it.

"You could go out of a morning with a groom." She turned a baleful look on him. "That is if you've bothered to come home the night before."

The horse snorted and ducked her head, as if agreeing, and Bakeley fought a smile. Now they were down to it. "I was hunting for Hollister last night," he said, keeping his voice low.

"I see."

"I must go out again. Shall we chat when I come back?"

"If I have time. I'm to be at home today for callers."

"Come away from that horse, love."

"In a bit," she said.

"Now."

"Why?"

"Because I want to kiss you and I'm not sure she'll allow it."

That won him a smile as he'd hoped it would. She patted the horse again, whispered something to her and stepped out of the stall.

He gathered her close.

A snort from the horse and a discreet cough from behind interrupted them. His mount was ready.

"I must go."

"And where is it you're going, Bakeley?"

"James."

"You will be Bakeley until you tell me."

He held his breath. There was no time to smooth this over, should she be upset with his mission, and he couldn't wait for her to change her clothing should she wish to accompany him. "I'm meeting someone who'll help carry out our plot," he whispered.

"And which plot is that?" she asked softly.

CHAPTER TWENTY-TWO

Sirena watched her husband assembling his answer from the bits and pieces of what he was willing to share. Galling it was, and she was a far way toward a hammering anger.

Part of his attention was on the wee horse behind her, and part on the twitchy mount waiting to take him away, and the groom who surely must be trying to eavesdrop.

Kiss her he would, and it would lead to nothing—his mind was not on amorous activities, nor on telling her the truth. What it was on, she wasn't sure, because he wasn't tipping his hand, nor were her fey senses working on him. Had he come to her in the morning—or had she smothered her pride and gone looking for him, she might have coaxed it out of him by her great skills at lovemaking.

For it was the truth—married less than a fortnight, and she'd been pining for him.

And perhaps that was why he'd avoided her bed. Men didn't like a clinging woman, even when they didn't have something to hide.

She must try anyway. She turned her head so their lips were in proximity, and after a moment, little sparks like fairy arrows began to play between them.

He stared down through heavy-lidded eyes, and her heart took a giant leap. This was a kind of power like her mother's and Gram's, and whether he had it over her or the other way around, she didn't know. She didn't care. She touched her lips to his and pressed her breasts into his chest, and the kiss was sweet and then sultry, and then smoking in the tiny gaps of air between them. It hurt to think how much she'd missed him in her bed, and to wonder if he was angry with her or if he even knew they'd had a wee falling out.

She broke the kiss and leaned around him. "Take Lightning outside," she told the groom.

When the boy led the horse off, she looked at Bakeley. "You didn't come to me last night."

"I didn't want to wake you when I came in."

The tenseness round his mouth told her he was skirting a secret. Very well. She'd try to draw it out of him. "That may be, but I think you were angry with me. I think you discovered a...a decision I made and were unhappy."

The glint that flashed told her she was right.

"What decision would that be?"

Anger sparked in her. "Don't play the dunderhead. I'm sure one of your whispering men told you I invited Lady Arbrough to the ball. I saw her at the dress shop and she seemed—well, she hasn't been unkind to me, and I won't be unkind to her."

"You're that confident in me?"

The irritation that laced his tone surprised her.

"You said your arrangement was over, and I believed you. She said the same thing, and I believed her. And no. I don't wish to share you with her, Bakeley." Or anyone else, but of course that was a fairy dream if ever there was one.

She sucked in a great breath and blinked hard. He'd married to spite his father, hadn't he? She'd married to have a roof and to find her brother. "Perry said your father would be shocked, but I don't think there's much will shock him, and I don't think he cares a hare's bottom what the *ton* thinks. Do you care? Or is that why you're upset?"

His eyes clouded and he lifted the comb from her hand. "I'll bring Pooka up for you to ride. But only when I'm around."

The great bloody fool. He was taking charge again.

Or thinking to.

"Very well, then." She forced a smile.

He took her elbow and marched her outside, where she watched him ride off, one of the Shaldon grooms mounted and following him.

And her heart twisted inside. At least he wasn't going off alone. She would count the hours until his return, whether to battle out their disagreement or to make peace, she wasn't sure.

And what battle, really, would they be fighting?

Madame La Fanelle herself, serene, and tight-lipped, and exquisitely polite, opened the shop door for Bakeley and ushered him in.

He would have to pursue his investment in Barton's enterprise more aggressively.

Madame curtsied. "This way. She waits in my office, as you requested."

He followed her down a narrow corridor to a small cluttered room.

Jocelyn sat at a desk, thumbing through fashion plates. The gaze she lifted to him was coldly amused.

Damnation. He had the ire of three women on him this morning.

He bowed. "I do apologize. Thank you for waiting."

"I hope it was due to pleasant reasons."

The insinuation was clear, but he would be damned if he'd give her intimate details of his married life.

"The wedding ball is requiring more preparations than anyone expected."

She smiled back tightly. "I'll decline the invitation if you wish."

He took Madame's chair behind the desk and looked around, wondering at the contents of this room. There were drawings and fashion plates, ribbons and trims, scraps of fabric and measuring tapes, but no lists of ordered ribbons and trims and textiles, no accounting books, no delivery schedules. Madame might bring clients here but her real work was done elsewhere.

How private it was, he wasn't sure. He lowered his voice. "My only consideration would be my new wife's feelings, but since she wishes you to come, that consideration is moot."

She blinked and he could not tell if she was hiding some sadness or plotting some mischief.

"Do not fear, Jocelyn. I shall not importune you in that way."

One eyebrow shot up. "In some other way then?" She studied him and laughed. "What are you up to, Bakeley?"

The tension eased, and he settled back as if he was talking to one of his friends at the club and not a woman who'd been in his bed.

"We need your help," he whispered.

"We?"

It was the *we* that had given her pause, not the issue of helping.

"Sirena needs your help."

"With what?"

He thrummed his fingers on the desk. Jocelyn gossiped like everyone else, and Sirena's past was none of the *ton*'s business.

"I won't bandy her secrets about, if that's what has you suddenly tongue-tied."

His face heated. "I must have your word on that. Not for my sake, but hers."

She nodded. "You have it."

He told her about Sterling Hollister's treatment of Sirena.

"So you rescued her from not just poverty, but disgrace should he choose to make the story known." Her voice had softened with a sentimentality he'd never seen in her. "She is safe now. No one can touch her if she is under yours and Shaldon's protection."

"Yes, she has protection, but what we would like for her is—"

"Revenge?"

He paused, remembering the wedding night conversation.

"Justice."

Her face froze and she sat up straighter. "Do not expect me to sleep with the man."

"If he lays but a finger on you, he'll answer to me and my brothers. But I've heard some tales recently that Lady Arbrough is capable of taking care of herself even in matters of combat."

"Have you?" Her dark eyes sparkled. "His lordship has been talking."

"Yes."

"He didn't approve of my marriage. One doesn't marry one's mark, he said. Had he been in town then, I might have exercised those combat capabilities on his person."

"Is that why you agreed to be my—"

"Bakeley. Stop. The possibility of inflicting pain on the old man by toying with his heir sweetened the chase for me, but do not fear that was the only reason I pursued you."

"*You* pursued *me*?"

She waved the question away. "My marriage was practical and friendly, but my husband's health issues... Ah, well, in spite of my services to His Majesty's Government, I went to Arbrough as a maiden and we both did our duty. However, after his death, I wanted to experience...the virility of a handsome young man. And I knew you would be safe. Sensible."

"Safe and sensible." His jaw ached with clenching it. Why not add *boring*.

"Safe and sensible with me, a woman you didn't love, and would never love. That is a compliment, Bakeley. I am sure you are reckless and feckless with Lady Sirena, which is how it must be when a man is head over ears with a woman. It's good you came to me to help her achieve justice. What is it you'd have me do?"

He was head over ears in love with Sirena?

He scratched a spot on his jaw that he'd missed with his hurried shaving.

Love? Was that what this was?

Lady Arbrough laughed. "Clever girl. The seduction has not all been one way, I see. Now, I have another engagement this morning, so if there's something you wish—"

"Yes." He blinked away the muddling thoughts—Jocelyn pursuing him, Sirena seducing him. "Yes, there is something I wish."

A while later Bakeley rose to escort Lady Arbrough out.

"Go ahead, Bakeley. I shall find my own way. It's not wise for us to be seen together."

"Perhaps." He took her hand and tucked it under his arm. "But come. Let us brave Madame together."

They'd talked long enough that the modiste had opened her shop to at least one customer, a plainly dressed lady, a maid surely, who she chatted with at the ribbon counter.

Madame left her and hurried to the rich viscount and wealthy widow. "May I help you with anything else, my lord, my lady?"

Just then the dark figure at the counter turned and shock spread across the maid's face.

Bakeley's breath froze. It was Barton, his future business partner.

He nodded to her and turned back to Madame. "Thank you for allowing us the use of your office." Then he bowed to Lady Arbrough. "Good day, my lady."

As he trotted down the steps and called for his horse, he calculated how long his next business with his father would take, and how long it would take Barton to return to Shaldon House.

An unmarked carriage waited a few doors down, for Jocelyn perhaps, though the rig must be a new one. The Shaldon coach was not around. Barton must have come alone and walked.

Blast it, he needed to get home to Sirena before Barton reached her with the tale.

*****

Sirena washed and breakfasted in her chamber. Lady Jane and Barton had gone out on errands, so she'd have to fend off visitors with no more than the aid of Lady Perry.

In no hurry to meet callers, she let Jenny help her into one of her new gowns and dress her hair in an elaborate, time-consuming coif of small braids and curls.

She eyed herself in the looking glass. "Put a daisy chain around my neck, and I'll look like the pony for the May crowning cart."

Jenny's lips firmed, and Sirena touched the girl's hand.

"Oh, this mouth of mine—don't be offended. It's lovely, it is, Jenny. You've a knack for turning me into a thing of beauty. It's only that I'm not used to it."

"You didn't 'ave a maid at 'ome?"

"Not one so skilled as you."

There. That had brought a smile.

"I took no offense, my lady. I should like it if ye be honest, and if it be that you don't like the 'air, or the dress, you must tell me. I'm not really Mrs. Gibson's lady's maid, you know."

"No?" Even so, surely Paulette would be wanting her back, wouldn't she? She drew the girl to the settee and sat next to her. "We haven't talked about this." She hadn't even thought about it. It had been selfish of her. "I've ever so much appreciated your help. If Paulette would allow it, and if you would be willing, would you stay with me? As my lady's maid?"

Jenny flashed a smile and then her brow wrinkled. "I'll ask her. She 'elped me out, she did. And, you should ask after me, what my background is, my lady. It's the way of it."

"All right then. Where are you from, Jenny?"

"From Seven Dials, madam. Lady 'Ackwell took me to live with her when she was still Miss 'Arris. And then I went to the 'ome in the country. And then she took me into service. And then..."

She stood and gripped her hands together. "I was attacked by the valet of one of the guests, and Miss Paulette insisted I leave with 'er."

"Attacked? At the home of Lord Hackwell?" Sirena could not keep the shock from her voice.

She nodded. "It wasn't 'is lordship's fault. 'Is lordship and Mr. Gibson stopped 'im, and locked 'im up, but his master got 'im released and 'e chased after us on the road."

Panic flickered within her. It was the thing she herself had feared that day running from her cousin. "He came after you?" She heard her own breathlessness.

Jenny shook her head. "It was Mrs. Gibson 'e was after. Mr. Kincaid chased 'im over a cliff. The man broke 'is neck and died."

Why was he after Paulette? She bit back the question. She wouldn't begin Jenny's service with gossiping. She would rather hear the answer from her husband, if he knew, and if he'd tell her. She couldn't ask Paulette until they'd become much better acquainted.

But, blast it, she *needed* to know. "If it's in the nature of gossip, you need not speak of it, Jenny, but I know so little of this family I've joined."

"The man's master spied for the French, and Paulette's father spied for the English. It went back to that, and Lord Shaldon trying to catch 'im up so he could be arrested."

"I see." She did. And now Shaldon was after another spy, the man Donegal, as well as Sterling Hollister. Someday she'd like to hear Paulette's side of the story. There would be a someday. If Hollister or Donegal didn't murder her.

The thought left her shaken. After a moment, she noticed Jenny's intense gaze.

She plastered on a smile and rose. "We shall talk to Mrs. Gibson. If she's agreeable, and you're willing, I should like to hire you."

Leaving Jenny all aglow, she went downstairs. A footman stopped her by the stairs and said the artist needed to speak with someone and he couldn't find Lady Perpetua.

At the ballroom door she paused, and let her heart fill with the pleasure.

It was a guilty pleasure, since she'd promised Perry she wouldn't have an early peek at this special gift.

It was a mad idea, this plan to chalk a drawing on the floor. It seemed daft in any space of time, but certainly so in less than one week.

At the first sight of it, her heart lifted. Spring burst upon the floor. Horses pranced about in a field of fanciful shamrocks and blossoming flowers.

In the far corner, a man was on his knees, a white-haired man standing over him. She recognized the older one as Old Nate, the man Perry said they called when there were walls to be painted or paper to be hung, or in this case, floors to be chalked.

He looked up and came to greet her, limping. Ah, so that was why he'd hired others for a kneeling task.

"Does it please you, my lady?" he asked.

"'Tis a marvel, it is. It seems a pity to dance upon it."

The dancing would erase the design. This truly would be fleeting beauty, like her brief honeymoon with Bakeley.

He nodded in agreement, and her heart hurt a bit more.

She pulled herself together. "And 'tis also a marvel that you've finished it in less than seven days. Even the Lord's creation could not proceed so quickly."

He smiled at that. "I need to ask about that, my lady. To complete the last part, my man here will need to work quite late tonight, perhaps through the night, as you will want him done before the flowers and the candles are arranged."

"Only one man? Cannot you send the others to help?"

"'Tis a special design he's adding to the corners, and he's faster than the others."

She craned her neck but could not see the drawing. Nor did the man look up. From here he seemed a man of middle age, fair-haired and built more for strength than for art, though his hand worked away. His attire was clean, his boot soles sturdy with no signs of holes. He seemed an entirely respectable working man.

Someone on Shaldon's staff could keep an eye on him. "Very well. I'll send along the butler to make the arrangements."

The man looked up then, and her breath quickened.

"But first, I'll just have a wee look at what he's doing."

She raised her hem and tiptoed along the wall, careful to step over the chalked lines. Her pulse built and clanged, stirring up memories from the deepest parts of her confused mind. The artist pushed up to his feet, and she could see, he was quite tall, his handsome face scarred on one side, from cheek to jaw. Blue eyes studied her with too much interest.

Had Jamie's eyes been that blue? Where, oh, where were her fey senses now?

She stopped outside his reach and angled her head to view the work.

'Tis Queen Brighid's quaternary Celtic knot, Sirena. Can you say it for me?

Her eyes started to fill. The outline on the floor was clear, and the man so like, but she couldn't be certain. She'd been but a child when Jamie left.

She took a breath and glanced back at the overseer who'd followed her. "Please go and find Lloyd. Tell him your request and that we've talked."

The old man nodded and left.

"And a good day to you, my lady."

Her nerves jangled more.

"And what would be your name?" she asked. "Donegal?"

His smile seemed kind, and she saw that a tooth was chipped. Kind or not, he'd had a violent life.

"It's as good an Irish name as anything to call me, Lady Sirena."

She swallowed the tears that threatened to form. *He knew her name.* Was this Donegal, or was it...him?

The quaternary cross—it must be him, and not some wishful thinking.

Except...Perry had spotted Gram's good luck charm in Sirena's room and asked to borrow it. She must have drawn the design for the artist.

Or perhaps, this was the man Donegal, and he'd seen Gram's charm round Jamie's neck before he'd murdered him.

Or tried to. She must keep faith that Jamie lived. And she must test this one.

"Why didn't you come forth to talk to me?" she asked.

"I could not. An Irishman can't be too careful, innocent though he be. I think you know that."

The words sent a chill through her. Did she know that?

And if he wasn't innocent, a traitor had found his way into Shaldon's abode.

He looked over her shoulder and then she heard the soft footfalls.

"What are you doing here, Sirena? It was to be a surprise."

"Keep my secret, I beg you, my lady."

She still wanted answers. "We shall talk later," she whispered and then said more loudly, "I'll leave you to go back to your work, sir."

He bowed and went back to his chalking.

Sirena caught up with Perry near the door and hustled her out. Whether Perry knew about the search for Donegal, she didn't know. She didn't want to inspire a visit from Shaldon, not yet, not until she'd had a chance to ask questions of her own. If her husband could keep secrets, so could she.

"I'm sorry. It was temptation's evil bite that made me do it. I just had to see."

"You were talking to that man."

Aye, Perry was Shaldon's daughter. She would need to tread carefully. "I interrupted him and he was being polite only. I don't even know his name. I was not being unfaithful to Bakeley."

That brought a smile.

"Old Nate said he's called Desmond. Come," Perry said. "I heard the front knocker moments ago. We'll have a visitor."

Her mind was jumbled with thoughts of the artist in that room and the earlier spat with her new husband. She needed to find out Bakeley's plan. She needed to find her way back to the ballroom and see what the man there was plotting.

And now to be poked and prodded by visitors coming to see Bakeley's scandalous new bride while she was tossed and scattered on the inside. It was a trial, it was.

She straightened her skirts. "Will I do?"

Perry squared her shoulders and lifted her chin. "Like this."

A laugh bubbled out and Perry joined in, linking arms. "Don't worry, Sirena."

In the corridor, a footman stopped them with news that the florist had come with the racks and vases for the next night's ball.

Sirena saw Perry's consternation. Perry was one to keep a firm grip on all phases of the planning, so much like her father and Bakeley.

"Go, Perry, and see to it. I shall brave this tiresome visitor alone."

"Are you sure? Oh, you'll be fine. It may be Lady Hackwell. She did say she would visit."

Outside the drawing room a footman handed her a salver with a card.

Her heart sank all the way to the leather heels of her new shoes and then rose again sweeping up every morsel of anger in her. Her hand shook with it, her lungs squeezing tight.

"Just the one caller, my lady."

She eased in a breath. The footman watched the door to the drawing room. And though his gaze had not lighted directly upon her once, she sensed he'd seen her discontent.

That wasn't good. She was supposed to play an English lady, not an Irish milkmaid. She set her face and entered.

The door, she noted, did not *snick* closed behind her and some of her tension eased. The footman was keeping watch.

Across the room, Sterling Hollister studied a fine piece of Sevres porcelain on the mantel. Wide shoulders, narrow hips, dark hair. It could have been Bakeley, but there was so much more true strength in her husband.

The oiled hinges of Shaldon House did not creak, nor did her heels clack on the polished floor, yet Hollister turned.

She stopped a few paces inside the door and curtsied. "Lord Glenmorrow."

He approached, too eagerly she thought, and came close enough to bow over the hand she put out to keep him away.

"Cousin Sirena." His beady eyes traveled up and down her person too boldly. "I must congratulate you on your marriage. You've done well for yourself."

"Won't you be seated?" She went to a narrow chair within view of that open door and waited for him to choose the more comfortable armchair. Instead, he pulled another chair from the round table and placed it near her.

Anxiety locked her knees together and an ache started in the back of her neck. "It is kind of you to visit," she lied. "Bakeley and I hope you have received the invitation to our ball tomorrow night and are planning to celebrate with us."

He smiled that oily smile that had preceded his first hint of an offer so many months ago. It took all her strength of will to keep her fists unfurled.

"Ah, so your husband is the generous sort and does not mind."

Her breath caught. Bakeley minded plenty, but his plans, she did not know, and that spiked a bit of anger.

And just how was she to respond?

He reached across and touched her hand. "You did not tell him." That smile grew more sinister. "Well, it shall be our secret."

She pulled her hand away, rose, and moved behind the chair. "I have no secrets from my husband."

Well, except for the man who was, even now, working away on the ballroom floor.

A thought flashed to run and get *him*, but she quickly tossed it away. Shaldon would only arrest him, before she could truly speak with him on her own.

"But Bakeley understands you are my only living relative."

He was on his feet again, moving closer, frowning. "What have you told him, Sirena?" He put a hand on her arm, his grip too tight.

Footsteps sounded in the hall. He dropped her arm and moved away.

I told him everything, she wanted to shout. Yet the truth might keep him away, and it might be essential for Hollister to attend the ball. If only she knew the plans.

"Do not worry," she said. "My husband is a sensible man."

The footsteps were drawing closer. "Not *so* sensible. He married *you*," he whispered.

"Lord Glenmorrow." The voice boomed across the room and her heart lifted. Bakeley entered, all stone-faced courtesy, and behind him was the Earl of Shaldon himself.

The gentlemen exchanged stiff greetings, and Bakeley made a show of kissing her warmly on the cheek. The way his dark eyes glittered, he was riled, yet she doubted Hollister could see it.

She smiled at the new arrivals. "Father, Bakeley, I am honored that you have come in time to meet my cousin."

Bakeley noted the tension in her. How could he not—it rolled off her in great waves. The ass had insulted her, or threatened her somehow.

Thank God, they'd made it in time. When Lloyd saw the visitor's card, he'd sent a footman running to get Bakeley who'd just picked up his father. Bakeley wanted to drive a fist into Hollister's smirking mouth, or put a sharp crease in his arse with the toe of his boot.

He leaned in to drop a kiss on her other cheek. "The footman said Perry deserted you." *And what were you doing alone with this man?* He led her to a settee and plopped next to her.

"Perry's gone to check a delivery. There's much to-do in setting up a ball, husband." She curved her lips up again in that approximation of a smile and he squeezed her hand, battling the rage that was threatening to choke him.

His father laid his cane upon a table—within reach of his hand—and settled into a large armchair. "Sit, Glenmorrow. Tell us, will we see you at this ball? My daughters tell me all the best are coming."

"I will be honored to attend, my lord."

"Though I don't recall that you and I have met before, I knew your brother."

"His death was a great loss." Hollister dipped his head sorrowfully.

A great loss to him, since he is dead. Bakeley felt Sirena's hand jump under his grip and he relaxed his hold.

Father's eyes tightened. "So you're Glenmorrow now, and yet I hear you're entering the Commons."

"Indeed. Happy to serve king and country."

Shaldon nodded. "Tell me, how do you find London?"

The conversation that followed diverted Hollister, yet Bakeley could see the man bending one ear to eavesdrop on them. Best to make the most of that.

He stroked the back of her hand with his thumb. "Have I told you today how lovely you look? That dress is very becoming."

"Thank you. Did your morning's business go as expected?"

"Yes, it did. And how was your morning?"

"Delightful. Your head groom—"

"Our head groom."

Her face broke into a smile, some of the tension easing. "Yes, oh, thank you. He does seem a competent man. Well, and we were discussing taking the new mare up to Cransdall a little later in the spring and see how her temper fares. Plus, 'twill be the proper time for most of the mares, he said, perhaps her also. Spirited she is, but your man thinks she'll do well, Bakeley, and so do I."

Hollister broke mid-sentence and turned his head their way. "You mean to allow her to take an active hand with your equine business?"

Bakeley gripped Sirena's trembling hand and channeled his own anger into cold boredom, or at least tried. It would be his sincerest pleasure to wrench the Glenmorrow title from this wretch. He managed a smile. "What say you, Father?"

Shaldon answered with his own rare smile. "The world is not aware, Glenmorrow, that it was Lady Shaldon who managed that enterprise, most ably, I may say, and Bakeley here after her. I heard tell you had that mad horse eating out of your hand today, daughter."

Her mouth softened and she blinked, eyes shining. "She reminds me of one my father's more recent mares and two of her foals. Have you sold all of the horses, Lord Glenmorrow?"

"I fear that I had to."

"Yes." She nodded. "That was probably wise. Especially if you won't be there to manage."

Perry came in then, followed by Lady Hackwell and two other ladies of their acquaintance, and Hollister took his leave.

While Shaldon made polite conversation with the ladies, Bakeley drew Sirena aside. "Good God, Sirena. After I picked up Father, Lloyd had sent a footman to tell us Hollister was here. But now we must leave. I'll explain everything later."

"Will you be back by dinner?"

"Yes, of course."

"You weren't back yesterday."

"I'm sorry. I told you, I was out with Charley, trying to run into that ass."

"And where are you off to now?"

"I'm off with Father for another meeting. All is shaping up. We'll talk tonight."

She frowned, studying him. "Will we then?"

He towed her out into the hall into a dim corner and locked her against him.

"Yes," he said, bending in close. "We'll make up for last night. And here's the proof of my good faith." He tugged her closer and kissed her until both of them were out of breath.

"There. Now, please trust me."

Her glassy-eyed look cleared and darkened. "I'm to go on kisses and good faith, then? And share information later?"

He heard Shaldon's voice speaking with the footman, and he stepped back, cupping her shoulders. "Yes. Keep the ladies nearby."

"Very well then, Bakeley."

Minutes later Shaldon sat frowning at him from the front-facing seat of the coach. "What do you suppose Hollister told Sirena before we arrived?" Shaldon asked.

Bakeley glanced out the window, his nerves prickling. *And we'll share information later?* All he'd been able to think about was comforting her, protecting her, kissing her. He'd not thought to ask her what she'd learned.

And, good God, he'd not taken the opportunity to talk to her about Jocelyn before Barton got to her.

He swiped a hand through his hair. "I don't know."

A long silence followed, and finally Shaldon spoke. "We shall fix him, my son."

He let out a long breath. "Indeed we shall, Father. And where are we going today?"

"Today we visit the Home Office."

And, he prayed, they'd make quick work of it.

Sirena picked her way through the dinner courses, barely listening to Perry and Lady Jane as they discussed the preparations for the ball.

"I suppose we should have a look," Perry said. "What do you think, Sirena?"

She lifted her gaze from her plate and sighed. "It's sorry I am. My thoughts were diverted by this excellent cheese."

Lady Jane reached over and patted her hand. "Bakeley is out on Lord Shaldon's business, else he would be home."

She hated to admit it—she *was* worried. Why had he not sent a message, after all his promises? This would make two nights' separation.

Perry smiled and glanced at Lady Jane. "He's completely besotted, so you have no worries. And the matter we were discussing was the floor. You've already snooped on my surprise, so we might as well all go and have a look at it. The artist is at work, I hear, and if we bring these candles we'll have enough light. And I know you're finished since you stopped eating at the first course."

Her hands tingled. She wanted more than anything to get into that ballroom and speak to the man at work there.

But if Perry was suspicious—no. He could stand in the shadows while they perused the art, and she would divert her friends. She would go back later and speak privately with this man who might know where Jamie was. Irish traitor, radical, what did she care? In Shaldon's home, there were plenty of servants to protect her.

She rose, took a sconce of candles, and followed Perry.

As they rounded a corner, the footman straightened up from his tired slouch.

"How goes it, Phillip?" Perry asked. "Did you draw the short stick over one of the new men?

"He's still at work, my lady," he said. "Lloyd wanted one of the old staff here, so I offered."

The doors to the ballroom were open, the light pooling in another corner of the room where a figure knelt.

In the dim light, the designs were mere lines and sweeps of shadings.

"The chandeliers and girandoles will brighten this entire room, you will see." Perry had read her concern, as usual. She was a cagey one.

Perry held out her branch of candles and Lady Jane peered closer. "Oh, I do see."

"It *was* beautiful in the daylight," Sirena said.

"However will they ready the chandeliers?" Lady Jane tiptoed around a white horse in full gallop and paused to study the dark center of the ceiling.

Sirena traced her path and sucked in a sharp breath. It wasn't a white horse galloping through the ballroom—'Twas a white unicorn, its yellow horn catching a glint of the candle flame. Had she had her hands free, she would have clapped them together and shrieked.

The artist had come to his feet and was waiting for them. He stood in front of his lamp, casting his own face in shadows.

"We've come to inspect your work." Perry advanced on him, her candles lighting his face. She stopped a good several feet away. "What is that you're working on there?"

Sirena's pulse quickened. Perry's voice crackled with an edge that said something had gone amiss.

"It is a special Irish design, your ladyship. As you requested."

The smug tone of those otherwise servile words, the lack of his earlier accent, sent the pounding of her heart higher into her ears.

"And quite a lovely one." Perry angled her head only slightly to call over her shoulder. "Will you tell us what it means, Sirena?"

An ache started in her chest and swelled into her throat.

Tell us then, wee Sirena. Tell us the story of the four points of this knot.

'Tis the four seasons, winter, spring, summer, and autumn, Jamie.

No, 'tis not that. Now tell us, iora.

'Tis east, west, north and south.

No.

The four gospels then.

Bah, you leave it again to me to tell, Sirena. Is it not then the sign of Brighid—hand, hearth, head and heart? Brighid, Queen of the Four Fires, Goddess of heaven, bringer of light, ruler of birth and new beginnings.

She eased in a breath and steadied her voice. "It is for you to tell, sir, what the design means."

He shook his head, eying her warily. "It is Irish, connected to some legend or other. I was given it to draw by the master."

Was this then the same man she'd spoken with today? Aye, the scar still carved a path down his cheek, his tooth was still chipped, but the way his mouth firmed sharpened the pain in her chest. Jamie's face had never been so hard. This was Donegal, and there was no softness in him.

"Come then," Perry said, "we hold the Irish in some esteem in this house. You must have some idea of the meaning."

He rubbed at his jaw, streaking it the white of the chalk. "Well then, 'tis a symbol of luck. A fancied-up, four-leaf clover."

Sirena's heart fell. The dark room seemed to swallow the light, and fear filled her as it had that day at the docks. Though this was but one man, the odds seemed much worse than that day. And she couldn't let Perry or Lady Jane be hurt.

She made herself chuckle. "And 'tis luck we will be needing to get everything ready in time for the ball. Best let him get back to his work. Will you be much later then, sir? It appears you're finished."

"I'm touching up where needed. It will be a while longer."

"Very well then." Perry herded them toward the doors.

Outside the room, while Perry spoke with the footman, Lady Jane linked arms with Sirena. *Oy*, but she was dying to hear what Perry was saying, impossible with Lady Jane drawing her attention away.

The three went up together, parting ways with Perry at her bedchamber door. Sirena escorted her former benefactor to her room, bade her goodnight, and went back down the stairs, a sick rage building within her.

The library, she had noted, was often Shaldon's last stop of the day. She would wait there for him, and for Bakeley. As much as she hated to admit it, she needed their help. Lady Bakeley she was, a weak English thing.

She found the butler and two footmen silently roaming the halls.

She pulled the butler, Lloyd, aside. "What are you doing?"

"We are just making some extra preparations for the ball tomorrow night. Do you not wish to retire, my lady?"

That was a bit cheeky and quite out of character for Lloyd. She looked past his shoulder. "You have extra men in the ballroom?" she whispered.

He blinked.

"That is a capital idea. I shall retire to the library to await my husband." He trailed behind her to the door, and she saw a glint of concern in his weathered face.

"I'll just add more coals to the hearth, my lady." He entered and closed the door behind him.

The butler himself feeding coal. Not the usual sort of servants.

Perhaps she could impose a bit more. "I should very much like it if my husband and his father come home soon. I should send a note, if I but knew the destination. I am not at all at ease tonight."

"Yes, my lady. And perhaps we should send the artist home?"

Send him home? Whoever he was, that would not serve Shaldon and Bakeley's needs, nor, she feared, her own. How had her goals become aligned so much with theirs that she would trap a fellow Irishman in the web of this English spymaster?

Only, perhaps he was not truly her sort of Irishman.

"And incur Lady Perry's disappointment? Let him work. Perhaps an extra footman on the door if any are still awake."

"As you wish." He bowed and left.

At the writing table, Sirena found a sheet of parchment and a pencil. Her hand began to trace the soothing form of the knot. Hand, hearth, head, heart. Every time her brother had come home from school or his travels, he'd told her the tale of it. And if the man in the next room did not know it, he was not Jamie.

She took in a ragged breath. If he was someone sent here to hurt them, Shaldon and Bakeley would take care of him, of that she was certain.

Perhaps being protected was not so bad.

And if he had information about her brother, Shaldon and Bakeley would thrash it out of him.

She squeezed her eyes shut. What had truly happened to her brother? And was he alive or dead?

A breeze ruffled her paper and sparked the fire. The window was open.

Fear galloped through her. She braced her fists on the edge of the desk. Too late, too late.

"You liked my design?"

The man with the scar, the man who was not Jamie, was looking over her shoulder.

CHAPTER TWENTY-THREE

Bakeley clutched the edge of the carriage seat as they turned a sharp corner. "What was the note you received?" he asked.

Across from him, his father remained silent, his face shadowed and unreadable.

His nerves jangled, and frustration gnawed at his empty stomach. "Did it have to do with the missing gunpowder?" Bakeley prodded. "And where the devil are we going, Father? This isn't the way home."

The meeting had been an interminable mix of waiting, talking, and speculating that stretched through the dinner hour. Radicals were gathering. Gunpowder had gone missing from a storehouse. Other matters were discussed, but Bakeley's presence had turned the talk into coded innuendo, each official talking around his own interest. No wonder the common sewers wouldn't work.

Hours into the ghastly event, a note was slipped into Shaldon's hands, and here they were now, headed to God knew where.

"Do you remember Fox?" Father asked.

"The Whig politician?" Charles James Fox was long dead.

"No. The American painter."

His skin crawled with memories and he blinked them away, not that Father could see in the dark. His memories of Fox were all tied up with his father's capture by the French, his own quick trip to Ireland for that hobgoblin horse, and his mother's sudden and tragic death.

"Yes," he said.

"He's come to London also." Father's flat tone belied an undercurrent of emotion, and damned if Bakeley could identify what that emotion was.

He'd soon find out, so he held his peace.

Bakeley set down the tumbler and rubbed his hand on his trousers, then stopped. It was the move of a green schoolboy, and rude to boot. Their host had fallen on hard times, but the drink was good, though the rest of the room was shabby.

He studied the glass again in the dim light of two candles and a smoking lump of coal. Perhaps it wasn't quite as dirty as he'd thought. He lifted it and let the amber liquid warm his throat.

Fox had excellent brandy, but it was a pity he hadn't more coal. The wall of tall windows in this strange little chamber had no covering to keep out the chill late winter wind that seeped through loose seams in the window caulking.

"Fox, you must let me help you." A fatherly kindness warmed Shaldon's words, one that Bakeley did not often hear.

Fox raised bloodshot eyes. Hell, he wasn't much older than Bakeley, but he looked it. His coat was worn, his neck cloth rumpled. Ten years earlier, he'd been better-dressed, healthier.

Ten years earlier, the man had gone from patron to patron, never keeping regular rooms. Now, he lived in this one room and another through a narrow door, left slightly ajar.

They'd startled their host, who was well into his cups. He'd not expected to see such a fast response to his note.

Now Father was dragging his feet. Why?

Bakeley glanced at that open door. "Is there someone else here with you?"

Fox laughed. "So you've grown into Shaldon's son, I see. Go and have a look, Bakeley."

Shaldon nodded. Bakeley took a candle and poked into the adjoining room, one hand upon the pistol in the pocket of the great coat he'd decided not to shed.

The room held a narrow bed and some neatly folded clothing and the acrid odor of paints.

Fox had spent months at Cransdall, painting portraits, a grand one of their mother, and one of the heir, the spare, and Perry together. Then he'd disappeared, shortly before Lady Shaldon's fatal accident. He'd gone to the Continent on the King's business, some whispered. Or he'd gone there to paint.

He ought to have earned enough commissions as a portrait artist to live better than this.

Though, perhaps this wasn't the artist's life. Perhaps this was the spy's life. One could never be sure with his father's acquaintances.

The men murmured in the adjoining room, their voices lowered now that he'd left them.

He raised his candle higher and strained to hear words while he looked around. Canvases lined the wall, a box of oils and brushes propped to keep them from falling.

No work in progress had been set upon an easel in that outer room with its uncovered windows, and he saw no easel here. Bakeley scooted the box with his foot, slid out a canvas, and held the candle close. It was a rough of a landscape, hills stretching in the background, a few scattered trees around a river.

His skin prickled. Fox had sketched out a view from the terrace at Cransdall. The next one was a similar country scene, with the figure of a distant woman, her features indistinguishable except for the spectacles she wore.

When Fox had spent those months at Cransdall, Perry had not worn spectacles.

His hand tightened around the candle holder. Fox had seen Perry, here in London, in person, perhaps in these very lodgings, while Bakeley was too preoccupied with Sirena to look after his sister.

He made a circuit of the room and found a battered round table piled with books. A loosely rolled paper lay on top.

"...Infernal machine...," Fox said, catching Bakeley's attention.

That term snagged at his memory. He shook his head. The rest of their discourse was unintelligible. He would look into it later.

He set down his candle and unfurled the rolled paper. This was a pencil drawing, a fanciful tableau of horses and...

He looked closer. Not horses. Unicorns. In all the corners, Celtic knots, and in the center, the coat of arms he'd learned to draw when he was old enough to hold a pencil.

His chest tightened. The ballroom floor design.

In the parlor, both men looked up.

"What is this?" Bakeley held up the paper and let the design unfurl.

"It's your ballroom floor, Bakeley. Lady Perpetua commissioned the design."

His stomach roiled. "I see. Who is that man chalking the floor?"

Shaldon sat up straight. "Old Nate's a good craftsman for following a design."

"Old Nate hired a crew," Bakeley said.

"Yes, I know."

"Yes, well, there's one man left, and Lloyd mentioned he's working late to finish."

When they'd returned to rescue Sirena from Hollister, Lloyd had also mentioned that Perry had found Sirena speaking with the workman. "We must go home, Father. Now."

A tic started near Shaldon's eye. He pulled a wad of notes from his coat.

Fox stared at the money in Shaldon's hand.

"You need it, and I trust you to pay me back. And I trust that any disputes among us have long been settled."

Fox took the money and flipped through it.

"Sirena and Perry are home alone," Bakeley said.

Fox's gaze narrowed. "Is he a tall man? Scarred?"

His hand fisted around the parchment. Was he? Damn, damn, he'd been negligent. "I don't know."

"Fair-haired?"

He'd barely looked in on the man. Bakeley closed his eyes and tried to retrieve the image. "He wore a cap."

Shaldon rose.

Fox stood also, wobbling. "I'll come—"

"No," Bakeley said. The man was ape drunk.

"My son is right. Get something to eat. You don't need to live like this. Come see me when you're ready to work."

At the door, Fox's voice stopped them. "My Lord," he said, and Bakeley caught the hard note.

Shaldon only waited.

"I...became acquainted with Hollister, you know, some time back. Not terribly useful, but I ran into him recently and he invited me for a drink. While I was with him, your man visited his quarters. I had the floor drawing with me."

"Thank you, Fox."

"I shall send over a watercolor in repayment."

Shaldon nodded, his face a shade grayer as he exited.

"That money will be a down payment on a portrait of his lordship," Bakeley said. "And you and I will talk more about the bespectacled girl in your picture."

The coach ride seemed interminable, with Bakeley's nerves stretched so tight they might burst from his skin. At this fashionable hour, when they hit Mayfair, traffic slowed. It was less than a mile to their townhouse, but a creeping mile it would be.

Anxiety gnawed at him. Perhaps the floor artist was Donegal, and perhaps he was not. How much could they trust Fox?

And, he reminded himself, they had a houseful of able servants to protect the women there.

"So, you employed a colonial spy to paint your family," Bakeley said.

Shaldon's hand tightened around his cane. "He would say he's never been a colonial. He was born after that war ended."

Father had dodged his question, but of course, the answer was an obvious one.

"Did he originally spy for the Americans?"

"He stopped here on his way to Paris to study art. And yes, to spy for the Americans. But he was not enthralled with the French version of *liberté*, nor with Napoleon."

"Yet he went back."

"It was necessary."

"Do you trust him?"

"He did me a good turn."

The coach shuddered to yet another stop, and Bakeley reached for the door latch. "I'll go the rest of the way on foot."

Shaldon called out to one of the grooms, and the man peeled off the back of the coach. Bakeley heard the pounding steps behind him as he raced down the nearest mews.

He must get to her before Father's web entangled her any further.

Sirena's skin rippled as fingers trailed along her neck. A quiver went down her spine and through her legs all the way to her trembling toes.

Help would be along soon. She must play this out. She must stall this man, whoever he was.

She squeezed her eyes shut, dredged up some courage, crafted a hurried plan. The man was looking for information on Jamie, Shaldon had said.

Feather-brained, she would be. A muffle-headed blonde lassie.

She squeaked and jumped up, scooting away from him. "Goodness. Goodness, you startled me." She pressed a hand to her chest. "Well, and why not use the door?" She batted her eyes and dredged up some tears that were all too real. "But, oh, never mind. Oh dear. There's a fine brandy on the sideboard there. I shall just pour us a dram...Jamie."

A big hand clamped on her shoulder. The same hand that had been raising her gooseflesh.

The candlelight made the scar come to life, wriggling and jumping with his chuckle. "Well then, why not a kiss for your long-lost brother?"

Her skin writhed. The accent had changed again. It was not Irish. Not Irish. She couldn't tell what it was—some English north country tangle.

"I'm in shock, Jamie." Real tears rolled down her cheek.

Blast it, she wasn't a weeper.

It was terror, it was. She'd not tasted fear like this since her cousin's attack, not even at the dock.

She swiped at her cheek and let her nose drip. The hand lifted, and he went to the sideboard.

He didn't like tears. This was good. Tears of happiness, they might seem, and she'd not even had to try to fake them.

She let them flow and sniffled. "Have you a clean kerchief, Jamie?"

One glass slapped the table and brandy gurgled, splashing over the rim.

"Do I look like a swell with a snot rag for the lady?" Smirking, he tipped back his drink.

She moved round the table, and he matched her, blocking her way to the door. "No, but I wouldn't expect that, though you are a gentleman, Jamie. You're a lord. Where ever have you been all these years? Mother's heart—"

"Do not be thinking of the door, your grand ladyship. I've locked it."

She took a step back. Her hands curled and she realized she still fisted the stout pencil. That, and her great act of stupidity wasn't much, but help would come and soon. The footman would have noticed him missing. Lloyd would come to check on her, carrying his key.

She gave her head a quick shake and let a few tears fly. "I don't understand."

Cold air rippled along her neck. She was nearer the window. He'd advanced though, keeping pace with her.

If he'd come in through the window, she could surely go out it.

"It's a long drop out that window, your grand ladyship."

"You came in that way?"

"Yes, but then I'm good with an upper-story window."

She was running out of ways to play stupid. "Who are you?"

"Did you not call me Donegal?"

"What do you want from me?"

"I want what you want, Sirena. I want your Jamie."

Her breath hitched. "Is he alive, then?"

He laughed. "Well then, you've finished playing the nick ninny, your grand ladyship."

Her grip on the pencil tightened. "*Is* my brother alive?"

"*Is my brother alive?*" He mimicked her in a high falsetto. "Mayhap he is." He stepped closer and chuckled. "You've no big clod-hopping boys here tonight like that day at the docks, your grand ladyship. No lord running up to rescue you."

She screamed, and his face twisted into a grin.

"There now. That footman won't come, yer butler is off to the kitchens and he won't hear you. The others are abed. And your man will stay out all night again."

She eased back. He was wrong. She prayed he was wrong. *Bakeley, where are you?*

"I have money—"

"Money? Well, I'll have it. But first I want a taste of what you shared with Glenmorrow before you made your grand marriage."

Her rump hit the window sash. Fear raced through her, numbing her hands.

His broken teeth gleamed yellow in front of her.

"You will stop right there."

The smell of brandy covered more putrid ones—dirt, sweat, and the decayed, rasping breath of a man thinking to take his pleasure.

The window was open. There'd be at least one groom in the still-empty stables, people traveling to parties, the watch making his rounds.

She sucked in those odors and screamed again, like a banshee of death.

She saw the fist and ducked. Not in time. The blow pounded the edge of her ear, knocked out her hair pins, and crashed into the window frame.

In the stables, a horse screamed. *Banshee.* If only the horse were here with her now.

Donegal cursed and drew back his fist again.

Bam, bam. "*My lady?*"

Lloyd. Lloyd was outside, pounding the door.

He glanced back. She yanked at her skirt and jabbed her knee into his cock, and heard a sharp rip of fabric.

Enraged now, he came for her, hands circling her neck, pushing her back through the window.

His fingers pressed and she arched away, struggling for breath, trying to scream.

Panic raced through her. She must make him let go. Her legs were pinned. He pressed against her, her only air his foul breath.

She had but a moment. He bent closer, eyes gleaming, lips pulled back. She flailed and struggled, and clawed, and—

The pencil. She swung her arm up and aimed at his eye. She missed, but the point hit something that caused a bellow and loosened his grip. One hand clasped his cheek. He grabbed for her, his hand dripping blood.

She drove her heel into his breeches. This time he doubled over.

They were battering the door. And why not use the key?

"*Lloyd,*" she shouted.

"Aye, bitch," he huffed. "I fixed the door. Fix you afore they break it. If you're dead, your Jamie will come." He pushed at his knees, still struggling for breath.

She looked around wildly. There were shovels and pokers near the fireplace. But he was bigger, and faster, and might wrest them from her before she could bash him.

Bam, bam, bam. Lloyd had taken up something heavier than his fist.

And Donegal would soon be recovered.

She yanked up her skirts and swung through the window, stepping onto the narrow frieze that girded the building.

Needing repairs, Perry had said. Old Nate would be engaging someone soon for the wood and the brick repair.

He lunged from the window, and she lurched away, grasping for a handhold.

There. Her fingertips tightened around the edge of a brick. She looked down. She could not see the ground below, but it couldn't be far.

There were lights in the stables. Someone would come for her.

Donegal stretched a leg through the window and paused, looking down.

Well, and he had somehow managed to come in that way, teetering on this fascia board like an elephant dancing on a tea saucer.

His other leg came through.

"*Help*," she shouted.

"*Sirena*." That bellowing voice was Bakeley. He was right below her.

"*Bakeley*," she shouted.

Donegal stepped out on to the same length of board where she tottered. It gave way.

She shrieked, and slid, hands scratching along the brick façade, finding no purchase until her toes hit a jutting casement above a ground floor window.

"Blast it." Her fingertips gripped the one other brick in the entire house needing tuckpointing.

"*Sirena, jump.*"

She heard scratching from the shadows. Donegal was perched on another window.

He was coming for her. Below her was all bricked gangway. The spymaster's home was not surrounded by bushes or trees that would obscure the windows or allow a climber in, no. Someone risking this climb would also risk a broken limb or worse.

"Come, love. I'm here." A hand gripped her ankle and relief flooded her.

"Bakeley."

"Slide into my arms, woman."

He pulled her foot from its perch and she shrieked, balancing on the one foot still supported by wood.

"Now," he said, and grabbed her other foot.

"Wait." She closed her eyes and reached a hand down for another purchase. He caught at her other leg and slid her along his body, while she braced her hands against the window, sliding until she was leaning on him, his arms locked around her, her bottom cradled against where his stiff manhood would be if he ever again felt any desire for her. His scent—leather, bergamot and horses curled around her too, and his breath came in great gulps like he'd just run all the way from Knightsbridge—or wherever he'd been. She began to shake in the same rhythm.

He squeezed her tighter. "*My God.*"

A thud sounded nearby.

"It's him." Her voice was a whisper, a mere breath.

Bakeley loosed his grip and shoved her behind him. The thud of two feet hitting the ground had been loud enough. The stealthy movement that came after, he sensed more than heard, and it was close.

The stitch in his side still pained, but it was nothing compared to the rush of panic, and then relief, and now rage sweeping through him.

Her trembling rattled him also. She tugged at his arm, trying to yank him away from the dark, invisible figure lurking.

He pulled the pistol from his pocket. "Go." They were near the servant's entrance. "Wait for me in the kitchen."

A loud crash sounded above and a beam of light burst from the library window, erasing the shadows around them.

Just in time, Bakeley ducked.

The fist coming at him shattered a ground floor window. Bakeley ripped a sharp blow to the man's jaw with his left fist, and the man went down.

Footsteps clattered, growing louder.

Blast it, he couldn't fire without risking hitting one of the servants.

"My lord! My lord! My lord!" Cries came from all around, above, from the back of the house, from the front.

He aimed the gun at the man. "You're cornered, Donegal."

Donegal burst to his feet and crashed into two servants. They snatched at him, missed, and looked to Bakeley.

"Get him," he cried. He shoved the gun in his pocket and joined the pursuit.

The villain ran down a walk, through the garden, into the mews. Servants reached for him. He was like oil, too slick to be held by the grooms when they grabbed him.

He burst through the mews, fled down the alley and disappeared, the two servants in pursuit.

Bakeley stopped and rested his hands on his knees, panting. When this was over, he'd best get back to his boxing and fencing.

"My lord." Lloyd hovered over him. "Are you hurt?"

"Where the hell was everyone?"

"The library door lock was jammed. They will catch him."

He shook his head. "They won't."

Sirena. He must get back to her.

Lloyd's boots trudged behind him back to the house. At the servant's door, he took a lantern from a groom.

"Sirena," he called.

The housekeeper hurried over, attired in her night robe.

"Shall I call for the surgeon?" she asked.

"Where is Lady Sirena?"

Lloyd looked at the housekeeper and the footman who'd joined them. "Where is she?"

"Sh-she's not here, my lord. I came down when I heard the shouting and she hasn't been here."

His chest tightened as if someone had ripped out his own heart.

Another footman ran up. "Mr. Lloyd, my lord, we have checked all the rooms. The ladies and the staff are safe and there are no other intruders."

"Did you see Lady Sirena?"

"No my lord."

His hands went numb. Sirena had been taken.

He fought for composure and lost. "Search again, damn you."

He went outside and circled the building. A clatter of hooves in the street reached them, and the muffled scream of a woman. The lantern slipped from his hands and he ran.

He spotted his father's coach turning the corner, but in front of the house, another carriage pulled away. Unmarked. Too fine to be hired.

A stocking-clad foot kicked out while a hand gripped the edge of the door, trying to close it.

Two horses, too fine to be hired.

Sirena. Sirena was in there.

He darted toward the square, judging the flow of the traffic. He'd catch a break when they reached the main street and the crush of traffic slowed them.

He ran, lungs burning, side aching, fists pumping against the air.

As they turned into Regent's street, a carriage crossed their path. The horses pulled up.

Bakeley reached it in time and yanked open the door.

He roared. Sirena lay sprawled, eyes closed, in the arms of a man—

No. Not a man.

"Take him."

Pain exploded in the side of his head, and he was yanked and pushed to the narrow floor of the coach.

CHAPTER TWENTY-FOUR

"There, there. Get it all out."

A man's gentle tones penetrated the fog in Bakeley's head, and the sound of retching that accompanied them slammed around inside it.

He put his hand to his temple and felt dampness.

"He's alert." That low timbred voice he knew. "Do you feel better now, Bakeley?"

He opened his eyes and turned, the mere act making his brain rattle.

A slim figure in men's clothing came into focus.

"Thank God." She leaned in close examining him.

Jocelyn. His mind raced, remembering. The carriage...Sirena abducted...

More retching sounded from somewhere behind him.

"There, there. This will pass very soon."

A woman moaned.

"*Sirena.*" He sat up. He'd been stretched on a brocaded sofa in an unfamiliar sitting room.

Blood speckled the flannel that covered a pillow. He pushed himself up to stand.

Jocelyn stood also and reached for him. He jerked away and the room spun.

She clamped a hand on his arm.

"Damn you, Jocelyn. I thought I could trust you."

"You can." The man behind him had spoken again.

Bakeley turned and sudden pain pulsed in his temple like the crash of a farrier's hammer.

Sirena sat next to the man, his arm wrapping her as she leaned over a basin held in his other hand.

Bakeley jerked out of Jocelyn's grasp. "Let go of my wife."

Sirena lifted her head and looked at him blurry-eyed. She pushed to her feet, wiping her mouth with the handkerchief she clutched. "Bakeley. Your head." She looked from Lady Arbrough to Bakeley to the man next to her. "What did you *do* to him?"

When Sirena wobbled, the man steadied her.

"Take your hands off my wife. Come here, Sirena."

She stumbled into his arms and he tucked her close, studying the man.

His fair hair was fashionably cut, as were his coats. Broad and muscular, his face had the edge of a man who lived hard.

Sirena took in a sharp breath and held the cloth to her mouth. He looked down into cloudy, unfocused eyes. They'd dosed her with something. One of her cheeks glowed a brighter shade of red and a bruise was blooming on her neck like a purple necklace.

Blood rose in him, sending the hammer pounding again. He forced his hand to unfist and stroked the tangled locks that spilled down her back.

Bloody hell.

He locked eyes with the man. "You'll pay for hurting her."

"No." The man rose, careful, wary. "Those bruises are Donegal's handiwork." His jaw hardened. "And how the devil was he working in your home?"

Shame fed the anger and the pain pounding through him. He'd failed her. He'd failed his whole household.

A soft hand touched his cheek. "It's true about the bruises," Sirena whispered.

He kept his eyes fixed on the man. "Yet, you drugged her."

"Only a bit of the *spongia soporifica.*" Jocelyn moved up next to the stranger. "We needed to move quickly and Sirena wouldn't cooperate. There is no harmful effect except for some nausea."

"I told you we should not use it, Jocelyn," the man said.

The gentle tone made Sirena stiffen.

Jocelyn had taken this man as a lover, and the intimacy upset her. His wife knew the man.

A wave of jealousy flowed over him and his brain muddled. He sorted through memories, looking for clues. Sirena at the ball. Sirena on the street. Sirena on the dock. What had he really known about his wife of one week?

Who was this man to her?

"And I told *you* she was no fool and would not come along easily. Bakeley, I am ever so sorry. If you both would have come willingly, it would have been easier. As it was, we barely escaped Hollister's minions."

"*Hollister?*" he cried.

"His carriage was entering the square."

"Hollister was on the street?" Sirena's trembling breath tickled his neck.

A chill went through him. "It's time for an explanation. What is going on? Why are you dressed in men's clothing?" He turned on the man. "And who the devil are you?"

Sirena swallowed a new wave of nausea and touched Bakeley's cheek until he turned back to look at her. Except for the dried spot of blood on his temple, and a disordered neck cloth, he looked as handsome as usual, even more so with a little rumpling.

He had come to her rescue in the garden, and then again in the coach. If her stomach wasn't already fluttering, it would be doing so for happier reasons.

As his eyes focused, she saw the clouds of his injury lift and a sharpness form. He glanced over her shoulder and then back at her.

No fool was her husband. He'd seen what she'd suspected between bouts of puking.

Another wave of nausea rattled through her, and she pursed her lips, inhaling deeply, pushing against her stomach's tide. "Yes..." She inhaled deeply twice. "*Oh.*" Her hand flew to her mouth. She jerked out of his grasp, just in time.

Only, when she could see again, there were spots on his buff-colored breeches. Ah, well, now that she noticed, they were muddied and bloodied, those breeches.

"Bring her here."

Jocelyn's command barely penetrated her quivering belly and the new spiral of pain in her head.

Bakeley lifted her—it was him, she knew the smell of him. The other man was plain soap and...and...

Her head lifted. Jasmine, damn him. Lady Arbrough's scent.

Her rump hit the sofa and she opened one eye to Lady Arbrough hovering at her head, ordering someone to bring tea, the woman's tightly packed breasts straining against the buttons of a black waistcoat. As if anyone would mistake her for a man.

The tea came and Bakeley whisked it away, sniffing it closely before he would allow Sirena to put the cup to her lips. Some dry toast appeared, and she sat up, testing her head and her stomach again.

Lady Arbrough and the man pulled up chairs, and Bakeley nudged her around to sit next to him.

"You see, Roland, I told you your sister was clever. I did not need to tell her I'd found you."

Anger rose in her and she clung to Bakeley. "Fast friends, indeed, Lady Arbrough. And if he is my brother, just when did you think to tell me you'd found him?"

"And why should we believe you are who you say you are?" Bakeley asked.

Why, indeed?

There'd been a portrait of Jamie, sketched by her mother. But after her death it had gone missing, and after that, she'd barely been able to remember her brother's face.

"Do you know," she said, "that man, Donegal. I thought for a moment he could be my brother, as Jamie might look all battered and scarred, and then, well, I had more than five words with him, and I knew that he couldn't be."

Bakeley stiffened next to her and a drop of blood spattered her arm. "You're bleeding again."

His blood had risen. She caught her breath. Aye, that glare was directed at her. He was angry she hadn't told him about Donegal.

She looked away and spotted the flannel covering the pillow and grabbed for it, taking a breath to quell her answering anger and gentle her touch.

She put the cloth to his nicked head and gritted her teeth, glaring back.

"Lady Arbrough," she said, "kindly bring me paper and ink or a pencil."

"I'll get it," the man said.

A small table appeared in front of her. Paper was set upon it, with an inkwell. The man set to work sharpening a quill and handed it to her.

Her hand shook and she blotched the first line.

"Let me do it, *iora*."

Her breath caught. *Iora*. Squirrel. It was the pet name Jamie had always used for her.

He dipped the quill and traced a half circle, the end points facing outward. Then he looped back for another at a right angle, and another, and a fourth, and one circle inside the center, and then he put the quill down and blew on the paper.

"Tell us the story of the four points of this knot, Sirena," he said.

She swallowed moisture and shook her head. Bakeley's hand covered hers, and she gripped it.

"Can you not then, *iora*? What will you guess? The four points of the compass? The four seasons? The four gospels?"

She pressed her lips together, blinked against a flood coming, and held her breath.

"Always, you leave it to me to tell. It's the sign of Brighid—hand, hearth, head and heart. Brighid, Queen of the Four Fires, Goddess of Heaven, Bringer of Light, Ruler of Birth and New Beginnings."

Air whooshed from her. She squeezed her eyes shut, hanging onto her husband.

"Breathe, love," Bakeley whispered.

She took in a sharp breath. "How *dare* you, Roland James Hollister. How *dare* you, Lady Arbrough." Her throat was raw from heaving and she squeezed her eyes again to hold back hot tears. "You drugged me. You struck Bakeley so hard, you might have killed the man I love. You say you were fleeing Hollister, but then why injure us? Why take us at all? We could have simply gone inside and—"

"You may not have been safe inside. We came as soon as we knew what was afoot. We know Hollister and Donegal had men amongst your household. The one who carted you out to the street, Lady Sirena, Obed recognized him."

Bakeley shot to his feet, still gripping her hand. "Then my father, my sister, they're in danger."

"No. It's Sirena he wants, to get to Roland," Lady Arbrough said. "I've sent a message. Your father will take proper steps. The graver danger will be at the ball tomorrow night. You've invited Liverpool."

"The danger to whom?" Sirena asked.

"You've invited dukes and ministers also, have you not?" Lady Arbrough asked.

"And they'll all feel safe at the home of Lord Shaldon," Bakeley said, staring off, frowning.

There was more he knew, and wouldn't tell her in front of these two, or maybe not at all.

"But why take me now?" she asked. "Why not wait until the ball?"

Bakeley's grip tightened as Lady Arbrough and her brother exchanged a look.

"We don't know. That would be a dispute between two villains, is my guess," Jamie said.

Lady Arbrough nodded. "It is good that you came to me for help, Bakeley."

Sirena's pulse quickened. When had he gone to Lady Arbrough for help? And why? And why his anger with her for inviting the woman to the ball?

Bakeley's heart raced. His father and sister were in danger, as well as the lady they'd taken in and the host of innocent servants. The Home Office had theorized a connection between Sterling Hollister and Donegal, but that they'd invaded his staff?

His mind ran through the list of new hires, as it had done the night the sewer had stopped up. "How long would you say his men have been in my father's house?"

Jocelyn held his eyes. "Very recently, we believe. Have you engaged new people?"

"*We?*" he asked.

She blinked.

"Who are you working with, Jocelyn? Besides him."

Sirena squirmed.

"I did mean just Roland, as well as his two men and a couple of mine. But now, of course, we shall include you and Lady Sirena and, very soon, Shaldon."

"Why did you not tell me you'd found my brother, Lady Arbrough?"

"'Twas my doing, *iora*," Sirena's brother said. "I asked Jocelyn to hold back until I was ready. I'd no idea you'd go off to the docks like you did."

She choked. "Since the docks, you knew? At the musicale? Oh, Lady Arbrough, you are deceptive. You would hide my own brother and expect me to play your friend?" She took a shaky breath. "And ready for what, Jamie? *For what?* Where have you been? Do you know that Sterling Hollister has sold off the last of the breeding stock?"

She could see that the rawness in her voice pained him. Blast her brother for upsetting her so.

"It's all right, *iora*." The man's voice softened again. "I'll buy the best ones back for you."

Tears rolled over her clenched jaw.

Bakeley pulled her to him. "We'll buy your favorites back, Sirena."

"No, ye shall not." Her brother glared. "They shall be part of her dowry. You whisked her off to marriage without a proper agreement."

She turned and glared back. "You're not listening, Jamie. I'm of age, and have been speaking for myself for years. I have a proper marriage agreement, no thanks to the Lords of Glenmorrow. My *English* husband has settled a generous dower from his own pocket for me and our children. And where were you when I was choosing a husband? My husband will pay for those horses, and you must allow it."

"I shall not, squirrel."

She scooted to the seat edge. "You must. And where have you been for these last many years? Mother—"

She choked and bit on her fist.

The lout was on his knees then, taking the raw fist, while Bakeley gripped the other.

"I was on the other side of the world. Sterling Hollister chased me to Belfast, and his man, Donegal, with him. They brought down that ship with a barrel of powder, but Gram's good luck held for I'd jumped to another near one."

"But they found Gram's Brighid knot."

"Aye. I put it around a dead man's neck before we left port. I didn't expect to be gone so long, but it took me years to get back, and when I did, I got word that Mother was gone, and others were looking for me. I would do you and Father no good so I left again. I've been around the globe more than once. I'm sorry I didn't get back in time to keep that bastard Hollister from hurting you."

"He didn't hurt me." She sniffed. "He did try, though. Bakeley is going to challenge his claim to the title and find a way to bring him down."

Or I could just kill him for what he's done tonight, and for what's he's planning.

The talk at the Home Office came back to him. Gunpowder was missing. And the graver danger would be at the ball...

Her brother was nodding at him. "I will thank you for your help with that, Lord Bakeley."

"You must claim the Glenmorrow title," Sirena said, "and be just and fair." She pulled her hand out of her brother's grasp, and turned, her whisper feathering Bakeley's ear. "What did you learn today? Will you speak of it in front of them? My head aches too badly to be entirely trusting."

The others were watching them closely.

"Come, Roland," Jocelyn said. "Let's give them a moment. I hear horses outside in the street. We're expecting a visitor."

"Hollister?" Sirena asked.

"There's always the possibility, but I believe we eluded him. No, I imagine Lord Shaldon will send Kincaid."

When the door closed on them, he pulled her close. "I asked Lady Arbrough to lure Hollister with the list of traitors' names we talked about. I met her at the modiste's, but only after I was told you had invited her to the ball. I did plan to tell you, but Father has had me running hither and yon."

She bit her lip, absorbing that information while he held his breath.

"Can we trust them? They are intimate," she said through clenched teeth. "He is tupping her."

"Does it bother you?" He stroked her cheek. "Because it doesn't bother me one whit."

She hunched her shoulders. "I would know how long they've been about this. How long before the musicale? Why? Why did he not seek me out? Why did he go to her?"

"She was one of my father's operatives. It's possible your brother knew her."

Her eyes searched his. "It was all a ruse then, her friendship. Even her...friendship with you?"

He gritted his teeth. He didn't want his wife's pity. "It doesn't matter. She means nothing to me."

But it wasn't pity that made her eyes flash. "'Tis dishonest. And what do I know of him, besides the pain that he's caused? He may have a wife. He may have children." She pressed her lips together. "It may be the way of these things, but it's not right."

His heart swelled, and he took her hand. "It will not be our way."

She bit her lip and would not look at him. "And when the children come and I am fair drained from chasing them and cross with my lot in life."

The picture warmed him. "We shall turn them over to their nursemaids, and I'll take you to bed and uncross you." He touched his lips to hers and she pulled away.

"Bakeley, I've been puking."

"It isn't catching." He retrieved the now tepid tea and handed it to her. "Sip this. Are you feeling at all better?"

"Yes."

He smoothed a hand down her side to the swell at her hip, provoking a hint of a smile.

"Can we trust them?" she asked again. "Perhaps we should sneak away back to Shaldon House."

Sneak away. Bink and Paulette had not trusted him when he'd gone to help them, had decided to sneak away from the safe house where he'd placed them, and it had almost cost Paulette her life.

"Let's see who my father sends in response to her message."

"Are you sure?"

"I've been through this before with Bink and Paulette. You've not heard that story?" He shook his head. "They tried to go it alone and it was a near thing."

"What happened?"

"Paulette was abducted."

Footsteps sounded outside the room and Bakeley jumped up. The door opened and Jocelyn entered, followed by Sirena's brother and Charley. Drawing up the rear was a large, foreign-looking man dressed in the same black attire as the others.

Charley looked bosky, yet Father had sent him. Bakeley had a good sense of what Bink had felt when he himself had been sent to help Paulette. Bink, a veteran of the Peninsular War, to be assisted by the heir, whose combat had been in Jackson's saloon and Angelo's studio. No wonder his brother had vanished.

Charley's eyes widened and some of his fog lifted. "Bakeley. You're bloodied. And Lady Sirena..." He looked at his brother. "I see now why I was pulled out of White's." He went down on one knee in front of Sirena. "My dear, who did this to you?"

"Oh, get up, Charley," she said.

Charley's gaze flitted between the two of them and he leaned close. "I know the fetching gentleman in the tight waistcoat, but who are the other two?"

His breath reeked of drink.

"Good heavens," Sirena whispered. "Bakeley, he's drunk. Shall we have to trust him also?"

He squeezed her shoulder. "Charley, you know Lady Arbrough. The fair-haired fellow is Sirena's brother, the true Lord Glenmorrow. The other man is the one who bashed my skull."

Charley swayed a bit struggling to his feet. He shook Sirena's brother's hand.

"Charles Everly, Bakeley's brother."

"Roland Hollister. And this is my man, Obed. I vouch for him."

For what that was worth.

Obed's head inclined. His hair was dark and stick-straight, his skin burnished, his features European, his eyes large and round, and golden— in other words, his nationality completely indeterminable.

Bakeley touched his head. The bleeding had stopped. "And I can vouch for his right hook."

"I beg pardon, sir." No expression wrinkled the foreign man's brow.

"Pardon granted, provided you use those fists on our enemies."

Sirena waved a hand. "Please, everyone, sit. Charley, exactly who pulled you out of White's?"

"One of the blood—er, one of Kincaid's Scotsmen. They are both hanging about outside. Whose snug *pied-a-terre* is this?"

"It is mine." Lady Arbrough took a seat. Sirena's brother quickly took the chair next to her that Charley was eying.

Charley grinned and carried a chair from the table. "You make an elegant fellow, Lady Arbrough."

Obed stood near the door and crossed his arms over his chest, reminding Bakeley of a picture he'd seen of a genie. All the man needed was a turban and flowing trousers.

It was not a group to inspire confidence.

"So," Charley said, "What is the plan?"

CHAPTER TWENTY-FIVE

Later, Sirena followed Bakeley into one of the bedchambers in Lady Arbrough's hideaway, where a Scotsman stood outside the door.

They would spend the rest of the night here—Shaldon's idea, Charley said. Given their injuries, her weariness, and the tumult at Shaldon House, Sirena was glad for it.

Compared to the bedchambers at Shaldon House, this room was simple fare, lacking ornamentation, and sparsely furnished. The bed would be a squeeze for the two of them, and they'd share a wash bowl and lamp. However, the deal table had been set with a bottle, two glasses, and a covered plate.

Bakeley poured some of the liquid.

She sniffed at it. "Laced with laudanum, is it?"

"It's hard to trust, isn't it? But no, I believe this is just wine. Will you have some?"

"No."

He sighed and set down the glass. "You must sleep."

"I'm not sure I can. Why not let me keep watch while you rest?"

He emptied his pockets of a tiny gun, a larger pistol, and a wickedly long dagger, and plopped onto the padded settee.

"Come." He patted the cushion next to him. "The fire is warm. Will you eat something now?"

Her stomach fluttered at the thought. "Not yet." She circled the table and trailed a hand over the mantel. More plain deal. This might have been a tradesman's lodgings, and not a terribly rich one.

She rather liked the lack of fussiness.

Bakeley looked at home here, also, legs sprawled like he had no cares in the world. The dim light cast shadows across his face, the flickering of the fire mirrored in his dark eyes.

He hadn't chosen the life of a titled nobleman. He'd been born into it, just as her brother had. Only, unlike her brother, Bakeley hadn't made a mess of his life.

He reached out a hand. "Come here."

The fluttering in her belly moved lower. She glanced at the door.

"I locked it. Come here."

They should not. He needed to sleep.

But...did he not almost always doze off after they made love? *And if Hollister kills me tomorrow, it will be the last chance for it.*

She pushed that thought away and crossed to him in three strides, standing over him. "You need to be my protector tomorrow, Bakeley. You need to sleep." She dropped to her knees and slid her hands along his thighs.

"What are you doing?"

"It occurs to me that I know a way to make you sleepy."

He let loose a shaky chuckle. "You were sick tonight. I had planned to be considerate."

"I'm not sick now."

She was terrified, and she must not let him know it, else none of them would be able to follow this through. "I've been missing my husband's touch." She let her hands travel up over his great hard member to his fall, unbuttoned it, and leaned down.

"No." He eased her chin up with one finger. "Not that way. That will be for some other night. There *will* be other nights, Sirena." He raised her by her elbows, lifted her skirt, and helped her stand. "Up, girl, on my lap."

Afterward, when she'd collapsed against him, he cradled her close, her heart beating with his, waiting until her breathing smoothed out. She'd been overwhelmed by the night's events, her worry palpable, her bravado shaken.

What to make of Roland James Hollister, he didn't know, and he sensed the same speculation in Sirena. Jocelyn had vouched for the man, but she was his *chere-amie* now—what sort of testimony could she offer?

Of all the players in this game, the only one he truly trusted was this bundle of woman whose hair was tickling his nose.

He stroked a hand down her back. In the council of war at the Home Office, they'd concluded that Sterling Hollister wanted many things—to acquire power through his radical colleagues, to ensure Roland Hollister stayed dead, to retrieve any evidence of his treason, and to accomplish it all without any blame pointing his way.

He wanted revenge on the late Lord Glenmorrow also, and one thing Bakeley was certain of—Sirena had thwarted him once. Perhaps he suspected she was the blackmailer.

The villain thought himself on the way to becoming a powerful man, destroying his enemies without so much as removing his gloves.

If all went as planned, they would strip him bare.

Unease settled over him. He thought about Shaldon's whispered conversation with Fox. Bakeley had shared all his secrets with Sirena, but he sensed Father had more.

Sirena patted the sable ribbon tied at her neck. A narrower, matching one twined through her hair which Jenny had braided and curled and piled atop her head.

A diamond brooch—Bakeley's mother's—had been pinned to the wide ribbon, and she wore the matching earbobs.

The necklace that was part of the set was back in the safe. She would wear that when her bruising had cleared.

"A bit more paint on her cheek, Jenny." Madame had personally supervised the final arranging of her hair and her jewelry and her dressing—or, as it had been, re-dressing.

When Madame arrived with the forgotten ball gown, Sirena had already been wearing the fine gold and red dress from her wedding.

The sight of it had given Madame pause.

While Jenny helped her out of the dress and her stays and into a new steel-boned set that Madame had made especially for her, there'd been some low conversation between the modiste and Barton. And then Madame had proclaimed the wedding dress exquisite, and then everyone had agreed Sirena should wear the new one, of a deeper shade of gold, and which, as it turned out, had been crafted with specially concealed pockets for weapons. Madame had whispered that fact to her as she'd stitched her into the dress.

Aye, the world was filled with ex-spies. If Barton or Lady Jane popped up and said she was working for Talleyrand, she'd not be surprised.

Madame handed Jenny a painter's brush, and the fine bristles whisked over her cheeks smoothing out the pink dabs there.

"Well, I look less like a bosky tavern wench now."

Jenny frowned.

"Do not be vexed, Jenny. I'm only having you on."

"She's nervous," Lady Jane said.

"I should say we all are." Paulette handed Sirena a pair of golden gloves and she worked them up over the scrapes on her hands. "You look like a queen, Sirena. Golden. Glowing."

"Like Brighid, Queen of fire," Perry said.

Upon their return to the house that morning, Sirena had shared the story of her brother, the quaternary knot, and Brighid with Perry, who'd rushed to write it all down.

"I am positively green with jealousy," Paulette said. "I would just like for once to be something other than little and dark."

"Jealousy?" Sirena said. "And you in your crimson gown? You look like a Spanish contessa. I should never be able to wear that shade without it swallowing me alive."

Perry pushed her glasses higher. She wore pale green, laced with silver and embellished with matching seed pearls and embroidery, and looked like a tall, bespectacled wood sprite. "You don't need to worry that Bink's eyes will stray, Paulette. They will be only on you, well, and perhaps—"

Sirena cleared her throat. Though a hoard of men had descended on Shaldon House early that morning, swarming the garden and the public rooms and even the cellar, Lady Jane, Barton, and Jenny were not privy to the night's undertaking. Though, knowing Jenny, she'd probably sniffed out the impending conflict. And the lord only knew what Madame had been told.

Perry had almost been left out, but Sirena had insisted Perry had to know. Bink had tried to keep Paulette home, and had finally told her why. After that, there was no holding her back.

Someone scratched at the door and Barton answered it.

Kincaid filled the doorway, dressed to the hilt in Shaldon livery. "All the dinner guests have arrived," he said.

Madame's back stiffened and she cast him a withering look. One that he returned.

Sirena swallowed a gasp. By all that was holy—Madame and Kincaid—here was a story she wanted to hear.

"We'd best go down," Lady Jane said. "Cook will be frazzled if we delay the first course." Lady Jane ushered Sirena's two new sisters to the door.

Jenny fastened Sirena's gloves, straightened her skirts and stood to examine her. The bonny girl clasped her hands together and smiled. Madame and Barton lined up next to her.

"We have done well," Madame said. "Perhaps one last thing. Turn this way, my lady."

Unseen by the others, she slipped a thin, sheathed dagger from her pocket into Sirena's and whispered. "Slash up. Avoid bone. *Courage.*" The last was said in the French manner.

"*Merci.*" Sirena's heart rattled against her stiff stays. Well, and she would need courage, no matter how one said the word. If all the dinner guests had arrived, then Sterling Hollister was here.

You are a brave girl. Shaldon's words to her that night in his study came back to her.

She straightened her shoulders and took as deep a breath as she could with these lacings. *Yes, I am.*

Bakeley took his place with his bride and sister for the receiving line and had his first good look at the floor. "I met your artist, Perry," he said over Sirena's elaborate coiffure. He'd complimented his lady's appearance earlier, lamenting the number of hairpins and braids he'd have to delve through later that night.

First the risk, then the reward, and later *would* come.

"*My* artist?" Behind her spectacles, Perry squinted. "You mean Fox. And what do you think of his design?"

"I think the Glenmorrow arms should be quartered with ours at the center of this canvas."

"I'm sorry, Sirena. There was not time for the research. I hope that you at least like it."

"Of course I do."

The first guests were announced and they entered, transfixed by the floor.

"Ignore your brother in this, Perry," Sirena said. "Your Fox's floor will be the talk."

Pink tinged Perry's cheeks at the teasing compliment. Or—Bakeley took another long look at his sister—perhaps it had been the mention of Fox.

The first lady in a long queue curtsied before them. They would sort out the wholly inappropriate Fox later.

Pleading poor health, Lord Shaldon was seated in a place of honor at the head of the room, with Kincaid and one of his liveried Scotsmen flanking him, and a real footman at Kincaid's elbow. Kincaid had sought Bakeley before the dinner, reminding him that one of his men would be on Sirena at all times, and that he himself should take no risks that might tip off the villain.

Shaldon would keep an eye on the room and the extra footmen-cum-guards—more carefully screened than the last group—would report to him throughout the evening. If things started to go sideways, Father could swoon and they would send everyone home.

Bakeley almost wished it would come to that.

At a break in the line, Sirena turned a bright smile on him. "It's very subtly done, I am noticing."

He followed the line of her gaze. Servants were circling near Sterling Hollister. Not for one moment had he been left unsupervised. Placed between Paulette and Perry at the small family dinner, he'd been peppered with questions about Waterloo on Paulette's side, and Irish politics on Perry's. Hollister's last condescending responses had carried an edge of irritation.

Now the man stood watching the receiving line.

"Counting the number of dukes, is he?" Sirena asked.

"Waiting for Liverpool." Perry whispered. "Oh, excuse me, Father is summoning me." She headed off into the crush.

"Deserter," Sirena muttered, nodding to the next couple in line. They greeted another string of guests.

The room was filling up, the rumble of voices making it impossible for the crowd to hear Lloyd calling names.

"Mr. A. Fox," he intoned.

Sirena edged forward to peer around Bakeley.

"Sirena." He caught her eye. "Another surprise invitation?"

She straightened, her smile growing wider as Fox appeared in front of them. The drunken lout from the night before was gone. Fox was shaved, groomed, and pressed, the same tall dark-haired fellow with a poet's demeanor and a blacksmith's strong build who'd visited Cransdall and painted all of them.

Fox bowed. "Lord Bakeley. Lady Bakeley."

"'Tis a pleasure to meet you," Sirena said. "Though I could have wished you'd arrived earlier. "The orchestra is tuning up and this great herd is already mucking up your wonderful design."

Fox smiled, showing white teeth.

"It is a great success," Sirena said. "You must dance on it yourself."

"I am not much of a dancer, madam, though I should be happy to try."

"Excellent. Though...my husband is expecting me to dance every dance with him, is that not shocking? So I must give my share of dances to Lady Perry."

Bakeley blinked. Fox and Perry—no. He must nip this matchmaking.

"I believe Perry is engaged to dance the first dance with Charles," Bakeley said.

"Your brother won't mind. The artist and his commissioner dancing together. I shall just go and find her—"

Lady Arbrough was announced, and a murmur spread throughout the ballroom.

"My dears." She curtsied, let Bakeley bow over her hand, and kissed Sirena on both cheeks.

"I'm so happy you've come," Sirena said, making sure the crowd watching would see only a contented bride, as they'd discussed.

"Do not worry. All is in place," Jocelyn whispered.

"I'm receiving a signal, Sirena," Bakeley said. They were to lead the first dance.

"The prime minister is not here."

"He'll be along in a bit."

Sirena opened her mouth and closed it. "Very well."

"Ready?"

She inhaled deeply. "Yes."

He squeezed her hand. "Be not afraid. I'm sticking to you tonight."

He led her through the crowd to the center of the dance floor where the chalked coat of arms was already mussed, and took her into his arms for a waltz.

"Wait but a moment, please." A booming voice drowned the tuning instruments. Sterling Hollister stepped out into the middle of the ballroom.

A bit too close. Bakeley's pulse raced. He released one of Sirena's hands and pivoted her away from her cousin.

"Speeches were not part of the program, cousin," Bakeley said with a show of annoyance.

"What, ho, interrupting a man with his bride in his arms?" That voice was Charley's.

A muscle ticked at the corner of Hollister's eye. He bowed. "I beg your indulgence to allow me to offer a few words as the head of Lady Sirena's family and her only living relative."

His pulse pounded, and next to him, Sirena bristled.

Father parted the crowd. "Well say it, man."

Hollister started on a meandering speech about the Hollister family.

"A ball," Bakeley murmured. "A ball seemed like such a good idea. What was I thinking?"

"I shall move him out of the way myself if he doesn't shut up soon." Charley had come up next to him. His stage whisper made Hollister flinch.

"He's killing time to put his plan in place," Sirena hissed.

"Yes."

He exchanged a glance with his father.

The doorways were covered. The house, garden, and mews had been swept through by every agent and runner they could come up with and many of them had suited up as footmen. Not everyone was here though, not the highest flyers. The new king was hosting an impromptu event that had peeled off the highest ranking peers.

"Lord Liverpool," Lloyd intoned over Hollister's speechifying.

Hollister halted, looked toward the new arrival and bowed.

Liverpool gestured that he should continue. Shaldon signaled the musicians and the opening strains of the waltz called them to order.

Bakeley tucked his bride a little closer than was considered polite for the *ton*. He didn't care. This was their dance.

What had it been since that first country dance together, a tumultuous two or three weeks?

She looked about her while they twirled, that pulse at her neck beating just above the ribbon that hid her bruises.

"You should smile at me," he said. "Do not worry. Not everyone is watching us."

She lifted her eyes to his.

"You are the only woman for me."

That coaxed a smile, but no comeback. They turned in the dance.

"She's doing it," Sirena said.

Jocelyn had cozied up to Sterling Hollister.

"We must not look. You must only have eyes for me."

"We make terrible spies, Bakeley."

He pulled her closer. "Thank heavens."

"Well, I do have a blade in my pocket. Madame gave it to me."

And it was his job to make sure she didn't have to use it. He dropped a kiss on her forehead. "I wonder, will the blade be on her bill? Now smile and stop watching the crowd."

She pulled her lips back dutifully. "We can't have Barton take business away from her."

"Hmm. Would they be amenable to a partnership, do you think? Ah...a real smile. Very good. Now, keep looking at me like I'm the center of your universe."

If only Sirena would truly see him that way. He spun her into a series of energetic turns.

Sirena danced with Charley, with Bink, and even with Fox, dreading the moment her cousin stepped up. At the edge of the ballroom, Shaldon mingled with Liverpool and the few of his ministers who were attending.

Hollister hadn't disappeared to pick up Lady Arbrough's list. He still roved about, chatting and mingling, angling for introductions to the rich and the powerful.

He was waiting for something, and it made her uneasy. Lady Arbrough was nowhere in sight. Her brother would be outside somewhere, ready to confront their cousin when Lady Arbrough led him out.

When a dance with one of Charley's friends ended, she let him escort her over to where Lady Jane sat with the older ladies.

A dowager countess studied her through her glass. "You are overheated, my dear. Red as a beet."

The lady next to her cackled. "And with that handsome Bakeley, who would not be?"

"It is the curse of fair skin as lovely as hers," Lady Jane said.

"Are you thirsty, cousin?"

The hair on her neck rose. She fixed a smile on her face and turned. Sterling Hollister's eyes gleamed.

"Parched, of course."

He snapped his fingers and a footman approached carrying a tray with two glasses.

Ripples of fear ran up her spine. This footman she didn't know. A bit older, a bit coarser than the usual strapping young men hired for that sort of work, he was not one of the regular staff. She hadn't met all the runners and agents dressed up to play footmen though.

She thanked him and took the glass. "And what are we drinking, sir?"

"Wine. What sort, you should know, as this is your ball. Come, cuz, a toast."

The old ladies tittered. She waved the glass under her nose and winked at them, stalling.

Any drink presented by Hollister could well be tainted.

Out of the corner of her eye, she saw a maid and a young footman hurrying her way. Shaldon's people. "I think not. My husband forbade all toasts until after his. Will you excuse me, ladies?" She curtsied without spilling a drop of the wine.

Hollister's hand clamped her arm and the wine did spill. The maid reached for her glass and signaled someone.

"We'll get this cleaned up, my lady."

Hollister still gripped her arm.

"Where did your footman get off to, cousin?" she asked. "He should be helping with this cleaning."

He smiled a fake smile. "He was not my footman."

"Of course not. But he was not one of ours either." She smiled back, and watched his eyes tighten.

The young footman stepped closer.

"Clean this up and stop staring at the lady," Hollister said. A country dance started up. "This is my dance, cousin."

His hand still clutched her forearm. She lifted her elbow and set some distance between them, allowed herself a frantic look around the ballroom. The footman followed her as far as the dance line forming. Lady Jane had stood up and was wringing her hands.

Bakeley moved quickly in their direction, bowing and ignoring attempts at conversation. Hollister nudged her into the line and stood next to a man she'd been introduced to earlier, one of Charley's friends. As the dance started, Bakeley tweaked the man's elbow and pulled him out of the line. "I'll fill in here, Penderbrook." He bowed to the lady across from him.

Hollister scowled, and Sirena's breath eased.

The dance began and they circled each other. "He's very protective of you, I see."

"He's a man of honor."

"Indeed. I was counting on it."

They separated, went to the corners of their group and did not join up again until the promenade.

"Though you will find, he cannot be with you every moment."

"Is that a threat, cousin?" She kept her tone sweet trying to catch this great ugly fly.

He laughed. "Will he call me out?"

"Duels are foolish, do you not think?"

"Very." He smiled.

They were nearing the end of their march, and she was nearing the end of her patience. This dragon needed to be poked to produce his fire. "Papa used to say, a duel resolves the disputes of men of honor. For everyone else, there's the horsewhip."

His ugly smile froze in place.

Trouble ahead, Sirena.

Blood lust coursed through her. Trouble, be damned. She kept her smile fixed and felt for the shiv in her pocket. At a turn, his foot went out, and she stumbled. When she looked down she saw the last quarter of Queen Brighid's knot. The three others had been smudged out.

Bakeley watched the interaction from his now distant place in the line. He and his young partner stood waiting to go through a new square one more time, and then down through the ranks to where Hollister's eyes bored holes into Sirena.

Something was wrong. A footman approached and hovered nearby, catching Bakeley's eye. He nodded to the man. Until he could get through the next wretched steps of the dance that would have to do.

He and his partner circled around and started down the middle.

When they reached the end of the line, she was gone. Hollister, too, and the footman.

CHAPTER TWENTY-SIX

Panic raced through him. He scanned the crowd. Kincaid hurried toward him, Bink on his heels, footmen handing their trays off and scattering to get out of their way.

"Out the door," Kincaid mouthed, flying past him toward the flapping French door near where Sirena and Hollister had been standing.

They sped out to the small terrace and down the steps to the back garden, and stumbled over a man on the ground.

The footman who'd signaled to him.

"The stables," the man groaned. "Hurry."

This should not be happening. It was Jocelyn's job to lure Sterling Hollister, not Sirena's.

A streak of gold flashed in the lamplight. Bakeley vaulted the concrete railing and raced toward her. Someone burst out from the shadows, but another body tackled that one.

Shaldon had men all throughout the garden, but so did Hollister.

The golden streak stopped and he caught up with them.

"I've got your back," Kincaid whispered.

Hollister had a hand clamped over Sirena's mouth and a knife to her neck.

Behind them, the music played on, the orchestra striking up a brisk Scottish reel. Whether the attendees noticed the commotion and poured out of the door, he didn't know. He couldn't take his eyes off the pair in front of him.

In the dim light from a garden lamp, Hollister's eyes glinted wildly, sending Bakeley's pulse racing. Sirena groped at the hand gagging her, her eyes wide as two pale gray moons. His own heart had climbed high into his throat.

Bink trundled up with a liveried man in tow, an older fellow whose face had been battered into a pulp. "Not one of your servants, I think, Bakeley."

"No, indeed." He made himself drawl the words. Hollister's blade was too close to that lovely neck. "I see you still have a way with your fists, brother."

"As needed, Bakeley. As needed."

He had a pistol tucked away, but there were other men here in the shadows, surer shots than he. Especially Kincaid. He needed to get Hollister talking.

"Are you all right, my love?"

Sirena blinked determinedly several times. In the corner of his eye, he saw her hand slip to the hidden pocket she had whispered to him about.

"Lord Glenmorrow," he said, "uncover her mouth. She won't scream, will she, my dear? What would be the point?"

She shook her head. Hollister released her mouth but slipped the hand down to fondle her breast. "Let her scream if she will."

She writhed and unleashed a stream of epithets that would have burned the ears of a stable lad.

Her cousin jerked her in tighter, his hand now at her waist.

"Ah, what a fine lady she is, with a mouth like a guttersnipe."

The lamplight around him was charged with red. Bakeley took a step closer.

"No." Hollister slipped the point of his blade under the ribbon. "This brown is a good color, Sirena. It will not show the blood."

"You have no honor, Sterling," Sirena said.

The knife pressed and sweat poured down Bakeley's back. "Ignore the chit," Bakeley said. "What do you want, Hollister?"

"What I want? You shall soon see. You with your muck men. There's enough powder under your ballroom to take out both your near neighbors and the mews in back."

"You would kill our horses?" he drawled.

The villain laughed harshly. "Everyone knows your horses are stabled elsewhere. But who cares about bloody horses? All the best of London, even the Prime Minister, will be killed in the blast and the fire that will follow. Except me. I'll survive. And the King will come looking for people to run his government and I'll be there."

Bloody fool. "You've enough powder to blow up all the witnesses, do you?"

"Where I don't have powder, I have men to finish them off. Except for this one. She shall give me what she wouldn't surrender at Glenmorrow, before she's rendered speechless. I'll take care of her myself."

"Everyone will wonder at your miraculous survival after attending the ball."

"I'll have left early. Everyone else will be dead."

"I think not," Bakeley said. "Why not put down the knife?"

While Hollister talked, Sirena was drawing her needle-thin blade.

"What of this man?" Bink tossed the battered footman face-first to the ground and put a foot on his neck.

Bink had seen Sirena's blade and was making sure the man didn't shout a warning. God, he loved his big brother.

Hollister shrugged. "Just kill him."

"You bastard," the man on the ground shouted.

Hollister's low chuckle sent more chills through Bakeley. Sirena's mouth had firmed, her hand clenching.

"Soon," Kincaid mumbled. "Keep talking."

Sirena willed her heart to stop clanging and captured the knife in the folds of her gown, grasping for Madame's instructions. *Up. No Bone. Courage.*

Pain jabbed at her and she took in a sharp breath. The bastard's knife pierced like a deep needle prick, and she could feel a trickle of moisture. Please God, let her not pass out.

Her husband went on, his voice smooth and measured, with a crisp edge that threatened damnation. Perhaps only she heard that. Perhaps Hollister was too stupid.

"Hollister," a gruff voice shouted. "Look what I've found."

Her heart dropped. A big man in a workman's kit shuffled out, Lady Arbrough trapped in his arms. His hat was drawn low, but even in the dark she could see the scar that traced a muddled path down his cheek. "Here's your blackmailer."

No. Her breath caught. Jamie was supposed to show up. Lady Arbrough was to set the trap, but

Jamie would bring the letter. They'd talked about it the night before.

Their plan had failed. Donegal had returned, Hollister had not fallen for the ruse, and where was Jamie?

Bakeley's gaze caught her, his tension lighting up the air around him. He gave a little shake of his head. What the devil he meant by it, she didn't know, but at least Hollister was too distracted to notice.

"Donegal," Hollister growled. "She was to stay in the ballroom with the rest. What are you about, you fool?"

"Hedging my bets," the man holding Lady Arbrough said.

"Damn you, Hollister," Lady Arbrough spat out. "You'll both be sorry. If I die, or if I disappear, a copy of the list will be delivered to the Home Office tomorrow."

"The Home Office will be a shambles tomorrow," Hollister said. "Is your fuse lit, man?"

"Aye, minutes to blow," the other man said darkly.

Hollister's arm tightened around her, his arm shaking with the tension.

"Let the women go." Bakeley had moved a step to the side.

"You may have that whore, Donegal, and I'll take this one. And before we're done, I'll show *you* the horsewhip, Lady Bakeley."

A trembling overtook her, but her fingers worked the blade out of its sheath, her hand stiffening upon the hilt.

Bakeley leaned closer. "Your quarrel is not with Sirena. Let her go."

His eerie calm floated out, surrounding her. Her breathing steadied.

"Let her go? No. She has a debt to pay. But if you keep moving this way, I'll gut her in front of you."

Hollister took a step back, his arm at her waist firming, her feet skidding. The heels of her dance slippers scraped the sharp edge of bricks and hot moisture trickled down her chest.

Bakeley stepped forward and stopped, constrained as if a force was pulling him back.

She gasped. Someone had come up in the dark behind him. They needed more time.

She writhed and squirmed and the sharp knife poked her. "*Ow*," she cried. "Leave off the pricking and stop dragging me. I can walk."

"How long is your fuse, Donegal?" Bakeley asked.

"It's a short one, then, isn't it? Should've blown by now."

Her heart lurched again and behind her Hollister froze.

He'd heard it too. This was not Donegal.

Bakeley's gaze stayed firmly upon her—he wasn't surprised. He'd known.

In the moment Hollister turned to look, she jerked away from his blade and swung round, driving her dagger into his waist. His hand flailed and struck her, and an explosion ripped through the air.

She was suddenly free. Floating.

Strong hands caught her.

"Sirena." That was Bakeley's voice, close to her ear, and it was the last thing she remembered.

"Up the backstairs, Bakeley." Charley was clearing a path, scooting servants out of the way. "Sure you don't need a hand?"

"Shut up." His heart was about to burst, not from the load in his arms but the load of almost having lost her. He'd promised to protect her and he'd failed.

She'd had to protect herself. Jenny met them in the kitchen and ran up ahead of them, opening the door to Sirena's bedchamber.

He laid her carefully upon the bed, and Jenny waved the vinaigrette under her nose. She didn't respond.

He snatched the vial from the maid and clamped a hand over Sirena's mouth. She sputtered, opened her eyes, and tried to sit up.

"Shhh." He stroked her cheek. "I'm afraid you fainted."

"Oh, no. I don't—"

"I know. But this time you did."

"Aye, milady," Jenny said. "You were out cold."

She collapsed against the pillow, dislodging a braid.

"It is these blasted stays. Hollister?"

"Is dead. Or wishes he was."

Her eyes clouded. "I k-killed him?"

"No. Kincaid shot him."

"And what of the gunpowder?" Her voice shook.

"Was discovered and defused hours ago."

She bolted up. "You knew? And you didn't tell me?"

"I...I..." He bit his lip. "In truth, I'd all but forgotten. We learned of missing gunpowder yesterday, in the meeting at the Home Office. Father had everything well in hand. I didn't want to worry you."

She mumbled something and fell back again.

"Is the Prime Minister safe?" Jenny asked.

"He's been at home reading reports all evening. The man in the ballroom is an actor. Well paid for this performance."

Sirena's eyes narrowed on him. "You didn't tell me that, either."

He swiped a hand through his hair. "No." Guilt gnawed at him. "But you are safe, and you were spared the worry."

She huffed out a breath. "Was I correct that the man holding Lady Arbrough—"

"Is your brother. Yes."

"And Donegal?"

"I don't know."

A red flush spread over her. "Or you're not wishing to tell me. You want to *spare me the worry.*"

"As of a few minutes before the ball, we didn't have him, and we don't know where he is. Word is he may be looking for a ship. We have men on the docks."

She pushed herself up. "Well, and I thank you for sharing that bit of bad news."

"And I regret it already. You're going pale again."

In fact, her cheeks had gone redder.

"We'll find him, Sirena. Meanwhile, your brother is donning his dress clothes to make a grand appearance. We need to complete the last part of this spectacle."

"The last part that you also forgot to tell me about?"

"Your brother is coming back to life tonight. Do you not want to be there?"

She extended her hand. "Help me up. Jenny, you must fix my hair."

"I must change your gown also, my lady. You have a gash here at the side, but the blood is on the bodice. Did you cut him then?"

Bakeley fell to his knees and smoothed his hand over the long cut in the gown. "Dear God," he muttered. Jenny was right, the speckles of blood were just under the neckline, and the ribbon she'd worn earlier was missing, revealing the bruise where Donegal's hands had squeezed.

Skirts rustled nearby, and he looked up into Madame's dark eyes. Barton had entered also.

"The corset worked," Barton said.

"It is like armor," Madam answered.

"Avoid bone. Slash up," Sirena said in a shaky voice. She reached for him and he stood, gathering her up with him into his arms. "Oh, Bakeley. Never keep secrets from me again."

His heart almost burst. "I should haul you off to bed right now," he whispered.

She took a deep breath and shook her head. "If Jamie is making a grand appearance, I must be there."

Madam stepped up. "My Lord. Your neck cloth is ruined. Will you go now and change it?" Her eyes swept over him. "And perhaps your coats and shirt. Your valet is just in the other room. Madame Barton, please bring out your lovely golden dress. These blood stains are fresh. If Mademoiselle Jenny starts on them tonight, perhaps they may be removed. The slash we shall mend, as though it never happened, you will see. Bring a wet cloth for these new cuts, Jenny and another length of that ribbon. Please to stand now, and turn around, my lady."

He left her in good hands and went down the hall to where the new, true heir of Glenmorrow was dressing.

Jocelyn had been lolling in a chair near the fire. She sat up when they entered.

"Is Hollister dead?" Bakeley asked.

"Yes." She lifted her glass in a toast. "He'll be discovered tomorrow, right after his treason is publicized. A suicide, don't you know, though I'm not sure how they'll explain the knife wound."

"He fell backwards onto his sword while shooting himself in the head," Sirena's brother said as he tied his neck cloth.

He did not entirely like Roland James Hollister, nor, he decided, Lady Arbrough. They were well matched.

"This was very troubling for Sirena," he said. "I doubt she's ever stabbed a man before."

"Of course." Jocelyn set down her glass. "Roland, we're both too hard. We've seen too much. We're sorry, Bakeley."

"We?"

She pursed her lips and looked at Sirena's brother.

"So, Glenmorrow, have you a wife somewhere in the Americas? It does matter to your sister."

A glint of humor entered the man's eyes. "You do love her. I'm happy for that. And no, I have no wife."

"That will please Sirena." It didn't matter a whit to him, but he wanted Sirena's happiness. "A wedding would please her even more. I'll see you in the ballroom."

He found his way back to his chamber where his valet was waiting and groaned. A wedding would make Lady Arbrough his sister-in-law.

Roland Hollister could take Jocelyn to America and keep her there. He and Sirena could find a good steward to run Glenmorrow for the man.

*****

Sirena had finished changing her gown, freshening her face and tidying her hair when Bakeley barged in to retrieve her. He seemed angry. She was shaking with it herself.

After all they'd gone through, he'd held things from her.

"Here it is my lady." Barton held the length of new ribbon for her to see. She'd stitched Gram's Queen Brighid's knot to the ribbon.

Her stomach fluttered as Barton fixed it around her neck, and she pressed a hand to her waist, the steel stays still firmly in place. Surely the good luck had been restored and 'twas safe to wear Gram's charm.

"Are you well, Sirena?" Bakeley asked.

She fingered the quaternary knot. "I've lost your mother's diamond brooch."

"To hell with the brooch. At least I didn't lose you."

She let out a breath. "You've no need to shout at *me*."

He looked at Barton and she hurried out.

"I'm not angry with you," he said.

"What else are you not telling me?"

He led her into the corridor and stopped on the landing, pulling her to him in a fierce, too short kiss. "I'm not angry with you. *Blast this ball*. I want it to be over. I want to well and truly ravage you tonight, Sirena, if you'll allow it."

A giggle bubbled up in her. She couldn't hold onto the anger. Not tonight. She could still hear the music below, the orchestra blaring, the jumble of voices carrying up the stairs. Had they been back at Glenmorrow, the ballroom would have emptied and the guests would have been wagering about her survival. These English had gone on as if nothing had happened in the garden. "To hell with Jamie. Let's go back to the bedchamber," she whispered.

He kissed her then, a long passionate melding like he was taking her into his soul.

And then he stopped and set her back.

"Another promise for later?" she asked, breathless.

"Yes. For now, we must see this through."

And what else was to happen that he hadn't told her about?

Lord Shaldon's face transformed when he spotted them, a look of relief sweeping away tension. She was starting to be able to see his moods.

He left the imposter prime minister and came to greet them.

He took Sirena's hand. "You're well?"

She nodded.

"Good. The supper dance can now start."

He waved to the musicians.

Bakeley led her onto the dance floor. The violinist pulled a note.

Lloyd's voice rang out over the crowd announcing an arrival. "Lord Glenmorrow," he intoned.

The crowd murmured, of course they did, having listened to Hollister droning at the start of the ball.

She teetered against Bakeley. Her cousin was dead. Donegal was missing, but what of that? With the full force of the English government, they'd find him. They must get this evening over, before all her loose threads unraveled.

She needed Bakeley's arms holding her, tonight and every night. Forever.

She was in love with this English lord.

The murmuring all around them turned to stunned amazement when Jamie appeared, looking magnificent in his coats, his hair brushed into fashionable disarray, the ugly fake scar washed away.

Whether he was true, or whether he was black of heart, she didn't know. He was her brother, and Bakeley was right—they must see this through.

Whispers started, the guests looking around, for Sterling Hollister perhaps, the other Lord Glenmorrow. Sirena latched onto Bakeley's arm and tugged him across the floor, pushing through the hushed conversations.

The talk of the Season they would continue to be, at least in the scandal sheets.

Jamie stood alone when they reached him. She reached for his hands, and then wrapped her arms around him. Shorter than Bakeley, he was, but still taller than her own self.

The gasping and whispers took her own breath away.

She released him and stepped back, next to Bakeley. "One for the ages, you are, brother," she said.

He smiled, and she saw her father before the drink had got to him. She squeezed back a tear.

"'Tis a warm welcome home, sister. Lord Bakeley, I am most pleased to meet you." They shook hands. "And, ah." He bowed. "Lord Shaldon. We meet again."

She stepped back and let Jamie be introduced to Lord Liverpool, and couldn't help but grin like a ninny.

Bakeley signaled and footmen scurried with trays, passing glasses all around.

Shaldon raised a glass. "Ladies and gentlemen, a toast. A *brief* toast."

The crowd tittered.

"A toast to my heir, Bakeley, and his new bride, the next Lady Shaldon."

"Here, here," Charley said.

Shaldon fixed him with a look, and he took the glass away from his lips.

"And," Shaldon said, "We're not only celebrating an heir's wedding. We are celebrating an heir's restoration. Raise a glass with me to the true heir of Glenmorrow, Roland James Hollister. God save the King."

Around her the room buzzed, and she found herself squeezed amongst these men, her husband, his brother, his father, and Jamie.

Bakeley handed off both their glasses and his arm came around her.

"No swooning," he said. "We shall leave that to Father."

She laughed heartily and looked up. Shaldon was laughing too.

Sirena stifled a yawn, as she and Bakeley saw the last guest out.

"Finally," she whispered. The rest of the family and Lady Jane had already gone up. "I thought they would never leave."

Bakeley bent for a kiss, and a throat cleared near by. Kincaid stood in the door, now dressed in shabby dark coats.

"What news?" Sirena asked.

A footman passed by within hearing distance. Kincaid's gaze tracking him sent a shiver up her spine until she recognized him. Phillip was one of the Shaldon regulars. The man passed down the corridor and she pressed a hand to her neck where the knot rested, where the bruising had begun to ache.

"Father is in the study," Bakeley told Kincaid. He held out his arm to her. "We'll follow you there."

"My lady." Phillip appeared again. "One of the grooms thinks he's found your brooch."

Lady Shaldon's diamond brooch. She pulled away from Bakeley. "In the garden?" she asked.

"I don't know. He's waiting by the ballroom terrace door."

"Get it from him, Phillip, and give it to Lloyd," Bakeley said. "Come with me, Lady Sirena."

Order her around, would he?

"No," she told the footman. "I'll be right along." The man nodded and stepped back.

Bakeley cupped her shoulder in his big gloved hand. "You want to be included."

She fingered the ribbon. She did.

And yet, she'd lost a brooch with diamonds that would feed all the Glenmorrow tenants for five years, one that had belonged to her husband's mother. She couldn't just let that go. What if the groom ran off with it?

"Will Shaldon and Kincaid talk freely in front of me, Bakeley? No. Not likely. Can I count on my husband to tell me the news?"

His brows furrowed, his lids worn down by fatigue. "Of course."

Truth to tell, she was just as tired, and with her cousin dead she wasn't sure she wanted to sit through Kincaid's blathering about Donegal. Find the man and be done with it.

"You go. Lloyd has a crew at work in the ballroom. I won't be alone. I'll just get that brooch and meet you in the bedchamber."

His eyes darkened. "Hurry then."

"I will. You do the same, or I'll come fetch you in my nightrail."

He leaned in and touched his lips to hers.

Her breath froze. Fear laced through her, and a vision of Bakeley, trapped.

Her hand went to the knot and she steadied herself.

"Are you well?" he asked.

Was she? She fingered the knot. The vision was gone.

She was tired. The evening's events were working on her. Bakeley would be with his father and Kincaid. He'd be safe.

"Yes," she said. "But, Bakeley, no more secrets. No more surprises."

"None," he said. "You'll know everything."

"You there. Phillip," he said. "Stay with her."

He kissed her again and hurried up the stairs.

She followed the footman through the ballroom, where lanterns had been brought in for the servants tending to spent candles.

The groom waiting at the terrace door was none other than the slender young man who'd saddled Lightning for Bakeley the morning before.

How had he fared in the wild melee earlier? An uneasy feeling settled over her. Her neck ached under the Brighid's knot. She didn't remember seeing this lad among the crowd outside, but then of course, she'd fainted, hadn't she?

"You've my brooch?" she asked.

"Aye, miss. That is, er, one of the boys from Kent found it when they were bringing the...er...new horse in." He reached a hand into his pocket and pulled it out empty, a look of consternation on this face. "Beg pardon, my lady. In all the excitement, I must have set it down and left it there. As bad as that Banshee, is this new mare—"

"Mare? From Kent?" She looked back. The footman had disappeared. She should tell someone she'd be in the mews.

But...a new mare from Kent with a wild disposition. That could only be Pooka.

Her heart filled with love. Bakeley had brought Pooka up as a surprise.

And her cousin was dead. She shoved past the boy and headed down the walk, heart pounding.

No more secrets she'd told him. *No surprises.* And all the while he'd had this one up his sleeve, and the joy of it bubbled up in her, making her laugh out loud.

She was going to visit a hobgoblin.

CHAPTER TWENTY-SEVEN

Kincaid was already reporting when Bakeley entered the study. Farnsworth was there also.

"Dunchatel," Kincaid said.

Farnsworth nodded to Bakeley. "The brigand's true name. Not Irish at all."

Father's face was grim. "Swiss. Had an English mother."

A chill went through him. "You know him."

"Yes."

"A cagey, traitorous weasel who'd go to the highest bidder," Kincaid said. "Worked with the Royalists in France until he started working against them. Ran off to Ireland when things got too hot."

"A wizard with explosives," Shaldon said. "Cadoudel employed him to build a bomb, a barrel packed with gunpowder and metal fragments that almost killed Napoleon." His mouth firmed. "And didn't."

He let out a breath. "The Infernal Machine."

"Yes," Kincaid answered. "And didn't kill us tonight, either, thanks to Bakeley's attention to the sewers. Nice and clean for the boys who crawled in there to remove Dunchatel's barrels."

"Where is he now?" he asked.

Kincaid frowned. "Still missing. We have men down at the—"

A sharp knock at the door silenced him. Bakeley opened it and recognized the footman they'd seen in the hall downstairs.

"Yes," Bakeley barked.

"It's Lady Bakeley, my lord."

Fear slithered up his spine. "What then, Phillip? I told you to stay with her."

"I'm sorry. She...she ran off to the mews with the groom who found the brooch."

He swiped a hand through his hair. "Go and see that she's all right."

"Yes, my lord, but she was going to see a horse just brought up from Kent. Pooka."

Pooka?

Pooka was in Kent. He hadn't sent for her. "Father, did you—"

"No."

He grabbed the man's arm, startling him, hauling him into the study.

Close set eyes, and a spark of fear.

His heart pounded inside his chest. He pulled the man up by his neck cloth. "How many years have you served us? That horse is in Kent." He shoved him to Farnsworth. "Find out what he knows. Kincaid, bring your pistol. Dunchatel is in the stables, and this traitor is one of his men."

He took the pistol Shaldon passed him and ran.

Sirena held her breath as she passed the place where Sterling Hollister had held her, heart buzzing, feet dragging, as if walking through a sucking bog, all of her lightness gone.

Something was wrong.

The groom came up beside her. "M-my lady?"

Twitchy, he was. Perhaps he'd seen the troubles with Hollister earlier.

She stopped and caught her breath. Her cousin was dead, Bakeley had said so. She'd slipped his noose. She needn't fear him.

And her husband had brought up her horse, her own horse, her Pooka.

She pushed through the stable door, and the quiet alarmed her. The stalls were empty, except for the wild black mare who poked her nose through the gate of the loose box. The fear that had slithered within began to pound through Sirena's veins. She touched Gram's good luck knot and let her senses roll out in all directions.

Pressure built in her nerves. Evil was here.

Banshee squealed and kicked at the slats, fear echoing.

She needed out. They both needed out.

She lifted the latch, pulled at the gate to free the horse, but a hand came up and banged the gate on Banshee's great nose, and Sirena found herself locked in a man's grip.

Fear choked her. Oh, God, his smell. Two nights in a row. This couldn't be happening.

Bam. Let me go let me go let me go.

Bakeley? Where are you Bakeley?

Banshee whinnied and thumped on the wood again.

She took a deep breath. "Let us go."

A chuckle. "Us? The groom who fetched you is mine. He's long gone."

Fool. She'd meant the horse.

Bam.

Banshee's eyes rolled wildly. She couldn't calm the mare if she couldn't calm herself.

Mid-breath, he jerked her hands back making her gasp. Ropes cut her wrists as he cinched them together.

Bam, bam, bam.

Bakeley. I need you, Bakeley.

Her cheek hit the box's gate and mashed against the wood, and another rope laced her waist through the slats until she was firmly tied. Chest heaving, she opened her eyes.

Banshee stared back at her, nostrils flared, ears and lips pulled back.

She closed her eyes and breathed out a moan. "We'll get out."

The mare lowered her head and pawed the scattered straw, fear momentarily calmed, and Sirena's with it.

"What do you want, Donegal? Sterling Hollister is dead. Why not go home to Ireland? Run away now, I'll not turn you in."

"Ireland is not my home. The Irish are pigs."

She heard the sharp scrape of a flint striking.

A fire. The words shrieked in her. Banshee raised her head, ears twirling and squealed.

A pungent smell sent the horse's nostrils flaring. Sirena craned her head around and spotted the lit end of a long piece of string that coiled in a wide circle around a barrel.

Terror washed through her and the mare. They were drowning in it together.

Bam. The wood slat burned her cheek. She tugged at the ropes, tied through the horizontal slot and tried to slide away from the latch.

Again. Strike it again. We'll leave together. Strike it again.

Bakeley, I need you.

A door crashed and a shot rang out, sending the horse into a frenzy. She felt a sharp pressure at her waist at the back.

Another knife.

"Let her go."

That low growl was Bakeley's.

"Try that again and I'll cut her."

Bam. Bam, bam, bam, bam.

"There's a fuse, Bakeley," she called. "Put it out."

The knife jabbed in deeper.

The stays were like armor, Madame said. Like armor.

Queen Brighid protect me.

Bam, bam, bam. The pounding rattled her teeth.

Her gaze focused on the latch of the gate. With each strike of Banshee's shod hoof, the screws of the mechanism loosened. With each crash, pain shot through her cheekbone. She didn't care.

Get out, Banshee. Get out, get out.

Blood pounding into his hands and feet, Bakeley took in the scene. Sirena had a knife to her back, and a horse likely to strike her ribs through the gate slats. And in the aisle, in the middle of a long, snaking fuse stood a keg,

Filled with gunpowder. An Infernal Machine.

Damn, damn, damn.

His father would be clacking his way through the garden with whatever loyal men he'd gathered, and it might not be soon enough

The fuse was lit, but long. Long enough for Dunchatel to make his escape.

Unless he planned to blow himself up with them.

He steadied his breath. "Why are you doing this? My lady and I have done nothing to you."

"But I have."

Shaldon had entered the stables behind him with more stealth than Bakeley would ever think possible.

"Isn't that right, Dunchatel. This is about our quarrel. Let the girl go. This is not her fight."

The horse continued to kick. Sirena was racked between the stallion and Dunchatel. If the stallion kicked the gate open, the point of the knife would sink into Sirena's back.

"She serves a purpose for me."

"More revenge," Shaldon said. "Against Roland Hollister. He got free, but you were on the ship that you sunk."

The man spat into the stall. "Aye, and against you, Shaldon. She and your heir will go up in mere moments."

"And you also."

"I'll be gone."

Bakeley took a step and Sirena gasped.

He froze. *Damn.*

"I can cut through the spine right here," Donegal said. "You might carry her out, but she will not—"

Boom.

A gunshot rent the air. Dunchatel's head spun around, bright blood streaking across his forehead. He stumbled, and in that instant the stall gate flew open, whirling Sirena back, knocking the barrel over and rolling it closer to the flaming fuse.

There was more pounding as one of their men beat at the back door of the stable.

Dunchatel struggled to his feet, heading for Sirena, knife in hand.

Bakeley roared and lunged at him, but dodged back when the terrified mare reared, her powerful hooves striking the air mere inches from him.

"The fuse," Sirena shouted.

The knife slashed, and Bakeley dodged again, drawing the villain away from Sirena.

Kicking and twirling, the horse reared. Bakeley ducked, just in time, but a shod hoof glanced off Dunchatel's head. The man lashed out blindly, missed, and Banshee struck him again, iron slicing the front of his face with a sickening crunch.

The mare squealed, terror and anger and the need for escape, filling the small space. Banshee's eyes rolled while Dunchatel's blood gushed, the scent of it mixing with the acrid odor of smoke.

And the fuse was still burning.

"There, my girl," Bakeley edged past the flailing horse. "Sirena, your song," he called.

"Shhhh." She coughed and cleared her throat, and began to croon.

All four feet plopped and Banshee danced from foot to foot, head nodding up and down. As the mare calmed, Sirena's song smoothed into a long soothing murmur.

"The fuse," Shaldon reminded him.

The gate and Dunchatel's body hid the fuse's lit end. Bakeley slid sideways past the horse and the gate holding Sirena and stopped.

Blood streamed, snaked along the seams of the brick floor, and reached the burning fuse before him, snuffing it out. He bent toward the barrel, and a hand clamped on his arm.

"Don't touch it, son." Shaldon emptied a bucket of water over everything.

*****

Banshee *tap-tapped* on the brick floor, her nerves all ajumble, just like the humans around her. Sirena pulled up a lullaby and crooned, smoothing out the panic, settling the fear.

She couldn't see a thing, all smashed tight as she was, but aye, from the way the men tiptoed and the hushed stillness around them, Banshee knew, and so did Sirena. Death had paid them a visit.

Someone came up behind her.

"Keep singing, love."

Her heart lifted and began to fill. She held still while Bakeley sawed at her ropes, and she sang. Banshee settled more, taking a step back, and then another, into the stall, and she sang. Not calm yet. 'Twould be a long while until either of them truly calmed down.

The ropes slipped away and she fell back into her husband's arms. "You came for me."

"Shhh." He pushed the stall gate, walking her forward, walking Banshee back and closing the gate.

Two other men entered the stable, a liveried footman and a well-dressed man who must be another one of her new father's spies.

"That gate latch is broken," Kincaid said. "Farnsworth, come see to that mad horse. I'm out of powder."

The well-dressed man raised a pistol.

Sirena gasped. "No." She jerked free, one hand extended, and moved in front of the pistol. "You'll not put her down."

"My lady, that horse just killed a man." Kincaid spoke soothingly, like she was mad also.

She felt Bakeley's strength next to her.

"She was frightened," she said, "and rightly so. As was I. She did it because...because I asked it of her."

Kincaid exchanged looks with Shaldon, and the third man. Aye, 'twas certain they thought she was as mad as the mare.

"Rather like a medieval destrier, Kincaid." Bakeley pulled her close. "We won't put the horse down, but we need to move her, love. There's a barrel of gunpowder in the middle of the stables."

"I'll do it my lady." The footman slid around the man called Farnsworth, and she recognized Johnny, Mr. Gibson's groom, all done up in fancy livery for their ball.

"She's been letting me handle her. Upset about all that's happened she is, and the blood's abothering her. I'll get her away from the smell and find her a place with the others. I'll take good care of her."

Tears filled her eyes and she blinked them away, pulling open the gate. Banshee nosed her skirt, and she stroked her head. "Thank you," she said. "You'll go with Johnny, and he'll take good care of you."

She talked and soothed, while Bakeley helped the groom gather the tack and lead Banshee out through the garden instead of the door at the back of the stables.

Donegal's body blocked that way.

"It's a pity," Shaldon said from behind her. "We wanted to question him."

She sucked in a breath and made herself look.

Bile rose in her. Donegal's ugly scar was a red, furrowed crater.

"We'll get that footman to talk," Kincaid said.

"There was a groom, also," Sirena said. "If you can find him. He lured me out here." Her eyes shot open. "But wait, what did the footman do?"

"He made sure Bakeley came out," Shaldon said.

Dear God.

She touched her Gram's knot. What a fool she'd been. The vision had warned her, yet she'd fallen straight into the trap over a horse and a diamond brooch. Bakeley might have been killed.

"I'll deal with this mess," Kincaid said.

The brooch. Perhaps it didn't truly matter, as Bakeley said. And yet...it would feed all of Glenmorrow for a long time.

"If you find the diamond brooch, Kincaid, you must let me know."

"Aye, I will, Lady Sirena."

Bakeley returned just then and pulled her close. "Come. Let's go in. Father will see to this."

"Kincaid will see to it," Shaldon said. "Don't blow yourself up, Kincaid." He followed them out.

"Is it really so dangerous?" she whispered.

"A keg of powder? Yes." She stumbled and he held onto her. "And that one is probably filled with bits of metal, the better to cause pain and suffering. Donegal wasn't Irish at all. His name was Dunchatel. He's a Swiss spy and bomb maker, and one of Father's old enemies."

She buried her face in his shoulder. "Oh, Bakeley. I'm sorry. The thought of him luring you out there to kill you...I did think the first time I talked to him he might truly be Irish," she whispered. "Else I would have told you..."

He gripped her shoulders. "You knew who he was before?" He frowned. "Before he assaulted you last night?"

She choked. Nodded. Shook her head. He hadn't understood what she'd said the night before. He hadn't suspected her of deception. She could have gone without telling him. Perhaps now he'd never trust her. Tears flooded her eyes and clogged her throat.

She swallowed them back and lifted her chin. "I suspected. I didn't know for sure. I talked to him one day and he was quite kind. I should have told you. It's only that, you're an English lord, and if he was truly an Irishman...and...and I wanted to talk to you and you didn't come home."

"I'm *your* English lord."

"Yes." She nodded. "Yes, you are."

"And you were afraid to tell me about an insurrectionist working inside our home because you thought he was Irish."

Oy, when he said it like that...

"You don't trust me, Sirena."

His gentle tone tore her heart to shreds, and she barely managed the breath to climb the stairs.

They stopped outside the door to her bedchamber and she took his hand. "I trust you, James. I l-love you. I was waiting in the library last night to tell you, only—"

"I didn't come home."

"I'll always want justice for the Irish, but..." She searched his face. "But I believe you want that too."

"Come." He opened the door and Jenny looked up.

"It's always so busy in here." He spun Sirena around. "Jenny, you may have the rest of the night..."

Bakeley's hands stopped moving along her laces, and tension crackled the air around them.

"Jenny, bring water and towels. My love, your suit of armor failed you."

She wriggled. "I feel nothing but metal stays poking me."

"Good sign." He worked on her fastenings until she was down to her chemise. With a sharp rip, he tore open the back, making her shriek.

"There was already a small tear." Bakeley pressed a wet cloth to her back, and she gasped.

"It's only a small cut, I think," Jenny said. "And the bleeding stopped. I think if you—"

What transpired behind her she wasn't sure. "That is, if you don't need anythin' else, good night, my lady, my lord."

She heard the door *snick* closed on the maid.

And then she was floating in Bakeley's arms.

"What are you doing?" she squealed. He kicked open doors and carried her through to his bedchamber, dumping her on the bed and ripping at his coats.

"You're mad," she said.

"For you. And I'm going to prove it."

EPILOGUE

One week later

Sirena clamped her knees and held on, laughing as she raced across the park in the early morning hours, the galloping of another horse next to her. When she reached the designated tree, they were neck and neck. She pulled her mount up, laughing.

"It's a tie," she said.

"You see," Bakeley said. "You were wrong. I've a horse as fast as your good Irish Connemara."

Pooka leaned over to nip at Lightning, who snorted and shied away, and it was Bakeley's turn to chuckle.

"Mother and son don't count," Sirena said. "We shall have to try Banshee against Pooka. You may let all your friends lay wagers."

"A public race? Only when Pooka is trained to the sidesaddle."

She pulled a face at him, and slipped back a few paces, making Pooka snort. The mare wasn't one to follow behind, but today, Sirena was playing Bakeley's groom, and another rider was drawing near, a lord or a gentleman.

The man tipped his hat and moved on.

"Riding sidesaddle is unnatural for me," Sirena said.

"Not for a lady."

"Shall I try it on you in bed, then?"

He gave her a dark look and laughed. "My dear, you may have a point there. Follow me." He wheeled the horse around and headed back toward home.

Nearby on the street, a carriage had stopped, the men inside watching the riders.

"He's happy," Shaldon said.

Kincaid grunted. "And Hollister and Dunchatel are dead."

"Yes. Now who is Charley's latest source and what has he gathered from her?"

The two horses with their riders trotted past.

"Not much. The boy's growing tired of chasing Spanish ladies. Drinking too much. It will catch him up sooner or later."

Shaldon knocked for the driver to move on. "Clearly, he's not yet found the right lady."

The End

A Note from the Author

Some time back while researching the British spy master, William Wickham, I came across a quote by Wickham about his experiences as the Chief Secretary of Ireland during Robert Emmet's rebellion. Of Emmet, Wickham supposedly said, "Had I been an Irishman, I should most unquestionably have joined him."

The stories of Emmet and of an earlier rebel, Lord Edward Fitzgerald, son of a duke, make for interesting reading, and are the background for Lady Sirena Hollister's story.

Of course, as usual, my characters and story are entirely fictional, and any historical errors are mine alone.

Many thanks go to editor Tessa Shapcott, and as ever, I'm grateful to my husband for his unfailing support and enduring patience, and to my son and daughter, and I'm excited that my first grandchild, Maddox James, arrived in time for this book's dedication!

I love hearing from readers! You can contact and follow me on Facebook, Twitter, Pinterest, and Goodreads, and at my website, AlinaKField.com. For special notices about sales and other news, please consider signing up for my newsletter at my website. I promise I won't spam you or sell your email address!

Best regards and happy reading!

Alina K. Field

Also by Alina K. Field

Rosalyn's Ring
2013

Bella's Band
2014, Soul Mate Publishing

Liliana's Letter
2015, Havenlock Press

The Marquess and the Midwife
A Christmas Novella
2016, Havenlock Press

The Ghost of Depford Hall
A Halloween short story, a sequel
to
Liliana's Letter
2017, Havenlock Press

Haunting Miss Fenwick
2019, Havenlock Press

The Duke She Despised
In the *Winter Wishes Regency
Holiday Anthology*
2019

Sons of the Spy Lord Series

Marrying Mr. Gibson
Previously titled *The Bastard's Iberian Bride*
Book One
2017, Havenlock Press

The Viscount's Seduction
Book Two
2017, Havenlock Press

The Rogue's Last Scandal
Book Three
2017, Havenlock Press

The Counterfeit Lady
Book Four
2018, Havenlock Press

Avenging the Earl's Lady
Book Five
2019, Havenlock Press